HOLLOW PEAK

Max Jeffries

ALSO BY MAX JEFFRIES

Altered Sense
Deadly Sense

For Dad

ONE

Colony of New South Wales,
Australia – December, 1861.

I n the eerie stillness of anticipation, three men lay silently in wait. Thick hessian masks that amplified the laborious rhythm of their heavy breathing concealed their faces. With slits cut barely wide enough to see out from, they would have to listen keenly. Contrasting the tanned masks, they wore thick black gloves and long, black raincoats that extended down to the tops of meticulously polished black leather boots. As the first rays of dawn filtered through the dense shrubbery lining the side of the muddy trail, the air became charged with a palpable sense of tension.

The Shadow felt his patience tested by the warm morning as the dew and remnants of the previous night's summer rain trickled down from the leaves overhead onto his mask. Now, hidden within the bushes, the wait was on the verge of reaching its climax. He reassured himself that his time would soon come and maintained a steely resolve. Glancing over his shoulder, he observed the two men beside him. They had left their true identities behind, naming themselves The Ghoul and The Banshee. Both lay patient in the morning's stillness, he knew their loyalty to him was unwavering, and together they would not disappoint.

Just when the weight of anticipation threatened to become unbearable, a gentle breeze rustled through the tall trees, carrying with it the distant sound of approaching horses from the west. The Shadow cast a knowing glance at his companions. Their moment had arrived.

The awaited carriage, making its return journey from the Bathurst gold mines to Sydney had taken longer than initially expected. However, considering the substantial load it bore, this delay did not catch The Shadow off guard. In fact, he willingly embraced the extended wait, fully aware that the potential reward justified the patience required.

Peering through the small eye holes of his hessian mask, The Shadow caught sight of the horse-drawn carriage gradually emerging in the distance. The exhilaration coiled in his muscles, causing a subtle twitch in his neck. Each passing moment heightened the tension, the culmination of a patient vigil finally reaching its conclusion.

Continuing along the muddied road, the two middle-aged guards in charge of the Royal Mail carriage displayed the weariness of a long night's journey. Both adorned with soft, round stomachs and bushy, dark beards which carelessly hung over their sweat-stained white shirts, they lacked the competent appearance of those usually trusted with the colony's precious gold supply.

An already long and exhausting journey, the relentless rain that persisted through the night further dampened their spirits, and they had discussed their shared desire for a hot meal frequently. As they neared the western limits of Sydney, the once firm ground beneath the wheels transformed into a sloppy, challenging terrain. The carriage travelled slowly, and the two horses walked lazily, fatigued. As they continued along the uneven track, the guards failed to see the deep hole hidden under bark and leaves until their front wheel fell into the ditch, halting the carriage in a sudden jerk that startled the horses and guards alike.

The guards snapped alert and quickly scanned their surroundings, but they saw only thick shrubbery and a long stretch of muddy dirt behind and in front of them under the overcast sky. Irate at the disruption, they grumbled, leaving behind their rifles in the carriage, and climbed out to investigate. They never considered the hole in the ground anything but an inconvenience.

Immobile and wedged deep in the hole was the cart's front wheel, and even with some encouragement, the spooked horses refused to pull it free. Suddenly, a slight rustling noise sounded from the bushes behind the guards. A twig snapping, perhaps. It caught the attention of the pair.

'What was that? Is something out there?'

The other guard squinted and peered through the thick undergrowth. The light breeze continued to sway the plants hypnotically. 'I can't see anything, probably just a bird. Help me move this wheel.'

Swift and silent, the three men emerged from their cover with purpose, their movements silent and calculated. The Shadow, not required, observed with a watchful eye as The Ghoul and The Banshee silently stalked the unsuspecting guards. Like whispers in the night, they navigated through the short, damp grass that bordered the road.

Without a moment's hesitation, the assailants closed in on the guards and deployed small knives with precision. They penetrated them deep into the sides of their necks. Executed with such speed and efficiency, the attack caught the guards entirely by surprise, and they never had the chance to mount a defence.

In the blink of an eye, the blades had found their mark. The guards' eyes widened with a mix of shock and horror. Their nauseating screams startled a flock of cockatoos, dispersing them from an overhead tree in a wild flap. Mud splashed, and blood spurted in volume, drenching the already damp ground. The guard's bodies soon convulsed into eventual unconsciousness. The Ghoul and The Banshee forced their blades in deeper before removing them and slashing at the front of their throats, allowing more blood to spill. Both guards were dead before they could even contemplate what had happened.

When their bodies surrendered into a limp deadweight, the assailants released their hold. They let them collapse to the ground with a sickening, lifeless thump. There, they straddled their victims and continued their brutal knife attack. Blood sprayed over their thick black coats and tan masks, and each stab was cruel and unrelenting. Behind the thick hessian, they laughed with every strike.

The carriage horses, still bound to their harnesses, continued to make a wild ruckus. Still in silent observation, The Shadow patted them gently on the nose, calming them effectively. He then whistled loudly, and moments later, three other large and saddled horses came bounding in his direction from somewhere deep within the thick bushland behind.

'Take as much as they can carry.' he instructed, his voice a muffled grumble underneath his mask.

After swiftly wiping their knives clean, The Ghoul and The Banshee retrieved small mallets from their pockets. Stepping over the mangled corpses of the guards, they climbed the wooden cart.

They forced open the locks, revealing the precious cargo within - raw, unrefined gold contained within two wooden boxes. Though lacking lustre in its present state, the unrefined material held the promise of transforming into a fortune once subjected to the refinement process.

They worked efficiently to collect their spoils however, the limitations of their storage soon became apparent. Unable to fit the entire amount into the leather satchels strapped to the sides of their horses, they handpicked the portion of most significant value, mindful of the need to maintain the horses' agility and endurance.

Mounted on their horses, The Shadow, still hidden by his hessian mask, surveyed his surroundings cautiously. Wary of potential witnesses. Satisfied they were alone, he smiled to himself. The once tumultuous scene had transitioned back into an unsettling quietude, interrupted only by the soft rustling of leaves in the breeze.

Beneath the still canopy, the lifeless bodies of the guards lay on the ground, surrounded by a sombre pool of their own blood. The aftermath of the swift and brutal encounter lingered in the air while their horses, finally calm, casually gnawed at the grass.

The trio rode east as fast as their horses could handle the steep, declining dirt road. Just before they reached the eastern foot of the Blue Mountains, they wrapped their blood-soaked raincoats, gloves, and masks in a tight ball and tossed them down a deep ravine where no one could ever gain access.

TWO

I t was not until over an hour later that a lone prospector headed to the gold mines at Bathurst stumbled upon the bodies
of the two guards. The prospector, a small and hunchbacked
old man bore the marks of a tough life. His thick, grey stubble
and thinning white hair hinted at the passage of time and the
trials endured along the way. From a distance, two horses caught
the man's attention. Tied to a carriage, they were entangled in a
ditch by the roadside. Intrigued by the unexpected obstacle, he
ventured closer to investigate, his curiosity tinged with apprehension.

As he approached, the grim reality of the situation unfolded
before him. The bodies of the two men lay sprawled on the
ground, their faces barely discernible amidst the deep lacerations
that marred their forms. The scene was further intensified by the
presence of a swarm of flies, their incessant buzzing filling the
air as they feasted upon the drying blood that pooled around the
bodies. Bearing witness to the grim aftermath of the ambush, the
once pristine earth now carried the tainted crimson hue of spilt
blood. The sight, coupled with the pungent stench of death that

hung heavy in the air, gave the prospector a wave of nausea. As he took in the harrowing sight, trying to comprehend what could have happened, his stomach churned again in a fresh wave of revulsion. Overwhelmed by a sense of dread and foreboding, he succumbed to a brief moment of panic before instinctively turning on his heels, the urgency of retreat consuming his thoughts. He retraced his steps with haste, eager to distance himself from the haunting scene that now lay etched in his memory.

After a brisk walk back eastward, the prospector traversed through expansive fields of sprawling farmland, the vast expanse starkly contrasting the grim scene he had just left behind. With each step, the weight of his heavy rucksack bore down on his weary frame, digging into his back and causing his hips to ache. Despite the physical discomfort, a lingering sense of illness still gnawed at him, exacerbated by the terror still coursing through his veins in the wake of his gruesome discovery.

As he made his way into the town of Penrith, nestled along the banks of the Nepean River, the subdued atmosphere reflected the early hour and the sombre mood that lingered in the air. The town centre, typically bustling with activity, seemed unusually quiet, the lingering traces of overnight rain leaving the wide dirt road of High Street damp and glistening.

Though hardly anyone had seemed to have ventured outside so early in the morning, signs of life flickered within the few open shops lining the street. The white-painted facade of a general store beckoned passersby with its wide-open wooden doors, extending an invitation, while the nearby barber shop buzzed with some activity as a handful of locals were being tended to.

To his left, the prospector gazed down a long, winding dirt road led to a sprawling wood mill dominating the distant horizon. Its imposing presence hinted at its significance as a cornerstone of the local economy, likely employing a sizeable portion of the town's population.

In his desperate search for someone to report to, the prospector's path intersected with that of two mounted police officers, their presence a reassuring sight. As the prospector waved them down, his demeanour tinged with hysteria, the officers dismounted from their horses and approached with measured steps. Clad in tidy black tunics adorned with bright brass buttons, the officers exuded an aura of authority. Long black waterproof capes draped off their necks, a practical yet striking contrast to the crisp white riding pants they wore.

'Can we help you?' the first officer greeted in a thick British accent, his voice resonating with confident maturity despite his youth. The officer was no older than twenty-one with a narrow, pale complexion and clean-shaven face. Still, complemented by short, dark hair, he accentuated an air of professionalism that commanded respect.

'A murder,' the prospector replied urgently, his breath coming in quick gasps. His efforts to steady himself were clear as he removed his dirty brown cap and shifted his weight from foot to foot.

'Steady yourself, for heaven's sake,' the older and larger of the two officers interjected, his voice resonating with a gruffness that mirrored the strength of his barrelled chest and the intensity of his dark, sunken eyes. Behind a thick, brown moustache that partially obscured his top lip, his features were weathered and dry.

'There are two men dead, no more than four west of here, at the foot of the mountains on Mitchell's Pass, just before the town of Glenbrook. There's blood everywhere. I'm afraid it's a horrific scene, sirs.'

'Did you see what happened?' The older officer asked as he scrutinised the man's anxious demeanour. His tone betrayed a hint of scepticism.

'No, sir, I just came across it. I'm making my way to Bathurst for the gold. There were two bodies covered in blood. I didn't get too close, sir. I was frightened. I came straight here to make the report.' The prospector's fingers twitched with an almost frantic energy as his gaze darted back and forth between the two police officers. His anticipation was discernible as he awaited their response.

'Why do you say murder, then?' the younger officer asked.

The prospector's eyes widened and his mouth sharply twitched in panic. 'Believe me, sir, what I saw could not have happened naturally.'

'Okay, slow down. What is your name?'

'Jonathon McNeill. I am just a humble labourer, and I don't lie or mean to cause you any trouble, but I need to report what I found. In fact, I feel quite ill just thinking of the scene.'

'Okay, Mr McNeill, are the bodies still where you saw them?'

'I assume so, sir. They were in plain sight. In the middle of the road. If you head west, you'll find them quickly, especially on horseback.'

'Good day, Mr McNeill. We will head there now. It's best you don't go too far away. For now, we may need to speak with you again.'

With a swift exchange of glances, the two officers acknowledged the urgency of the situation. They excused themselves, swiftly mounted their horses, and headed west in a fast gallop; the rhythmic beat of hooves echoed against the backdrop of the quiet town still waking.

The morning sun, breaking through the overcast sky, cast its warm light upon the officers. The air hummed with anticipation as they delved deeper into the thickening foliage, the canopy of trees growing denser with each passing moment. Navigating the sharp, twisting incline with determination, they pressed onward when suddenly they beheld the scene that had spurred their hastened journey.

In the distance, the grim scene unfolded before them. Blood pooled on the ground, staining the earth a morbid crimson, while the mangled bodies of the fallen guards lay in a tangled heap upon the road. The horses, still tethered to the carriage, whined and snorted in agitation, their patience worn thin from being tethered and immobile. Surrounding them, patches of grass lay trampled and depleted.

As the officers drew closer, their eyes took in the gruesome sight that awaited them amidst the lush, ankle-high grass and the glistening leaves of the thick trees lining the soggy dirt road. With each step, the grim tension hung heavy in the air, and there, amidst the tranquillity of the bush, lay the evidence of brutality. The blood-soaked earth bore witness to the horrors that had unfolded.

Having dismounted nearby, the officers left their horses. They moved with deliberate steps toward the mangled and contorted bodies, their senses assaulted by the aggressive buzzing of flies that swirled above the scene in a frenzy. The officers stood over the bodies, engulfed in a maelstrom of horror and disbelief. The eyes of both slain men remained wide open in a silent scream of terror, holding within them the echoes of the horrors they had witnessed in their last moments. Miller felt his fingers tremble, and his breathing became rapid and shallow. He looked away from the bodies and tried to draw long breaths. He tried to convince himself he was a far more experienced police officer, one equipped to handle such a scene, but his physical response to the scene betrayed the confidence he had tried to portray.

'Sergeant Palmer, I've seen nothing like this before,' the young officer whispered through a hollow gaze, as though he was about to be sick.

'Nor have I, Constable Miller,' Palmer replied. Miller thought Palmer was remaining stout, but he also detected a grimace in his eyes as the colour drained from his face, and it seemed he too was trying to keep his breakfast down. He continued, wiping the sweat from his forehead. 'Look at the carriage and the uniforms. This was a gold escort. Perhaps someone robbed them on their way to Sydney.

'So an ambush, then?' Miller said.

'Looks that way. They probably never saw their assailants coming.'

'But someone butchered these men. Just look at their faces and chests. It seems someone stabbed each of them at least fifty times. Why this level of violence?'

'Son, I do not know,' Palmer said as he released the two horses from the carriage and watched them run to the east, down the incline toward Penrith.

'What do we do?' Miller asked, now turning away from the bodies. He had seen enough.

Palmer sighed and also averted his gaze. 'Well, we don't see murders like this in these parts, and I am not trained to handle such a thing, but I know someone who I think can help. A contact and friend at the Sydney police. I'll write to him and request that he attend as soon as possible.'

Palmer walked back to his horse, pulled out some paper and ink from a saddle pocket, and drafted the letter to his colleague working in Sydney Harbour's patrol.

'Constable, take this and ride to The Rocks police station in Sydney. It's for the attention of Inspector James Walsh. Make sure he gets it and that he leaves immediately.'

Miller took the note, but he found the strange assignment puzzling, as it would consume valuable time in the early stages of a murder investigation. 'That's nearly a full day's ride. Is this really necessary?'

'Indeed, it is. You best leave right away.'

'Who is this inspector, sergeant?'

'The best investigator I know. I will make preparations for Chief Inspector Noland to be notified of the murders, and I will then remain with the bodies until you return. Something tells me we will need all the help we can get.'

THREE

One month earlier...

The dank and filthy square-rigged convict ship battered against the freezing wind of the Atlantic Ocean as it slowly made its way along the Clipper Route, having departed from the south of England, bound for the west coast of Australia. When the ship first set sail, the weather was bitter, and it rained for the first week of the voyage, leaving the prisoners stuck below deck in confined and inhospitable quarters shared with rats and human waste. Weeks later, as it neared its destination, the rain disappeared, and the air became warmer and more humid. This, however, caused rougher seas, and even after his prolonged time onboard, Henry Hobbs still could not gather his sea legs, resulting in being sick more times than he cared to remember.

As the days had slowly turned into weeks, the tension on board reached its boiling point. The ship had exceeded its capacity, and fresh provisions were no longer available. Soon, the effects of malnutrition and deprivation took their toll. The passengers' already frayed nerves were stretched to their limits, causing a pervasive sense of irritability and unrest. The oppressive atmosphere only amplified the waves of sickness that swept through the ship, leaving no corner untouched by illness.

Since they left, two men had died from fever, and many others infected with its crippling symptoms. To save the threat of plaguing the entire ship, the deceased had been unceremoniously cast overboard, and the infected were quarantined to a tiny room below deck. Listening to the echoes of sickness from beneath them, those unaffected still feared the worst.

Hobbs, a solitary figure amidst the chaos of the overcrowded ship, preferred the solace of his own company to the clamour of conversation that permeated the cramped quarters. Like many aboard the vessel, Hobbs was an Englishman bound for the distant shores of Australia, condemned to exile. While others aboard the ship succumbed to the weight of their despair, Hobbs remained steadfast in his resolve, refusing to yield to the torrents of emotion that threatened to engulf him. In the quiet moments of the evening, he retreated into the recesses of his mind, grappling with the harsh reality of his fourteen-year sentence and the uncertainties ahead.

Hobbs possessed a quiet demeanour, not out of timidity, but a keen sense of observation and a penchant for speaking only when necessary. Standing at six foot three, with a robust build and a broad chest, he cut an imposing figure among the cast of fellow convicts. His physical stature marked him as one of the more capable men aboard, a fact not lost in the vigilant eyes of the guards, who wasted no time in assigning him the most arduous and backbreaking tasks.

He toiled under the scorching sun each day, his thick, sandy-coloured hair providing scant protection against the relentless glare bouncing off the ocean waves. Despite his best efforts, his pale English skin proved ill-equipped to withstand the harsh rays, and after the first day, he found himself badly burnt. With each passing day after, the relentless assault of the sun continued and left his skin continually scorched and peeling. His flat, broad nose and wide jawline endured the sun's fury, and the delicate lines of crow's feet deepened with each persistent squint, an attempt to shield his light green eyes from the harsh glare bouncing off the water's surface.

In the rare moments of respite from the relentless labour, Hobbs spent his free time on the edges of the ship, his sturdy frame often anchored against the thick, wooden taffrails as he gazed out into the boundless expanse of the ocean. With each wave, he braced himself against the relentless sway of the ship, his stance wide and sturdy, his knuckles whitened with the strain of a tight grip. Knuckles, which were slightly deformed from a rough upbringing and the rigours of street fighting. Raised in the slums of London amidst the tumult of a boarding house frequented by transients, Hobbs learned early on to fend for himself. His parents, preoccupied with the demands of their work running the house, had offered little guidance or supervision, leaving him to navigate the city streets alone.

In his youth, Hobbs had forged his own path, his sheer physical size and innate wit serving as his most formidable weapon. Street fights and underground bare-knuckle boxing matches became a means of survival and a way to earn a meagre living in his youth amidst the harsh realities of life in London.

The weeks eventually turned into months, and as the journey drew to a close, Hobbs couldn't help but notice the profound changes his body had undergone since embarking on the arduous voyage. Tugging at the fabric of his convict-issued cream-coloured cotton shirt and trousers, he marvelled at the transformation that had taken place beneath the surface. Gone was the familiar weight that had once anchored him to his former self, replaced by a leaner yet harder physique. Throughout the journey, Hobbs estimated he had shed at least fifteen pounds from his previous two hundred and ten-pound frame. The thin layer of subcutaneous fat accumulated over the years, a remnant of a more comfortable existence characterised by careless dietary habits, had melted away. Where once there had been softness, now there was hardness—a dense, sinewy mass of muscle honed by the rigours of life on the ship with little food.

'Land! Land!' came a sudden cry from a young convict early one cloudless morning as he pointed from the starboard side to a growing mass appearing on the horizon.

Abandoning their brooms and mops in a flurry of motion, Hobbs and the remaining men on deck rushed to the side as the silhouette of the West Australian coast slowly emerged on the horizon. Hobbs and the others gazed out in wonder at the first sight of land in weeks. A bitter voice spat loudly behind them, 'I wouldn't get too excited if I were you.'

It was the voice of the miserable and sadistic shipmaster known only as Mr Lloyd. He was a stocky man of about fifty, with a perpetual red face, thick white mutton chops, and an equally thick white moustache. He was completely bald, and apparently self conscious about this as he wore a black forage cap day and night. Hobbs recalled during one windy afternoon early in the voyage, Lloyd's cap had blown off his head and tumbled across the deck. Watching him panic and hurry after it, a handful of young convicts cheered, enjoying Lloyd's embarrassment and fluster. After he quickly reclaimed the cap, Hobbs and the other convicts discovered the cruelty the man was capable of. Lloyd ordered his fellow guards to deliver the punishment of lashings to anyone who had so much smirked at the mishap. A punishment that was both swift and brutal.

Although every convict received routine physical punishment, Hobbs had found himself singled out and relentlessly scrutinised, punished by Lloyd on a near daily basis. Despite his attempts to keep to himself, Lloyd's unwarranted beatings, often in front of the other men, seemed to be a regular occurrence for no valid reason.

'If you knew what was coming to ya on the land, you'd beg me to stay on the ship,' Lloyd continued with a smug grin. 'Now get back to work before we hand out floggings.'

Hobbs didn't know what his new life would look like, but staying on this ship with the rats and the relentless churn of sickness, made worse by Lloyd's presence, was not something he wanted to experience any longer.

To taunt the convicts and further add to their irritability and anguish, no person was permitted to leave until the following day after the ship had docked at Fremantle. As Hobbs stared out at the land before him, longing to get off the Godforsaken ship, the dense and green bushland was a foreign sight to him, as was the humidity he could feel in the air. It starkly contrasted the usual dreary and cool London city weather.

The guards consumed the old and meagre amount of food that was left over for dinner that evening, leaving none for the convicts, which Hobbs thought may not have been a bad thing given the state it was in. Diarrhoea and vomiting had already caused severe problems on board, and he had no issue with the guards eating the convict's share, even if it meant he and the others went hungry.

With the gradual emergence of dawn following a restless night, the guards summoned the convicts once more to duties aboard the ship. The convicts were primarily assigned to cleaning, interspersed with minor repairs aimed at readying the ship for its return journey. In a rare display of mercy, the weather extended a gesture of kindness. The morning unfolded beneath a canopy of overcast skies, offering a respite from the sun's relentless glare. The air was calm, the wind gentle, providing a soothing balm to their sunburnt skin and a welcome reprieve from the harsh elements they had endured for months.

Hobbs received an old mop with several missing plies and was given the unenviable task of cleaning the ship's stern, with explicit instructions to pay particular attention to the whipping post where the remnants of past lashings lingered. Yet, as he surveyed the scene before him, he realised the futility of the task. For weeks, the blood from the merciless lashings had soaked into the wooden deck, stubbornly resisting all attempts at cleaning.

As he continued his best in the impossible task, Hobbs reached to his back and, through his thin linen shirt, felt the raised welts from his own lashings at the hands of Lloyd. Aside from his own beatings, Hobbs had also witnessed many savage floggings upon others on the ship. The crew administered most of these beatings for even the most minor infractions, such as taking too much food at supper or minor scuffles on deck. Often, the punishment didn't fit the crime, and some men could never fully recover from the damage the cruel cat-o'-nine-tails whip inflicted.

While he continued to mop, Hobbs looked around the deck and carefully eyed each man on board. *Man* was a loose term, he thought. Most were young and scrawny, and whilst he knew the land in the distance intrigued them, he knew they were terrified of what was to become of them. The fear of the unknown. He could see it in their eyes. Though their crimes may have warranted punishment, he seriously doubted this extreme sentence would be proportionate to the offences they had committed.

The convicts spent their last night on the tattered hammocks below deck. Hobbs struggled to sleep as he stared at the sagging hammock above him, and through the snores and grunts of the other convicts, he pondered about what was ahead of him in this unfamiliar country.

The following morning, as the sun rose, casting a warm glow over the ship's deck, the convicts gathered in weary silence, their hunger gnawing at their insides like a relentless beast. The guards, unmoved by their plight, callously denied them breakfast and gathered them in a single file, preparing to disembark.

The guards, their faces etched with disdain, lowered a wooden walkway with deliberate slowness, the creaking of its hinges a haunting refrain in the stillness of the morning air. At Lloyd's hostile command, the convicts obediently filed off the ship, their footsteps echoing against the wooden planks as they made their way toward the waiting docks of Fremantle.

Hobbs was toward the end of the line, waiting to get off the ship. When he finally touched the wooden boardwalk, he felt a sense of relief when his old leather boots made contact with the firm platform, anxious about what was to come but grateful to be away from the sea. With a deep inhalation, he filled his lungs with the crisp, clean air of the unfamiliar land, the scent of eucalyptus and salt lingering on the breeze. As he slowly inhaled again and stared at the clear sky, Lloyd pushed him forward from behind.

'Hurry up!' he yelled, brandishing a thick wooden baton.

Hobbs avoided eye contact with Lloyd, but silently complied and walked forward along the rickety, sea-damaged boardwalk behind the convict shuffling in front of him.

The single-file line of weary convicts continued walking further inland until they reached a wooden warehouse about one hundred yards from the shore. The large double doors were wide open, and as Hobbs and his fellow prisoners entered, he saw a completely empty wooden building. There were no windows or furniture inside except for a single desk where a guard sat behind it with a pen, a bottle of ink, and a ledger. A lit candle provided a tiny amount of flickering light, just enough to illuminate a book and the bottom of his pale, bearded face. From the back of the line, Hobbs could just make out a black tunic and a stiff black cap worn by the guard. Next to the guard and behind the desk stood another, again dressed in all black, including the black cap. He was short and thin, and the pile of grey, ragged clothes beside him almost towered over him.

'Keep moving forward,' Lloyd called out. 'A sorry lot we have here, officers.'

'Mmmm, looks like it,' the seated guard said, lowering his tiny, round glasses and inspecting the mass of new convicts before him.

Hobbs watched the line move quickly as the men in front had their details recorded. After recording their details, the men were issued a new set of clothes and then instructed to turn back around and return through the same door as they entered.

'Name,' the seated guard asked without looking up as Hobbs reached the front of the line.

'Henry Hobbs.'

He dabbed at the ink bottle and wrote something in his ledger.

'Move to the left and collect your new clothes. We will burn your old ones after the inspection.'

Hobbs complied with the guard's command, accepting the bundle of worn clothes handed to him. When he returned outside, he squinted as his eyes readjusted to the daylight. As soon as they did, someone took him by the arm and ushered him around the back of the wooden warehouse.

'Strip!' an additional guard demanded. This one was much older and stockier than the other two, but wore the same neatly pressed tunic and stiff black cap.

Hobbs paused, meeting the guard's gaze with unwavering resolve. Time seemed to stand still as he watched the guard take a deliberate step forward, the wooden baton raised menacingly above his head, poised to strike.

'Are we going to have a problem?'

'No,' Hobbs replied slowly, staring straight back at him.

'Then strip.'

He stripped his clothes, carefully removing the small gold ring from the bottom of his boot, which he had kept concealed during the long journey. He tucked it in his palm, and the guard pointed toward a large wooden box. Hobbs threw the old clothes in there and stood naked before the guard. His chest and abdomen muscles bulged and looked well-defined while his fist clenched tightly around the ring buried deep within his palm.

The guard approached him and inspected his body from head to toe, paying particular attention to the thick, sandy hair on his chest and on top of his head while Hobbs.

'Enjoying yourself?' Hobbs asked blankly, distracting the guard from looking any closer at his clenched hand.

'Shut your mouth. You've been on that disgusting ship for months. Everyone gets checked for lice and ticks.'

Clearly irritated at Hobbs, the guard conducted his inspection quickly, stepped back, and swung his baton around. 'Next!' he called out. 'You. Put your new clothes on.'

Hobbs unfolded his newly collected garments comprising a thin grey shirt and a pair of grey trousers with the letters 'PB', for Prison Barracks, stitched down the side of the legs. The legs had buttons down the entire side, which he presumed were to support ankle shackles while still keeping one's pants on. He slid his feet into the new pair of black boots and discreetly pushed the ring he had kept secure down the side. The new uniform was, in fact, far from new. It was stained and smelled of mould and dried vomit. Hobbs wondered who last wore these clothes and what happened to them. Once dressed, he sat on the hard ground and fastened his boot buttons up to the top of his ankles.

The guard continued, 'Move over to the side of the building with the others. A carriage will be here soon.'

Hobbs's gaze swept over the scene, taking in the sight of approximately fifty other men gathered together in the shade behind the wooden warehouse. Each man, clad in the same grey attired uniform of a convict, wore tired expressions and carried a subdued demeanour. Not a word passed between them; the weight of exhaustion, hunger, and nerves was simmering in the air. Hobbs approached the group and silently joined their ranks. Like them, he carried the burden of weariness and uncertainty.

Several large wooden carriages pulled by two horses arrived at the warehouse a short time later. Armed guards holding long rifles climbed down from the front of them and used a thick, rusted key to open the back door to the carriage. There were no windows inside it, just one at the back door, protected by thick iron bars. Hobbs peered inside and saw nothing except two long benches on either side. He figured only fifteen men could fit inside.

Several guards began dividing the group without saying a word. They simply walked through the mass of convicts and, using their batons, pushed them into smaller groups of about twenty. No one, including Hobbs, had enough energy to ask questions or even offer any resistance. He was pushed into a group of men similar to his own large size, and he figured they were probably being separated based on physique. This would likely mean the larger and fitter men would be required to perform more gruelling and physically demanding labour, just as they did on the ship.

As Hobbs and the convicts of similar size gathered together, a lone guard dressed in the familiar black tunic stepped forward from the ranks. 'All of you, inside the carriage now.'

'Where are we going?' a voice in the middle of the group nervously asked.

The guard ignored the question and moved to the back of the group, poking those at the back of the huddle with his wooden baton, urging them forward. They filed inside, and as Hobbs correctly guessed, the carriage was designed for no more than fifteen men. The group of twenty uncomfortably crowded in, and he found himself wedged tightly between two men on the wooden bench. When the carriage was full with the large group, the guard slammed the door shut and locked it. Darkness and silence swiftly swallowed Hobbs and the group, aside from occasional deep breathing and claustrophobic whimpers.

The horses soon picked up to a canter, and Hobbs, alongside his fellow convicts, began the bumpy ride to their unknown destination.

FOUR

As the carriage eventually came to an abrupt halt, the once-quiet interior erupted into a racket of indistinct murmurs, the air thick with anticipation and uncertainty. Desperate for answers about their new whereabouts, Hobbs and the other convicts inside strained to peer through the narrow cracks between the wooden planks that formed the carriage's walls. His efforts, however, were thwarted by the sturdy construction that barred the view. Despite Hobbs' best attempts, the darkness remained impenetrable, and the unknown was still yet to reveal itself.

After another ten minutes had passed, the men remained trapped inside the carriage, and a few of them became overheated, restless, and irritable. Now that the carriage had stopped moving, claustrophobia was spreading, and some hyperventilated violently around Hobbs, who simply closed his eyes and controlled his breathing, ignoring everyone else around him. Just when it appeared insanity would take the better of the group, the rear door of the carriage unbolted and swung all the way open.

Bright sunlight poured into the carriage, and Hobbs squinted as he struggled to adjust.

'Everyone out now and form a single file in front of the carriage,' a loud voice demanded.

There was no orderly exit. The convicts were desperate to breathe fresh air and regain some personal space. Hobbs finally made his way out of the cramped space and took in his new surroundings. Beside him, dense clusters of green foliage adorned the landscape, their canopies swaying gracefully in the arid breeze. Yet, it was not the tranquil scene that commanded Hobbs' attention. Instead, his gaze remained fixed on the enormous structure before him. It was an imposing sight: an immense grey limestone building, its towering presence dominating the landscape. Several levels high and spanning hundreds of yards wide, the structure seemed to stretch across his entire field of vision, casting a formidable shadow over the surrounding terrain.

'Welcome to Fremantle Prison,' a guard called out from behind the group of convicts.

The group fell into their single file formation again, standing in silence as they awaited further instructions. Moments later, a figure emerged from the shadows—a man of roughly forty-five, his long brown beard cascading down to his broad chest in unruly waves. Dressed in a black tunic adorned with a gold-coloured belt and large buttons, the man exuded an air of authority as he approached with measured steps. His attire, complete with a stiff black cap, mirrored the standard-issue uniform that Hobbs had grown accustomed to during his time in captivity, only with the addition of a brightly coloured gold belt.

'My name is Comptroller General Robert Dawes. This here is my prison,' he said, sweepingly extending his arm toward the prison, commanding fresh attention to the imposing structure behind him.

'You are here because you broke the law. As such, we will put you to work and believe me, you will work hard. But we believe your hard work will contribute to the development of this colony.

Dawes, exuding an air of casual authority, strolled leisurely past the line of convicts, his hands tucked behind his back. Flanking him, two guards, identical in appearance save for the absence of a gold belt, fell into step.

'I have only one rule here, and it's quite simple,' he continued. 'Do whatever the officers tell you to do. Simple. If you do this, you will not have any problems.'

With a subtle nod to one of the guards, Dawes pivoted on his heel and retraced his steps, disappearing again through the imposing entrance of the prison's enormous front doors.

'Inside now. Single file!' a guard suddenly bellowed, his voice echoing sharply as he brandished his wooden baton with authority, punctuating his command with a decisive wave.

As they entered through the large doors, Hobbs looked around at what was to be his new home. He was no stranger to prisons, and this one resembled the English facilities he was so familiar with. Hobbs figured he was currently standing in the main yard. As the group approached the centre yard, he felt the crunch of small rocks under his boots.

The prison, fashioned in the expansive shape of a U, enclosed the yard within its stern walls. Hobbs observed that the architectural form enveloped the space, creating an enclosed atmosphere. Beyond the U-shaped structure, his gaze extended to a backdrop of terrace houses and limestone buildings in various stages of construction adorned with skeletal scaffolding frames.

Hobbs heard a loud whistling noise and, along with the rest of the group, turned around and looked at a guard standing on a wooden box.

'My name is Officer Wardell, and I am the chief guard.' Wardell was about the same age as Hobbs, and even standing on the wooden box, he was still well shorter than him. He had an arrogant-looking smirk behind yellow crooked teeth too big for his mouth. His thin face stretched out to show more of his rotten teeth as he continued to grin obnoxiously. He smoothed out his tight-fitting tunic and continued.

'You all heard the Comptroller General and his only rule here, so I won't repeat it, but let me say this: I have been at this putrid place for five years now, and I am irritable. I will not tolerate foul behaviour. If you cross me, it'll be lashings or days locked in the irons under the blistering sun. Or, sometimes, both. You will all start work immediately on the buildings you see behind you. The area is expanding, and you will be a part of this construction. We will soon split you into groups, and work will begin shortly.'

When Wardell stood down from his box, several guards began grabbing convicts by the arm and separating them into smaller groups. As they continued to sort through the men, Wardell approached Hobbs and looked him up and down.

'Are you a labourer?'

'No.'

'Excuse me?'

'No,' Hobbs said a little louder, knowing exactly why Wardell asked him to repeat his answer, but he couldn't bring himself to stroke Wardell's ego by using any inflated title that he had selected for himself.

Wardell quickly drove his baton into Hobbs' stomach, and he curled over, winded by the sharp blow. Hobbs looked at Wardell, and as soon as he saw the smirk on his face, he did everything he could to conceal the pain and not give him the satisfaction. He stood back up quickly and towered over the chief guard.

Wardell grinned. 'You're pretty tough. Most men don't get back up that fast from a good hit like that.'

Akin to Lloyd, Hobbs disliked the man increasingly with every second he spent in his presence.

'That resolve will work well here unless we crush your spirit, which is likely inevitable. From now on, you will address me as sir, understand?'

Hobbs sighed. 'Yes, sir,' he reluctantly uttered, only to avoid another strike.

'Better. So, seeing you aren't a skilled labourer, I have another way to put a big chap like you to work. You'll be on limestone duty. We source all the limestone for the construction here locally, so you join that crew, lugging it around wherever it's needed. After a few days, I promise you'll be too tired to annoy me. Now move over there to the far left side of the yard.'

Wardell lingered and looked directly at Hobbs. Waiting.

Despite his irritation, Hobbs wanted nothing more than to avoid attention. He tried hard not to roll his eyes and grunted, 'Yes, sir.'

'Good, now get to work.'

Hobbs met two more men, quite a few years younger than himself, but about the same size. They stood by two guards, who then opened a wooden door and instructed them through it. They slowly walked along a cold corridor with stone walls. The ground was wet as water continued to drip through from above.

They continued along the corridor and passed some tiny cells, all of which were unoccupied. The walkway echoed, and Hobbs could only hear the slapping of leather boots on the ground. As they reached the end, a guard unlocked another door, and Hobbs and the other two men walked through. They found themselves back outside and near a new construction site.

Looking around, there didn't appear to be much construction work occurring, aside from about a dozen men lugging enormous blocks of limestone and laying them in a neat stack by the side of the new building beside two more guards.

'Fresh lot for you,' the escorting guard said.

'Good, we are finished here, but now we need to move all this stone inside.'

The guards pushed Hobbs and the other two toward the slabs of stone and returned through the door they came from.

Hobbs looked at the other men who had taken a break to catch their breath. They had sweat and dirt on them, each with a sunburnt face and rough, calloused hands.

The limestone guard said, 'These men have just finished with the last lot of stone out here. Now, it needs to get inside immediately to be smoothed and shaped, so construction on the new wing can continue. Understand?'

Yes, sir,' the convicts, including Hobbs, replied. Their tone was more vigorous, layered with fear after witnessing Hobbs' earlier punishment.

'Now they have been working all morning, and they are going to keep working, but you are all fresh, and I expect you to double their efforts.'

'Cheap labour to spare the British treasury,' Hobbs thought.

'Sir, we haven't eaten in over a day. We are weak,' the young convict next to Hobbs said.

The guard gritted his teeth, and with a flash, he had struck the man hard on his left shoulder with a forceful blow of his baton. The convict fell hard onto the ground, clutching at his arm.

'Help him up,' the guard said.

Hobbs and the other convict took the injured man by the waist and helped him back to his feet.

'Thanks,' he groaned, while Hobbs gave him a gentle pat of encouragement. As Hobbs observed the young man, a pang of empathy washed over him. Despite not knowing the details of his crime or background, he couldn't help but notice the youthfulness etched into his features—barely eighteen years old, perhaps even younger. Reflecting on his journey and the circumstances that had led him to this place, Hobbs couldn't shake the feeling that the young man, much like himself, may have become ensnared in a web of circumstances beyond his control. In that moment, amidst the harsh realities of prison life, a flicker of compassion stirred within him - a recognition that no one, regardless of their transgressions, deserved to be subjected to such harsh treatment.

The guard kept his baton in his hand while he gave additional instructions. 'You eat when we say, drink when we say, sleep when we say, and work when we say. Right now, you work. Start moving the stone inside the construction site.

Hobbs joined the rest of the group and picked up his first bulky piece of limestone, overwhelmed by its weight. A gnawing hunger gripped him as he surveyed the daunting pile of limestone yet to be shifted. With each glance at the arduous work before them, he resigned himself to the fact that it would be quite some time before he would eat.

He carried the first piece of stone along a long, narrow dirt path to the site of the half-completed building.

'Put that down there,' another convict drenched in sweat said.

Hobbs dropped the stone and turned to walk back to repeat the process. When he left the new building, he suddenly felt a firm hand grasp him by tightly on the shoulder. Hobbs turned around and saw a man covered in grime and sweat. His matted black hair was wet and flat on his scalp, and his thick stubble and sun-damaged face made him look older than he probably was. Hobbs guessed that the man was in his early thirties and had a similar height and build to him, which was perhaps why he was assigned to the stone lugging detail.

'I know you,' the man said, glaring at Hobbs with hostility.

'No, you don't,' Hobbs replied flatly.

'Yeah. Yeah, you're a bobby from London, aren't ya?'

'I'm a convict.'

'Nah, that's it. I knew I'd seen you before. You pinched my brother.'

A small cluster of fellow convicts had gravitated towards the unfolding dialogue, their curiosity piqued by the exchange. Hobbs cast a quick glance around, noting the conspicuous absence of the guards.

'Don't deny it, you are,' he said, poking Hobbs in the chest with a single finger.

Hobbs glared at the man. 'Do not poke me,' he warned.

The man stepped forward, inches from Hobbs' face, staring into his eyes.

'What do you want?' Hobbs asked, tensing his arms.

'Admit it. My brother was Alfred Dayton. He was hanged because of you. All of us Dayton's wanted your head after that.'

'I don't know you, and I don't know your brother,' he said, turning his back on him.

Dayton's firm grip on Hobbs's shoulder jolted him backwards and his muscles tensed instinctively. With a swift turn, Hobbs faced a giant, clenched fist hurtling at his nose at alarming speed. Reacting instinctually, he dodged the incoming blow and moved with fluid agility. In a split-second counterattack, Hobbs unleashed a powerful right hook aimed squarely at Dayton's jaw. The impact reverberated through his fist as Dayton let out a sharp cry of agony, and his jaw dislocated under the force of the punch.

As the group of onlookers gasped in disbelief, Hobbs stepped back. His chest heaved with the intensity of the moment.

Dayton shook his head and tried to correct his now displaced jaw, but it was too disfigured and his bottom lip was hanging crooked. Hobbs figured this would have been enough to stop the man, but he could see pure rage in his eyes and knew this wasn't over.

'You filthy pig,' he slurred. 'You might not remember, but I could never forget your face.'

'Stop it. Either get your jaw looked at or just get back to work,' Hobbs said calmly.

Dayton ignored him and charged at Hobbs. He tackled him around the waist and dragged him to the ground hard with everything he had. As he fell backwards, Hobbs tucked his legs toward his stomach, slid his knees against Dayton's heavy body, and drove him off with a powerful kick.

Hobbs quickly got to his feet at the same time as Dayton charged again. This time, Hobbs skipped sideways and drove his leg hard into the side of Dayton's right knee. It broke instantly, and he collapsed on the ground in an agonised scream. Suddenly, a pair of guards charged over and Hobbs watched as the remaining convicts fled the area.

'What's going on here?' a guard asked when he saw Dayton curled over on the ground in writhing pain, groaning, and nursing his shattered leg and jaw.

'I was defending myself,' Hobbs said.

'Defending yourself?' he said, looking Hobbs up and down, examining his entire body. 'You don't have a mark on you, and look at him.'

Hobbs shrugged. 'He's not much of a fighter, I guess.'

The guard waved his hand, and two others swiftly grabbed Hobbs by his arms. 'You're going to see Wardell. He'll sort you out.'

FIVE

Wardell stood alone in the centre of the main yard, the tendrils of smoke curling lazily from his thin wooden pipe as he surveyed the scene with a detached air. Amid this solitary moment, Hobbs found himself forcibly brought before him by the firm grip of two guards.

'What's all this about?' Wardell asked, spitting a piece of loose tobacco to the ground.

'This man just beat up on another. Left him with a broken knee and a messed up jaw.'

'Why?' Wardell asked sternly, looking directly at Hobbs with his teeth clenched.

'He came at me. I was defending myself.' Hobbs said. From what he could decipher from his brief interactions with Wardell, Hobbs knew this reasoning would likely not prevent him from unwanted attention, yet he decided he would tell his version truthfully.

Wardell glared at Hobbs.

'Sir,' Hobbs added after taking a slow, deep breath.

'There's not a scratch on you.'

'I was defending myself. I did nothing wrong but protect myself from an assault.'

'So you were just attacked, unprovoked then?'

'Correct, sir.'

'Why?'

'He believed me to be someone he knew back in London.'

'And who might that be?'

Hobbs tried to hide another deep breath, but failed when it turned into a sigh. He had only been at the prison for a few hours, yet he had already attracted too much attention. He wanted to leave his past behind and become just another convict until his sentence was complete, but evidently, that would not happen. His chest felt tight and his muscles were still tense from the brawl, yet he continued with the truth.

'A police officer,' he mumbled.

'Hmm. What's your name, convict?'

'Henry Hobbs, sir,' he replied, detecting a faint smirk behind Wardell's thin lips.

'You know,' Wardell said, walking closer to Hobbs and spitting another piece of loose tobacco inches from Hobbs' boots. 'I thought you looked like trouble from the first moment I saw you. You have an unusual presence about you. You don't seem as...' Wardell paused for a moment, as though contemplating his words as he glanced at the sky. 'Let's say, broken as the other men who arrived here with you. I couldn't put my finger on it. You were just somehow different from the rest of the slackers here.'

Wardell took a deep drag from his pipe, blew smoke in Hobbs' face, and smiled the same arrogant smirk as he wore earlier. 'But you know, I heard there was going to be a police officer coming in today. Word travels fast, even from all the way in England.'

Hobbs didn't speak and kept his eyes locked on Wardell's. If word of his arrival had arrived with him from London, he knew it could not be good and he tried to bury the panic that was swirling inside him.

'So, you're the inspector who punched his superintendent and stole five pounds from him?'

Hobbs remained silent.

'Answer me when I ask you a question!'

'Sir, I stole nothing.'

'But you don't deny the assault.'

'No, sir, I do not.'

'Well, your superintendent sent word that his attacker was coming. Told us what you did and to really look after you,' he said with another sly grin.

'He isn't my superintendent. Not any more, sir.'

'You're damn right. You're a convict now, and you belong to me. Ten lashes for today. Administered by myself this afternoon.'

Wardell turned to one of the guards. 'Put him inside a cell until then.'

'I did nothing wrong, he attacked me!' Hobbs roared, suddenly losing control of the composure he tried to maintain as a flood of emotions quickly surfaced. Before he could protest further, the two guards who had escorted him to Wardell snatched him under the arms.'

Wardell took a drag from his pipe and shrugged. 'Mr Hobbs, I simply do not care.'

With a smug smirk stretching across his face, exposing his yellowed and decayed teeth once more, Wardell stared at Hobbs with a twisted satisfaction as the guards forcefully escorted him away.

Dragging him across the courtyard, they led him into the foreboding depths of the large U-shaped building, where they unceremoniously thrust him into a dark and cramped stone cell near the entrance. Thick iron bars guarded the cell, which contained no semblance of comfort. No bed, no blanket, or water.

Seated upon the hard floor, Hobbs gingerly nursed his red and swollen knuckles, tender from the heavy punch on Dayton's jaw. In that solitary moment of reflection, he grappled with the stark reality that his past life and employment had followed him across continents. It was a chapter of his life that he had hoped to leave behind, buried in the depths of tragic memories. Yet, as the current events unfolded, it became painfully clear that his past refused to leave him.

As the hours dragged on in the oppressive darkness, Hobbs' body grew weary from the unyielding stone floor of his cell. Aches and pains gnawed at his muscles. Hunger gnawed at his stomach, thirst parched his throat, and exhaustion weighed heavily upon his limbs. But perhaps most agonising of all was the suffocating isolation and the thought of the inevitable physical punishment he would soon receive.

Exhaustion eventually overcame him, and he slipped into a light sleep, his head nestled against his knees. Yet, just as his sleep deepened, the jarring clatter of a heavy keyring against iron bars startled him awake. He blinked groggily as the heavy door opened. Without a word spoken, two guards materialised and with a firm grasp, they hauled Hobbs to his feet.

As they escorted him out of the building, the searing afternoon sun momentarily blinded Hobbs, as its intense rays pierced through his disoriented state. Squinting against the glare, he struggled to focus his vision, only to be confronted by the surreal sight unfolding before him. Hundreds of convicts and scores of guards stood in eerie silence, encircling an ominous A-shaped wooden rack at the centre of the yard. Still reeling from the disorienting brightness, Hobbs surveyed his surroundings with bewilderment. Through his blurry vision, he discerned the contours of a smaller yard nestled behind the main U-shaped building from which he had just emerged. With a sinking realisation, Hobbs understood the significance of this space - it was the punishment yard, a realm of retribution where iron rings tethered individuals to endure hours, even days, under the scorching sun.

Navigating through the crowd, the masses shifted, creating a pathway that reshaped around the impending spectacle of the wooden rack. Atop a wooden pedestal, Wardell exuded an air of theatricality, gripping a tightly coiled whip in his hand. His smirk, aimed directly at Hobbs, infuriated him.

'Gentlemen, you have been called here to witness this convict's punishment for fighting. I do not tolerate aggressive behaviour. I have always made it clear that destructive behaviour under my guard will not go unpunished.'

In the solemn hush of the crowd, the two guards dragged Hobbs toward the ominous wooden rack. With a swift and forceful motion, the two guards tore his shirt from his body and firmly bound his limbs to the rack's weathered restraints. As he lowered his gaze, he saw the stained earth beneath him, knowing it bore witness to the countless lashings given out in this very spot.

After being flogged more times than he cared to recall during the voyage to Australia, Hobbs was all too familiar with what was coming. The anxious anticipation, the memory of the searing pain, and the relentless sting of the whip all haunted his thoughts. As he awaited the lashes, a gnawing fear gnawed at him—a fear not only of the excruciating torment to come, but also of the fear of his old wounds reopening, leading him to bleed out on the spot.

Amidst the crowd's sombre silence and having been in their position several times, Hobbs knew none harboured any desire to witness the brutality that was about to unfold. Yet, he understood all too well that the spectacle of punishment served a dual purpose: to instil fear in the masses, ensuring absolute compliance while causing Hobbs a profound sense of agony and humiliation.

'Ten lashes with the cat!' Wardell cried out as he dropped the end of the whip, allowing it to unravel by his side.

Hobbs turned to his side and saw the cat-o'-nine-tails whip gripped tightly in Wardell's hand with its nine short plaited rope ends. It was a cruel instrument, meticulously crafted to exact maximum suffering. Each dense length of the braids bore hard knots at their tips, designed to intensify the pain and tear open the skin upon impact.

He tensed, every muscle in his body coiled in anticipation of the impending pain. Yet, in a cruel twist, Wardell lingered for a moment. Hobbs knew the pause would have served as psychological torment and intensified the uneasy apprehension that gripped both Hobbs and the audience.

Wardell's first blow landed squarely in the centre of Hobbs's back, slicing him open with brutal efficiency. The searing pain radiated through his body as the ropes coiled around his ribcage, threatening to crush the very breath from his lungs. Despite the overwhelming agony, Hobbs clenched his teeth with unyielding resolve, making a silent vow to himself not to scream. In that harrowing moment, as pain and determination collided, Hobbs steeled himself, refusing to give Wardell the satisfaction.

The second strike found its mark higher on Hobbs's back; the sickening crack of the whip on flesh echoed through the air. Agony surged through Hobbs as he felt the searing pain intensify, blood trickling down his back as his legs threatened to give way once more. Light-headedness enveloped him, a dizzying haze clouding his senses as he fought to maintain consciousness.

On the third, Hobbs's entire body convulsed. The agony tore through him, threatening to unravel his resolve with its relentless intensity. Yet, amidst the searing pain, he glimpsed Wardell. The frustration that stretched across his face ignited a fresh resolve within Hobbs, now compelled more than ever to remain silent.

After enduring seven more agonising lashes, Hobbs teetered on the brink of collapse. As Wardell concluded the punishment, casting the blood-soaked whip aside, he struggled to remain upright, supported solely by the shackles of the wooden rack.

Two guards approached and untied Hobbs, but his weakened body betrayed him. He crumpled to the ground, unable to muster the strength to remain upright. Despite his efforts, the tremors wracked his limbs, leaving him utterly dependent on the guards to hold him upright as Wardell strode toward him, grinning.

'You might think you're pretty tough now, but we will see you handle your lashings tomorrow, the next day, and the next after that.'

Gripped by profound weakness and exhaustion, Hobbs felt a surge of rage growing within him as Wardell's smug face loomed dangerously close. Despite experiencing overwhelming pain and fatigue, Hobbs recognised the truth hidden behind Wardell's sadistic satisfaction - that Wardell was not merely perpetrating an isolated incident, but deliberately and continuously assaulting him to shatter his spirit and, ultimately, take his life. Though his eyelids drooped heavily with fatigue, Hobbs summoned the last of his strength and, fixing his gaze unwaveringly upon Wardell, broke free of the guards holding him up and launched his head forward as hard and fast as he could. His forehead connected with Wardell's nose with a sickening crunch, flattening it against his face. Around him, the other convicts looked on in stunned silence, their gasps mingling with whispers of disbelief while a few scattered cheers rang out. The guards responded and tackled

Hobbs to the ground, but he didn't care. If Wardell intended on torturing and eventually murdering him, he would go down fighting.

Wardell, still howling in agony and clutching his broken, bloodied nose, regained his footing and charged at the restrained Hobbs with unbridled fury. His fist collided with Hobbs's stomach with brutal force, causing his knees to buckle. Yet, before Wardell could unleash another punch, a commanding voice reverberated through the yard, freezing him in his tracks.

'Enough!'

Comptroller General Dawes marched toward Hobbs and Wardell with every ounce of his authority behind every step.

'What is the meaning of this?' he demanded.

'This convict just struck me,' Wardell cried, blood still leaking from his crushed nose.

'Is this true?' Dawes asked, looking directly at Hobbs.

'Yes, sir. After the threat of daily punishment for no reason,' Hobbs replied.

'You are Henry Hobbs, the ex-Scotland Yard Inspector, yes?'

'Yes, sir,' Hobbs grunted.

A collective gasp rippled through the crowd of convicts at the revelation, their inaudible whispers swirling through the yard.

'Yes, I thought so. On your first day here, you assault a fellow convict and then assault my chief of guards.'

Hobbs remained silent. He knew that no words he could offer would adequately address the gravity of the circumstances.

'I do not want troublemakers in my establishment. I am here to represent the British Empire and to ensure this colony's economy grows, which can only happen with hard-working convicts. I am not interested in petty rivalries or unfair punishment.'

'He should hang for what he has done,' Wardell said, his voice strained as he held his head back, attempting to stem the blood flow.

Hobbs decided to change his tact and respond. A last attempt to defend his actions. 'I have only ever acted in self-defence. The assault on the convict earlier was in response to him attacking first, and I only struck Mr Wardell because of what he said to me about further punishment.'

'Is what the convict said true?' Dawes asked the guards holding onto Hobbs.

Both fidgeted nervously, hesitating to offer a response.

Tell me the truth. What was said?' Dawes asked sternly.

One guard sighed and reluctantly answered, 'Yes, sir, what the convict said is true.'

'Right,' Dawes said. 'Wardell, go clean yourself up. As for you, Mr Hobbs, perhaps you are being honest. Still, you have already attracted enough troubling attention to yourself in a brief amount of time. My introductory statement stands. I don't want troublemakers here. We are trying to establish a thriving colony, and there is no place for men like you. As such, I am sending you away.'

'Away? To where?' Hobbs asked.

'Cockatoo Island in Sydney, the heart of the colony of New South Wales. Fresh convicts are no longer sent there, but repeat offenders are. There, they manage the worst of the worst. Men like you who continually flaunt the rules and commit further offences. They are better placed to manage difficulties. I don't want anyone like you at my facility. Men like you cannot be rehabilitated, and are counterproductive to our community. You leave tomorrow on a supply ship already scheduled for the East Coast. I will complete all the transportation paperwork. For now, you will go back to your cell until morning.'

SIX

December, 1861.

Constable Edmund Miller burst through the front doors of The Rocks police station in Sydney Harbour in the late afternoon, the exhaustion evident in his flushed face from the hard ride he had endured. After tethering his horse outside, allowing it a much-needed drink from the wooden trough, he scanned the station's foyer for Inspector Walsh.

'What's wrong, son?' A burly, middle-aged sergeant with a thick, bushy beard asked, peering down from his small framed glasses behind the counter.

'I need to see Inspector Walsh immediately,' Miller said hurriedly. His breathing was rapid and shallow, and sweat ran down his forehead as he fidgeted and nervously peered beyond the sergeant and into the back area of the station.

'What's this all about? And for heaven's sake, relax, boy.'

'A double murder at the foot of the mountains, just past Penrith. I have a letter for him,' Miller said, waving Sergeant Palmer's letter above his head.

'The inspector isn't here now, but I expect him back any minute. Just sit down, take a breath and try to stay calm please.'

Miller settled into a seat near the front door, and his grip on the letter tightened as he tapped his feet anxiously against the ground. His abrupt entry into the police station created a minor disturbance, prompting a few constables to peer curiously from the back of the station. Even an old drunkard, confined to a small cell behind the sergeant, stood up to glimpse the commotion.

'Who was murdered?' the prisoner asked, pressing his face against the thick steel bars. Miller didn't respond, but the drunk stood up against the bars, waiting for an answer before belching loudly and wiping his mouth and cheeks with the sleeve of his whiskey-stained shirt.

'Sit down!' The sergeant called out before turning back to Miller. 'So, why do you need Inspector Walsh out west?'

'I was sent with this letter to find him. We seek his investigative expertise.'

The sergeant pondered momentarily and then nodded.

'Well then, make yourself comfortable. He shouldn't be too long now.'

Miller sat back on the wooden bench by the front door, exhaling deeply as he attempted to calm his racing thoughts. The gruesome images of the two murdered guards lingered in the forefront of his mind, and he couldn't fathom how he would ever erase the haunting memory of what he had witnessed.

Anxiously trying to pass the time, Miller gazed around the station, which was weathered and dusty, with remnants of horse droppings tracked through the foyer from outside. The only source of light filtered in through a long, narrow window on the left side of the stone building, offering a glimpse of Sydney Harbour beyond. Miller looked through the window and observed the tranquil, deep blue waters under the clear, cloudless sky. Watching the people outside, he noticed they moved with a greater sense of urgency compared to Penrith's slower pace of life. Sweaty men in rumpled shirts hurried along the water's edge, hauling large crates while urgent steam whistles pierced the air.

A short time later, a man of around forty, slim and fit with broad shoulders, entered the police station. He removed his bowler hat and placed it on a stand near the front door, revealing a prominent nose over a thin moustache, thick dark eyebrows, and wavy black hair. He wore dark trousers, black boots, and a cream-coloured shirt held up by brown suspenders. Despite his blank expression, Miller thought he exuded both confidence and approachability.

'Excuse me, sir', Miller said, addressing him courteously. 'Are you Inspector James Walsh?'

'I am. What can I do for you, lad?' he replied chirpily with a thick English accent.

Walsh looked Miller up and down as he combed his hair back carelessly with his fingers. Despite the sweat dampening his hair, his expression showed no discomfort from the heat.

Sir, I am Constable Edmund Miller. I have a letter from Sergeant Samuel Palmer from Penrith.'

'Ah yes, Samuel Palmer, we go a long way back. I trust he's well?'

'He is good, sir, but here, you need to read this,' he said, handing over the letter.

Walsh tore open the envelope, removed the letter and looked at Miller sharply before he began reading.

Dear Inspector Walsh,

I hope you are well. It has been too long since we last spoke, and I wish I had written more pleasant news, but I am afraid this is not a personal letter. I am writing to request your investigative expertise. This morning, someone murdered two gold guards and the scene is more gruesome than anything I have ever seen. I fear news of these murders will spread through the community, particularly to the Gold Guard and Royal Mint. The Penrith police station has not yet employed specialist investigative officers and relies solely on the mounted unit. As such, I seek your expertise and guidance in managing this case with the utmost care and urgency. Constable Miller will assist you as required; you will find him most competent. We will inform our Chief Inspector and make arrangements to accommodate you here. If you can assist, please do not delay. I recall from a previous training seminar you spoke of the importance of crime scene preservation, and I have endeavoured to do this.

Yours Faithfully,

Sergeant Samuel Palmer

Miller watched Walsh read the letter slowly, methodically. He paused twice, glancing up at Walsh without speaking, before rereading it.

'Follow me,' Walsh finally said, returning the letter to Miller.

He ushered Miller to the far side of the police station, where he found a modest office with an unobstructed view of the harbour. Shelves lined with stacks of paperwork and an array of leather-bound books adorned the space. A sturdy wooden desk dominated the centre of the room. Taking his place behind the desk, Walsh gestured for Miller to sit.

'How old are you?' Walsh asked.

'Twenty-one, sir.'

'How long have you been a police officer?'

'Two years.'

'You have an English accent too.'

'Yes, sir, I was born and raised in London. I married three years ago, and my wife and I moved here looking for adventure.'

Walsh smiled. 'Plenty of that out here.'

'Yes, sir, there is,' Miller said, his throat tight as he again replayed the gruesome scene of the murders in his mind, anticipating when Inspector Walsh would address the topic.

'Do you enjoy your work?'

'Very much so, sir.'

'Have you seen the crime scene?' Walsh asked as Miller exhaled. He was grateful to leave the small talk and pleasantries to discuss the purpose for his visit.

'I have. It was awful.'

'What are your theories?'

Taken aback, Miller reluctantly answered. 'Sir, I am just a simple mounted constable. I have no experience, so I have no useful theories.'

'Well, surely you must have some after seeing the scene. Sergeant Palmer wrote you were competent, and my friend would not say that unless he meant it.'

Feeling a mix of embarrassment and pride at his sergeant's words, Miller straightened up in his chair and adjusted the cuffs on the sleeve of his black tunic. 'Well, sir, I believe an ambush occurred on their gold run back to Sydney.'

'Was anything stolen?'

'Some gold, but not all of it.'

'Why do you think that was?' Walsh asked, his gaze inquisitive, yet kind, fixed on Miller.

'I think they could not carry it all. The entire load would have had considerable weight.'

'Good. That makes logical sense. And that tells us what?'

'I guess they were on foot or on light horseback. They probably sought a quick getaway.'

'I agree. You also said '*they*'. I, too, think we are looking for more than one offender to take down two armed gold guards. How were they killed?'

'They were stabbed. Many times and all over their body. I lost count of the number of wounds.'

Walsh sat silently for a moment while his gaze drifted toward the ceiling.

'Do you think this was a robbery gone wrong?' he eventually asked.

Miller shook his head. 'I'm not so sure. The level of violence seemed unnecessary if you ask me. Beyond just performing a robbery, anyway.'

'Good. And I do ask you, and if I ask you such things again, I want you to always answer me with what's on your mind. Every tiny detail helps, and it is better voiced than kept to yourself. A team is better than one man, and so far, everything you have told me has been insightful. I have learnt much without even seeing the scene. So, do you understand how I want you to work with me?'

'I do. Does that mean you'll help?'

Walsh stood up. 'Yes, of course. We will leave soon. First, I need to stop at home and speak with my wife. Wait for me here. I will be back shortly. Take your horse around the back for a rest and some shade. There's hay and water there. We will leave shortly; there is no time to waste. These slain men deserve justice.'

SEVEN

Walsh arrived back at the police station astride his sturdy yellow palomino, the saddle pouches laden with supplies. With the sun casting long shadows, he guided his horse to the rear of the station, where Miller was grooming his own horse.

'Let's go, Edmund. We have a long ride ahead of us, and we need to get to the scene while it is as fresh as possible.'

'Yes, sir, I'm ready.'

They journeyed westward in silence for the first several hours. While Walsh maintained a composed exterior, his mind churned with what lay ahead. Even busy with his thoughts, he was keenly aware of Miller's occasional gaze in his direction, and he sensed the younger man's apprehension.

Miller was the first to break the silence. 'If you don't mind me asking, sir, what brought you here from England?'

'I don't mind you asking at all. My story is much the same as yours. I arrived five years ago from Scotland Yard. The police here sought an experienced investigator to develop and lead the Sydney detectives, and I saw it as an excellent opportunity. My wife and twin twelve-year-old sons took a little longer to adjust, but this is now home. That is how I know Sergeant Palmer. Over the years, he has taken part in training programs I have facilitated. He is a clever and experienced police officer, and I trust his judgement. If he is out of his depth here, it must be bad. Hence, I did not wish to delay.'

As the sun dipped below the horizon, casting hues of orange and pink across the sky, they pressed onward a little faster. With the onset of night, the air turned cooler, a welcome relief from the day's heat.

'How long do you need at the crime scene?' Miller asked.

'I don't know yet. I have to see it first.'

'It'll be late by the time we arrive and finish up. You are welcome to stay with my wife and I for the night. I expect Sergeant Palmer will have some accommodation set up for you by tomorrow if you need to stay a while.'

'I appreciate that, Edmund, thank you.'

As midnight neared, Walsh and Miller approached the crime scene, where they found Sergeant Samuel Palmer guarding the area, surrounded by lanterns that cast flickering light. Leaning against the rear wooden wheel of the carriage, Palmer appeared to be dozing off. Walsh felt the heavy air with the scent of death mingling with the citrus aroma of nearby trees, while swarms of flies buzzed incessantly.

Even from a distance, Walsh could discern the grim sight. The bodies of the guards lay contorted and mangled across the road, and rigour mortis had set in, rendering their limbs stiff and unyielding. Blood had pooled around them, seeping into the earth in all directions, and their faces endured several brutal wounds, rendering them unrecognisable even from afar.

'Samuel!' Walsh called out as he dismounted and tied his horse to the carriage.

Palmer woke in a fluster and smiled, his sleep-ridden eyes blinking against the lantern light. As Walsh approached, he straightened up and extended his hand, and the pair greeted each other like old friends.

'Thanks for coming, inspector.'

Walsh clapped Palmer on the back. 'You're welcome. I just hope I can help. The situation sounded bleak in your note.'

Walsh looked down at the bodies, his outward expression unreadable, but inwardly, horror mingled with disgust as he contemplated the scene before him. The brutality of the murders stirred a deep sense of revulsion, prompting questions about the depths of human savagery that could lead to such savagery.

'These poor men,' he eventually said. 'Edmund here has already filled me in on the details.'

'Good,' Palmer replied. 'I sent word back to town for the doctor to come up and take the bodies for an autopsy. He should be here shortly, but I wanted things to be intact when you arrived.'

Walsh nodded thoughtfully and began a slow, methodical examination of the bodies. Circling around them, he crouched down to inspect the victims more closely. Walsh lifted their chins with gentle yet deliberate movements, revealing the deep gashes on their necks. Proceeding with caution, he unbuttoned their blood-soaked shirts, revealing further evidence of deep lacerations consistent with the wounds on their faces.

'Have you searched the area during daylight?' Walsh asked.

'Yes, sir,' Palmer replied. 'For many hours right after I sent Edmund to find you.'

'Did anything strike you as unusual?'

'No. I couldn't find a murder weapon or any physical evidence at all. The carriage itself was equipped with the usual supplies.

Plenty of food, water, Scotch and camping items. It's all still in there.'

Walsh glanced up at Palmer, his expression betraying a sense of concern. 'Edmund was right. This is extreme violence beyond that of a traditional robbery,' he said, wiping his hands clean on the dewy grass next to the road.

Palmer nodded in agreement. 'And no witnesses either, as far as we know. A prospector found the bodies early in the morning on his way to Bathurst. Still, we will continue to canvas for anyone who may have seen something.'

'And the prospector? What do you think, sergeant?'

'Just an old man, sir. He was terrified. Trembling with fear, in fact. I don't believe he could be involved.'

Walsh nodded thoughtfully. His instincts suggested that with the precision displayed in these murders, they were unlikely to find any witnesses. Given the clear force involved, it seemed improbable that a single elderly man could have been responsible. He stood back up and looked at the back of the carriage, which was still open. Several lumps of gold remained, but it was clear it had been disturbed. He stepped back from the carriage and thought about the precise location where he was standing.

'Interesting.'

'What is?' Palmer asked.

'I think nothing is accidental, sergeant. I believe someone purposefully chose this tight passage of road here as the ambush point. Look how narrow the landscape becomes here. The trees and shrubs are much closer to the road, almost like a funnel. It would seem like the perfect waiting spot as opposed to the open road a little further east or west, where the guards would have seen the men approaching or hiding.'

'Oh, I see, so you don't think they followed them? Or just came across them and attacked as an opportunity?'

'No, I don't. The guards are armed and trained. They would have been able to at least mount some kind of defence. Anyway, first things first, these men need to be identified for the sake of their families. Sergeant, in the morning, I would like a constable to ride to the goldfields in Bathurst and get a copy of the schedule from the Mint employees. It is a long journey, I understand, but it is crucial. Tell him to be discreet. There are already enough problems in the mines with theft and violence. They don't need the other guards fretting over this. Still, they must increase their security as a precaution, so please advise them to consider their protocols.'

'Yes, sir.'

Walsh examined the surroundings again, but the limited moonlight struggled to penetrate the dense treetops, hindering his vision. Despite the challenges, he felt compelled to explore the scene further. Picking up a lantern, he walked away from the road, moving beyond the short stretch of grass until he reached the edge of the bush marked by thick shrubs.

'Edmund, come here please and bring another lantern,' he called out.

When he did, Walsh continued. 'All the branches and leaves are squashed,' he said, pointing at the bushes. 'My instincts were accurate. It was an ambush, and I think they were lying here in wait.'

Miller lifted his lantern, illuminating the area where Walsh had pointed out the damage to the bushes.

'So that means...' Walsh said, his voice trailing off.

He stood abruptly, his sentence hanging in the air, and turned his gaze back to the carriage, which remained stationary on the road beside the two bodies.

'Sergeant, is this where the carriage was when you arrived here?' Walsh continued.

'Yes, sir. I have not moved a thing.'

'See that hole in the ground where the wheel is stuck?'

'Yes,' both Palmer and Miller replied simultaneously.

'I think someone created that as a trap.'

'But there are holes everywhere on this road. It's always been dangerous around here,' Palmer said.

'Ordinarily, a hole this big, the guards would see and could steer away from, but look underneath the wheel.'

All three officers crouched down and shone their lanterns at the stuck wheel.

'Look underneath it,' Walsh said. 'There are twigs and leaves crushed under the wheel. I think whoever killed these men covered this hole as a means of concealment. When they became stuck and climbed off the cart to investigate, they were ambushed.'

'Yes, I see,' Palmer said. 'So what do you think?'

'I don't know yet,' Walsh replied, his tone serious. He then cast another glance at the two bodies, his expression marked by concern. 'But I haven't seen something like this since I was in London. Even then, never with this level of violence.'

EIGHT

They remained at the crime scene for another hour, enveloped in silence as Walsh grappled with the shock and overwhelming nature of the gruesome murders. Though he didn't voice it, he was wrestling with the challenge of devising a viable investigative plan. Suddenly, the distant, slow rattling of a heavy carriage shattered his quiet contemplation. As it drew near, he observed its bright white paint, with a single horse pulling the lengthy vehicle while two men rode at the front.

'This is the doctor arriving,' Palmer said. 'He is the practitioner contracted to conduct all police-related medical business in the area.'

As the horse came to a halt, the two men dismounted. One was an older, stocky individual with thinning grey hair, a voluminous grey beard, and a bulging stomach barely contained by a long white apron. He waddled over to the police officers, accompanied closely by a small teenage boy of about sixteen or seventeen. The boy wore a similar white apron hanging loosely on his slight frame.

'Good evening, Doctor Andrews,' Palmer called out.

'Good evening, sergeant, or should I say morning?' he replied.

'Yes, quite so, I expect. I must admit, I've lost track of time up here,' Palmer said before gesturing to Walsh. 'Doctor, this is Inspector James Walsh from Sydney, who is assisting with this investigation, and you already know Constable Miller.'

Walsh nodded respectfully.

'Evening inspector, Doctor Bill Andrews, is at your service. This is my junior assistant, Fred Bartlett. Apologies for our delay. Now, what do we have here?'

Walsh provided the relevant information. 'Two deceased males with a thick laceration of both their throats, which I suspect were the fatal wounds. Also, multiple stab wounds to their faces and torso, seemingly made post-mortem when they couldn't have struggled against each thrust. But I will leave this up to your trained medical opinion.'

'Hmm, I would say you are correct, inspector,' Andrews said, crouching by the bodies and waving his lantern over them. 'Deep lacerations on both men appear to have severed the carotid arteries; this would have resulted in rapid and extreme blood loss. I would expect these other bodily stabs to be made post-mortem after the heart had stopped beating, hence less blood on the chest wounds, but I will take them with me and conduct a detailed autopsy. Fred, come here and help me, please.'

Walsh noticed the young assistant's nervous demeanour as he approached, observing the slight trembling in the boy's legs with each hesitant step.

'It's okay, son,' Walsh said faintly.

'Help me turn them over, Fred,' Andrews said.

Andrews placed his hands under the shoulders of the first body and directed Fred to assist.

'Come on, boy,' Andrews said impatiently as Fred hesitated. 'Sorry, officers, we don't normally deal with things like this. It has been many years since I've managed a post-mortem on a murder victim, let alone of this nature. Mostly, we deal with farming accidents and natural causes. This would be Fred's first of its kind.'

They turned the body over and observed no injuries on the back of the first man. Replicating the process, they found the second man's injuries were almost identical to the first, with no injuries evident on his back either.

'Interesting. They were wounded only on their anterior sections,' Andrews said. 'Help me get them into the cart, will you? I'll take them back to my practice for a more thorough examination.'

All five men struggled to handle the dead weight of the men, but eventually, and one by one, they slid their limp bodies into the back of the white carriage and sealed it shut.

'Come by and see me soon for my examination results,' Andrews said, climbing to the front of the carriage and taking the reins.

'Thank you, doctor,' Palmer said.

'Sergeant,' Walsh began. 'This matter is quite peculiar and complex. I'd like to stay as long as possible and work on this investigation. I'd also like Constable Miller to assist me.'

'Of course, anything you need, inspector. All of us here at Penrith appreciate your help.'

'Things have been quiet in Sydney of late, and I have a competent team working for me there. Although I may still have to manage things back home, I will help as much as I can. Edmund, is the offer for accommodation and your hospitality still available?'

'Of course, sir,' he said.

'I will set up something for you tomorrow,' Palmer said. 'There is a police-owned vacant terrace down from the station you can use for a while.'

'Great. For now, let's get some rest. Sergeant, please take the carriage and the gold back to the police station and arrange for someone to take it back to the Mint tomorrow. They will expect their gold; for now, the gold itself won't give us any more clues. Explain to them what's happened and let them know someone will inform their colleagues in Bathurst. In all that has happened, try to give them peace of mind to ensure we are working hard to solve these murders.'

'Yes, sir.'

'And Edmund, lead the way to your home; I'm tired and imagine you are too, after spending the entire day riding.'

Palmer tethered his own horse to the golden carriage, and the three of them rode back into Penrith, Palmer, with the gold carriage behind. Upon reaching town, Palmer veered left at the fork in the road toward the police station. Miller continued further east, with Walsh trailing closely behind.

'Here we are,' Miller announced as he rode into the front yard of a quaint wooden home. Its light cream façade contrasted with the bullnose tin roof, while a wrap-around verandah adorned with two rocking chairs moved gently in the breeze next to the front door. Lining the verandah was a well-cared-for garden full of rose plants and lavender.

'A cheerful home,' Walsh said. 'The garden is lovely.'

'Thank you, sir. My wife enjoys gardening, and I try to keep up with maintenance. Follow me out the back to put the horses away.'

They proceeded down a dirt driveway on the right side of the house, arriving at an open stable with space for two horses. The officers tethered their horses and observed them greedily indulge in hay and water. Walsh then retrieved his luggage from the saddle and awaited an invitation to enter the house.

'They'll get a good rest here,' Miller said. 'Anyway, follow me inside. Jane, my wife, will be asleep and the floor creaks, so we will have to step carefully.'

They climbed the few wooden steps leading to an entrance on the verandah, extinguishing their lanterns before stepping through the back door and proceeding down a narrow hallway.

'Here,' Miller whispered, opening a white-painted wooden door. You can sleep in our spare bedroom. I hope it is adequate and comfortable enough.'

Walsh peered inside. A solitary bed, pressed against the wall beneath a lengthy window illuminated by the moonlight, was the sole piece of furniture in the room.

'Perfect,' he whispered in reply. 'Thank you again. Let's get some sleep, and I will see you in the morning. We will have much to do.'

NINE

Walsh struggled to find the sleep he had hoped for. He tossed and turned on the narrow bed beneath a scratchy blanket, his mind consumed by thoughts of the murders. Just as he finally drifted off into a light sleep, the east-facing window abruptly stirred him awake at dawn. With a sigh, he lifted his legs from under the blanket and let them rest on the hardwood floor, absently rubbing the coarse stubble on his chin.

Repeatedly, he replayed the murder scene in his mind, attempting to map out the most effective strategy for the investigation. Yet, a coherent plan for how to proceed still eluded him. He sat on the edge of the bed, grappling with his frustration while the sun rose, casting its warm glow throughout the room.

As the sound of pots clattering down the hall reached him, he rummaged through his small bag in search of a fresh shirt, still clad in the same trousers as the day before. As he finished adjusting his black boots, Walsh heard a soft knock at the door, accompanied by the faint squeak of the hinges as it cracked open.

'Good morning, sir,' Miller said, poking his head inside the room.

'Good morning, Edmund.'

'If you would like to use the bathroom, it is down the hall. You are also welcome to join Jane and me for some breakfast.'

'Very kind, thank you, I would love to.'

The kitchen, though small, was warm and charming, nestled in the middle of the house. Miller sat sipping tea, already dressed in his uniform, while Jane bustled about the kitchen, preparing porridge in a large pot over the stove; the aroma wafted through the small window that overlooked the neighbour's side garden. She wore a long green floral dress that complemented her slim physique. The dress had a modest design, reaching her ankles with sleeves extending to her wrists. Like Miller, she was in her early twenties, her long brown hair fashioned in a tight bun. Her porcelain-smooth skin seemed almost flawless.

'Good morning, inspector,' Jane greeted with a bubbly London accent.

Miller stood up and formally introduced the pair to each other before gesturing towards a chair for Walsh to sit in.

'Tea?' Jane offered.

'Please,' Walsh replied. 'And thank you, Mrs Miller. I wanted to say how much I appreciate your hospitality at such short notice. I understand you probably only found out about me staying here the first thing this morning, but I am very grateful.'

'It's my pleasure, inspector. Edmund spoke highly of you, and we are both glad to make you feel comfortable while you are away from your own home.'

'Well, again, thank you,' he said as Jane slid a bowl of hot porridge in front of him. 'You have a beautiful home,' he added.

'Thank you. We are both thrilled to be here and, hopefully, we will raise a family. Do you have children of your own?'

'I do. Two boys.'

'And I understand you moved out here some years ago. Did it take you long to settle?'

'It has had its challenges, but the boys are enjoying it. My wife found it hard at first, but she is happy now and prefers warmer weather here. I do, however, get homesick occasionally.'

'Well, Edmund and I have had the same struggles. We have no family here, but this town has been great for us. Although what Edmund told me happened at the foot of the mountains is quite frightening.'

'Indeed, it is, but please don't fret, Mrs Miller; I expect this was a targeted attack, and you have nothing to concern yourself with.'

Edmund cleared his throat. 'Jane, would you please give the inspector and me a moment alone? I think it's time for us to plan out our day.'

'Of course. I need to walk into town and pick up some things. I will be back shortly.'

Once Jane had left, Walsh started on his porridge. 'Your wife is very kind, and I appreciate your hospitality.'

'It's a pleasure, sir, so what's on for today? Am I still staying on this case with you?'

'Yes, you are,' he replied, taking a mouthful. 'I have been giving this a lot of thought, and honestly, it kept me awake for most of the night.'

'Well, it wasn't just me then; I was up most of the night, too.'

Walsh took another spoonful of hot porridge, then momentarily folded his arms and thought. 'Edmund, it has been a long time since I have investigated a homicide even remotely like this. I must admit, I am a little out of practice. I said nothing to Sergeant Palmer last night, but I have a strong feeling whoever did this will kill again. Why wouldn't they? Whether their goal was to kill, rob or both, they were highly efficient and successful. I think those responsible are extremely dangerous, and at the moment, I'm unsure how best to proceed with the case in a timely manner. So I have pondered my options and think I'll need some help with this.'

'You need help? But Sergeant Palmer said you are the best.'

Walsh smirked. 'Kind of him to say, but I'm far from the best, son.'

'So what do we do then?'

'For now, I want you to see Doctor Andrews and see how he is progressing with the autopsy. As for me, I need to go back to Sydney for a while.'

'Sydney? Why?' Miller asked with an expression of surprise, as though he assumed Walsh was stepping back from the investigation.

Walsh frowned. 'It is part of the reason I have been up all night. I need to return and speak to an old friend I believe can help.'

'Another police officer?'

'Not exactly. Well, not anymore,' Walsh said.

'Who then?'

'A convict.'

'You're joking?' Miller replicd as a look of disbelief swept across his face.

'No, Edmund, I'm not. His name is Henry Hobbs. He was an inspector like me at Scotland Yard and my closest friend. We worked together for many years, and he was the most gifted investigator I ever knew.'

'So what is he doing here as a prisoner?'

'He has only recently arrived from the records I have seen, but I believe I know what happened to him from letters I received. His story is one of tragedy, and unfortunately, since I left England, I have been unable to be the friend I wished I could be.'

'Can we trust him, though?'

'Edmund, I would trust Henry with my life.'

'I apologise, sir. I didn't mean to challenge you. I'm just a little confused, that's all. How did he end up here?'

'As I understand it, he arrived in Australia about two weeks ago. He was on a ship that arrived at Fremantle in the colony of Western Australia, where convicts are still being sent. Just yesterday, I spoke to the Commander in charge of Cockatoo Island in the Sydney Harbour, who routinely provides me with a list of fresh prisoners on the island. I take this manifest for precautionary reasons, as the island falls under my station's patrol area. I carefully review the names of new inmates, as those sent to Cockatoo Island are re-offenders and usually the worst of the worst. I like to be aware of who is there and what crimes they have been convicted of. To my surprise, I saw my old friend's name on that list, and his intake information indicated that he had been sent to the island because of apparent behavioral issues in Fremantle. From London to Fremantle and now to Sydney, I would like to believe that fate is bringing us back together. Right before you sought my assistance, I was, in fact, making plans to visit my old friend.'

'Inspector, I still don't understand.'

'You see, Edmund, I used to correspond with Henry every month or so since I have been in Sydney, but a few months back, my letters stopped being responded to. Then, another former colleague at Scotland Yard sent me a letter informing me that Henry had been arrested on assault and theft charges and that authorities were sending him on a convict ship to the colony of Western Australia. The letter detailed his framing by his superintendent and the travesty of the trial, in which Henry never stood a chance.'

Miller couldn't conceal his hesitation and appeared somewhat cautious of Walsh pursuing this avenue as an investigative option.

'But then a transfer to Cockatoo Island? What kind of trouble could he have gotten into?'

'Knowing Henry, he must have attracted the wrong attention in Fremantle. He has been through pain and suffering very few people could understand, and, well, he is not one to back down from a confrontation either.'

'Are you sure they will even let him help you? I mean, they sent him to the island for a reason.'

'Do not worry about that, Edmund. I have a good and trusting relationship with all the guards on Cockatoo Island. When I explain the situation, it will be fine. They will allow him to be released into my custody. That is, if Henry is willing. I fear he may not be the same man I once knew.'

'But you think he will be able to help?'

Walsh nodded. 'I do. I really mean that. There is no one better.'

Miller remained silent, his contemplation clear in his furrowed brow and thoughtful gaze. Walsh sensed his hesitation and understood the underlying concern.

'Okay, Edmund. Let me convince you this is the right thing to do for the sake of this investigation. About eight years ago, back in London, Henry and I had just received promotions to inspector, and they assigned us a homicide to investigate together. This case was unusual because it was relatively high profile, considering the victim was a judge. He was a good man and a righteous officer of the Courts whom we had both known and respected for a long time. Judge Stephens was his name, and he was one official who dedicated his life to upholding the law and acting with integrity, which, contrary to what you may think, was rare in London. One night, his body was discovered after a large party. Someone stabbed him to death and left him in an alley, where he remained undiscovered until the following morning. Together, Henry and I began interviewing everyone who was at the party. However, even after speaking with nearly one hundred guests, we were no closer to discovering what happened. It appeared his attendance at the party and his death was, in fact, not connected. Henry's careful examination of the crime scene told him that Stephens' death was slow. Blood trailed in every direction leading into the alley, and he believed the judge put up a strong fight. Henry then vowed to fight just as hard to find who was responsible. From reviewing the messy crime scene and the body of the judge, he believed at least two people were responsible for the murder and that they would have considerable defensive wounds. Still stuck, though, Henry insisted we retrieve the clothing Judge Stephens wore that evening.

'I had my constables look over the clothing immediately following the murder. Still, they found nothing remarkable, just an excessive amount of blood and tearing, as you would expect. Well, Henry saw something different. A tiny red fibre underneath the lapel of Stephens' coat. Henry immediately deduced there was a struggle during the attack and that the judge must have torn the clothing of the assailant. He identified that the fibre was a fine silk and concluded that only the most affluent in London could have afforded it. I did not think this would be a good lead; after all, it was just a silk fibre, but Henry became obsessed with it. He knew it would be the key to solving this case, but it went unsolved after several weeks.'

Miller's curiosity was now visibly palpable, and as he listened intently and wide-eyed to the account of dedication and meticulousness in the investigation, Walsh saw his initial concerns about Hobbs had dissolved.

Walsh continued. 'One day, he was raiding an opium den, looking for some men with outstanding warrants he believed were hiding out there, and as he was searching, he saw it. A red silk shirt made of the same fibre he had obsessed with for so long. The owner of the opium den, a man of Chinese descent, wore it. Henry quickly pulled him aside and interviewed him while his team successfully apprehended several men on outstanding warrants. As it was, the shirt was one of two imported from

China and made of the highest quality silk available. The den owner had one, and later he found out that a second one was gifted to a high-level organised crime syndicate member. Henry maintained the murderers would have had defensive wounds and, further, would have needed to be physically large and strong to successfully overpower and kill Judge Stephens, who himself was a large man. The den's owner was short and slight, with no scratch on him, and it was quite apparent that he was not the person we were looking for, so Henry cut a deal with him. If the den owner could provide information on the owner of the other shirt, Hobbs would ignore the fact that he had helped conceal wanted criminals. He agreed and gave up the name of the owner of the other shirt. The name given was Norman Reynolds, apparently an old associate of the opium den owner when they used to organise underground dog fights. We knew the name. Reynolds was a key figure in the London underworld and, along with some other crime groups, ran most of the organised crime in London. Extortion, robberies, gambling, murder for hire, you name it, the Reynolds' family were involved somehow. Reynolds himself was a known killer, along with his closest associates. Still, before this, we had never been able to pin him for anything.'

'So, Henry solved the case?' Edmund asked.

'Yes. The next day, we gathered a large team and raided a warehouse by the docks, where the Chinese den owner told him Reynolds spent considerable time. After a messy gunfight, Henry apprehended Norman Reynolds and one of his brothers. They had the marks of old defensive wounds; bruises, and scratches along their arms and necks. We later discovered the red shirt within the warehouse and it matched the fibre found on the judge's clothing. When presented with this overwhelming evidence, they both confessed fully and were later hanged. We learnt they had killed Judge Stephens in retaliation for sending their father to the hangman years earlier for armed robbery offences.'

'That's impressive,' Miller said as he nodded in approval, his expression reflecting a growing confidence in the potential of involving Hobbs in the investigation.

'It was. Unfortunately, we lost some of our men during that bloody raid, including a young detective working as Henry's assistant, but that's the kind of man I am talking about. He is staunch, determined, and has a tenacious mind and impeccable attention to detail. I rarely solved a complex murder investigation without his guidance.'

'Inspector, if you think he can help solve the murders, I look forward to meeting him.'

'Good, I'll leave immediately after breakfast. Please tell Sergeant Palmer where I'm going. I will return as soon as I can. I must say, though, I am somewhat apprehensive about seeing Henry after all these years. After everything he's been through, I just hope he is the same man I remember.'

TEN

Since he arrived at Sydney Harbour's notorious Cockatoo Island, Henry Hobbs became entrenched in the relentless Sydney convict routine, which consisted of gruelling manual labour and deplorable living conditions that were far worse than those in Fremantle. Renowned for housing the most notorious and recidivist offenders, the island's company was not one he would typically keep. Nonetheless, he found a few men who were likeable enough to help pass the time.

During the days, the convicts toiled away at the recently constructed Fitzroy Dock, the largest dry dock in Australia. Hobbs and his companions were responsible for tending to the ships berthed at the dock, which involved scraping, cleaning, and painting under the unforgiving Sydney sun. Rest periods were scarce, and the work was unrelenting.

The guards, although just as cruel as those in Fremantle, fortunately, showed little interest in Hobbs specifically. Instead, their punitive actions targeted a select group of convicts who seemed to invite trouble without regard for the brutal consequences. Floggings and beatings were common occurrences, often turned into grotesque spectacles witnessed by the rest of the prisoners. It echoed the public floggings in Fremantle that Hobbs himself endured. Through conversations with fellow prisoners, Hobbs discovered that waves of infection and disease ravaged the island, claiming multiple lives before subsiding, only to resurface again. Medical care was virtually nonexistent, forcing convicts to fend for themselves while still obliged to complete their daily tasks.

He rarely slept soundly at night, confined within a stifling sandstone chamber. Its thick door was securely locked, devoid of windows, with twenty other men crammed inches apart on narrow cots. On top of that, the rations provided were dismal: watery porridge, stale bread, and tough, sinewy meat served in meagre portions twice daily, scarcely sufficient to replenish the energy demanded by the exhausting labour each day.

For the past two days, Hobbs and a young convict named Peter Buckley, with whom Hobbs had formed a bond, cleaned scum and dried algae off the hull of a docked ship. Buckley, the son of a convict sent to Australia years ago for stealing horses in the southeast of London, shared his story with Hobbs as they toiled away one warm afternoon. Born and raised in Sydney, Buckley had unfortunately inherited the same inclination for thievery as his father. He was convicted of cattle theft two years prior, leading to his transfer to Cockatoo Island because of his prior convictions for similar offences years earlier. He recounted his circumstances to Hobbs, explaining how he had stolen cattle from wealthy farmers to support his struggling family. Hobbs felt sympathy for him, having also faced his own unfair, severe punishment and understanding all too well the actions desperate men might resort to.

As the sun reached the centre of the sky, signalling midday, a piercing steam whistle echoed through the dockyard. Instantly, the convicts dropped their tools and sought refuge from the scorching sun on the warm stone ground or against the hulls of the ships, wherever they could find slivers of shade. They savoured each precious moment of respite, knowing that when the whistle blew again, they would be back to toil. Hobbs and Buckley sought shelter against the shadow cast by a large ship, wiping the sweat from their faces with their grimy grey convict uniforms. Meanwhile, guards in their crisp tunics patrolled the docks, wielding heavy wooden batons.

'Hot today,' Buckley said, running his hands over his bald scalp. He was a robust figure in his early thirties, boasting a muscular build and pasty white skin reminiscent of Hobbs's complexion. He recounted having been bald since his late teens, his round face and thick arms devoid of hair save for his bushy black eyebrows. Hobbs couldn't help but wonder if there was a single follicle on his body aside from the eyebrows.

'Just like yesterday and the day before that,' Hobbs remarked, wiping away more sweat from his forehead, which still stung from the perpetual exposure to the sun. Despite the discomfort, his skin was gradually adjusting to the harsh elements, but he feared his face now resembled leather more than flesh.

'And it will be tomorrow, I expect,' Buckley said, smirking at the pointless small talk. He turned to face Hobbs, who was attempting to dry his sweaty hair with his sleeves.

'We've known each other for over a week now, but I don't feel I know anything about you. I mean, you know my story with the cattle, and then, well, I've spent the last three years on this island, but what's yours?'

Hobbs weighed the question thoughtfully. He had deliberately refrained from sharing much about himself to protect his past. Still, as the pair formed a friendship, Hobbs recognised that having a companion on the island would make his time here less arduous and isolating.

'I was a police officer back in England. A detective.'

'Oh, is that right?' Buckley replied, wide-eyed with surprise. 'That's the last thing I imagined you did for work. I mean, you're a tough-looking fellow, but a police officer? How in the hell did you end up here?'

Hobbs sighed. He knew this question would follow, but he didn't have the energy or the strength in his heart to explain the reason in detail.

'The long story is one for another day, but the short version is I was having a pretty tough time and drinking a lot. A lot of police actually drink heavily, and normally, I could deal with it myself, but my superintendent had it in for me. I never knew why. Maybe he was jealous or felt threatened by me, but whatever it was, the man never liked me. I could work around this, though, and it never really bothered me, but one day, I was drunk and feeling sorry for myself working on a difficult murder investigation I just couldn't solve. He barged into my office and told me to close the case and move on to the next one. I looked up at him and saw he was smirking. Something inside me snapped, and I punched him square in the face. I broke his nose, and then he had me arrested on the spot. Things only got much worse for me then. It wasn't enough to satisfy his ego after he fired me. He wanted to see me severely punished for breaking his nose, so he must have falsified some internal financial records, which made it look like I was stealing police money. He set me up, and the fraudulent evidence he produced was overwhelming. The Court believed the testimony of the superintendent over mine, so they shipped me off here for the assault and theft convictions.'

'Oh, so you shouldn't even be here. I mean, you didn't take the money, did you?'

'Of course not,' Hobbs snapped, glaring at Buckley.

Buckley raised his hands. 'Sorry, I didn't mean to offend you.'

Hobbs sighed. 'It's alright. A fair question, I suppose. I punched my superintendent, though. And now here I am, and I can do nothing about that now.'

'Well, for what it's worth, I am sorry about all that happened to you.'

'I don't need your pity, Buckley. Back home, I have had my share of people pitying me; I'm just trying to deal with what's now in front of me.'

'Understood. So, did you leave behind a wife or children in England?'

'No,' Hobbs replied sharply as the steam whistle blasted through the air. 'Let's get back to work.'

Hobbs stood up and adjusted his trousers before climbing back on deck to resume his work. He attempted to conceal the tremor in his lip caused by the weight of the last question.

ELEVEN

obbs and Buckley engaged in casual small talk for the rest of the day. Hobbs reminisced about London and his work with Scotland Yard, while Buckley shared anecdotes about growing up in Australia. He described life's challenges as a farmer in a country where such work is incredibly demanding. From the constant physical exertion and battling regular bushfires, floods, and long periods of devastating drought, he claimed it was not a simple life. Despite his efforts, Buckley said he had barely made ends meet, and whenever he had a successful harvest, the elements seemed to find a way to destroy it. He reasoned it was this struggle which drove him to steal livestock to feed his family.

As the sun dipped below the horizon, the piercing sound of the steam whistle echoed across the dock, marking the conclusion of the workday. Drained and sunburnt, Hobbs and his fellow convicts trudged back to the barracks under the watchful eyes of the guards, moving in single file. Once inside, the guards directed them to the mess hall for their evening meal.

The bustling room teemed with convicts, nearly spilling over with the hungry men awaiting dinner. At the back of the line, and despite the expected disappointment of the meal to come, hunger gnawed at Hobbs, and he knew he would devour whatever was given to him. Rows of long wooden tables filled the space while the queue for the serving area snaked its way outside the room. Finally reaching the front of the line, a gaunt, elderly convict, who seemed too frail for dock labour and had likely been relegated to kitchen duty, handed Hobbs a meagre portion of sloppy meat swimming in a thin, grey coloured gravy.

Balancing his tray precariously, Hobbs navigated the maze of long wooden tables lining the hall, finally finding a spot at one that was already packed with hungry convicts, gorging their woeful meals. He settled in next to Buckley and another inmate named Stephen Collins, whom he had recently met. Collins, like Buckley, had received a sentence to the island for repeated livestock theft offences. Despite his legal troubles, Hobbs took a liking to Collins, who he found chirpy and affable, and Hobbs thought he possessed a certain intelligence and dry wit that intrigued him.

As Hobbs dug into his meal, he listened to Buckley and Collins bantering about the dubious origins of the meat they were served. The prevailing theory, amidst laughter, was that it might have been sourced from a passing flock of seagulls spotted earlier that morning. Despite the jokes, Hobbs was too hungry to dwell on the origins of their dinner.

As he continued to eat in silence, occasionally smiling at the banter, Hobbs looked around the dining room and couldn't shake off a growing sense of unease creeping over him.

'Something doesn't feel right,' he said.

'What do you mean?' Collins asked.

'Look around. There's a certain tension in the queue. Look at the faces of everyone waiting for food. They are anxious.'

Buckley and Collins glanced at the cluster of men in the queue, as if attempting to discern what had caught Hobbs' attention.

'I don't see anything,' Buckley said.

'Everyone's just tired and hungry,' Collins added.

'No, this is different. Who's that over there, at the front of the line?' Hobbs asked, pointing to a small middle-aged man with fuzzy black hair sticking up in every direction. His face was sporadically twitching, but his eyes were wide open, and Hobbs had yet to see him blink.

'That's Ellis Burton, he's a lunatic,' Buckley said.

'Well, he very well may be, but tonight's different. Look at his eyes. He's focused and determined. He's dangerous. His body language is bold, but his fingers are twitching. Something's about to happen. All the people behind him have taken a few steps back, and it looks like he's talking to himself.'

'How could you possibly know something will happen?' Collins asked. 'Besides, he's always talking to himself.'

Hobbs observed the serving queue intently as Collins and Buckley resumed their meal. Moments later, he watched as Ellis Burton seized a metal tray from the counter and struck the guard monitoring the front of the line directly in the centre of his face. The force of the blow surprised the guard, causing him to tumble to the ground without being able to brace himself from falling. Two more guards hurried over as the rest of the room erupted into cheers, relishing the rare spectacle in their bleak existence. Burton gave a sinister chuckle, and his actions now surpassed his reputation for madness. His sinewy yet strong arms and legs thrashed wildly in every direction, landing a powerful right-footed kick squarely in the genitals of the second guard. The guard doubled over in howling agony, dropping to his knees. Despite the third guard's attempts to restrain him, Burton seemed impervious to pain. A blow from the guard's baton to Burton's upper arm did little to slow him down. Instead, Burton retaliated with a solid punch to the guard's nose, causing him to stagger backward.

The fight escalated rapidly. Taking advantage of the guard's disorientation from the nose strike, Burton tackled him to the ground, unleashing a barrage of relentless punches to the guard's face. His screams echoed through the room, mingling with the crowd's cheers.

'He's going to kill him,' Hobbs said, standing up.

Collins shook his head. 'Nah, more guards will come in any second. They will break this up before you know it, and Burton will cop a major flogging.'

'The guard will be dead before that happens,' Hobbs said as he ran toward the fight, pushing his fellow convicts out of the way. When he reached the frenzy, he drove his knee deep into the side of Burton's face. It didn't seem to affect him in terms of a registered pain response, but it knocked him off the guard he had almost punched to death.

'What are you doing?' Burton roared. He still had the same deranged look in his unblinking eyes.

'Back off, the fight's over,' Hobbs said.

Burton's scream pierced the chaotic atmosphere as he redirected his fury towards Hobbs, his eyes blazing with unbridled rage.

Hobbs stood firm as Burton charged towards him. He tensed every muscle in his body, and with swift reflexes, just before impact, Hobbs sidestepped and delivered a powerful elbow strike to the side of Burton's head, sending him crashing to the ground in an unconscious heap. The crowd, momentarily stunned, erupted into cheers. Hobbs then realised these men didn't care who was fighting or who was winning; they just sought entertainment.

More guards responded to the clamour, racing in to find the three injured guards sprawled on the floor, while Hobbs stood upright amidst the chaos. As they rushed forward to apprehend him, the guard who had been struck in the genitals waved them off, still nursing his injuries with one hand while gesturing with the other.

'No, it was Burton. This convict saved us,' he groaned.

In disbelief, the guards looked at Hobbs, but quickly assisted their colleagues back onto their feet before they carried the still-unconscious Ellis Burton outside.

The eyes of every convict in the room remained on Hobbs as he returned to his table.

'That was amazing,' Collins said.

'Not really. Ellis Burton is clearly very disturbed in the head. But he would have killed that guard. They should lock him away in an asylum, not here.'

'You still didn't need to get involved.'

'The guard didn't deserve to die just for doing his job. Chances are Burton didn't even realise what he was doing, though, and I do pity him for that, but that guard probably has a family, and Burton would have killed him.'

Buckley smiled. 'Well, you certainly won over the group here. Burton is a pest. He isn't like everyone else; he's always starting trouble with whomever he can.'

Hobbs simply shrugged and returned to his dinner.

TWELVE

$\mathbf{A}$s Hobbs exited the dining hall, a few of his fellow convicts laughed and offered him pats on the back for rendering Ellis Burton unconscious, granting them a brief respite from his frenzied outbursts. Hobbs, however, took no pleasure in his actions and brushed off their congratulations. He had always harboured empathy for those plagued by illnesses of the mind, recognising that their suffering was often misunderstood. Reflecting on the words of a modern and wise physician from London, Hobbs understood mental afflictions could be as debilitating as any physical disease, yet society often marginalised those afflicted. Dodging the last of the applauding convicts, Hobbs quietly returned to the sleeping barracks.

That night, like the ones preceding it, Hobbs endured fitful sleep in the cramped quarters shared with twenty other men amidst the loud snoring and belching. The thin mattress on his old cot provided little comfort, and the unsupportive frame offered no respite from the discomfort of loose springs digging into his lower back. As a result, the following morning's labour proved even more arduous, with his body already weary from the restless night.

The guards paired Hobbs again with Buckley and instructed them to resume algae and scum removal on the outer hull of the same ship they had previously worked on. The ship would depart later in the evening, and the cleaning and maintenance convict crews were warned to have the ship spotless by then or else they would be severely punished. The sunburn on Hobbs' face and arms was stinging again, and as the sun rose, the harsh reflection from the water made the day feel hotter than it was. He climbed on deck, reached over to the hull and continued to scrape off the thick layer of algae as hard as he could to prevent any unnecessary attention from the guards, especially after what had happened last night. Just before midday, when he figured they would finish their duties earlier than expected, a guard strolled over to the side of the ship.

'Hobbs,' he called out.

Hobbs, who was now lying on his chest on the edge of the warm stone dock with an outstretched arm scraping algae with a metal spatula on the lower part of the ship, ignored the call.

'Hobbs!' the guard repeated.

Buckley panicked and tapped his shoulders. 'Guard's here. You better get up.'

Hobbs slowly pushed himself up and turned to face the guard in his pressed black tunic.

'You've got a visitor,' he said.

Hobbs raised his eyebrows, genuinely taken aback by the announcement. 'A visitor? Here on the island? Who is it?'

'Just follow me to the Commander's office.'

The guard walked away, and Hobbs followed. He cast a puzzled glance back at Buckley, who shrugged in response, also confused at the demand.

Hobbs and the guard walked in silence along Fitzroy Dock through the centre of the island toward the western end. The guard kept his gaze fixed ahead, pretending Hobbs wasn't following him. Sensing his reluctance to engage, Hobbs decided against asking more questions.

As they neared the administration building, a sense of quiet enveloped them. The only access was via a narrow dirt road flanked by dense shrubbery. The further they walked, the more distant the sounds of the convicts' barracks and the bustling Fitzroy and Sutherland Docks became. Looking in the distance, Hobbs couldn't shake the eerie feeling of isolation surrounding the sandstone building. However, as he neared the outer perimeter, its bright garden, neatly trimmed grass, and large open windows on both the ground and upper floor offered a surprisingly inviting ambience.

The guard unlocked the tall iron gates, which creaked as he pushed them open, gesturing for Hobbs to enter. As he approached the building, he noticed a private dock at the back with a small ferry moored to the wooden pier.

'Inside, Hobbs,' the guard directed.

Hobbs held his ground and looked once again at the facade of the building.

'Now, Hobbs.'

Through the gates, the breeze wafted the fragrance of the garden's vibrant summer flowers towards Hobbs, prompting him to close his eyes briefly and savour the moment. It was the first time he had encountered such a fresh and pleasant scent in months.

When they reached the front of the building, Hobbs paused, waiting for further instructions. With the strict treatment of minor indiscretions on the island, he hesitated to barge in through the front doors on his own accord.

'Go up the stairs and into the second room on the right,' the guard said.

Hobbs paused briefly, momentarily considering what awaited him inside, then climbed the three wide stone steps to the large wooden door left slightly ajar. He climbed the stairs to the upper floor, taking notice of the open door of the room he was instructed to enter. Anticipating that he would be questioned about last night's altercation, he took a deep breath and entered the room with caution.

The room exuded an eerie emptiness, furnished only with a round wooden coffee table and a couple of chairs. Each step Hobbs took echoed against the floorboards, amplifying the sense of solitude in the room. His anticipation grew with each passing moment, half-expecting a guard or even the Commander to walk in at any second. Yet, as the silence persisted, so did his unease. He couldn't shake the replay of last night's altercation in his mind and assured himself that he had acted appropriately. He tried to convince himself that he wouldn't face repercussions, bolstered by the belief that the guards involved would corroborate his version of events. To distract himself from whatever was to come, he drifted to the far end of the room and peered out of the large window facing east, casting his gaze upon the docked ships on the other side of the island, including the one he had toiled on for the past few days. Amidst his contemplation, the sound of approaching footsteps broke the silence.

He turned and saw a familiar face standing at the threshold.

It was the face of his old friend, James Walsh.

'Hello, Henry,' he said.

Hobbs struggled to mask his surprise. His gaze lingered on his old friend, scanning him from head to toe in a deliberate, measured manner.

'Hello, James.'

THIRTEEN

Walsh immediately closed the distance with a warm and tight embrace. Hobbs was startled and initially reacted slightly slower, but eventually reciprocated. Walsh was almost overwhelmed with the emotions and memories that instantly resurfaced in the presence of his old friend. He took a moment to gather himself. 'It is good to see you, Henry.'

'What are you doing here?' Hobbs inquired, his gaze still wide with surprise lingering on his old friend.

Walsh waved his hand in a flurry. 'In a second. Tell me, how are you being treated? My stomach has been churning every day since I received the news about your situation. I needed to get here and see you as soon as I could. I only wish I could have done something for you.'

'James, I'm fine. I mean, as fine as can be,' Hobbs said.

'You look terrible,' Walsh said as he surveyed Hobbs. His gaze lingered on the new, thick creases surrounding his eyes, evidence of the toll the past few years had taken on him. Saddened by the sight of his old friend clad in convict rags, Walsh suddenly felt self-conscious in his pressed trousers, neat shirt, and holding his expensive bowler hat. Though thrilled to see Hobbs again, Walsh couldn't shake a sense of discomfort, fearing that Hobbs might not feel the same way after enduring so much. During his brief journey to the island, Walsh grappled with uncertain feelings about facing his old friend again. Now that they were reunited, a hint of unease tinged his excitement.

'Yeah, I've not been eating or sleeping well. I need a good hot shave and a haircut,' Hobbs said, his tone devoid of emotion.

A lot had transpired since their last correspondence, and Walsh couldn't help but sense the peculiar tension in the room. He found himself at a loss for words, uncertain how to broach the sensitive subjects that needed addressing.

'When they sent me to Sydney, I assumed you were working close by,' Hobbs said, breaking the silence. 'So they let you visit the convicts?'

Walsh nodded and offered a small smile.

'Sit down with me,' Walsh said, offering Hobbs one of the wooden chairs.

As Hobbs settled into his seat, Walsh let out a heavy sigh. 'Henry, I'm so sorry about Emma. I wish I could have been in London with you then, but it was impossible to get back with everything happening here. Reading your letter about what happened just broke my heart. I felt utterly useless.'

Hobbs lowered his gaze and shook his head. 'It's okay, James. Anyway, you were always at least a month out of date by the time my letters would have arrived.'

'I just wish I could have helped you with everything. Emma's case, and just being there for you. And then, when I found out about the assault and theft charges, my heart broke again. I'm sorry all this happened to you while I lived here on the other side of the world.'

'James, please, you started a fresh life here. I understand,' Hobbs said. 'And besides, Superintendent Gowing was a disgrace of a man and a coward to boot. There would have been nothing you could have done. I should never have been surprised by his reaction, not after the way he had treated me and my entire team. He's just a jealous, spiteful man. But he still got the last laugh, anyway. Look at me now. Far from home and sentenced to clean ships and eat scraps at this disgusting place.'

'For what it's worth, I wish I could have seen his face when you punched him. I can't believe he got away with setting you up.'

'After I was arrested, my team investigated the allegations, but he covered his tracks and planted the fraudulent receipts in my office. Everything pointed to my guilt. Besides, the judge who presided over my trial was so corrupt and loyal to him, it probably wouldn't have mattered. He wanted me gone, and he got just that.'

'It's just so wrong. After all you went through, Gowing still wanted your head.' Walsh took a deep breath and composed himself before he continued. 'Were you getting close to solving Emma's murder?'

Hobbs flinched, and his eyes watered. 'No. Whenever I thought I got close, I was actually getting further from solving it.'

Walsh closed his eyes, feeling another sharp pang in his stomach as he thought about the murder of Emma Hobbs. He had been the best man at their wedding ten years earlier, and never had he seen a better-matched couple. She was vibrant and wore her colourful personality on her sleeve. The first time Hobbs introduced Emma to him, Walsh remembered him saying to be prepared to meet the most beautiful woman in the world, and he was not lying. She had magnificent long, flowing brown hair and wide green eyes against her flawless complexion. Walsh always found it amusing that while Hobbs was tough and gritty at work, Emma had the power to make him melt in her hand, turning him into the softest, most gentle man around her.

Walsh and his wife, Helen, cherished their time with Henry and Emma, and the four became the closest of friends. They grew so close that James and Helen Walsh were uncertain about accepting the Australian posting, fearing they would leave their dear friends behind. However, Hobbs had always been supportive of his decision.

After settling into their new Sydney home for several years, the day Walsh received the dreaded letter about Emma's death, Helen was beside herself, and both were unsure of what to do from the other side of the world.

Hobbs's letter was mostly incoherent rambling, and there was no doubt he was drunk while writing it. Walsh recalled how it detailed an evening when someone had gained entry to their townhouse and murdered Emma in cold blood.

In his letter, Hobbs stated that as soon as he entered the front door of their townhouse, something felt amiss. He called to Emma from the hallway, but there was no response. As he made his way through the hallway, a sense of unease settled over him, causing the hairs on his arms to stand on end. He quickened his pace, his heart pounding. His first instinct was to check upstairs to see if perhaps Emma was feeling unwell and had retired to their bedroom for a nap. However, when he reached the top of the stairs and opened the double doors to their bedroom, everything appeared undisturbed. The blanket on their wooden four-poster bed was neatly tucked in, and everything appeared to be in order. He left the bedroom and checked the bathroom, where his legs nearly gave out beneath him. The bathroom window was wide open, and the pink curtains fluttered against the breeze above the tub.

Walsh knew Hobbs had always maintained strict security around the home and emphasised the importance of keeping windows closed when he wasn't home. However, the day Emma was murdered, the exceptionally hot weather made it understandable to be tempted by the cooling breeze through the open window. Recalling that dreaded letter, Hobbs had recounted how he turned and bolted down the wooden stairs, taking two steps at a time. He raced through the hallway, checking each room as he passed, and found that nothing appeared to have been tampered with.

The last room in the house was the kitchen, in the back corner on the ground level. What he discovered next, Hobbs wrote, literally knocked the wind out of him.

Emma Hobbs lay cold and still on the kitchen floor, surrounded by cups, plates, and pans strewn about as if in the aftermath of a great struggle.

Hobbs' letter further detailed how he wept and crouched down next to his dead wife. Her neck bore the telltale marks of strangulation, and her once bright, kind eyes were now vacant and lifeless. All that made her Emma was now lost. Her personality, vibrance, and essence vanished in an instant.

The neighbours were the first to respond when they heard Hobbs' anguished cries from within the home. They hurried over to investigate, only to find him on the kitchen floor, clutching his wife's lifeless body. His team of detectives then arrived to manage the scene, but despite their exhaustive efforts, they found no clues at the house. There were no witnesses to the crime, and no credible suspects emerged from their investigations.

Walsh vividly remembered how the penmanship in the letter frayed as Hobbs recounted the harrowing sight of Emma's lifeless body on the kitchen floor. He almost felt the tremble in Hobbs' hand as he wrote those words. Subsequent letters revealed a mind beginning to unravel. Hobbs' once meticulous work suffered as he plunged into an obsessive quest, revisiting every criminal he had ever encountered, convinced that his wife's murder was an act of vengeance for past arrests. Despite interviewing hundreds of individuals, all with solid alibis, Hobbs descended into a spiral of despair and obsession. His subsequent letters became increasingly illogical, bearing the weight of heavy drinking and the torment of an unsolvable crime. Even from across the world, Walsh sensed his friend battling dangerous inner demons.

'I miss her, James. Every day,' Hobbs mumbled.

'I know you do. Emma was a wonderful woman, Henry. Helen and I miss her too, and I wish things could return to how they once were. After everything you have been through, they sent you here. There's simply no justice in your story.'

'I'm trying to make peace with it, but I feel I am constantly surrounded by darkness and despair. James, I can't let it go. If I were back in London, I probably would have just drunk myself to death. Emma wouldn't have wanted that, but that's where I was heading, and truth be told, I didn't mind. I still cannot see any purpose in my life without Emma.'

'She would not have wanted you to rot in chains on a convict island. You have a purpose. I truly believe that, and you won't find it in this place. You do not belong here.'

Hobbs shrugged, but Walsh could sense the weight of memories bearing down on him, overwhelming his emotions.

'So you've come for a visit, then?' Hobbs said, clearly wanting to change the subject.

'Well, not precisely, Henry. As much as I have missed you, I'm here for your help.'

'If you have yet to notice, there's not much I can do to help anyone. I can't even piss without asking permission.'

'It's a double murder. I know multiple offenders are involved, and my gut tells me they will strike again.'

'You'll work it out, James. You always do,' Hobbs said, disinterested.

'I always worked it out in London because I had you. I can't do this one on my own. I have not seen murders like this since I've been here.'

Hobbs paused for a moment and nodded. 'Still, I'm no good to anyone right now.'

'Well, I spoke with the island's superintendent, and you will be free to leave with me in my custody while you assist in the case. I said you do not belong here, and I mean that. Come with me, Henry.'

'To help the police in this colony?'

'Yes.'

'The police here are a mess, James. Understaffed. Under-re-sourced. There's no unification of departments, and ex-convicts fill the patrol numbers. Also, how can anyone expect to solve anything without a proper investigative squad?'

'That's political and out of my control, Henry, you know that. There is talk of an amalgamated police force with new legislation being discussed, but that's not relevant here. I want you to help me prevent more people from being killed. And more people *will* be killed. These murders were cold and callous. I've seen the crime scene, and everything there told me they will kill again.'

Hobbs shook his head and folded his arms. 'I'm not the same person I was, James. The last murder I worked on was Emma's, and I couldn't solve that.'

'I don't believe that for a second. There's no one like you. Help me, Henry, please?'

Hobbs paused as his gaze drifted out the window.

'I have a ferry docked, ready to go. What do you say?' Walsh said.

Hobbs remained silent, his stare fixed.

'Don't let yourself waste away here. Please help me. I'll make sure you are looked after. You have my word. Let me get you away from this place.'

'First, tell me about the murders,' Hobbs said.

At least two assailants stopped two armed guards on a gold delivery in their tracks and murdered them about forty miles west of here, at the foot of the Blue Mountains past the Nepean River. Their throats were sliced open, which I believe to be the cause of death. They were then stabbed at least fifty times each in their faces and torsos. Most of the gold was taken, but not all. There were also no defensive wounds. This was a planned ambush where the guards never stood a chance. Henry, I've never seen this kind of rage in a homicide.'

'A robbery gone wrong?'

'I don't think so. That may have been the end goal, but it doesn't explain the overkill and post-mortem injuries.'

Hobbs remained silent a little longer.

'Okay,' he eventually said.

'Okay?'

'Okay, I'll help if it gets me off this island. But I cannot promise anything.'

Walsh stood up as if he had known all along that Hobbs would agree and clapped his hands together. 'Thank you, Henry. We'll leave immediately. You'll stay at my house tonight. Helen and the boys would love to see you.'

Hobbs briefly smiled, and Walsh couldn't help but wonder how long it had been since he last did so.

'They are both twelve now, if you'll believe it,' Walsh said. 'However, first, we'll get you a haircut, a shave, and perhaps some new clothes.'

'Yeah, I've gotten used to the stench, but I suspect Helen won't appreciate it. And these clothes should be burnt. I would hate to think of some other poor soul wearing these putrid rags.

'I've already signed the paperwork for your release. Let's go,' Walsh said, patting Hobbs on the back as he stood up.

'That was presumptuous of you.'

'It's been many years, my friend, but I still know you.'

FOURTEEN

Hobbs looked back at Cockatoo Island, shrinking in the distance as the small steam-powered ferry approached the shores of Sydney. The sea breeze provided a welcome respite, gently ruffling his wavy hair as the ferry cut through the waters. Small waves lapped against the edges of the ferry, creating a soothing sound that seemed to drown out much of the angst he had felt since arriving in Australia. Instead, a calming sense of peace washed over Hobbs. Though he still carried a painful burden, he couldn't ignore the sudden liberation he felt. He took his boot off and removed the ring from the bottom, gazing at it, rubbing the smooth edges slowly before placing it in his trouser pocket. Hobbs felt some tension melt away as he gazed at the ring he had successfully kept safe and hidden for so long.

'It was Emma's,' Hobbs said. 'Her wedding band. They never knew I had it.'

He sat down on the edge of the ferry next to Walsh, and neither spoke for a moment. It felt like old times, and Hobbs knew Walsh sensed it. Despite the constantly looming sense of failure and dread since Emma's murder, Hobbs couldn't deny the happiness he felt. In fact, he knew it was the happiest he had been in months.

Walsh finally broke the silence. 'It really is good to see you, Henry. When I heard you were being shipped off to Fremantle, all those thousands of miles away, I never thought I'd see or hear from you again.'

'It's good to see you too, James. But I need to ask you a favour.'

'Sure, anything.'

'I don't want your pity, alright? I'm not drinking anymore, and I don't need anyone feeling sorry for me. I'm managing things fine on my own.'

'Are you, though?' Walsh asked sceptically.

'Yes, James, I am. Now, please, enough.'

'Okay, I understand. But are you going to tell me what happened in Fremantle? As I understand it, you were transferred here because of behavioural issues.'

'I think Gowing must have sent word that I was being transported there. One guard took a particularly nasty interest in me.'

'So what happened?'

'To the guard? I broke his nose.'

'Well, you haven't changed, have you?'

Hobbs shrugged nonchalantly and turned his gaze towards the approaching cityscape.

Hobbs wasted no time disembarking when the steam ferry docked in Sydney Harbour. Stepping onto the dock, he drew in a deep breath, the salty tang of the sea air filling his lungs. His gaze lingered back on Cockatoo Island once more, now a mere speck in the harbour's vastness. It sat isolated, a solitary outpost amidst the shimmering waters.

As Hobbs observed the city's skyline, he felt a sense of calm wash over him. Sydney seemed to breathe with a different rhythm, a freshness in the air that invigorated his senses. It was a welcome change from London's shadowed lanes and towering structures. Gone were the perpetually overcast skies and murky alleyways. Here, the streets were broad, bathed in sunlight that danced off the harbour waters. All around him, existing buildings stood tall, and several new buildings were under construction.

Walsh followed Hobbs off the ferry and gave him a hearty slap on the back. 'First things first,' he declared. 'I'm taking you to my barber, then a tailor.'

They strolled together through the bustling harbour streets, where brand new carriages rolled by, drawn along the cobblestones by sturdy horses. Men dressed in smart wool trousers, linen shirts and hats, and women adorned in long dresses bustled about, engaged in the local Sydney trade. As they continued on, Hobbs couldn't help but notice the puzzled looks and murmurs from passersby. It served as a reminder of his dishevelled appearance, while not forgetting he was still clad in his ragged convict attire.

A few hundred yards of leisurely walking through the city, weaving in and out of the bustling streets, led them to the small barber shop at the harbour's end. The old, frail-looking owner warmly greeted the pair. Walsh sat at the front of the store by the street-facing window, indicating that it was just Hobbs in need of attention today.

The barber expertly shaved Hobbs' rough face and gave his thick sandy hair a modern trim, crafting a smooth comb-over with the sides neatly levelled to his ears. After his shave and haircut, Hobbs felt closer to his usual self. He had always presented himself immaculately, and was even slightly fastidious, likely a remnant of his acute attention to detail cultivated during his law enforcement career. Although that aspect of his life had been taken from him, he now at least felt that he presented himself immaculately once again.

Their next destination was the tailor's shop just down the street from the barber's. At Walsh's insistence, Hobbs collected two pairs of navy trousers and three crisp white button-down shirts at the tailor's shop just down the street from the barbershop. He also selected navy suspenders, a sleek black overcoat, and a sturdy pair of new boots. As Walsh settled the bill, Hobbs treated himself to a new dark brown Derby hat to complete his ensemble.

'That's better,' he said, looking at himself in the mirror and nodding in approval.

'Good choice. That's the same hat as mine,' Walsh added. 'But at least you look like a detective again.'

'And I expect I'll wear it better,' Hobbs said with a playful smirk.

'If you say so,' Walsh chuckled. 'But this isn't London anymore, Henry, so be prepared to change those shirts often. There will be some hot days ahead of us. You probably won't need that coat either.'

They stepped out of the store, greeted again by the lively sounds of the streets. 'So, what do you think of Sydney?' Walsh asked.

'It's different,' Hobbs said. He glanced around at the new streets again, taking in all the activity, but then realised Walsh was right. He wouldn't need the coat anytime soon.

'I guess it's just an old London habit of taking a thick coat everywhere,' Hobbs said, slinging it over his shoulder.

Walsh smiled. 'Are you hungry?'

'Famished.'

'Good. It's only a short walk to my house from here. When I told Helen I would visit you and try to get you off that island to help me, she knew you'd agree. I daresay she has already set a place for you for supper.'

After another ten minutes of walking through Sydney's residential backstreets of newly constructed stone terrace homes, they arrived at the suburb of Miller's Point, greeted by the vernacular wattle and daub home of the Walsh family. At the far corner of a quiet street, well beyond the noise of commercial Sydney, other similarly humble single-story homes surrounded it. Walsh opened the small wooden gate, and Hobbs followed him toward the front door. Neatly trimmed grass bordered the dirt pathway leading to the entrance. The front garden was well-tended underneath a large window overlooking the dining room, providing a serene ambience. Looking through the window, Hobbs noticed five place settings arranged around the long wooden table.

Before they reached the steps to the front door, Hobbs heard heavy footsteps from within, accompanied by the sound of boys loudly bickering with each other. The front door swung open quickly, and a sweet and familiar face greeted Hobbs.

'Good evening, Helen,' he said with a smile.

'Oh, Henry, it's so good to see you,' she replied warmly, stretching her arms to invite him inside. Helen was barely five feet tall, yet her presence was anything but small. She effortlessly captivated those around her with a vibrant personality that seemed to fill the room. Hobbs quickly remembered why he and Emma had cherished their time with James and Helen. Wearing a long, cream-coloured, light cotton dress, Hobbs knew Emma would have loved Helen's Australian attire had the weather in London allowed for such a light dress. Her green eyes sparkled in contrast to her long auburn hair, tied in a loose bun. Approaching forty, she had aged gracefully, retaining the youthful looks and smooth skin of a woman a decade younger.

As Walsh and Hobbs stepped into the home, Helen hugged them both. When she embraced Hobbs, she expressed her sorrow for Emma's death. As tears pooled in her eyes, Helen re-counted her regret and helplessness at being so far away.

'Honestly, Helen,' Hobbs said. 'I was no joy to be around, and I worry I am still not.'

'Nonsense. I've missed you very much. And I know James has, too. I'm just glad you are now off that filthy island. You should never have been there. Now come in, and we will eat soon; you probably haven't had a proper meal in months.'

Hobbs strode down the corridor, passing several closed doors, and headed toward the kitchen nestled at the rear of the house. As he entered the kitchen, its grandeur struck him. High wooden ceilings stretched overhead, adorned with a magnificent hanging chandelier, adding an air of elegance to the room. Despite its unassuming exterior, the home revealed itself to be much larger and more impressive within.

Walsh affectionately patted the backs of the two twelve-year-old boys waiting in the kitchen. 'Boys, you remember Mr Hobbs, say hello,' he said warmly, prompting the boys to acknowledge their guest.

Hobbs offered a warm smile to the two boys, who bore a strik-ing resemblance to their father. Despite their efforts to appear confident, he could sense their uncertainty. The last time they had seen their father's friend, they were only seven years old, and now, he felt like a stranger to them.

'Hello, Mr Hobbs,' they said in unison with a slight bow of their heads.

'Hello, boys,' Hobbs replied with a gentle smile, acknowl-edging their polite greeting. 'Now, let's see here. You must be Timothy, and you must be Adam.'

The twins giggled, 'I'm Timothy, and *he's* Adam, sir.'

'Well, of course you are,' Hobbs said. 'And look at you both. You two are nearly men.'

Hobbs couldn't help but notice the boys' prideful stance and imagined how their stature might change with time. He could foresee them reaching six feet tall in just a few short years, especially considering their current size for their age.

A short time later, Helen brought the steaming dishes of roast lamb and potatoes into the dining room, and Hobbs marvelled at their aroma. After barely surviving on tiny portions of scraps and foul meat for so long, the sight and scent of the delicious meal was a genuine gift.

After Timothy led the Grace, Hobbs savoured what he considered the best meal he could remember, surrounded by wonderful company. When they had finished, the boys cleared the table. Meanwhile, Hobbs enjoyed continuing the conversation with his old friends.

'Emma would have loved it here,' Hobbs said.

'Yes, she would have. We miss her every day,' Helen said. 'Even though it had been so long since I had seen her, our regular letters were so comforting to me. And even after all these years, and at such a distance, when she was gone, I felt so lonely.'

'As I did too,' Hobbs softly replied as he felt his words choke and knot in the back of his throat. 'As I still do.'

Helen reached over the table, her hand extending towards Hobbs with a sympathetic expression. As their hands met, her voice lowered: 'James told me everything that happened afterwards: your firing, the court case, and you being sent here. It was just awful. I am truly so sorry.'

Hobbs nodded his head, though he didn't relish the pity. In fact, he felt discomfort at the attention, yet he respected Helen enough to allow her to express whatever sentiments she felt compelled to share.

'Thank you for dinner, Helen. It was wonderful. You're right; it has been a long time since I have had a proper meal.'

'You're very welcome. It was my pleasure. I'm sure you are also exhausted and in need of a proper bed, so I've made up a room for you down the hall.'

'Henry and I will leave early tomorrow,' Walsh added. 'We must travel back to Penrith as soon as possible and return to work.'

'Of course. James told me about these killings, Henry. So awful.'

'Yes, sounds that way,' Hobbs said, not wishing to talk about these terrible murders in his friend's family home. 'So I should get some sleep, I think. I'm sure we have a big couple of days ahead of us.'

Hobbs excused himself and made his way to the spare bedroom. There, he undressed and collapsed onto the soft mattress with a sigh of relief. He retrieved Emma's wedding ring from his pocket, rolling it between his fingers for a moment before tucking it under his pillow. The bed offered a comfort he hadn't experienced in a long time, and within less than a minute, he fell asleep.

FIFTEEN

The pungent odour permeating Doctor Andrews' makeshift coroner's room, nestled at the rear of his medical practice, nearly overwhelmed Constable Edmund Miller. Despite the foul scent of death, Doctor Andrews, accustomed to its presence, paid it little heed as he quietly moved among the ceramic tables where the bodies of the two guards lay, motionless and cold. With a throat clearing and a deft adjustment of the long, stained white apron hanging from a hook behind the door, he proceeded without hesitation. While the room simmered uncomfortably warm, and the air remained stagnant, Miller's visible grimace betrayed his discomfort.

'I insist on keeping the room sealed to avoid a swarm of bugs entering and disrupting my work,' Andrews said.

Miller attempted to maintain his distance, feigning attention from the corner of the room. Yet, even as he kept his gaze averted from the bodies, the sight of glass jars behind him, brimming with formaldehyde and preserving human organs, sent a shiver down his spine. The recent discovery of formaldehyde and its applications added an unsettling layer to the scene. Andrews, intrigued by the chemical's properties, explained his fascination to Miller, advocating for long-term storage and frequent organ dissection to deepen his understanding of the human body. Miller nodded, but truthfully, he wasn't interested in Andrews' strange studies and found the doctor a tad peculiar and eccentric.

The doctor's jittery assistant, Fred, tentatively entered the room with cautious steps and secured a white apron around his waist, his demeanour betraying an equal measure of nervousness to Miller's own. Unlike Miller, however, Fred couldn't find solace in hiding in the corner; constantly under Andrews' direction, he was thrust into the forefront of the operation. His first task had him help roll the bodies back onto their backs, facilitating Andrews' examination of the ruptured organs within their chests and stomachs.

'Fred, take notes for me,' Andrews demanded as he dove both hands into the first guard's open chest cavity. As he continued his examination, Andrews dictated to Fred, who was standing by with a pencil and ledger.

'COD - severed carotid artery resulting in fatal blood loss. The laceration is one-half inch thick, almost identical in length and depth on both men.'

Andrews looked up at Miller while his hands were still inside the body. 'You know, Constable, earlier, something piqued my interest. Concerning the fatal injuries. Now, given the scene, I still believe you are looking for two separate assailants, but the throat slashes were almost identical. As though the same hand made them.'

'Two men of the same size and strength, then?' Miller asked.

'Perhaps. That would be the most likely scenario. Also, consider that both assailants had the same callous intent. There is no evidence of hesitation on either cut. Just deliberate, strong, smooth slashes on both men.'

Miller's throat tightened as the doctor withdrew his hands from the gaping chest cavity, revealing the gruesome extent of the wound. He couldn't help but recoil slightly as Andrews gently tilted the head of the first guard, exposing the severity of the injury. The sight alone made Miller's stomach churn while Fred distracted himself by burying his face in his notes.

Doctor Andrews continued his examination in silence, which involved removing and examining the guard's insides with various primitive-looking tools. After a moment, he dictated again. 'The first guard, five feet ten inches, approximately forty-five to fifty years of age, fourteen stone and three pounds. Name unknown. A total of thirty-seven puncture wounds were made with a knife of approximately six inches long. Eleven punctured the neck, face and skull, nine punctured the lungs, twelve in the stomach and five punctured the bowel area. All made post-mortem.' Andrews slowly made his way over to the second guard and repeated the same procedure. 'Total of thirty-two puncture wounds, again all made post-mortem. Ten punctures to the face with what I would describe as an identical bladed weapon in shape and size. Nine to the chest, piercing the lungs, two through the heart and eleven through the stomach.'

Fred appeared visibly pale, and Miller couldn't shake the suspicion that he might succumb to nausea. Beginning to feel ill himself, Miller was suddenly grateful for Sergeant Palmer's earlier practical advice; he had wisely chosen to skip breakfast.

For the following hour, Doctor Andrews meticulously measured the guards' organs, his focus unwavering as he dedicated his findings to Fred. Then, with a somewhat careless hand, he stitched their torsos back together, a task done efficiently yet lacking finesse. However, when it came to the neck wounds, Andrews devoted extra care to ensure the closures were neat and precise. Miller knew this precise attention was for the eventual funerals.

'Doctor, are you now finished?' Miller asked as Andrews wiped his bloody hands on his apron.

'Yes, lad, we have a stab count, and there is no doubt the cause of death is what your detective identified at the scene. Fred, head over to Mr Duncan at the funeral home and have him come and collect the bodies. Constable, have you been able to identify these men yet?'

'Not yet, but I expect an officer to return momentarily with the transport ledger from Bathurst.'

'Well, our work here is done. I will prepare a report on my findings, detailing my professional opinions, which you can collect tomorrow.'

Miller wore a relieved smile as he quickly exited the putrid room. Bursting through the front doors, he welcomed the sunshine and clean air, seeking respite from the lingering stench of death. To his disappointment, however, the outdoors failed to provide the anticipated relief, as the scent seemed to cling to his senses, trapped in the tiny hairs within his nose. Before returning to the station, he knew he needed to wash and change his clothes.

Hobbs and Walsh left Sydney just before dawn, urging their horses to their limits as they raced to the west. Despite the fatigue that threatened to slow them down, they pressed on, making intermittent stops along the way for brief breaks. After several hours of relentless travel, they finally reached Penrith. Slowing down to a trot through the town centre, the small police station soon appeared.

Surveying the building, Hobbs couldn't hide his clear lack of enthusiasm. Dismissing the modest appearance of the station, they secured their horses outside, tethering them to a water trough. Hobbs and Walsh silently observed the building as the horses eagerly lapped the water.

'The building itself doesn't matter, Henry. It's the work that's done inside,' Walsh eventually said, as though he knew precisely what Hobbs was thinking.

Hobbs shrugged at Walsh and turned his attention back to the building before them. Its resemblance to a cosy two-bedroom cottage rather than a typical police station struck him as peculiar. He mused that it might have been someone's home before its transformation, noting the wooden patio by the front door - a feature uncommon in police stations he had encountered. A narrow pathway led from the street to the front door of the yellow stone building, and with a creak, Walsh pushed open the round handle. Stepping over the threshold, Hobbs found himself pleasantly surprised by the interior. Despite its modest size, it appeared to be a respectable-looking police station.

Hobbs noticed an ageing but sturdy looking man, whom he detected as the station sergeant sitting behind the counter, engrossed in his newspaper. Despite his relaxed demeanour, the sergeant exuded an undeniable air of authority, unmistakably the one in charge of the station. Beyond the counter, a row of wooden desks sat in an orderly fashion, serving as workstations for the station's constables. As Hobbs peered further into the station, he caught sight of the cells at the rear. Thick iron bars framed the small, confined spaces, with straw strewn across the floors and thin beds resembling those he had slept on at Cockatoo Island.

'Welcome back, inspector,' the sergeant greeted from behind the wooden inquiry desk, tucking his newspaper away.

'Thank you, sergeant,' Walsh replied as he turned and gestured toward Hobbs. 'I trust Edmund advised you I was recruiting an old colleague. Sergeant Samuel Palmer, allow me to introduce Inspector Henry Hobbs.'

'Ah, yes, he did, sir,' Palmer replied, looking Hobbs up and down as though he were sizing him up.

'It's just Henry Hobbs, sergeant,' Hobbs offered, glancing back at Walsh. 'I am no longer a police inspector.'

Palmer's discomfort did not go unnoticed by Hobbs, but it didn't faze him. Disregarding the unease, Hobbs extended his hand and smiled. Palmer seemed to overcome his initial hesitancy and responded with a smile and a firm grip.

'Why don't I show you where you can stay while you are here? We have a townhouse that would be suitable for you both.'

'That would be excellent, thank you, sergeant,' Walsh said.

Palmer led the men back out to the front of the station and walked past a few small cottages just down the street. 'These are government-owned cottages,' he said, continuing down the street until he reached the last house. 'Here we are, gentlemen.'

The tiny cottage bore a similarity to the police station, constructed from the same type of light-coloured stone and likely built around the same time. As Hobbs, Walsh, and Palmer walked through the neglected front garden, the sparse grass crunched underfoot, betraying its lack of care. As Hobbs ascended the wooden stairs to the front door, Palmer swung it open, and a rush of stale air immediately greeted him. Stepping into the foyer, Hobbs looked down a short hallway that provided a direct line of sight through the back door to the unkempt yard beyond.

'The house has two bedrooms, both just off the hallway here. I expect this will be adequate?' Palmer asked eagerly, as though he was waiting for some kind of approval.

'Yes, it will be, thank you,' Walsh replied as Hobbs continued walking down the hallway, the hardwood floors creaking under his heavy boots, where he found a small wooden dining table next to a modest kitchen with a wooden bench and tall cupboards. A subtle smile crossed Hobbs' lips as sunlight poured through the open curtains of the kitchen window above the sink. His thoughts drifted to Emma, thinking how she would have loved the humble charm of this home, even in its somewhat neglected state.

'Yes, thank you, sergeant. It's nice,' Hobbs called out, now from the dining room, his gaze fixed absentmindedly on the backyard beyond. In his mind's eye, he pictured Emma wandering freely through the garden, embracing the warm Australian weather. As Hobbs shifted his focus back to the present, a shudder rippled through him, serving as a painful reminder of Emma's absence.

'Well, I'll let you get settled then,' Palmer said.

'That won't be necessary. We have work to do and will unpack our things later,' Walsh said.

While Hobbs remained absorbed in the yard, Palmer drew closer to Walsh. 'Constable Miller told me your friend is a convict. Is this true?' he said in a hushed voice.

Walsh took a step back and looked Palmer directly in the eye. 'You have nothing to be concerned about. He is a fine man and a brilliant investigator. He was involved in a complicated issue back in London and should never have been sent here in the first place. I expect you to trust my judgement and ask that you refrain from speaking of this matter again. Do we understand each other?'

Palmer's initial startle gave way to a composed nod. 'Yes, sir, I absolutely understand. I apologise. A friend of yours is a friend of mine, and I shall not mention the matter again.'

After a moment of awkward silence, Palmer spoke as he paced toward the front door. 'Very well then, I will meet you back at the police station as soon as you are both ready and provide you with a briefing on the current developments.'

SIXTEEN

Upon their return to the police station, Hobbs found a noticeable surge in activity compared to their earlier visit. Palmer had resumed his post behind the wooden counter, but now the once-quiet cells housed two dishevelled-looking drunks engaged in a rowdy argument. As Walsh and Hobbs approached the front counter, Palmer promptly rose from his stool and silenced the rowdy argument by delivering a sharp kick to the cell bars. The bullpen area near the cells was also busier, with several more police officers, including Miller, donned in smart black tunics, engaged in lively conversations as they huddled around wooden desks.

Walsh swung open the hinged door next to Palmer's front counter and stood in the centre of the room with Hobbs. Acknowledging their presence, Palmer offered a nod before clearing his throat, instantly demanding the respect of everyone in the room. The constables swiftly halted their chatter and turned their attention towards the guests.

'Men, this is Inspector Walsh and his associate, Mr Hobbs. As you probably heard, I have summoned Inspector Walsh here to assist in the murders at the foot of the mountains. I expect you will show them your complete respect and diligence. Miller, Bryson and Davidson follow me.' Palmer turned and gestured to an office at the rear of the station. 'Inspector, this is an empty office used when the district Chief Inspector visits. You can use it to manage your investigation.'

Hobbs glanced into the small office. Despite its size, it featured a sturdy wooden desk with a solid chair positioned to overlook a window that provided a view of the stables. A stack of aged paperwork, likely abandoned police reports, occupied a corner underneath a cluster of spiderwebs. The mess and absence of additional furniture or personal touches led Hobbs to surmise that the Chief Inspector's infrequent visits to Penrith didn't warrant the effort of transforming the office into a more personalised space.

'This will do just fine,' Walsh said as he opened the window behind the desk and felt a rush of fresh air enter the stale room.

Palmer entered the office, followed by the three young constables. 'Gentlemen, this is Constable Victor Bryson and Constable Gerald Davidson, and inspector, you know Constable Miller already. Mr Hobbs, Constable Miller has been assisting Inspector Walsh thus far.'

Hobbs nodded thoughtfully as he observed the trio of young men before him. Taking in their distinct features, he noted the contrasts among them. Miller, slight in build, had large, bright blue eyes and a boyish appearance that belied his stature. In comparison, Bryson and Davidson boasted larger frames and thick, muscular arms. However, their smooth, youthful faces hinted at a certain naivety and inexperience.

Bryson's shallow green eyes and sharp nose, paired with thinning blonde hair combed over in a manner reminiscent of Hobbs', caught his attention. Davidson, in contrast, sported tiny, piercing brown eyes and dark brown hair slicked straight back, accentuating his broad forehead. Though Hobbs surmised they were likely a few years older than Miller, who appeared to be the youngest among them, neither Bryson nor Davidson seemed to be a day over twenty-five.

As Hobbs continued to observe their expressions and body language, a habit ingrained in his nature, he noticed distinct differences in their demeanour. Miller exuded a sense of reservation, even shyness, as he held himself with a certain modesty. In contrast, Bryson and Davidson stood with chests proudly puffed out, eager and awaiting any instructions that might come their way.

Palmer continued, 'Bryson and Davidson here have returned from Bathurst with the ledger that identified the deceased guards. Bryson, if you would.'

'Yes, sergeant. Sirs, we have identified them as Robert Hall and Lawrence Miller. They were both locals of Bathurst and had been part of the gold guard for the past twelve months.'

'I trust you have notified their families?' Walsh asked.

'Yes, sir, we took care of that personally,' Bryson said.

'Wives?' Hobbs asked.

'Yes, sir,' Bryson replied. 'They were both married.'

'A difficult task that must have been for you both.'

'Yes, sir,' Bryson said.

Walsh continued, 'Constable Miller, please inform the undertakers of this information. No doubt their families would like to prepare a funeral as soon as possible.'

'Yes, sir,' he replied courteously.

'Tell me about the gold transport ledger,' Walsh continued.

Davidson said, 'We spoke with the Royal Mint representatives. They briefed us on the process and reiterated twice weekly that they weigh, count, and load up the gold purchased from the mines in a carriage with a receipt to be taken to Sydney. They said the guards always carry weapons.'

'How did they react to the news?'

'Well, of course, they were devastated; they lost their gold, and what they said were two of their best men,' Bryson said. 'Though we did not speak in specifics while the investigation was taking place, they assumed it was a ground of bandits. A robbery gone wrong.'

'*Is* taking place, constable. Not *was* taking place. We will find those responsible, do you understand?' Walsh said sternly.

Bryson's cheeks turned red. 'Yes, sir, of course.'

'Are they worried about their next gold delivery?' Walsh asked.

'They have already confirmed the successful delivery of the latest shipment to Sydney. Do you really expect more killings?'

Walsh paused and glanced at Hobbs. 'That will be all, gentlemen. Thank you. Edmund, please wait behind.'

Bryson and Davidson left the office quietly, and Walsh waited for them to leave before directing his conversation to Miller.

'Edmund, I would like to formally introduce Inspector Henry Hobbs, my old friend and colleague I was speaking to you about. I expect you will get to know each other as the investigation continues.'

Miller's nervous smile betrayed a sense of apprehension as he met Hobbs' gaze. Hobbs offered his large hand, which Miller accepted with his own clammy hand.

'Hello, Inspector Hobbs.'

'He's the inspector here,' Hobbs replied, pointing at Walsh. 'You can call me Henry. I am no longer an inspector, nor even a police officer, for that matter.'

Miller looked slightly taken aback by the informal gesture. Nonetheless, he acknowledged it with a nod.

'What did the autopsy reveal?' Walsh asked.

'Doctor Andrews confirmed what you said about the cause of death being severed carotid arteries. He said each fatal wound was, in his opinion, precise, confident even. You'll recall the multiple stab wounds on both men. According to Doctor Andrews, someone made the subsequent stabs post-mortem. He is preparing a report as we speak.'

'Thank you. We will speak with the doctor shortly. That will be all, Edmund. Please now inform the undertakers of the guards' identities. This is most important; they deserve a proper funeral.'

'Yes, sir.'

Palmer closed the door after Miller left and sat by the old stack of papers. Walsh sat behind the desk, and Hobbs took the third seat next to the desk.

'I also made arrangements for the Chief Inspector to be notified about the murders, but he has yet to respond,' Palmer said.

'Who is he?' Walsh asked.

'Bernard Noland. He was a captain in the British Army.'

'Does he come to Penrith often?'

'No, sir, while he oversees the Blue Mountains, Hawkesbury and Nepean river patrol areas, he spends his time closer to Springwood in the Mountains. I usually oversee day-to-day operations here.'

'Well, regardless, we will continue with our investigation. I trust he will have no problem with our help in this case?'

'I expect not. He will likely be grateful if anything. There is no one else qualified this far west of Sydney.'

'Well, we shall do all we can,' Walsh said, looking at Hobbs.

'So, how do you plan on proceeding?' Palmer asked. His eyes darted back and forth between Hobbs and Walsh, unsure of whom to direct the question to.

Hobbs answered. 'I would like to first speak with the doctor who performed the autopsy. Then, tomorrow morning, I would like to visit the crime scene. From there, I cannot predict how the investigation will turn out. I will let the evidence direct us from there.'

Palmer nodded. 'Very well. Doctor Andrews is the person you will look for. You will find his practice on High Street.'

SEVENTEEN

A soft bell rang as Hobbs pushed open the wooden door to Doctor Andrews' medical practice. The foyer greeted him in silence, yet a hushed chatter emanated from the rear of the building.

'Doctor Andrews,' Walsh called.

A moment later, the portly figure of Doctor Andrews appeared, his round face peeking around the corner as he stroked his grey beard.

'Oh, hello. Inspector Walsh, isn't it?'

'It is. We would like to have a talk about the autopsies.'

'Sure, come on back.'

As they walked down the hallway, passing the regular examination rooms, an unmistakable smell wafted through the air and hit Hobbs with an unsettling force. Doctor Andrews apparently sensed his reaction to the strong odour.

'Yes, the smell. It has been a little warm of late. I try to keep this heavy door closed. I do suspect the bodies will be removed soon, though.'

Walsh, who was fanning the air away from his nose, nodded. 'It's okay. The smell is not foreign; it's just impossible to get used to. Doctor, this is Henry Hobbs, my old friend and colleague from Scotland Yard. He is assisting me with this investigation.'

Upon noticing the blood staining Andrews' hands, Hobbs discreetly kept his own behind his back, refraining from extending a handshake, instead offering a nod and a smile.

'Pleasure to meet you, Mr Hobbs. And good timing. I have finished my report. Excuse the hands, I have just completed another autopsy. Natural causes, do not worry, but the contract as the local medical examiner keeps me busy.'

'I would like to see the bodies of the gold guards if I can,' Hobbs asked.

'Certainly. I have already stitched them back up, though.'

'That is no problem.'

As Andrews led them to a large table at the rear of his surgery, Hobbs took in the scene with a mixture of intrigue and unease. The room resembled an old, warm, and blood-stained operating theatre, its floor lined with fresh straw. However, instead of the sterile atmosphere of a doctor's surgery, it reminded him more of a butcher shop. Crude-looking tools hung from large hooks, casting long shadows in the dim light, while organs floated in glass jars, their forms distorted by the liquid within.

Hobbs approached the covered bodies, his hands steady as he removed the white sheet that concealed them. What met his gaze was beyond anything he had anticipated: two blue, sunken faces bore witness to the violence they had endured, each marked by several crudely stitched wounds. Though no stranger to gruesome homicides, the brutality and ferocity of what he saw momentarily startled him. Putting his shock aside, his focus shifted to the cause of death, and his eyes homed in on the large, freshly stitched neck wounds that spoke volumes about the savagery of the attack.

'Doctor,' Hobbs said.

Andrews slowly waddled over to the large table in response and waited for Hobbs to continue.

'Given that they have been stitched up, it is not easy to tell. However, the wounds on both necks appear slightly more profound on the left side. Do you agree?'

'I would,' Andrews replied.

'I believe what we have is a sneak attack by two right-handed assailants. By the look of these wounds, they are smooth but deliberately aggressive. Both men do not exhibit any signs of defensive marks on their bodies, suggesting they were slain at the same time. If the killings were not simultaneous, I would have expected some level of a fight by the last victim.'

'This is indeed my opinion as well. I have detailed such in my report.' Andrews said.

'Did you notice any other damage to the throat during your autopsy? Bruising, scratches?' Hobbs asked as he continued his inspection of the bodies.

'No, just this wound,' Andrews said.

'Which supports the theory there was no struggle. The guards definitely did not see their attackers coming. A very steady hand killed them at the same time. There was no hesitation here.'

'Yes, I found that fascinating. It was as though the assailants were highly confident in what they were doing,' Andrews said. 'Have you seen much of this before, Mr Hobbs?'

'Not exactly. Well, actually yes, I have, but this is a little different.' Hobbs said. 'The overkill is very extreme. This level of violence is uncommon, and to see this in two men who kill simultaneously, well, I've never investigated something like that before.'

Hobbs paused for a moment while continuing to examine both bodies closely. After a moment, he stepped away from the slab. 'I think we are done here. Thank you, doctor. I've seen all I need.'

Andrews handed Walsh several pieces of paper containing notes and diagrams. 'Here, take the report. If you have any more questions, do come back.'

Hobbs and Walsh exited the surgery as the sun dipped below the horizon, casting a warm glow. Despite the approaching night, the evening retained a lingering warmth as they made the short walk back to their terrace house.

'James, what you said to me on Cockatoo Island, I agree,' Hobbs said, taking a deep breath of clean air. 'These people are going to kill again. You don't display this much anger to kill only once.'

'Any ideas on where to go from here?'

'No. Not yet,' Hobbs said. 'But I want to see the crime scene. I need to see what the killers saw.'

Upon their arrival at the terrace, they found some bread, cheese, and ham left on the table, along with a note from Palmer. *'I have put your horses in the stables at the back of the police station for the night. Enjoy your dinner.'*

'Well, it was a long day of riding, and I still have some sleep to catch up on. Let's eat and then get some rest. We have another big day tomorrow,' Hobbs said.

Hobbs prepared for bed after an enjoyable dinner filled with tasty food and pleasant company, during which he and Walsh reminisced about their early days as investigators together in London. He couldn't help but feel a sense of gratitude towards Walsh for rescuing him from the godforsaken island he never deserved to be on. The opportunity to reconnect with his old friend in such a meaningful way tonight was something Hobbs never thought he would experience again. However, even now, reunited with Walsh, Hobbs couldn't shake the sense of loneliness that had haunted him since the night he lost Emma. Despite their camaraderie and shared memories, the void left by her absence seemed impossible to fill. No matter what he did or who he was with, the wound remained raw and unhealed.

Feeling the weight of Emma's ring one last time for the day, Hobbs allowed himself a moment of quiet reflection before drifting off to sleep.

He opened his eyes and found himself wearing a crisp black dinner suit as he strolled through a lush, grassy meadow. Hand in hand with Emma, the warmth of the morning sun bathed them in its golden light. Emma's radiant presence illuminated the scene, her long, brown hair cascading freely in the gentle breeze. Her green eyes sparkled with joy, her face adorned with a serene beauty that seemed to defy time. Wearing her favourite sky blue dress and bonnet, she carelessly twirled dandelions between her fingers while strolling through the grass.

They settled against the trunk of an old oak tree. This idyllic spot held a special significance for them - it was where Hobbs had asked Emma to be his wife. As he leaned back against the tree's base, a sense of pure bliss washed over him as Emma curled up beside him, her head resting against his shoulder.

Suddenly, a chilling sensation crept through Hobbs' body, sending shivers down his spine as he felt his wife's touch grow cold. Panic surged within him as he turned to her, but she was gone. As dread consumed him, Hobbs rose to his feet, his heart racing with each bewildered step. The once vibrant grass now lay brown and dry beneath his feet, a stark reminder of the desolation that surrounded him. Frantically, he called for Emma, his voice echoing into the empty expanse, yet met with only deafening silence.

Hobbs woke with a loud gasp, his shirt heavy with perspiration. He unbuttoned it and threw it on the floor as he caught his breath. The dreams had sporadically appeared since the murder of his wife. Although he longed to see her, his dreams were the only chance to do so, but the terror he felt when she was always taken from him at the end of each sequence was renewing his agony. When they first began, and during long periods of heavy drinking, Hobbs rarely knew whether he was asleep or awake. The days often blended together, and while he felt pain, he also felt nothing, like an emptiness he could not seem to fill.

He struggled to push away the creeping headache, but the haunting images of her murder flooded his mind, unrelenting. The wooden floor of their London townhouse groaned beneath his feet as he crossed the threshold. A cold draft brushed against the back of his neck, raising the hairs on his arms. The stillness surrounding him was unnatural and oppressive. The usual symphony of Emma's movements—her footsteps, the clinking of dishes, her soft humming—was conspicuously absent, replaced by a suffocating silence that made his skin crawl.

When he had entered the kitchen, the sight hit him like a physical blow. Emma was there, her skin ghostly pale, her vibrant hair spilling over the shoulders of her favourite blue floral dress. Deep scratches and red ligature marks covered her pale neck, and her body was impossibly still, unnaturally fragile, as though a single breath could shatter her.

Hobbs felt his heart nearly burst in his chest, the pain spreading in waves through his frozen body. He stood paralysed, his legs like lead, his eyes locked on hers. Those once lively, expressive eyes were now glassy and hollow, staring back at him with an almost accusatory intensity.

A jagged sob escaped his lips as guilt surged through him, choking him. He knew it was his fault. He failed her. He should have protected her. The thoughts echoed in his head, each one heavier than the last. His knees gave out, and he collapsed onto the cold floor, his body convulsing with uncontrollable sobs. He clawed at the tiles, his cries raw and guttural, a sound ripped from the depths of despair.

Time lost all meaning as he howled into the silence, his anguish reverberating through the empty house. When the neighbours finally found him, crumpled and trembling, he was barely conscious, his cries reduced to hoarse whispers. His vacant, tear-streaked face betrayed the truth; Hobbs had been broken beyond repair.

Hobbs groaned as the images replayed themselves, over and over. He pressed his palms against his damp forehead, trying to will the memories away, but they clung to him, sharp and vivid. Finally, with a heavy sigh, he swung his legs over the edge of the bed and forced himself to the kitchen to find some water.

'Can't sleep either?' Walsh asked, sitting at the round table and massaging his head.

'Bad dreams. What's your excuse?'

'This case, I guess.'

Hobbs found a jug of water on the table and fetched a cup from the kitchen before joining Walsh at the table.

'We've been stuck before, James. You and I will solve these murders. We always did.'

'We worked in the city. We often had witnesses. This place is brutal, Henry. It's isolated and barren. It just feels different.'

'Humans are the same no matter where you go.'

'With this level of violence, I don't think these men are human.'

'We will find them,' Hobbs said before taking a long drink.

'Are you okay?' Walsh finally asked.

'I'm fine.'

'Henry?'

Hobbs sighed. 'I dream occasionally. About Emma mostly.'

'Do you want to talk about it?'

'No. There's nothing to say. I miss her, and I always will. Sometimes, I enjoy the dreams. It gives me a chance to be with her again, even if it's only in my mind, but sometimes it's too hard when I wake up and remember she's truly gone.'

Hobbs took a deep drink and stood back up. 'Try to get some sleep, James, or you won't function as you'll need.'

Walsh nodded, and with that, Hobbs returned to his bedroom and failed to follow his own advice. He stared at the ceiling for what must have been hours before he finally fell back asleep.

EIGHTEEN

As dawn approached, the three figures clad in hessian face masks and new black raincoats lay in wait, their eyes peering through small, roughly cut slits, scanning the horizon for the next gold carriage destined for Sydney. Positioned on opposite sides of a narrow passageway located approximately five miles west of the town of Springwood in the lower Blue Mountains region, they remained hidden amidst the dense shrubbery. At its narrowest point, the passageway spanned a mere four yards in width, its confines shrouded beneath the thick canopy of overhead foliage. A slender dirt road, barely wide enough to accommodate a single carriage, stretched in a straight line in either direction.

While The Shadow stood in hiding at a distance, The Ghoul and The Banshee lay waiting in the nearby shrubs, still damp from the overnight dew, looked at each other and nodded. They felt exhilarated. The intoxicating rush of blood from their first kill was still hot in their veins, and the anticipation of what was to come this morning was almost overwhelming. Never had they experienced a sensation like what they felt days earlier during their savage attack on the gold guards, but they knew they would not have to wait long until their next opportunity.

They looked at each other and knew their thoughts were aligned. Both truly felt like haunting spectres, and their chosen names never felt more appropriate. They didn't know why they desired to kill, but it was all they could think about. It felt at times like an impulse, something even beyond their conscious control, and they knew it wouldn't be too long until they had their chance again. Their recruiter and leader, The Shadow, forbade them from any reckless behaviour that would draw attention to themselves, and they would not disobey, but something inside them burned to hunt and kill everyone they met. The itch began sometime ago, when together they slaughtered a sheep which had wondered from its flock. Soon after, killing animals could not quench that growing thirst. Now, they knew their only targets could be their fellow man.

Having meticulously set their trap, they settled into an eerie calm as they waited in the stillness of the morning. Hours passed in silence, each moment stretching into eternity as they remained vigilant for any sign of movement.

Then, at the passage's far end, The Shadow reached into a sack and released several pigeons into the sky. Their wings beat against the damp branches and leaves, creating a soft rustling that served as a subtle signal to the other two men lying in wait. With keen anticipation, the others recognised the cue – the gold carriage was drawing near.

With swift precision, The Ghoul and The Banshee sprang into action, igniting a pile of dry leaves to create a smouldering heap in the middle of the road. As the flames licked the air and smoke billowed skyward, they fed the fire with larger sticks, fuelling its growth until it roared with intensity. Once satisfied that the blaze had consumed enough fuel, the pair retreated to their designated hiding spots on opposite sides of the passageway. Armed with knives and polished Pattern 1853 Enfield Rifles by their side, they remained poised for the impending confrontation.

As the sound of hooves echoed through the passageway, the pair tensed, their senses attuned to the approaching carriage long before it came into view. Painted a deep red, the heavy wooden cart emerged from the shadows, propelled forward by two sturdy horses. At the front, a lone guard guided the reins with weathered hands, bony shoulders, and arms visible beneath a dirty white shirt. The guard appeared aged, possibly in his late fifties, his weathered black cap offering little protection against the elements. A long rifle lay on the empty seat beside him.

As the gold carriage ventured deeper into the narrow passageway and neared the flames, the horses grew increasingly agitated, their senses overwhelmed by the flickering firelight and smoke. Despite the guard's efforts to maintain control, their panicked whinnies filled the air as they strained against the reins.

He soon managed to pull them to a stop; however, now the guard was caught in a precarious position. He could not move past the flames, as the road was too narrow, and because it was too narrow, he had no room to manoeuvre a turnaround. The fire would have to be extinguished.

The Ghoul and The Banshee patiently waited.

The guard banged on the wooden carriage behind him, a signal for assistance. Shortly after, another guard emerged from the carriage, groggy and disoriented. In his early thirties, with a large black bushy beard and a thick barrel chest, it was clear he had been roused from a deep sleep. Hastily pulling up his suspenders to his shoulders, his eyes widened in shock as he recoiled at the sight of the rapidly growing fire.

'Fetch some blankets so we can put it out. It's the only way to get through!' The driving guard said in a panic.

The second guard, looking irritable, rubbed his eyes and grumbled, 'What's happened?'

'I don't know, but we have to put it before the whole bush goes up in flames!'

As the gravity of the situation dawned on him, the groggy guard snapped to attention. Recognising the urgency of the growing fire, he quickly opened the back of the carriage. He retrieved several thick blankets that he had been resting on. With a sense of urgency, he handed some blankets to the driver as they both began to smother the flames.

Their efforts with the thick blankets proved effective in stopping the spread of the fire. As the guards extinguished the last flickers of the blaze, they stepped back, panting from the exertion.

The Ghoul and The Banshee moved swiftly, their rifles trained on the unsuspecting guards. With calculated precision, they took aim, mindful to inflict injury without delivering a fatal blow. Death would have to wait. In unison, they pulled their triggers, the crack of gunfire piercing the air as the shots found their mark, piercing both low in their calves.

The guards screamed in agony as they fell hard to the dirt ground, their hands clutching desperately at their gaping wounds. The Ghoul and The Banshee wasted no time, quickly emerging from hiding in the bushes and closing in on their whimpering targets.

The older guard, immobilised by pain and unable to pull himself from the ground, raised his hands in surrender, pleading for mercy with wide eyes full of terror. However, his pleas fell on deaf ears as The Ghoul delivered a swift and merciless blow. With a chilling efficiency, the blade sliced through the old guard's pleading hands, leaving him defenceless against the impending onslaught. The next strike descended toward his neck, and it carved a deep and fatal wound as the air filled with the sickening sounds of spurting blood and anguished cries before he took his final, gargled breath.

The second guard, his terror palpable in the trembling of his limbs and the fear in his eyes, remained defiant despite the searing pain radiating from his wounded leg. Clenching his teeth against the agony, he summoned every ounce of strength within him, determined to resist his assailant's merciless onslaught. Even as he grappled with his attacker, now positioned behind him, choking him with a vice-like forearm, he refused to yield to the overwhelming odds stacked against him. Each punch and clawing motion aimed at his attacker's arm and side was an act of sheer desperation, but it failed to deter his attacker. Despite the futility of his efforts, the guard fought on, clinging to the slim hope that as long as he continued to resist, there remained a fleeting chance of escaping.

The Ghoul, having just dispatched the older guard, swiftly closed the distance to the younger guard, wrestling violently against the grasp of The Banshee. Without hesitation, he delivered a barrage of powerful, flat punches to the guard's face and arms, further disorienting him. As the guard reeled from the blows, The Ghoul seized the moment and ruthlessly plunged his knife into the guard's stomach. The agonising pain from the fresh wound served as a brutal distraction, robbing the guard of the remaining fight within him. Gasping for breath and writhing in pain, the guard's resistance waned. Sensing the opportune moment, The Banshee released his choke hold, allowing the wounded guard to slump forward. With a swift and merciless motion, he brought the blade across the guard's neck, spilling volumes of blood from his arteries. The Banshee, panting after the fight, kicked the guard's lifeless body onto the ground.

'He put up a good fight,' The Banshee said between heavy breaths as he wiped his blade on the damp grass.

'Nothing good comes easy,' The Ghoul replied.

Standing amidst the aftermath of their ruthless onslaught, The Ghoul and The Banshee surveyed their handiwork with a chilling sense of satisfaction. Dusting themselves off, they stood beside the lifeless bodies of the guards, their dark coats stained with the deep red hue of blood.

The Shadow, having retrieved three horses from the bushes, joined the scene of carnage. Guiding the horses, and from behind the hession mask, he cast an icy gaze upon the lifeless bodies of the guards sprawled on the ground.

'Good. Load up as much gold as possible. We leave immediately,' he said.

'We will,' Ghoul said. 'But there's still something we need to do first.'

With cold precision, The Ghoul and The Banshee approached the lifeless bodies of the guards, their movement devoid of remorse as they brandished their knives.

NINETEEN

Hobbs woke to a cloudless morning, his room bathed in a gentle warmth that foreshadowed the impending heat. Acknowledging the hot day ahead, he dressed and rolled the sleeves of his white shirt beyond his elbows, leaving the top two buttons undone.

After a night marked by restless tossing and turning, Hobbs finally fell asleep in the early hours of the morning. As he strolled from his room and made his way to the kitchen in search of a cup of tea or coffee, he found Walsh seated at the table, wearing a neatly pressed grey shirt and sleek black trousers.

'Good morning,' he said, raising his coffee cup.

'Morning,' Hobbs replied. 'Did you get back to sleep at a reasonable time?'

'Not really, hence the coffee. You?'

No, not really,' Hobbs said, fetching a cup for himself. 'I'll be okay, though. I sleep very little nowadays anyway, and I think my body has become accustomed to that.'

Walsh frowned but didn't address the comment. Instead, he changed the topic. 'Well, are you ready to leave shortly?'

'Sure. I expect we will have a big day; the sooner we begin, the better.'

'Agreed. Why don't you make some porridge? You'll need a full stomach, and then we will go.'

'Not hungry,' Hobbs said as he poured himself some hot coffee and drained the cup in a few mouthfuls.

They left the house together and made the brief journey back to the police station. Upon arrival, they discovered that the only occupant within was Palmer, who greeted them with a nod of recognition as they entered.

'Good morning, inspectors,' he said gleefully.

Hobbs winced imperceptibly, but overlooked Palmer's momentary lapse regarding his current position within law enforcement.

'It's quiet in here,' Walsh said.

'Everyone is out for the day. Our patrol covers a large area, but my men are competent and do their work with little supervision. Constable Miller was the first to leave this morning, but I have arranged for him to meet us at the crime scene mid-morning. Shall we make our way there?'

'Yes, we will get our horses and leave immediately,' Walsh said.

They made their way to the rear of the station house, where the stables stood nestled in the shadows of trees growing overhead. They eventually reached the far end of the row, passing by several vacant pens, where their horses patiently awaited them. Already prepared and laden with supplies, Hobbs and Walsh led them out of the stables, followed closely by Palmer.

They journeyed in silence, with Palmer forging ahead while Hobbs lingered at the rear, lost in his contemplations. The rugged and unforgiving terrain stretched out before him, a stark departure from the familiar bustling streets of London and the gentle English countryside he once knew. Navigating the uneven paths posed a challenge for him, as his riding experiences had been confined to leisurely jaunts through the English country-side. The weight of his thoughts pressed upon him, and his mind drifted to memories of Emma and their idyllic countryside retreats.

'Here we are,' Palmer soon announced after they had climbed a rough and steep slope.

They dismounted and secured their horses to a tree nearby. As Hobbs glanced around, he spotted Miller, who was reclining against the trunk of another tree.

'Good morning,' he said.

Good morning, Edmund,' Walsh replied.

Hobbs ambled through his surroundings with deliberate slowness, absorbing the scene in its entirety. Casting his gaze skyward, he noted the expanse of blue stretching endlessly above. Turning his attention downward, he observed the long grass swaying gently along the dusty roadside, sheltered beneath the dense canopy formed by the towering trees that flanked the nar-row passage. Taking careful note of his surroundings, Hobbs scrutinised the shrubs lining the roadside and detected the faint impression of a recent disturbance.

'That is where we believe they sat in wait,' Walsh said.

Amidst the shrubs, Hobbs positioned himself with a vantage point overlooking the dirt road where the hole in the ground had trapped the carriage. He dissected the crime scene in his mind, analysing each component for potential clues. He then carefully examined the flattened shrubs, scouring them for any trace of evidence that might offer insight. Yet, despite his meticulous examination, it revealed nothing.

He strolled back to the road, where he found the execution scene. Patches of dirt still bore blood stains, but the elements did an excellent job cleaning the ground. The blood would soon vanish completely with more rain and regular traffic.

'I don't expect we will find much from this scene,' Hobbs said. 'But I agree with you, James. This was a planned ambush. Based on the bushes where the men were lurking and what we saw in the autopsy, it was a surprise attack. From the damage to the shrubs, we are dealing with at least two men.'

Walsh walked over to Hobbs, leaving Palmer and Miller standing by a large tree. He did not want them to hear what he was about to say.

'I'm stuck, Henry. I believe they will attack again, but this scene does not give us anything. No witnesses, no evidence.'

'There is some evidence, James.'

There is?' Walsh said, a startled look crossing his face.

'Not physical evidence, but behavioural evidence.'

'What on earth do you mean?'

'This scene tells me the men were patient. They then quickly turned that patience into sheer aggression. We are dealing with people with no compassion for their fellow man. Yes, it was a robbery, but it's not that simple. It is as though a robbery was a second thought for them. Why the overkill? It was unnecessary to commit the robbery. This level of violence was almost unnecessary. There would be few men capable of this level of savagery. I can see absolutely no remorse.'

'Fine,' Walsh replied, 'but how does that help us find them?'

Hobbs lowered his voice, careful to avoid being overheard by Palmer and Miller. 'I don't know.'

They stood together in a momentary silence. Despite Hobbs's efforts to maintain composure and conceal any hint of deflation or apprehension, he couldn't help but feel that Palmer and Miller could sense the underlying tension.

'Everything okay?' Palmer called out.

'Yes, sergeant, we are just deciding what to do next.' Walsh replied.

As Hobbs continued his contemplation of the crime scene in silence, the unmistakable sound of hooves thundered from the west. Glancing in the direction of the noise, he saw a lone figure in the distance, riding at a gallop toward their narrow passage. As the rider drew nearer, Hobbs and Walsh maintained their stance alongside Palmer and Miller. Nodding with what Hobbs detected as relief when the rider saw the uniforms worn by Palmer and Miller, he dismounted.

'Officers!' the man called out. His breaths came in ragged gasps. He was a younger man in his early twenties, with rough features, sun-damaged skin, and muscular arms. He wore denim pants and a denim shirt with a wide-brimmed hat.

'What is it, son?' Palmer asked.

'I'm glad I found some police. Two men are dead!' he said, panting and leaning over his knees to catch his breath. Hobbs and Walsh became suddenly alert to his words and rushed over to the man.

'What did you say?' Walsh asked.

'Two men are dead. A few miles west of Springwood. I found them this morning while I was out riding. There was blood everywhere. It was a gold carriage. There was something else. The side of the carriage had a message written in blood. I went to the Springwood police station, but there was no one inside. I left a note on the door but needed to find someone fast. I thought there would be some police further east. I have been riding hysterically for the last hour, trying to find someone.'

Hobbs and Walsh ran back to their horses, and after climbing on them, Hobbs called back, 'Where exactly?'

The young man, still looking terrified, raised his arm in the direction he had just come. 'Go west up the mountains, through the town of Blaxland, and then further along past Springwood. As the road bends around a shallow creek, you will find them in the shadows where the road reaches its narrowest point. They are not hidden.'

'What was written on the carriage?' Hobbs asked.

The young man gulped and spoke nervously. '*Good luck.*'

Hobbs and Walsh looked at each other nervously, then wasted no time leaving the area. They kicked their horses and began riding.

'Edmund, you and Sergeant Palmer record everything this man has said and meet us there when you are done,' Walsh called back.

As they galloped side by side, Hobbs turned to Walsh. '*Good luck?* A taunt. I can only imagine that is a message for us.'

TWENTY

Hobbs and Walsh thundered through the rugged terrain in silence. As they reached the town of Springwood, they pressed on with urgency as they rode recklessly through the bustling town centre, drawing both confusion and irritation from the townsfolk. Ascending a steep hill beyond Springwood, their horses slowed. Despite their fatigue, Hobbs and Walsh urged them onward, driven by their determination to reach the crime scene they suspected lay just ahead.

As they reached the crest of a hill overlooking a long and narrow creek, Hobbs caught his first glimpse of the murder scene from about one hundred yards away. The horses slowed to a steady pace, their hooves muffled by the soft earth of the dirt road beneath them.

At the forefront of the scene stood the Royal Mint carriage bearing large red letters that had once dripped with fresh blood, now dried and hardened. Even in their faded state, the chilling words were unmistakable, stark against the carriage's surface: GOOD LUCK, printed in bold capitals.

'This scene is pretty fresh,' Hobbs said as he disregarded the ominous message and strode purposefully toward the bodies of the gold guards, each sprawled facedown in the dirt amidst a pool of drying blood. The sun was high in the sky, and light filtered through the dense canopy, casting streaky shadows.

Walsh disconnected the two horses from the stranded carriage, and they trotted off to the side of the road, where they began munching on the leaves of the surrounding bushes.

Stepping back from the bodies, Hobbs directed his attention toward the back of the wooden carriage. A pile of gold lay within, but it was evident that someone had disturbed the stack, visibly reducing its contents by what appeared to be a significant amount.

A few yards away from the road, the grass sloped gently toward the creek. As Hobbs explored the area, he stumbled upon a curious discovery: a tiny burnt-out stick, unmistakably remnants of a self-lighting phosphorus match. He carefully collected the stick and retraced his steps back to the road.

'James, someone lit a fire,' he said. 'Look here, a matchstick. And there's a burnt patch right in the middle of the road. It must have stopped the horses in their tracks.'

'So what are you saying? Someone lit a fire to stop the carriage?' Walsh said.

'Yes. As a trap. Like what we saw at the first crime scene, just done differently,' Hobbs said, inspecting the black ash on the ground by the carriage. 'It appears localised to the path, and no surrounding bush is burnt. They lit it, I'm sure of it. It was controlled and precise, and then it was extinguished. The trap worked efficiently, too. It would have spooked the horses, and the guards would have thought nothing of it. The blankets by the road were probably used to put it out.'

Hobbs picked up the blankets and saw the burnt patches. 'Yes, that's exactly what they did,' he said to himself.

'Henry, look at this,' Walsh said as he crouched down by the bodies. 'This seems different to what I saw in the first scene.'

Hobbs leant over the two bodies and saw what Walsh was referring to. Gunshot wounds to the lower legs of both guards.

'And then see here,' Walsh said, picking up the stiff, cold arms of the larger of the two guards, covered in bruises. 'Defensive wounds. They saw them coming this time. It was an ambush, but they saw them coming. This guard tried to fight them off. His arms and face are covered in scratches and bruises.'

'Same cause of death, I would say,' Hobbs said. 'Their necks were sliced open in the same manner as the first murders.'

'So, no doubt it's the same men.'

'No doubt at all. There would not be many people capable of brutality and overkill like this, especially in such a sparsely populated area. The killing, though, is slightly different, but it's the same men. Those cuts were made by the same hands. Cutting someone's neck is an extreme act of personal violence. It is intimate and messy, and it sends a clear message. A message of dominance. These are people who are looking to have complete control over their victims. To me, these men are trying to prove their strength and power. And I think they are really trying to frighten and get our attention.'

'Well, they have it,' Walsh replied. The crime scene is also almost identical to the last. It's another narrow passage. It offers seclusion, and once you enter, it is too difficult to turn around and take a different path. In fact, this seems to be the only path to get through to Springwood.

'What is further west of here?' Hobbs asked.

Walsh jogged back to his horse, dug through a pouch on the saddle, and found an old map of the Blue Mountains Palmer had packed. He traced his finger along a narrow line west of their current location.

'A small town called Woodford, I believe. About seven or eight miles away,' he said.

'And then Springwood is back to the east, the town we just went through?'

'Correct.'

'Surely someone saw something then,' Hobbs said. 'Something unusual, either just before or after the murders. Some strangers, perhaps. Or men acting unusual. And now we have a time frame. Judging by this scene, I would say these killings occurred within the last few hours.'

'I'll head to Woodford. It'll be a tough ride through the mountains, so I won't waste any time,' Walsh said.

'Good, I'll wait here for Miller and take him to Springwood. Remember, James, be open to anything the locals might offer. Even the smallest of clues could help. Then meet us back at Springwood for dinner when you're finished?'

'Agreed. See you later.'

Walsh climbed back on his horse and galloped west.

Alone in the stillness of the bush, Hobbs continued his examination of the crime scene. The lifeless bodies lying before him gradually succumbed to the inevitable pull of coldness as a swarm of flies invaded the area, feasting on the thickening blood pooled on the ground.

Miller and Palmer arrived a short time later, their expressions a mixture of disbelief and horror as they beheld the gruesome scene before them. Wide-eyed and stunned, they stood silently for a moment. Hobbs allowed them to take in the brutality of what had occurred in this very spot only hours earlier.

'So it's what we feared,' Miller eventually said. 'They killed again.'

'Yes,' Hobbs replied. 'This time, it's different. We have defensive wounds and gunshot wounds. They have changed their method. Change is good. It can lead to more evidence and often lead to mistakes, so this autopsy will be crucial. I want to know all we can about the ammunition and firearms used.

'Sergeant, I would like you to contact Doctor Andrews in Penrith. I appreciate this is a little further west than his usual jurisdiction. Still, it will be important for the same doctor to perform the autopsy. I need to know his medical opinion compared to the first murders.'

As Palmer prepared to leave, the distinct sound of approaching hooves reverberated, alerting Hobbs to the noise coming from the east. A formidable-looking figure astride a horse emerged from the shadows of the trees, clad in a black tunic with a matching cap, fluttering in the breeze as he rode purposefully toward the crime scene.

Palmer looked at the figure approaching and scratched at the stubble on his chin. 'Oh, this is not ideal.' His voice carried a mix of angst and irritation as he addressed the unexpected arrival.

'Who is this?' Hobbs asked.

'Chief Inspector Noland. The commander of our entire region. As I said when we met, he mostly works out of Springwood, near his home. I wrote to him about the first murders, and now he must have seen the note left on the station door. He won't like this one bit. Four murders in his command in a short period, without much of a lead.'

'No genuine lead yet at all, unfortunately,' Hobbs reminded.

Noland drew closer, remaining atop his horse as he came to a stop beside Palmer. His imposing figure boasted a large, rounded chest and an even larger stomach supported by thick, sturdy legs. Despite his age, which must have been well into his fifties, he exuded an air of strength, authority and experience, and his steely gaze surveyed the scene with intensity. A voluminous grey moustache covered his top lip and cascaded down to the bottom of his jaw. As he removed his cap, wispy strands of silver hair framed his mostly bald head.

'Good day, Chief Inspector,' Palmer said.

'Sergeant. What's all this then? I saw the note on the station door, and I'm sure you could appreciate my serious concern.'

'Of course, sir, it is awful news. Two more gold guards were murdered, and like the first attacks, the thieves also stole gold from the carriage. Some gold, but not all of it.'

'These murders likely took place earlier this morning,' Hobbs added. 'Perhaps even just a short time before someone reported it.'

Noland turned sharply and stared directly at Hobbs. 'And you are?' His expression contorted into a snarl as he dismounted from his horse. His formidable stature came into full view as he towered over Hobbs, revealing a figure an inch taller than Hobbs and considerably broader despite his excess weight. Adjusting his belt, which bore a holster housing the same sidearm carried by Palmer and Miller, a Dougall Transition Revolver. Noland's frown and twitching lip made him appear to be ready for a confrontation.

Palmer answered, 'Sir, this is Henry Hobbs. As I wrote in my last report, Inspector Walsh from Sydney is assisting the investigation, and Mr Hobbs here is his associate.'

'Associate?' Noland said, raising a bushy eyebrow.

Hobbs always disliked others speaking for him, so he moved closer to Noland. 'That's correct. I worked with James Walsh at Scotland Yard.'

Noland continued his stare at Hobbs. An icy silence filled the warm air as Hobbs stared back. 'And now what, Mr Hobbs?' he sneered.

'And now nothing. I'm just here to help. I have investigated many murders over the years, and my expertise has been requested. With the lack of resources here, I would say any help I can offer would be sincerely appreciated.'

Hobbs saw Noland's lip twitch again while he continued to glare at him. Hobbs maintained his resolve to not be intimidated and simply stared back at Noland, unblinking. Noland looked away first and turned to Palmer.

'So, what do you think, sergeant? Any leads so far?'

Palmer hesitated and looked back at Hobbs.

'I asked *you* a question, Sergeant Palmer, not Mr Hobbs.'

'Nothing yet, sir, but we will keep working as hard as possible,' he eventually replied.

'See that you do. That's four murders in under a week. I'm sure you can understand the pressing seriousness of the investigation.'

'Absolutely, sir. We are all concerned and will work as hard as we can.'

'Do you have adequate resources to investigate these matters?'

Palmer again glanced at Hobbs. 'Yes, sir, we have the matters under control,' he said.

'These murders are now our number one priority. Do you understand that?'

'I do, sir, absolutely. We will work our very hardest.'

'Good. I don't want our communities to panic. Now, where is Inspector Walsh?'

Hobbs spoke up again. 'He has gone to the next town in the west to see if anyone saw anything. Constable Miller and I will head east to Springwood to do the same.'

'Very well, then. And Mr Hobbs, I trust you to know your place? You are working for the police at Inspector Walsh's request, not mine. I don't want trouble from outsiders. If at any time you get in the way, I will see your removal from the investigation and the entire area, too.'

'I am simply here to help.'

Noland nodded and circled the crime scene himself, examining the two bodies, when suddenly, a loud rummaging was heard from within the bushes at the side of the road.

Hobbs turned to the bushes quickly as Noland, Palmer, and Miller drew their revolvers, aiming them toward the noise. The sound was too loud to be a small animal, and soon, he detected movement within the shrubbery. This close to a gruesome double murder crime scene, Hobbs was prepared for anything. Still unable to see the source of the noise, he crouched low, poised to react in an instant, his heart racing with anticipation.

TWENTY-ONE

As the rustling drew nearer, the tension thickened, and the officers maintained their grip on their revolvers. Hobbs clenched his fists, prepared to confront whatever was in the bushes. He saw a shadow loom before a tall, slender figure stepped out from behind a tree. Seemingly unfazed by the piercing gazes fixed upon him, he emerged onto the roadside without a hint of concern at the guns pointed toward him. The man was young, no older than eighteen or nineteen and Indigenous with long, curly black hair cascading over his shoulders. He wore loose-fitting dark trousers paired with a brown cotton shirt left unbuttoned, offering a glimpse of his slender yet well-defined stomach and chest muscles.

The officers eased their tension, gradually lowering their firearms. Hobbs straightened up, unclenching his fists and releasing the tension from his muscles as he drew a deep breath.

'What are you doing out here?' Noland snarled.

The stranger promptly responded, 'looking for berries.'

'Constable, search this man,' Noland demanded.

Miller paused and briefly looked at Hobbs before complying with the direction. He walked over to the man and gave him an apologetic look. He didn't respond, but offered no resistance as Miller patted him down.

'He is not armed, sir.'

'Of course I am not armed. I'm not hunting this morning,' he said.

'Are you sure about that?' Noland asked, moving aside as he pointed to the two bodies behind him.

He remained silent, his response limited to slightly widening his eyes in reaction to seeing the bodies. Hobbs noted this subtle reaction.

Noland advanced toward the young man, his gaze intense.

'Did you do this?'

'No, I didn't.'

'So why are you here, then?'

Hobbs quickly interjected. 'I believe he answered that question.'

Noland maintained his intense stare but now fixed it on Hobbs as he approached the young man with measured, calm steps.

'Sir, did you see anyone in this area this morning? Likely more than one man,' Hobbs asked.

Eyebrows raised, he replied, 'sir?'

'Yes, well, I'm sorry. I do not know your name.'

The young man remained visibly startled, his expression reflecting surprise at the unexpected show of respect. 'No one has called me that before.'

'His name is Yarran,' Noland said, taking a few steps back. 'He's a tracker. A wanderer through these areas. A nuisance and a busybody.'

Yarran shifted his gaze downward, his nervousness evident in how he avoided eye contact, focusing instead on the ground beneath him.

'Yarran, my name is Henry, and as you can probably tell, there have been some murders this morning. I'm tasked with assisting on the case, and I'd like to know if you saw or heard anything.'

'No, I didn't. I have been deep in the bush all morning, and just now is the furthest to the east I have been.'

'He can't help,' Noland said.

Hobbs ignored him. 'Did I hear correctly that you are a tracker?'

'Yes, that's correct.'

'Would you be so kind as to look at this scene? I would understand if you said no, given that it is quite gruesome; however, if you can tell me anything, I would appreciate that.'

'He will do no such thing,' Noland interrupted. 'This is a police investigation, and at the moment, Yarran, you are a suspect.'

'I do not believe he is,' Hobbs said.

'Excuse me?' Noland asked, trying to stand over Hobbs, who ignored the attempt at the dominating tactic.

'Look at his hands, fingernails, clothes, hair, Mr Noland. There is no blood on him. Now, either he washed and changed his clothes in the bush, which I find unlikely, or he is innocent. Plus, his expression when he saw the crime scene. It was a pure surprise. Minor details such as these matter, Mr Noland.'

Ignoring Noland's sudden red face and contemptuous expression, Hobbs continued before he could launch into an ego-driven lecture.

'Mr Noland, let me try to solve these murders. We can use all the help we can get. There is no place for foolish pride here.'

Noland's face turned a darker shade of crimson as his anger grew. Hobbs knew Noland was not accustomed to being challenged or addressed in such a manner. Grunting in frustration, he returned to his horse.

Climbing atop, he glared at Hobbs once again. 'Mr Hobbs, you either solve these murders with Inspector Walsh, or I have you arrested for hindering an investigation and recommend that Inspector Walsh's employment be terminated.'

He spurred his horse more forcefully than needed and rode eastbound toward Springwood.

Palmer, his complexion now pale, finally spoke up. 'I hope you know what you are doing, Mr Hobbs. Chief Inspector Noland is not one to tolerate any confrontation or disappointment.'

'I'm not worried about him, sergeant,' Hobbs said nonchalantly and turned back to Yarran. 'So Yarran, will you care to look? Any clue could be incredibly valuable to our investigation.'

'Sure, I can look if that's what you want,' he said slowly, almost cautiously.

'Fantastic, come over and tell me if you can learn anything from these horse tracks.'

As he walked toward the road, Hobbs remained near the bushes, allowing him space to examine the scene quietly.

'I really hope you know what you are doing,' Palmer said.

'I don't really, but can it hurt? I have relied on members of the public to help with investigations back in England, so I don't see how this is any different.'

'But using the Indigenous People? He hasn't even received a formal education.'

'School does not always breed an intelligent person. Life experiences can be just as important, if not more important, in one's development. Just let him try.'

After a moment of watching Yarran pace around the bodies, Hobbs walked over while Yarran was leaning over some deep hoof prints in the wet dirt.

'Do you see anything?'

Yarran paused and looked back at Hobbs. 'Why did you stand up for me, Henry? You don't know me.'

'Everyone is a stranger at some point. Now tell me about these prints you are looking at.'

Yarran nodded. Hobbs interpreted Yarran's nod as a sign of satisfaction with his answer and proceeded with his examination.

'Horses came from the east.' Yarran then moved over to a new patch of hoof prints and continued. 'These track marks are not as well formed, but definitely made from the same horses. It appears they walked here and then galloped back the way they came. I can see the tracks headed back east are more hurried, so not as deep.'

'So no track marks tell you they may have gone west instead?'

Yarran took another look at the ground. 'No, they went east. The other horse's tracks that you can see came from the west and this carriage here followed them.'

'So that would be the gold carriage arriving?' Hobbs looked back at Palmer and Miller. 'Well then, the tracks support what happened after the murders. The killers went back toward Springwood. That's where we will go.'

'There's something else,' Yarran added. 'Look here, the tracks heading back east. There are three distinct sets. Three different horses, not including the horse which would have pulled the carriage.'

Yarran walked back to the area where the bodies were left and silently examined the ground once again. After a moment, he looked back at Hobbs.

'There are also three different boot prints. That is not including the ones these murdered men are wearing.'

'Three? You are sure?' Hobbs asked.

'Yes. Look here, they are different sizes and widths.'

Hobbs looked closely but could only really distinguish a difference once Yarran pointed to specific features in the footmarks.

'Yes, I see that.'

Hobbs offered his hand to shake, which Yarran, at first looking surprised, accepted.

'Thank you for your help, Yarran. Might I suggest you head back home now? I suspect Mr Noland is quite irate, and I think you should stay away for a little while.'

'I am Wiradjuri, so my home is well beyond here. Past Lithgow. I will just camp in the bush tonight.'

Hobbs nodded. 'I am not knowledgeable about your culture, but you speak English well.'

'It is my second language, but it helps me find tracking work for farmers when their livestock wanders off.'

'And you're comfortable sleeping out here in the bush?'

'I enjoy being with nature, roaming through all parts of the mountains when I am not at home. We can learn a lot from our natural surroundings. My people have done this since the beginning of time.'

'Well, thank you again. Take care of yourself, Yarran.' Hobbs turned back to Miller and Palmer as Yarran nodded and walked back into the bush behind them. 'Edmund, you and I will go to Springwood. Sergeant Palmer, can you arrange for the doctor to collect the bodies? Where are your other constables?'

'Out on patrol, I expect. They had left before I arrived at the station this morning.'

'Well, I understand you still need a patrol in Penrith, so perhaps alert the Springwood Constabulary to see if they can assist you in removing the rest of the gold to have it taken to the Mint.'

Hobbs removed his hat and wiped a thick line of sweat that had now formed around his forehead. 'Four murders now on the gold route, word will spread quickly, which concerns me. We are not far from mass panic.'

TWENTY-TWO

'That was impressive back there, your interaction with the native tracker,' Miller said as the pair continued riding back toward the town of Springwood.

Hobbs slowed a little and looked Miller directly in the eye. 'Edmund, a good detective needs the ability to adapt. Use your surroundings and explore all possibilities. Yarran may or may not have been able to assist, but we would never know without asking. Always ask questions. Remember that okay.'

Miller nodded. 'I will.'

It was midday when they arrived back in Springwood, and upon their return, they saved time by splitting up.

Hobbs provided some final instructions before they went their separate ways to complete their enquiries. 'Edmund, speak with everyone in the stores and anyone else you pass in town about what they saw in the morning. Ask them if they saw anything out of the ordinary, both at the times before the murders and after. Even the smallest or seemingly insignificant details can be important. However, refrain from disclosing specific information to anyone, especially the fresh clue about three men being involved or what was written on the carriage. Allow them to tell you what they saw; we will later interpret this as relevant or not.'

'Yes, I understand,' Miller said.

'Good lad. Encourage those you speak with to give you a full recount of anything they may have seen before you, then probe in with more specific questions to clarify what they have said, but allow them to do most of the talking. Believe me, an excellent investigator listens more than they speak. I'll meet you in the centre of town later.'

Hobbs strolled past the town's pub, a quaint old brick building adorned with a wooden verandah that wrapped around its sides. Three elderly men sat outside, leisurely sipping tall glasses of cold beer and idly watching the day unfold. Perfect, Hobbs thought. If anything out of the ordinary happened, these men would have likely seen it.

'Gentleman, I was hoping to have a moment of your time,' Hobbs said, talking from the street to the old men huddled around a small round table. Each wore large floppy hats and dirty, sweat-stained linen shirts. Their faces, wrinkled and sun damaged, were flushed red, and their unsteady posture in the chairs suggested they had spent much of the morning drinking at the pub.

None responded; instead, they raised their glasses and swayed even more. Their eyes were bloodshot and cloudy.

'I just wanted to know, while you've been here drinking, have you seen anyone unusual pass through?'

'Strange question,' one of the men said. The wrinkles on his face were deep, and his moustache was so thick that his lips were completely concealed.

'Yes. I'm helping the police look for something. So have you?'

'Just you,' he said.

'How do you mean?'

'You aren't from around here.'

Hobbs nodded appreciatively; at least the drunks were somewhat observant.

'Have you seen anyone else not from around here?'

'No. Just the usual crowd. We sit here most days. Men heading off to work, children running around. You're the first stranger. What's this all about?'

Hobbs ignored the question and scanned the street up and down. It was the main road, and he reasoned that if a foreigner travelled through town, they would likely use this direct route to the east or west.

'How about a drink?' another asked as he drained his beer, leaking some of the large mouthfuls on his ragged beard before wiping his mouth clean with his dirty sleeve.

'No, thank you. So you're sure you've seen no one else?'

'Sure as sure can be,' he said.

'Thank you for your time,' Hobbs said.

Hobbs persisted in questioning as many people as possible while skilfully dodging inquiries about the true purpose of his inquiries. He conversed with the town's pastor and even engaged a group of children playing with a large ball in front of the small local school. No one had seen anything that raised his suspicions. Hobbs felt frustrated as he realised this lead had turned into a dead end. When Miller returned shortly after, he echoed the same sentiment. No one had seen anything that could aid their investigation.

'Everyone said their day had been typical. No strangers at all, and nothing unusual,' he said, sounding deflated. 'Do you really think they came this way?'

'Well, they either came back this way as Yarran said, or if he was wrong, they continued west, and James will hopefully have some information for us.'

'I hope so. I don't like the idea of four murders happening without us having so much as a single suspect.'

'Be patient, Edmund. Let's have a drink in the pub while we wait for James to return.'

They walked into the same pub that Hobbs had spoken with the old men earlier and were welcomed by the lively chatter of patrons. They opted for a table outside, where the late afternoon sunlight filtered through the lush foliage, casting a warm glow over the rustic wooden furnishings. As they settled into their seats, Miller ordered a pint of lager while Hobbs opted for hot tea, served to him in a thick ceramic mug.

'You don't drink alcohol, Mr Hobbs?' Miller asked.

'Henry,' Hobbs corrected.

'Oh, right, sorry, Henry.'

'No, not anymore. It did me no favours back in England.'

As they finished their first round, Hobbs took charge of the next. When he refreshed his tea, his mind momentarily drifted to thoughts of James and his progress.

'Do you miss England?' Miller eventually asked, breaking the silence.

'Sometimes, but I have no purpose there. Not anymore.'

'No wife? Or children.'

Hobbs flinched and quickly swallowed a large gulp of air, making him gasp. It was an involuntary reaction, and he felt a sudden surge of anger rise within him at the question. In an instant, cherished but now sorrowful memories flooded his mind's eye, and he felt his hands clench under the table. Anger quickly replaced itself with a feeling of foolishness and he quickly composed himself. His rage or self pity did not belong here. It was an innocent question, and not Miller's fault for raising what was a routine enquiry.

'My wife died, and no, we had no children,' he said in what he hoped was a composed and balanced tone.

Miller had just taken a sip of his beer and choked a little. 'Oh, I'm so sorry, Henry. I did not know. Forgive me.'

'It's alright, Edmund. Perhaps we should discuss something else, though.'

Miller's face become red, and an awkward silence filled the air. Sensitive to Edmund's obvious discomfort, Hobbs redirected the conversation, steering it away from what he knew would soon grow to an uncomfortable tension.

'What about you? From the strength of your accent, you only moved here recently?'

'Indeed. When I married, my wife and I moved here from England. I'm from Kent originally. Where did you learn how to be a detective? I would very much like to become an investigator someday.'

'A noble career choice,' Hobbs said. 'I learnt my trade from many fine investigators, starting with my first inspector. After that, I was fortunate enough to work under very competent police officers back in London before being promoted. They taught me everything they knew and, most importantly, taught me to question everything and always trust my instincts. The rest, I'm afraid, is all from painful experiences. I have made many errors and miscalculations in the past, but how we learn from these mistakes is important. Do you understand what I am saying?'

'Yes,' Miller replied. 'It's not ideal to make mistakes, but it is part of how we learn.'

Hobbs sipped his tea and nodded. 'You have a good head on your shoulders, Edmund. You are calm and clearly dedicated; you will be a fine detective someday.'

Miller smiled as Hobbs drained the rest of his second cup of tea.

'When this case is over. What will you do?' Miller asked.

'That I do not know. I don't have any purpose back home. I don't believe I have one here either.'

'Will you have to go back to Cockatoo Island?'

Hobbs shrugged. 'I suppose I will have to. I have a conviction, so according to this colony, that is where I belong.'

'Do you have any family at all back in London?' Miller asked.

Hobbs shook his head. 'I have no family left. Both my parents have long since died, and I am an only child. When I lost my wife, I lost everything.'

Miller averted his eyes and fumbled with his fingers, still cradling his half-finished pint.

'I hope you're hungry,' Hobbs eventually said, again sensing the quiet uneasiness from Miller. 'I expect James to arrive soon, and I would like to eat here tonight. It has been a long time since I ate at a pub.'

About thirty minutes later, Walsh wearily entered the town. Hobbs noticed him riding slowly, appearing fatigued. Calling out to him, Walsh dismounted, tethering his horse at the front of the pub. The tired animal eagerly indulged in a much-needed drink from the nearby trough.

'I had no breakthrough at Woodford,' Walsh said, taking off his hat and slumping into the empty chair beside Hobbs. 'No one saw anything out of the ordinary. How were the enquiries here?'

'The same,' Hobbs said. 'No one saw anything unusual, nor did anyone see anyone other than the locals.'

Walsh exhaled. 'Let's get something to eat. I'm tired and hungry.'

They abandoned their outdoor table and entered the pub, finding a new spot in a quiet corner. They ordered another round of beers, a fresh tea for Hobbs, and three servings of shepherd's pie. As the sun dipped below the horizon and the end of the workday drew to a close, the pub swelled with patrons, filling every available table and leaving only a smattering of stools at the lengthy wooden bar. A vibrant energy filled the room as drinks circulated, voices rose, and laughter echoed off the walls. Hobbs,

Walsh, and Miller found themselves speaking with raised voices to be heard over the lively chatter and jovial banter.

'I think the killers are locals,' Hobbs said.

'You do?' Walsh asked.

'Well, think about it. You went west, and I went east. Our killers must have gone either way, and no one saw anything out of place. Only a local could have returned to town without someone noticing something, or at the very least, they could easily blend in. I spoke to some men at this pub who had been drinking out on the balcony most of the day, and they saw nothing unusual.'

'Drinking?' Walsh questioned. 'Were they even reliable?'

'Well, regardless of whether they were a little drunk, they were confident they did not see a stranger. The same went for everyone both Edmund and I spoke with. Nothing unusual, and we spoke with almost every shop owner in town.'

Miller nodded.

Hobbs continued. 'I also believe there are three men. I was fortunate enough to find some help from a local tracker who happened across the scene while we were there?'

'Who was this tracker? You trusted him?'

'His name is Yarran, and yes, I trusted him. He gave me no reason not to. He examined the scene from a different perspective. It was quite interesting, in fact.'

'And he told you three men were involved?' Walsh asked.

'Yes. From boot prints. And this matches our theory of at least two men being involved. He was also sure they headed east after the murders, which would have led them right through Springwood.'

'Well, anyway, this complicates things. It could be any of thousands of people then, and we still have no witnesses.' Walsh said. 'We're still stuck, and things are now escalating.'

TWENTY-THREE

After a brief wait, the pies arrived, steaming hot and fragrant. They ate in silence; the aroma filling the air as Hobbs savoured the hearty meal. Exhausted from the day's events, the comfort of the food was a welcome reprieve.

'Should we be concerned if the killers are local?' Miller asked when they had finished eating.

'In a way,' Hobbs replied. 'They clearly have the ability to blend in, but at least now we can narrow down our searches. We likely are not looking for vagrants and travellers, rather someone within the local community. But importantly, I still believe we are looking for a team. I will always look at the positives in a case like this. Every clue is a win.'

'What if they strike again?'

'We will do everything we can to avoid that.'

'But you do think they will kill again?' Miller asked.

'Unfortunately, I think they will continue until they are stopped.'

'What's the plan, then? We can't let more people die.'

'I want to go to Bathurst,' Hobbs said. 'The gold transport process needs to be seen from the beginning. Every single step in their processes and who has access to the gold and records. I'll talk to the gold guards and arrange with the Mint representatives to have us go undercover inside a gold carriage.'

When Walsh and Miller said nothing, instead they cast perplexed looks, bewildered by the idea, Hobbs continued, 'I want to set the bait and possibly catch them in the act.'

'So let them ambush *us*?' Walsh asked on the edge of his seat.

'Or if you look at it the other way, *we* ambush them,' Hobbs replied.

Walsh settled back in his chair and exhaled with a shake of his head.

Over the raucous laughter and chatter, the sound of breaking glass shattered the air, followed by the sharp cry of a distressed woman. Hobbs glanced up to see a man in his early twenties, clad in soiled overalls, towering over a petite and visibly frightened woman. His demeanour was imposing, and his voice boomed menacingly inches from the woman's face. Those nearby kept their distance, unwilling to intervene in the escalating scene. As his intoxicated tirade continued, the man's bellowing voice slurred with each word, his unsteady weight shifting back and forth. It was evident that he was on the verge of violence, fuelled by the effects of heavy drinking. The woman, her face a portrait of fear, seemed all too familiar with the impending danger, her body instinctively recoiling. With a forceful shove, the man suddenly pushed her against the edge of the bar, causing her hands to collide with the sharp fragments of broken glass strewn across the wooden surface, slicing through her skin.

From a safe distance behind the protection of his wooden countertop, the bartender cried out meekly, his voice barely audible over the racket of the crowd. 'Douglas, go home. You're drunk.'

'Mind your own business!' the man responded hostilely, maintaining intense eye contact with the terrified woman.

The pub had become quieter as people stood by and watched, too afraid to offer a challenge. Hobbs stood up and walked over to the woman who was now nursing her cut hands, his footsteps echoing against the hushed atmosphere.

'Are you okay, miss?' he asked, taking her hands and examining the damage.

The man named Douglas pushed out his large chest and roared at Hobbs. 'Hey, stay out of this! She's my wife. Mind your own business!'

Hobbs ignored him and continued speaking with the injured woman. 'I think you need to see a doctor. Come with me. I'll help you find one.'

'Who do you think you are? Stay away from my wife!' the man roared as he roughly shoved Hobbs in the shoulder.

Hobbs released his gentle hold of the crying woman and stood in front of her. 'She's your wife?'

'That's right, now piss off.' The stench of alcohol on the man's breath was pungent, but Hobbs did not take a backward step.

'And you hit your defenceless wife, do you?' Hobbs asked calmly.

'She's my wife, and it's no business of yours!'

Hobbs turned around and took a glimpse of the cowering woman behind him, clutching at her bloody hands, her eyes wide with fear.

In a fraction of a second, Hobbs grabbed the man by his hair and slammed the side of his head down hard on the wooden bar. As he collapsed onto the ground, Hobbs drove his knee up into the man's chin, cracking his jaw as he fell face down onto the floor.

The pub crowd gasped, and then silence fell over the room as they peered at the man's body withering on the floor.

'Come on, I want to find you a doctor,' Hobbs said to the now hyperventilating woman, with tears running down her face. 'What's your name?'

'Edith.'

'I'm Henry, Edith. Does he hit you often?' he asked.

The woman gasped in between cries and hurried breaths. 'I can't be with him anymore. We've only been married for six months, but I'm frightened all the time. I can't take the beatings anymore. I thought he would change, but he frightens me when he drinks.'

'And he drinks often?'

'Every day.'

'Do you have family nearby?'

'Yes, my brothers work on a farm near here.'

'Can I suggest you stay there for a while, maybe have them collect your things?'

She nodded again.

'Okay, come on then, you're safe now.'

'No one has ever stood up for me like that before, and I never know what to do when he turns so violent like that, so thank you. I mean, if my brothers were here, they probably would have killed him, but they are always on the farm working; they don't know what Douglas is really like.'

'Thanks are unnecessary. Let's just take care of your hands. From now on, have your brothers look after you.'

Hobbs glanced at his table as he walked the woman out of the pub to see Miller's look of surprise as Walsh tapped him on the shoulder. 'Let's go, Edmund.'

'What just happened?' Miller asked, looking at Walsh.

'He never had much patience for men who are violent toward women. I suspect now he has become even less tolerant of the behaviour. Now, let's ride back to Penrith and get a good night's sleep. I'll tell Henry to meet me back at our cottage. We leave for Bathurst first thing in the morning.'

TWENTY-FOUR

Even though he was exhausted from the late-night events in Springwood, Hobbs woke early the following morning. He shuffled into the kitchen and poured himself a cup of coffee before stepping outside to breathe the fresh morning air. Shortly after, Walsh joined him, and they stood together, sipping from their porcelain cups.

'How's the lady from last night?' Walsh asked.

'She will be fine. I found a doctor in town to wrap her wounds, but the damage was done. It was clear she had been a victim of prolonged abuse. I just hope she finally stays away from that brute she calls a husband.'

'Well, you have always been righteous in that regard.'

'Even more so since I lost Emma.'

'As long as you won't be too reckless. I don't want you losing control,' Walsh said.

Hobbs paused and waited for Walsh to finish what he knew he wanted to say.

'It's your proposal to ride in the back of a gold carriage and act as bait for a team of dangerous killers that has me concerned.'

There it was, Hobbs thought. He had been waiting for Walsh to voice his reservations about his plan. 'Why? Because you think I have nothing left to lose since Emma's gone?' he said.

Walsh took a step back and raised his hands defensively. 'No, Henry, not at all. I just want you to remember who you are and all the good we've done over the years.'

'All the good we've done has left me with persistent nightmares and nothing but the memory of my wife.

'Do you want to know what really frightens me, James? I'm scared one day I'll wake up and forget her face. Forget her smell, her laugh, and I just can't afford to let that go.'

Walsh sighed sympathetically. 'I just want you to remember what Emma would have wanted for you. To live and love your life. Just be careful, is all I'm saying.'

'So I shouldn't have taken out that thug and helped that lady? Emma would not have wanted a woman trapped in a cycle of abuse.'

'It's more than that, Henry. It's this ambush plan of yours to ride in the back of the gold carriage. It's risky, that's all.'

'Well, James, how else do you suggest we further the investigation?'

'Look, you know I trust you. I just want you to have a clear mind, free from recklessness.'

Hobbs remained silent.

Walsh slowly nodded, understanding that the conversation was over. 'Well, come on then, let's get going. We have a big day of riding. It will take a couple of days to reach Bathurst, so we should get a good start before it gets too warm. I told Edmund to meet us at the station at first light.'

'I'm ready,' Hobbs said, finishing the rest of his coffee.

Walsh paused for a moment. 'Henry, before we leave, I need to know if you are truly sure this is the best tactic.'

'Right now, we have nothing. We have a somewhat limited suspect pool, yet at the same time, we can't narrow it down. It could be anyone in these mountain towns. We need to get ahead of them. If they don't take the bait, we are in no worse position.'

'Alright, Henry. We'll do it your way.'

When they reached the Penrith police station, they discovered Edmund by the stables, diligently finishing the preparations for their three horses before their upcoming journey.

'Good morning, I have almost finished preparing the horses. I have packed some food too. My wife has made rabbit stew we can reheat tonight for dinner.'

'Sounds delicious. Well, at least let me help,' Hobbs said, finishing adjusting the stirrups on his horse. 'I think that's about it. Let's get started.'

'It is a very rough trail ahead, and it will take some time, so the sooner we leave, the better,' Miller added.

Just before departure, they bid farewell to Palmer, who came by to ensure everything was in order.

'Travel safe,' he said. 'By the time you get back, I expect Doctor Andrews will have completed the autopsy reports for the last two victims.'

'Thank you, sergeant,' Walsh called out, his voice trailing behind him as they galloped toward the foot of the Blue Mountains.

As they approached the site of the first murders, an eerie atmosphere hung in the air, reminiscent of the brutality that had occurred there. Though the dirt had absorbed the copious amounts of blood spilt last week, the scene still exuded a sense of unease. Continuing their journey, they encountered the second crime scene later in the day. Despite removing the carriage at Palmer's request, the recently dried blood still stained the earth. Hobbs expected that soon the blood would be completely absorbed into the ground or washed away by rain, much like what had happened at the first crime scene.

They stopped for lunch a little further west and settled on the dry grass in an open paddock while their horses grazed nearby. Eager not to linger unnecessarily, as soon as they and their horses had eaten, they resumed their journey along the winding dirt roads, ascending the sharp incline of the Blue Mountains. By the time they neared the peak in the centre of the vast mountain range, the sun had begun its descent, casting warm hues across the landscape. They chose a suitable spot to camp for the night, and Miller skilfully started a fire. He then reheated his wife's stew in a cast-iron pot, and Hobbs savoured every spoonful, grateful for all the wonderful food he had eaten since his release from Cockatoo Island. Full from the hearty meal, they each chose a soft spot on the grass, and just as the fire was dying, Hobbs fell asleep.

Hobbs sat under the massive oak tree, his bare feet gently caressed by the long grass swaying beneath him. Emma sat beside him, her eyes closed, basking in the moment. No words were necessary; they found solace in each other's quiet presence, enveloped by the soothing sounds of rustling leaves and distant bird songs in the early afternoon. Emma leaned against Hobbs, resting against his legs. He closed his eyes, finding a simple peace in the warmth of his wife's head resting on his lap, her hair flowing freely in the gentle breeze. At that moment of tranquillity, Hobbs felt her presence so vividly. However, when he opened his eyes, he was met with the sight of desolate surroundings instead of his wife. The once vibrant oak tree behind him now stood lifeless, its branches barren and skeletal, as if ravaged by fire. The dead grass beneath was cold and uncomfortable against his legs, and a sense of eerie emptiness filled the air. Hobbs's heart raced with panic as he scanned the barren landscape for any sign of his wife. The emptiness within him grew with each passing moment, gnawing at his insides like a relentless hunger. Tears welled up in his eyes, blurring his vision as he desperately called out for Emma, his voice echoing through the lifeless expanse. But there was no response, only the eerie silence of the dead countryside that felt suffocating.

Hobbs's heart pounded against his chest as he jolted awake, his breaths ragged and laboured. Sweat covered his forehead as he scanned the dimly lit surroundings, his senses still reeling from the haunting remnants of his dream. The fire's dying embers cast flickering shadows across the campsite beside the rhythmic breathing of the still fast-asleep Walsh and Miller.

He found his water flask and took a long, soothing drink while the echoes of the dream lingered in his mind. Sitting in the quiet darkness, he thought about the recurring dreams - a mix of pure joy, followed by pain when she vanished, and he woke. He often wished he would remain sleeping forever. To live simply, inside his head, amongst the field with the woman he loved more than anything.

Back in London, this relentless pattern of despair and the longing for a life outside his mortal existence had driven Hobbs to alcoholism and the edge of death on more than one occasion. Wasting away in despair, and clinging desperately to his dream fantasies with Emma, Hobbs found himself on the verge of self-destruction. After several nights of heavy drinking, thoughts of ending his own life crept into his mind. Yet, something he couldn't understand always restrained him. He never knew why he stopped himself, but life, even as it was, filled with pain and emptiness, clung to him. There was a fiery determination deep in his gut that compelled him to persevere. To refuse surrender. It was as though a small piece of his late wife still clutched onto him, holding him to life.

Ultimately, he realised it was Emma's memory that rescued him from the depths of his torment and stopped his drinking. Following his arrest for punching his commanding officer, he spiralled into depression, grappling with the repercussions of his mistake – an ending of his career and then his own freedom. Yet Emma's presence persisted, a beacon of light in his darkness. Her memory and essence enveloped him, urging him to rediscover the zest for life he once possessed. Though lost and in agony, the thought of her provided comfort. Her memory, securely locked away in his mind, became something that could not be taken from him. It was that which kept him going and not the bottomless whiskey bottles he had been drowning himself in.

The morning sun filtered through the crevices of some distant rocky hills, rousing all three simultaneously. Walsh prepared their breakfast - a hearty, if somewhat lumpy, porridge cooked over the crackling fire. As it simmered, Hobbs attended to the horses, guiding them to a fresh patch of grass for their breakfast. Satisfied and fuelled, they resumed their westward journey, descending the opposite slope of the mountains, bound for the town of Lithgow.

They rode through the bustling yet relatively small town without stopping, pressing westward across the rugged terrain down the mountains. Their journey became more arduous as an afternoon thunderstorm descended, intensifying the already challenging conditions. By nightfall, they sought a spot to camp, but the relentless rain left them without a dry space for a fire.

Instead, Hobbs suggested they consume the remaining rabbit stew cold and find their own resting places by the thickest canopy nearby and underneath overhanging bushes with the broadest leaves to keep as dry as possible.

The rain persisted throughout most of the night, and sleep proved elusive. However, with the arrival of the next morning, a clear day greeted them. They pressed on in near silence, overwhelmed by exhaustion, and by late afternoon on the third day, they finally reached the outskirts of Bathurst.

TWENTY-FIVE

Bathurst bustled with activity and vitality, boasting newly constructed buildings and bustling shops, its population exceeding Hobbs' expectations this far from Sydney. It was so busy, in fact, that they went largely unnoticed amidst the vibrant atmosphere, even despite Miller donning his mounted police uniform. The gold rush had propelled Bathurst to newfound prosperity, evident in the burgeoning wealth that adorned the town. Tailor shops, cobblers, and restaurants lined the streets, fuelled by the influx of money and the growing population. As they made their way deeper into the town, it became apparent that the prosperity extended beyond the urban landscape, and rows of grand houses lined the streets behind the main thoroughfare. As Hobbs observed herds of well-dressed women and children engaged in the day's activities, the atmosphere reminded him of the centre of Sydney, albeit on a smaller scale. Yet, still, it had its own lively energy.

Hobbs soon observed a wave of prospectors making their way towards the western edge of Bathurst. Among them, a stark contrast emerged: some donned fresh attire and brandished brand-new mining implements. In contrast, others appeared cloaked in tattered rags, their aspirations of fortune apparently still needing to be realised. These men bore the marks of exhaustion and hunger, and it seemed the quest for gold they embarked upon today might very well be their last.

As they departed from the town centre, the mass of prospectors gradually dispersed, splintering off into smaller clusters, each seeking their own secluded corner amidst the rugged terrain of mountains and streams in pursuit of their golden dreams. Along a serene valley flanked by rolling hills, a small creek came into view, where several figures huddled by its banks, meticulously panning for gold with oversized steel dishes. With a nudge to his horse, Hobbs urged it into a trot, closing the distance towards the group ahead.

'Good day,' he said as he approached. 'I am looking for the Royal Mint representatives. Do you know where I can find them?'

The men ignored Hobbs and remained absorbed in their panning, their attention fixed solely on the swirling waters within their pans.

Hobbs dismounted and approached the group.

'Excuse me,' he repeated, tapping one of the crouching men on his shoulder.

Hobbs met the gaze of the man and his companions, a group of Chinese descent. Their weathered faces were partially shielded from the harsh glare of the sun by oversized floppy hats.

'Chinese,' Walsh called out. 'They probably don't speak English. They came here after the American gold rush. This area is full of Chinese miners and panners.'

Hobbs smiled and courteously nodded at the group, a gesture reciprocated by warm smiles and respectful nods before they resumed their panning.

'Come on, let's keep riding; the creek probably widens further west, and I expect we will find the Mint's tent established there,' Walsh said.

As they continued alongside the creek, its width expanded and the current quickened. Along the water's edge, more prospectors stood in a familiar stance, mimicking the technique of the Chinese men, plunging their iron pans into the rushing stream. Though the process demanded patience, Hobbs understood the rewards were not always as substantial as those found deep underground or within the confines of a gold mine. Yet, this method was accessible and remained a cost-effective means of pursuing the elusive gold, with these very creeks boasting a proven history of yielding sizeable nuggets.

Further upstream, as the landscape inclined, Hobbs noticed an improvised settlement coming into view. Several large tents dotted the area, with men bustling about, manoeuvring wooden wheelbarrows amidst them. As they neared, the purpose of these tents became clear - it served as the operational hub of the region. Within them, makeshift stores had sprung up, offering a variety of goods, including clothing, mining equipment, and refreshments. Groups of men lounged under open canopies, drinking coffee, and Hobbs overheard several regaling each other with tales of past triumphs, likely embellished for dramatic effect as he could not imagine the sheer volume of gold some men claimed to have found. Meanwhile, another tent at the top of a grassy hill attracted a steady stream of visitors, their hands clutched tightly by their sides, hinting at their protection of something valuable.

'I would say this is the tent,' Hobbs said, pointing to the queue outside. 'What else would a person hold so tightly?'

Securing their horses to a sturdy wooden post, they weaved their way through the bustling crowd and climbed the hill toward the tent. Reaching the top and standing at the rear of the queue, Hobbs looked out at the breathtaking scene below.

Across the valley, he saw what appeared to be hundreds of small tents and makeshift shelters encircled by dying bonfires, casting flickering shadows. A mass of men toiled amidst the vast expanse, their figures silhouetted against the backdrop of rocky terrain. With pickaxes in hand, thousands chipped away at formidable boulders. At the same time, many more groups ventured into the depths of what appeared to be underground mines, likely created some time ago with the aid of copious amounts of nitroglycerin explosives.

Walsh strode forward with purpose, leading the way and parting through the weary group of men waiting to sell their hard-earned gold. He pressed on until he reached the forefront of the tent, where three figures clad in wool suits occupied a wooden table, perspiring profusely in the stifling heat that hung heavy within the confines of the tent. Next to them, two heavily built gold guards maintained a watchful eye, dressed in black tunics and rifles at the ready. The men behind the table were busily receiving small, dirty clumps of unrefined gold from the equally dirty-looking men and weighing them on scales. In return, these men were being issued with their payment. Hobbs saw several small metal boxes behind the table where the gold was being temporarily stored.

Walsh made it to the front of the queue and introduced himself. He requested to speak with the supervisor immediately, to which one man raised his arm.

'Perhaps it would be best for my colleagues and I to speak with you in private,' Walsh said.

'Yes, of course, sir. Please follow me.'

They were led through the back of the tent where a wooden gold carriage was parked, similar in description to what Hobbs had seen at the last murder scene. Propped against the cart stood two robust young men, their suspenders hanging loosely and their shirts unbuttoned as beads of perspiration glistened upon their exposed chests.

'If you gentlemen would excuse us,' the supervisor said. The men nodded and immediately left.

'My name is Clarence Pearson. I manage the Royal Mint's business here in Bathurst. I fear I know what this is about, having heard the awful news of our guards during the previous gold deliveries.'

Pearson spoke with a refined English accent, leading Hobbs to surmise that his tenure in Bathurst was relatively fresh. It seemed probable that he had received a promotion from London to be elevated to this position. A man of short stature and portly build, Pearson, aged around fifty, sported a dense brown moustache and possessed a round, bald head that left little room for a discernible neck.

Walsh removed his hat and cast a sympathetic glance. 'Yes, Mr Pearson, quite right. I am leading the investigation into these murders. These are my colleagues, Mr Henry Hobbs and Constable Edmund Miller.'

Pearson greeted Hobbs and Miller with a nod. 'These are very troubling times, inspector. A large amount of gold is being found here, and we require it to be conveyed to Sydney. Still, it is difficult now to find such men for the job without offering them more money and heavier artillery. In addition, the Mint is becoming concerned about its financial losses. We cannot keep the gold here either; it is not safe for the long term.'

'Mr Pearson, rest assure that we understand all your concerns and we are putting in our maximum effort to solve these murders. This is what brings us here, in fact. We have an investigative plan we wish to implement, but we would require your approval.'

'Anything. Anything at all, inspector. The sooner we can return to normal, the better for our business. The miners up here are already becoming restless as there is chatter about the Mint lowering the purchase price for their gold to recoup their earlier losses. I don't think these men will accept that either. It is often tense around here as it is, what with the Chinese and the Americans moving in on the fields. I fear a full-scale riot will occur if people are not being compensated appropriately.'

'I completely sympathise with you, Mr Pearson. We do not wish any trouble for you here, and that is why I would like to propose something to you, and for it, I would need your two best guards.'

'Of course. Russell and Saunders. The two young men who were here moments ago. But I must say, even they are beginning to feel uneasy about what has recently occurred.'

Hobbs took a step closer and offered his plan. 'Sir, what we propose is for us to accompany your guards on their next delivery to Sydney. I suggest we will hide in the carriage's rear and lure these men out. I expect they will plot an ambush on the carriage, which we will counter. They will probably not be expecting reinforcements in the back of the carriage.'

'So my guards will be offered as bait?'

'In a way, yes. This is why I want to use your most astute and fit men. There is, however, an element of danger in this.'

Pearson shuffled on his feet and pulled at his moustache. 'This makes me feel a little nervous. I mean, we have had problems with bushrangers in the past, and robberies occur from time to time, but from what I have heard about these murders, they were horrific. Senseless, in fact.'

'They were indeed, and I do understand your reservations, but unfortunately, we currently have very few investigatory leads, and I fear they will strike again. We now need to be proactive with this investigation.'

'Well, officers, if you believe this will finally put an end to this, then I will allow this to take place. However, I will advise my men to be heavily armed on the journey, taking every precaution.'

'Good, I too would advise this,' Hobbs added. 'We are dealing with several highly perilous men. Now, when is the next gold carriage scheduled to depart?'

'First thing tomorrow morning,' Pearson said, 'but I can have it brought forward if you wish.'

'No. We want everything to remain as scheduled. Nothing changes, do you understand? Also, the only people to know about this plan are yourself and the two guards.'

'I understand. So you all wish to fit in the back of the carriage.'

'Not I,' Walsh said. 'I wish to remain here and review the logs and records. There may be a clue here.'

'It will be Edmund and I,' Hobbs said.

'Very well, the gold carriage will leave from here at sunrise tomorrow.'

'Good day, Mr Pearson. We will be here first thing in the morning.'

TWENTY-SIX

Upon their return to the bustling town centre of Bathurst, Hobbs spotted a recently constructed hotel that looked clean and comfortable, at least from the outside. After making the suggestion, Walsh and Miller agreed to dine and sleep there for the night. After settling the bill for their accommodations, they opted for the additional service to house their horses in the hotel's stables overnight. This ensured they would be well cared for, enjoying a night of food and rest before embarking on the journey back to Penrith with Walsh, following his local inquiries.

After Hobbs bathed and changed his shirt, he regrouped with Walsh and Miller downstairs in the large open-planned bar and restaurant area for dinner. Walsh and Miller drank pints of lager while Hobbs opted for a tall glass of cold water. Despite the hotel's current state of near emptiness, the bartender assured them that at nightfall, it would soon teem with miners after a gruelling day in the fields. With a hint of amusement, the bartender added that they would be able to discern the day's successes by observing the miners' dinner choices.

Hobbs, Walsh, and Miller sat at a round wooden table at the heart of the hotel and promptly ordered roast lamb with potatoes, which arrived shortly after. As they ate, a surge of patrons flooded in. True to the bartender's earlier remark, Hobbs quickly identified those who had enjoyed fruitful days at the mines; their laughter filled the air as they generously bought rounds of drinks and large steaks. However, the overall ambience in the room remained distinct from that of the lively Springwood Hotel. Amidst the crowd, only a handful of miners were rowdy, and most sat in quiet, clearly recuperating from the day's toils under the sun or mourning their ill-fated endeavours, returning home empty-handed.

As they finished their dinner, the hotel reached its capacity. Though a minor increase in noise occurred due to the arrival of a small group, the atmosphere remained predominantly sombre. Hobbs headed to bed, seeking all the rest he could get for what he expected would be an uncomfortable day confined within the cramped gold carriage. The small, modest hotel bed, wedged against the wall in the compact room, wasn't the most comfortable he'd slept on. It emitted a peculiar odour and felt uneven beneath his back. Yet, his standards had lowered over the past few months, and it was far better than any convict cot he had slept on. After inspecting Emma's ring in his palm with care one final time for the evening, he fell asleep within minutes and remained undisturbed for the entire night.

Hobbs was in a deep sleep when Walsh knocked forcefully on his door just before daybreak. It had been dreamless and restful, and his mind briefly pondered the thought of sleeping forever. Emitting a low groan, he shifted in bed before begrudgingly rising and dressing. Descending the creaky staircase soon after, he found Walsh and Miller seated at the same table from the previous evening, both eating bowls of porridge and accompanied by steaming cups of coffee.

'Come on, Henry, eat something quickly and let's go.'

'Thank you,' Hobbs said, taking the bowl offered by Walsh. 'So what specifically are you going to be looking for here, James?'

Walsh swallowed his coffee and wiped his mouth. 'Anything out of the ordinary. I want to go through their delivery records. Find out who packs the carriages and who else may be privy to the transport information. I will follow you from a safe distance for a few miles to make sure you aren't being followed. After that, I will approach everyone employed by the Mint here in Bathurst and speak with them.

'Very good,' Hobbs replied. Give us a day's head start and then make your way back along the gold route, where if all things go to plan, you will probably find us at either Springwood or perhaps Penrith with our offenders. Dead or alive, that remains to be seen. That choice will lie with them and their actions.'

When they returned to the Royal Mint's tent, Hobbs observed a striking contrast in the surrounding fields compared to the previous day. The tents and swags remained, but he guessed most of the miners were still sleeping. Only a few early risers were tending to small fires and brewing tea or coffee in billy cans. Despite the scattered signs of activity, an eerie silence enveloped the area.

Behind the tent, Russell and Saunders packed crates beside the wooden carriage that had been stationed overnight, working quickly and methodically. It looked in good condition, and the two dark brown Arabian horses looked fit and healthy, ready for their long journey. Despite the guards' brisk activity, no one in the vicinity seemed to take notice of their preparations, and everything appeared ordinary to Hobbs. '*Good*', he thought, relieved that no one was suspiciously monitoring them.

'Good morning,' Hobbs said, inspecting the carriage. 'I trust your supervisor has informed you we will be your travel companions.'

Russell nodded and wiped his brow as he dropped another large crate. 'We have. We spoke at length with Mr Pearson. You must be Mr Hobbs,' he said, offering his hand. Saunders, too, shook Hobbs' hand before introducing themselves to Miller.

'And this is Inspector James Walsh,' Hobbs said, pointing to Walsh, who was already intrigued by a pile of records bundled on a table at the back of the tent, but quickly refocused his attention.

'Good morning, gentlemen, and thank you for your cooperation,' he said. 'I will not be joining the trip, but I will follow from afar, until you leave Bathurst to ensure you are not followed. I will then return to sort through the schedules and records here with Mr Pearson.'

'Sure. Mr Hobbs, are you certain this plan of yours will work?' Saunders inquired, wiping sweat from his brow as he and Russell completed loading the carriage with the weighty crates of gold and other supplies. Despite the early hour, they looked like they had been working for hours, perspiring and breathing heavily. Hobbs had no doubt that these men were seasoned veterans, as their weathered hands and tanned skin testified to many years of rugged outdoor labor.

'Not entirely,' Hobbs replied. 'But it is a viable lead. As I understand it, there has been a successful gold convoy between now and the last murder. I suspect these assailants are not attacking every route, so it is possible that we will not find them. At the moment, we do not know of any distinct pattern or reason they choose certain carriages.'

'They'd be fools to attack us,' Russell said, accompanied by a short laugh.

Hobbs disregarded his overconfidence. 'I should mention, the prospect of luring these men into a dangerous ambush is dangerous, but if we don't act soon, I fear more deaths will occur.'

'Saunders and I could probably handle them on our own,' Russell said. 'We are fit, well trained and heavily armed.' Hobbs thought he detected a look of offence at the idea they could not protect their own load.

'I expect you are,' he replied, noticing again their powerful barrel-shaped chests and thick arms. 'However, a total of four men, with two being hidden, will offer a greater advantage and an element of surprise. I had already pondered the suggestion of simply suggesting more overt guards. However, this may spook our suspects into hiding, and besides, you cannot maintain a staffing roster like that for long. Soon, you will be forced to return to a normal routine, and I would imagine the killings would then resume.'

Hobbs caught Russell rolling his eyes, and just as he ignored the guard's overconfidence, he also ignored this display of arrogance, but now directed his conversation directly to Russell. 'So, Mr Russell, this is the only way for us to take an advantage.'

'Well, of course, we are happy to oblige, Mr Hobbs. I should warn you, though, you and Constable Miller will find the back cramped and uncomfortable,' Saunders said, while Russell remained silent.

'We will be fine. I trust there are some long arms in there for us also?'

'Yes, sir, one rifle each.'

'And how long do you expect the trip to take, assuming we are not interrupted?"

With four people and the amount of gold we are pulling, it will be slow. It will take at least four and a half days, if not five, to reach Sydney.

'Fine. Well, we are ready when you are.'

Miller entered first, followed by Hobbs, who squeezed into the cramped, sealed carriage, immediately sensing the claustrophobic confines. They situated themselves on opposite ends of the carriage, their knees drawn up to their chests in discomfort. Hobbs and Miller located a rifle each and carefully positioned it atop the stack of gold and provisions, ensuring quick accessibility.

'If I see anything suspicious, I will raise extra gold guards and the Bathurst police; otherwise, I will allow the plan to continue as discussed,' Walsh said, peering into the carriage.

'Thanks, James,' Hobbs said.

'Good luck, Henry, you too, Edmund. Be careful.'

'You two alright in there?' Saunders asked.

'As good as it can be,' Hobbs replied.

'Here are some canteens with water. I expect it will get quite hot inside there. Knock on the front of the carriage if you need anything. I will not lock the back should you need a fast escape.' And with that, Saunders shut the door, causing the carriage to become nearly pitch black.

Moments later, they felt the abrupt jostling of the carriage as their journey begun.

TWENTY-SEVEN

'Are you alright, Edmund?' Hobbs asked, hearing only the rattling movement of the carriage and Miller's heavy breathing.

'Yes. It is just a little hot in here. And cramped.'

'Take a sip of water, and then just try to relax and slow your breathing. Force yourself to take longer breaths instead of faster, shallow ones.'

'I've done nothing like this before.'

'Just trust your judgement and your training.'

Miller's hands fidgeted atop his Pattern Enfield Rifle, which lay across his lap.

'You've fired rifles like this before?' Hobbs asked.

'Yes. Many times.'

'Good, so you are as well prepared as you can be; however, a real gunfight, fighting for your life, is different to any training. Do not waste your ammunition. Now, if we are attacked, a rush of panic will try to take over. Remember, a still target is not like returning fire to a live, moving target. Fire carefully and be prepared to take cover to reload. If you do not have time to reload, you must innovate and find an alternate method of both defence and attack. Most importantly, trust yourself. We will look out for each other.'

'I've never shot someone before.'

'I hope that doesn't change, but that will not be up to us. I pray these men surrender first. That our surprising presence and counterattack will unsettle them enough.'

'Have you killed someone before?' Miller asked nervously.

'Yes, Edmund, I have. But I do not take it lightly. It was my life or his, but I still wish I was not put in that position to begin with.'

'Do you think about it often?'

'Sometimes. But I remember after it happened, talking about it with my wife and I....' Hobbs stopped.

'Henry? Are you OK?'

Hobbs remained motionless, his mind adrift in memories. Recollections of the challenging days at work flooded his thoughts, and there were countless, each one leaving its mark. Yet, amidst those troubles, Emma had always been his beacon of confidence and compassion, a pillar of support through his chaotic days with Scotland Yard.

Hobbs snapped back to attention. 'I'm sorry. It's just my wife. I miss her. Little things seem to always creep into my memory and remind me of her. She was my biggest supporter and a strong shoulder to lean on when times were tough.'

'No, I'm sorry,' Miller said. 'I didn't mean to upset you.'

'It's not your fault. Mostly, the memories are pleasant. But they are just memories. That is all I have left.'

Miller glanced down at his feet, and Hobbs sensed his unease.

'You know, you remind me of a young Detective Constable I had working for me in London. He was a good lad. About your age, too.'

Miller smiled weakly and nodded. 'I'm glad I can work with you and Inspector Walsh. Thank you for the opportunity.'

Hobbs nodded, then closed his eyes, allowing thoughts of his former assistant, Detective Constable Benjamin Webster, to flood his mind. A bright young man of twenty-one, Webster bore a striking resemblance to Miller, both in appearance and in their shared attitude and aptitude for investigations. Each day, Webster trailed alongside Hobbs, diligently taking notes and posing a myriad of questions, his timing always impeccable. To Hobbs, it felt as though Webster was consistently on the same page as himself, and their professional rapport was seamless. He had always envisioned that in just a few short years, Webster would likely earn a promotion and evolve into a skilled lead investigator in his own right.

Hobbs still vividly remembers the day Benjamin Webster was murdered. During the raid on Norman Reynolds' warehouse at the London docks, orchestrated in connection with the murder of Judge Stephens, Webster, accompanied by two uniformed constables, fell victim to Reynolds' ruthless crew. Hobbs attributed much of the success in unravelling the case of the murdered judge to Webster's invaluable assistance. Witnessing him cut down by a piercing rifle round straight through his chest was a devastating blow. Despite having only worked together for five months, Webster's murder left Hobbs shattered. Although he later witnessed the shooter meet justice through the hangman's noose, the profound sense of grief lingered on.

During the aftermath of Benjamin Webster's death, Emma provided solace and counsel to Hobbs, as she unfailingly did. Inside the dark carriage, he summoned a mental image of Emma's radiant smile. 'You are a good detective, but an even better man,' she had whispered to him in bed on the night of the funeral. Her large eyes were staring deep into his own, and her long hair flowed over her blue nightgown. Hobbs tucked it behind her ears and managed a weak smile.

'It is just unfair. Webster was a good man, too and far too young.'

'No, you are right. It's not fair. But I know you would never intentionally endanger one of your own men, Henry. She kissed him on the forehead and tucked herself further under the blankets.

'Time will heal everything. Goodnight.'

Hobbs opened his eyes and turned his gaze toward Miller. Reflecting on his entire career, he couldn't escape the bittersweet nature of it all – the painful losses of those closest to him contrasted with the satisfaction of quenching his thirst for solving crimes and bringing the worst of humanity to justice. In moments of introspection, he grappled with whether the torment was a worthwhile trade-off for his achievements. Now, facing the prospect of continuing without Emma, the burden seemed almost unbearable.

They journeyed in silence for the next few hours, grappling with bouts of nausea induced by the carriage's unstable rocking over the uneven terrain. As the midday sun beat down relentlessly upon the carriage, they endured heavy sweat, and Hobbs developed a nasty headache.

'Where do you suppose we are now?' Miller asked, his voice strained.

'No idea. Well, out of Bathurst, though. I expect somewhere along the open road between towns. James would have left our trail long ago. We are on our own now.'

'I don't even know what time it is.'

'Me either, and I don't know about you, but I could do with a break from being in this carriage,' Hobbs said as he knocked hard on the wooden panels and soon felt the wheels slowly stop.

Before anyone could open the carriage for them, Hobbs collected his rifle and pushed through the doors, eager for fresh air. Stepping out, he filled his lungs. Looking around, Hobbs surmised they were likely between towns, currently surrounded by an expanse of open and flat terrain. Stretching out before them were vast green plains interspersed with gently rolling hills that extended as far as the eye could see.

Russell had climbed down from the front of the carriage to see what the problem was. 'Everything OK?' he asked.

'Everything is fine. Just time for a stretch and some relief,' Hobbs said.

'I thought you had heard something. Why do you have the rifle?'

'No, we heard nothing, and I just think it is best to always be prepared. I don't believe there is anything out here, though. This landscape is too open for our killers.'

When he returned, Russell was unpacking a satchel. 'Well, we might as well have something to eat,' he said. 'I packed cheese and bread. We can eat and then keep going until dark. We will camp for the night in a spot Saunders and I often use.'

They ate and stretched out on the soft grass for half an hour until it was time for Hobbs and Miller to climb back into the carriage and continue east while it was still light.

After enduring several more hours of a bumpy and uncomfortable ride, the carriage finally came to a halt again. As Hobbs swung open the door and stepped out, he saw they had pulled off to the side of the quiet road beside a small, fast-running creek. The waterway was flanked by slender trees and enveloped by swaying long grasses. The sun was just about to set, and Hobbs felt hungry again.

'We could probably catch some fish here; we usually stop here on each journey, and there are usually plenty in this stream,' Saunders said as he and Russell unpacked some fishing poles and swags.

'I'll light a fire then,' Hobbs said.

Miller and Saunders took the poles to the edge of the creek and baited the hooks with some pre-packed worms while Russell led the horses to the creek's edge for a long drink.

True to their efforts, after about twenty minutes of patient angling, Miller and Saunders successfully hooked two sizeable Silver Perch. They prepared the fish and, ten minutes later, had them roasting atop the fire, started by Hobbs.

'Where are we now?' Hobbs asked.

'Not far from Lithgow. We are making pretty good time. I don't suppose we are under any threat camping here?' Russell asked with a smirk.

'You sound cynical.'

'Well, Saunders and I can take care of ourselves. It is a pity what happened to our fellow guards, but that will not happen to us.'

'They were ambushed, Mr Russell. Taken by complete surprise, ambushed and murdered, and do not forget that. It could have happened to anyone.'

'We can take care of ourselves. I dare them to even try it on us.'

Frowning, Hobbs grew increasingly frustrated with Russell's nonchalance. 'We are prepared, and we have an advantage with Miller and me riding in the back, but do not be complacent.'

'You think you know better than us? You think you know these roads better than we do?'

Russell was now starting to irritate Hobbs even more, and he spoke sternly, glaring at him as he did. 'I'm not saying I do, but I have seen the victims and the level of violence left behind on their bodies. I just warn you to be vigilant and not underestimate this situation.'

'We should all finish eating and get some sleep,' Miller said.

'Good idea,' Hobbs added, still eyeing Russel and sensing the growing tension would not resolve tonight; he stood up and walked away. 'I expect another long day tomorrow.'

'We will leave before sunrise,' Russell said.

As the fire slowly dwindled to a dull red ash, the four men fell into a deep sleep under a clear sky lit up with thousands of stars. They each clutched their rifles close to their chests, hugging them for the entire night.

TWENTY-EIGHT

The Shadow, The Ghoul and The Banshee, cloaked in their disguise of hessian masks and dark raincoats, reached their designated waiting spot just as the first light of dawn crept over the horizon. They concealed their horses deep within the bush, then assumed their positions near the side of the road, ensconced in the shadows.

The Shadow calculated that they might have to endure a lengthy wait, but he remained undeterred. He knew the gold carriage would inevitably pass through this narrow passageway near Lithgow before it reached the Mountains. Anticipating heightened vigilance from the guards; he deemed it prudent to shift locations, preserving the element of surprise.

He knew as the carriages drew nearer to the base of the Blue Mountains on their final stretch before the outskirts of Sydney, tensions would inevitably escalate, fuelled by rumours of the recent murders. However, on the western side of the Blue Mountains, before the ascent to its peak, the guards would be unsuspecting of their impending ambush.

With careful planning and unwavering commitment, the three men embarked on the long journey to locate their optimal hiding spot. They ventured deep into the terrain, nestled within dense shrubbery by the roadside, flanked by trees that offered good concealment.

The Shadow had unequivocally articulated his instructions: set the traps, execute the ambush, and leave with all they could carry. With their planning complete, success now hinged on patience, precision, and swift execution.

Before the sun rose, Russell nudged Hobbs, Saunders, and Miller awake. He was already dressed in his tall black boots, stained trousers, and white shirt, sipping hot tea.

'Let's go, come on, wake up. Have some tea, and let's get moving; we have a lot of ground to cover.'

Hobbs pulled himself off the grass, which was still wet from dew, and felt some light rain brush his face. He eyed the boiling water in the billy can over the small fire, which was the only source of light during the pitch-black morning as thick, dark clouds blocked the moon. The air felt sticky, and Hobbs sensed heavy rain was due to fall at any moment. He fetched himself a cup of tea as Miller and Saunders eventually joined him. After a quick drink and a stretch, Hobbs and Miller checked their surroundings. They satisfied themselves that there was no one around and that they had yet to be identified as having camped there overnight. He took a deep breath, bracing himself for another rough day of travelling inside the cramped carriage.

Hobbs lost all perception of time and space in the back of the carriage, but heard the splatter of heavy rain hit the roof. He was unfamiliar with the territory and relied on Russell and Saunders to be their eyes and ears and alert them to any potential danger.

He found it difficult riding in the back of the carriage with no
way to anticipate any oncoming danger. Still, he did their best to
remain vigilant, and his hands rested on the loaded, heavy rifle
across his lap.

As the carriage steadily approached the narrowing of the road,
the men concealed behind their hessian masks tensed with eager-
ness. The rhythmic clopping of the horse's hooves grew louder,
resonating through the stillness of the morning air. The Shadow's heart quickened its pace as it approached. His keen eyes
fixed upon the two guards positioned at the front. Their demeanour appeared relaxed and seemingly indifferent, lost in the
haze of drowsiness or perhaps boredom. Meanwhile, The Ghoul
and The Banshee inspected their matches and handled multiple
bottles of ether, their openings stuffed with long rags.

The sudden onslaught of glass bottles hurling towards the carriage caught Russell and Saunders off guard. The projectiles
shattered upon impact, sending shards flying and igniting a
chaotic frenzy. Startled by the sudden attack, the horses reared
in fear. The guards quickly scrambled to assess the situation, yet
before they could fully grasp the severity of the onslaught, at least
four more bottles hurtled towards the carriage, setting it ablaze
in a matter of seconds. The stench of burning wood mingled
with the pungent odour of ether as the flames grew in intensity.
Desperate attempts to douse the flames proved futile as the fire
swiftly consumed the carriage, spreading with relentless voracity.
Even when Russell attempted to smother a small patch of flames

with a blanket, his efforts only fuelled the fire further, as the fabric became engulfed in the blaze.

Amidst the chaos, Hobbs and Miller sprang into action. Responding quickly, they pushed open the rear doors, rifles poised and ready for whatever awaited.

The relentless rain pelted down, adding to the chaos as Hobbs scanned his surroundings for the source of the trouble. The carriage, now engulfed in flames, made Hobbs' stomach twist, and his instincts quickly sharpened as he realised what was happening: they were being hunted.

By the time his eyes adjusted to the bright flames pouring over the carriage, Hobbs saw the men wearing strange brown masks, made of hessian, charge toward them from about thirty yards away. They aimed rifles at Russell and Saunders, firing at their chests. At that moment, Hobbs realised the guards were not holding their rifles, rather welding only thick blankets to put out the fire.

His heart raced, and he choked on his breath as he raised his rifle toward the three men bounding toward them. Hobbs watched as the masked men moved the muzzles of their rifles toward Miller and came to a halt about fifteen yards away from them. Hobbs processed the attackers quickly, calculating his plan - react, adapt, improvise, overcome. He knew the masked men would not have expected reinforcements to emerge from the carriage. Still, to his shock and disappointment, he was not expecting Russell and Saunders to have neglected their weapons or even this level of precision in the ambush so far west from the first two crime scenes. He held his aim, fired and the nearest, and missed.

Miller's arms trembled as he levelled his gun while Hobbs reloaded. His heart raced, and time seemed to slow down as terror surged and overwhelmed his senses. He fired, but his bullet missed and his arms continued to shake as all three assailants targeted him. Before he could evade or reload, a hail of bullets hammered into his chest, taking his breath away with a soft, pained gasp. Before he could process his impending death, he collapsed to the ground next to the bodies of Russell and Saunders as the carriage continued to burn and the horses bucked wildly.

'Noooo! Hobbs screamed as he watched Miller's lifeless body slump limply in front of him.

The masked assailants now closed in on Hobbs while they reloaded their rifles. They did so with trained efficiency, and the next wave of rapid crackle of fresh gunfire shattered the air, mingling with smoke and gunpowder. Hobbs dove to his side, evading the muzzles of the rifles, and when the trio were rapidly reloading again, Hobbs rested on his knee. He steadied himself. He knew he needed to restrain his emotions from the terror of what had happened to Miller if he wanted to put an end to these men. Hobbs watched as their hands moved quickly, priming their muzzles and almost ready to fire again. Drawing a deep breath, he trained his rifle on the largest of the three assailants. With precision, he squeezed the trigger, sending a bullet hurtling towards his target. The shot found its mark, striking the assailant's right shoulder. With a cry of agony, the man crumpled to the ground, his weapon slipping from his grasp.

Hobbs swiftly shifted his rifle in his hands. With no time to reload, he was prepared to use it as a club towards the other two assailants, who darted forward with alarming speed. Yet, despite his agility, he realised his efforts were in vain as they closed in, both with freshly loaded rifles pointed at him.

The sudden crack of gunfire reverberated through the chaos, and agony tore through Hobbs as the bullet tore into his left thigh, sending shockwaves of searing pain coursing through his entire body. His knees buckled beneath him, and he collapsed to the ground, his head swimming with dizziness. From his vantage point on the ground, Hobbs glanced to his side and saw Miller's lifeless body, blood staining the front of his shirt. The stark reality hit him like a sledgehammer – Edmund Miller was dead.

As Hobbs made a feeble attempt to rise from the ground, he heard the ominous sound of approaching footsteps, and the masked men closed in with purposeful strides. With waning strength, Hobbs lifted his gaze and met the chilling gaze of the assailants, their eyes cold and unyielding behind the narrow slits of their masks. Before he could muster a defence, a surge of searing pain ripped through him as one of the assailants plunged a knife into his stomach.

As the knife was removed from his body before being driven in deep for a second time, Hobbs gasped and took an agonised deep breath. Panic set in, and he struggled to take in any oxygen as the blade sliced through his abdomen. Hobbs felt the intense pain as thick pools of blood dribbled onto the ground, and he began to lose his vision along with any fight still left within him. As everything went dark, the last thing he heard was a high pitched, taunting laugh.

Regathering themselves, the assailants acted with ruthless efficiency, carefully calculating their actions amidst the chaos. Most of the gold carriage was swiftly consumed by the raging flames, fuelled by the accelerants from the shattered bottles, casting an ominous glow upon the morning. The panicked horses, over-whelmed by the chaos and smoke, broke free from their harnesses and galloped away in a frenzy.

'Hurry,' The Shadow winced from the ground. He was clutching his arm, trying to control the bleeding, but managed a weak whistle, calling three horses from deep within the bushes.

The Ghoul and The Banshee sprinted to the rear of the blazing carriage. Ignoring the fire, they quickly gathered as much gold as they could carry, stuffing it into sacks slung across their shoulders. With the gold secured, they rushed to the aid of the injured Shadow, who was still writhing in pain on the ground.

'Are they all dead?' he asked, groaning and clutching his arm to control the bleeding.

'Yes,' The Banshee replied.

'The two in the back were armed and waiting for us,' The Ghoul added.

'Yes. They anticipated our ambush and were prepared to counter our attack,' The Shadow said.

'They were easily managed, though. Although it was a surprise. Are you able to ride?'

'I'll be fine, just help me up. And rip off some of your shirts. I need to tie something around the wound to stop the bleeding. But quickly. We need to leave immediately.'

Amidst the escalating inferno of the carriage fire, the four men who had come up against the gold passage assailants now lay silent and motionless on the cold, wet ground. The relentless rain mingled with the growing pool of their own blood.

TWENTY-NINE

Hobbs regained consciousness slowly, and his vision swirled in a haze.

Alone and in agonising pain, he mustered every ounce of strength, rolling onto his stomach to inch closer to Miller's lifeless body. The rain intensified, drowning out the flickering flames of the gold carriage fire, and the wet ground dragged heavily against his aching body. Blood mingled with rainwater, and each slight movement reopening wounds caused him to bleed further. Finally, within arm's reach of Miller, a solitary tear traced a path down his cheek before he succumbed to unconsciousness once more.

Beneath the relentless downpour, Hobbs' eyes flickered open again, his senses still blurred by pain and disorientation. Looking up, a shadowy figure loomed over him, its identity obscured by either the storm or perhaps his disorientation. The mysterious figure knelt beside Hobbs, applying pressure to his wounds before assisting him to his feet and gently positioning him across a horse's front. With the figure steering the horse, they departed from the grim scene, leaving Hobbs to cast one final, hazy glance back at the haunting scene. With one last look at Miller's bloodied body, his vision dimmed once more as he lost consciousness for the third time that morning.

After a long period of nothing but profound darkness, Hobbs woke beneath the warm midday sun on a cloudless day. With a sense of complete peace, he folded his arms behind his head and allowed his gaze to drift towards the sky.

'Henry, it's time to wake up,' Emma said, kneeling beside him and holding his hand. Her vibrant blue dress brought out the sparkle in her eyes, and her smile was instantly warming. With her other hand, she brushed her fingers through his thick, sandy hair. Hobbs met her hand, and their fingers locked.

'I don't want to go. I want to stay here. With you,' Hobbs said as tears pooled in his eyes.

Emma smiled and shook her head. 'You can't. You need to wake up.'

Tears were now flowing down his cheeks. 'I miss you. Please, just let me stay.'

'I can't. It's not your time, Henry. Wake up.'

The searing agony surged back, slicing through Hobbs' leg and stomach with merciless intensity. Gradually, he pried open his eyes but could barely see. From what he could make out, he was in unfamiliar surroundings that stirred a sense of disorientation within him. Struggling to rise, he was swiftly subdued by his pain and sunk back into the thin mattress beneath him. Someone had removed his shirt, revealing the thick bandages that wrapped his body.

'Henry, try not to move too fast,' a familiar voice said from the corner of the room.

The figure walked over to the side of the bed and handed Hobbs a cup of water. 'Drink it slowly.'

'Yarran?' Hobbs groaned as his vision slowly became clearer.

'Yes. Try to stay calm. You are going to make a full recovery,' he said in a slow, calming voice. Yarran had now tied up his long hair at the back, and he had rolled up the sleeves of his blood-stained white shirt past his elbows.

Hobbs drank greedily, and as his eyes completely adjusted to his new surroundings, the small room revealed itself. It housed only a solitary, thin bed with no windows, yet thin streams of light seeped through the gaps between the wooden panels, casting faint patterns across the confined space.

Hobbs squirmed in the bed, his surprise and restlessness momentarily eclipsing the throbbing pain that gripped his body. 'I don't understand. What's going on? Where am I?'

A deep groan then escaped Hobbs' lips, his restlessness intensifying the already tremendous pain that spread through his entire body. A surge of panic quickly accompanied the pain, and his trembling hand instinctively sought the outside of his blood-soaked trousers. His fingers fumbled until they encountered a small lump nestled in his pocket. A sigh of relief escaped him as his touch confirmed Emma's ring was still there.

'I found you by the burnt-out carriage this morning, and I brought you to my village. You have a couple of puncture wounds from a blade, and we were able to remove the bullet from your leg. Fortunately for you, the gunshot caused no major harm, and the knife wounds seemed to have missed all your vital organs.

I expect you will make a full recovery, although you will be in pain for some time.'

Hobbs continued to struggle restlessly under his heavy bandages. 'What of the men I was with? Constable Miller?'

Yarran bowed his head, but just before his eyes reached the floor, Hobbs saw a brief look of regret in his eyes. 'I am sorry, Henry, you were the only one I found alive.'

Hobbs found himself engulfed in a whirlwind of emotion, and he sobbed in between weak coughs that wracked his weakened frame. With each slight convulsion, the searing pain surged, clawing at his sides with relentless ferocity.

'It's all my fault,' he mumbled. 'It's all my fault. I thought the worst before I passed out, but I did not want to believe it.'

'I'm sorry. I really am, but there was nothing I could do. You lost a lot of blood. You needed attention straight away. I did what I could in the bush, but you needed to be brought back here as a matter of urgency.'

Hobbs brought his hands to his face, muffling his sobs. 'Edmund is dead, and it's all my fault. It was my plan. We tried to ambush the killers, but it was a disaster, and now good men are dead. I was reckless. Arrogant and reckless.'

'Please, Henry, I'm sure it is not your fault. The first time I met you, I understood you to be a man of integrity. I am sure you did everything you could have. But now you need to stay as still as you can. Your wounds could open up again if you are not careful.'

He knew deep down Yarran was right, but Hobbs couldn't relax. Amidst hurried breaths punctuated by waves of pain and remorse, fragmented memories of the attack flooded his mind. His recollection was hazy, but several images entered his mind's eye: the engulfing flames of the carriage, the figures wearing strange masks, the chilling sight of the slaughtered gold guards, and finally, Edmund Miller's lifeless body.

His mind conjured the haunting image of Miller collapsing to the ground after being shot. The memory lingered, vivid and stark, as Hobbs himself teetered on the precipice of consciousness, overwhelmed by crippling agony and blood loss.

He wiped his eyes dry and tried to sit up again. 'What is that smell?'

'That would be the tea tree oil and crushed snake vine,' Yarran said, soaking a bloodied rag in a bowl of water by the bed. 'Both were used to treat your wounds.'

'Yarran, where am I?' Hobbs asked, looking around the room, trying to focus his still partially foggy and teary vision.

'You are on Wiradjuri land with my people. Just west of Lithgow.'

Hobbs shook his head. Perhaps it was the blood loss or severe pain, but he struggled to piece it all together. 'But I don't understand. What happened? How did you find me?'

I was foraging in the bush when I saw the smoke. Then I came across two spooked horses. I took one of them and rode toward the smoke, and that's when I saw you. Unconscious but breathing. Only just though. Your breathing was not steady, so I took you here as fast as I could.'

Feeling suddenly warm, Hobbs pulled the blanket off and inspected the heavily blood-stained rags and bandages wrapping his stomach. 'Thank you,' he breathed. 'I just wish Edmund didn't have to lose his life.'

Yarran didn't respond and wrung out the rag of cloth from the bowl of water and mopped the thick beads of sweat forming on Hobbs' forehead.

'Did you see the men who did this?' he asked. 'They wore tan masks made of hessian. I expect that, in their disguise, they would have looked unusual. That is if they kept them on after.'

'I'm sorry, I did not see anyone. Here, take another drink,' Yarran said, handing Hobbs another cup of water.

As Hobbs drained the last drops of water, a woman entered the room, her presence silent yet commanding. Petite, with aging yet smooth dark skin and wearing a long red dress with delicate shoulder straps, her short, curly hair framed her face with an air of quiet strength. Barefoot, she moved with purpose towards Hobbs and without speaking; she inspected his blood-stained bandages, her hands moving with practised care. As she murmured in a dialect unfamiliar to Hobbs, Yarran responded in kind.

'Henry, this is Yemmel. She is good with natural medicines, and she treated all your wounds.'

'Thank you,' Hobbs said, bowing his head.

'She does not speak English,' Yarran said.

Hobbs nodded. 'Please thank her for me.'

'Henry, say *mandaang guwu*.'

Hobbs looked back at Yemmel and bowed his head again. As he did, he did his best at responding in her native tongue, '*mandaang guwu*.' Still, he felt the pronunciation was a little off.

Yemmel offered a faint smile and nodded before leaving the room.

'She saved your life. Some of my people were quite startled when I brought you back here and were unsure why I did. However, when I told her about our first meeting and what had occurred this morning, she did everything she could. Now, please, rest.'

Hobbs remained as still as he could as the memories of the morning replayed in his mind on a relentless loop. Everything had gone so horribly wrong, and he sobbed again for Miller.

'Yarran, where is the bullet from my leg?' Hobbs asked in a moment of clarity and composure, his mind automatically directing his attention back to the investigation. 'When it struck me, I don't believe it went all the way through.'

'No, it didn't. It is here,' Yarran said, collecting the small, dented bullet next to the bowl of water that Yemmel had extracted and handed it to Hobbs.

Hobbs examined the squashed metal round. 'This is an expanding conical bullet,' he said. 'It is made of rather soft lead.'

'Does that tell you anything?'

'No. Not at the moment. However, I do know the Pattern Enfield rifles use these bullets loaded through the muzzle. They are widespread and used all around the British Empire. In any case, I would like to keep it.'

'Sure, it belongs to you more than I. Now please rest some more. If you are hungry later this evening, you are welcome to join us for supper.'

Yarran stood back up and turned to leave just as Hobbs took him by the hand.

'Yarran, thank you.'

Yarran nodded and left.

Hobbs retrieved the bowl filled with cool water and washed away the grime and dried blood from his face with the damp cloth. His thick stubble and messy hair demanded extra attention, requiring vigorous scrubbing to rid them of the stubborn stains. Finally, overcome by exhaustion, he let the cloth slip to the floor, and fell fast asleep.

THIRTY

Later that evening, the lively sounds of singing and laughing woke Hobbs. The room was now near pitch black, and he knew he had slept through the afternoon. Alone in the small room, he noticed a newfound ease in his movements despite the lingering ache of his wounds. Gently exploring his body, he saw two neat stitch marks on his belly and one on his thigh. Though he expected scars, the wounds appeared clean and stitched neatly. The faint scent of tea tree oil still hung in the air as he mustered the strength to rise slowly from the bed. Pulling on his blood-stained white shirt, its buttons left undone, he limped towards the door.

When he opened the door, Hobbs discovered that the room he occupied was a single-room hut. As he stood at the threshold, his gaze swept across a cluster of similar structures nearby. Some others were the same size, while others were larger, forming what seemed to be a modest village. Walking down the three wooden steps, he headed towards the back of the hut, drawn by the lively cheers and the aroma of a crackling fire.

A large fire blazed in an open plain, and around it, about thirty or forty men and women wearing white paint on their faces and bodies danced in unison, synchronised to the swaying flames. Hobbs observed their dance as he manoeuvred cautiously through the gathering, his presence drawing little notice from the group.

Yarran called out to Hobbs, 'You are awake,' as he made his way over to him. He had put on a new outfit; a red loincloth tied around his waist, and he had also covered himself in white body paint.

'Are you hungry?' he asked.

'Yes. I am, actually,' Hobbs replied truthfully, noticing the pang for the first time since he had woken. 'My body still aches, though.'

Yarran walked over to the edge of the fire toward a large bench while Hobbs remained still, watching the rhythmic dancing. A moment later, he returned carrying a wooden plate with a generous amount of meat on it.

'Eat,' Yarran said, pushing the plate toward Hobbs.

'What is it?'

'Kangaroo tail. Delicious.'

Hobbs looked around and saw several men, women, and children feasting on the meat, using only their hands. Hobbs picked up a thick bit of the dark meat and took a small, cautious bite.

The meat melted in his mouth, and to his surprise and delight, it reminded him of a lean piece of beef. 'It's actually delicious, thank you, Yarran.'

Yarran smiled and escorted him closer to the fire, where they both sat down on tree stumps.

'I don't expect you to dance, seeing as you are still injured, but please eat.'

As he settled down slowly, mindful of his wounds, Hobbs observed the playful antics of the young children around him.

Their laughter echoed through the noise of the singing and dancing. While some giggled at Hobbs, their attention quickly diverted to the dance and their wooden clapping sticks. Suddenly, a slightly older child, a boy of perhaps eight or nine years old, approached him and, without speaking, smeared white paint across his face. With a mischievous laugh, the boy ran off towards the fire. Hobbs, still startled, looked at Yarran and couldn't help but smile.

'Do not worry, it comes off,' Yarran said, taking a seat next to Hobbs. 'I have told everyone about you and your kindness towards me when we first met. Most here are happy to have you with us.'

'Most?'

'Some elders are not so accommodating to white men, but I have assured them you mean no harm and that you will soon be on your way.'

Hobbs nodded. 'Yes. While I greatly appreciate everything you have done for me, I expect my friend James will be worried about me. No doubt, by now, someone would have found the crime scene. Either way, he would probably have realised I'm missing by now. I'm afraid he would likely fear the worst. Especially if he has found out about Edmund Miller's murder.

'I am sorry about your friend too, but please do not rush. You almost died, and you need time to rest.'

Hobbs lowered his head and took a deep breath. 'Well, thank you for dinner and everything you have done. You're right. I think I might get some more rest.'

'Can I come with you when you are fit to leave?'

'Excuse me?'

'I would like to come with you if I can. If needed, I can provide help with the investigation. I know these areas well.'

'Yarran, I appreciate what you have done for me, but look what's happened. It is a very dangerous investigation, and these men are still at large.'

'I understand the risks, and I don't need anyone to look after me. You could use my help.'

Hobbs studied Yarran. Although his face was covered in white paint, it was resolute, waiting patiently for a response.

'Okay, Yarran,' he eventually said.

'Okay?' Yarran responded with a slight inflection, which Hobbs detected as a tone of surprise.

'Yes, okay. You can come with me. I am not one to turn away the possibility of assistance in a case such as this, as long as you appreciate the risks.'

'Good, and I do. Now come with me. Before you go back to rest, you can learn a little about my people.'

Yarran guided Hobbs through a group of dancers and toward a low-burning fire away from the noise and the main group. He saw three older men dressed in small red shorts and wearing full white body paint. They sat patiently next to each other on a thick log, stared at Hobbs with flat expressions, and then looked at Yarran. They did not speak.

'*Muyulung*,' Yarran whispered. 'Elders.'

A group of boys arrived and walked past Hobbs without speaking. Like Yarran, they had long, curly black hair and thin frames. Hobbs figured they would have been about eleven or twelve years old. They each sat cross-legged on the ground in front of the Elders.

The Elders looked at Hobbs one more time with the same vacant expression and began speaking to the group of boys in their native tongue.

'The Muyulung are talking about Biami,' Yarran said.

Hobbs remained silent and watched on intently.

'Biami is the sky father, and soon, these boys will travel to the Bora. Our people's initiation site where they will become men.'

'What are they saying about Biami?'

'They are talking about the stars. Look up at the sky,' Yarran said.

The night sky was clear and littered with bright stars surrounding the glowing moon.

'The story is reflected in the stars. Look, follow my finger.'

Yarran traced his finger in front of Hobbs' eyes, making an invisible line, following the stars sparkling in a neat row. 'Can you see? Gugurmin. The emu in the sky. The stars and the sky are very significant. It is the interaction between the land and people. Do you see it?'

'Yes. Yes, I can actually see it,' Hobbs said, now looking at a cluster of stars that actually resembled the shape of an emu when pointed out to him. He traced the stars with his eyes and saw the bird's round body, long neck and beak.'

'My people have watched the stars since the beginning of time. As it moves across the sky at different times, we know the right time to search for emu eggs.'

Hobbs continued to look at the giant emu in the night sky. Now that he was shown the great bird in the stars, it was all he could see. Looking back at the Elders, he glimpsed one now glaring at him with a stony expression.

'We best be going now. I think you need more rest,' Yarran said.

'Are they okay with me being here?'

'They are just not used to white men under our care, but they also know you cannot understand them. Nevertheless, it is time to leave. Biami is sacred, so the words they are speaking form particular initiation rites. They do not allow women to attend the Bora, and the same rule applies to you, a white stranger.'

'I see. I don't want to offend anyone here.'

'Come. Rest some more,' Yarran said, leading him away.

THIRTY-ONE

Hobbs eased his way back to his hut, each step a reminder of his enduring pain, but despite his discomfort, sleep came quickly. The following morning, as sunlight filtered through the cracks of his wooden shelter, he woke to discover a plate with an array of colourful berries resting beside his bed. He must have slept deeper than he realised because he didn't hear anyone come in, but ate every berry with gratitude.

Throughout the day, Hobbs drifted in and out of sleep, his body demanding the rest. As the afternoon waned, the figures of Yarran and Yemmel quietly returned. With care and concern etched upon their faces, they gently roused him from his sleep and examined his wounds.

They had a soft conversation together in their native language, and Yarran translated. 'Yemmel says you are healing well.'

She applied some cool, thick balm to his wounds, and although her touch was gentle and careful, it still made him shiver and recoil.

'Are you feeling better?' Yarran asked as Yemmel redressed his stomach and leg bandages.

'I am, yes. We should leave tomorrow.'

'If you think you are ready,' Yarran said.

'I think I will be. Remind me, Yarran, how do I say thank you again?'

'*Mandaang guwu.*'

'*Mandaang guwu,*' Hobbs said, this time being more attentive to the subtleties of the accent and speaking a little closer to Yarran's pronunciation.

'Get some more rest, and we will see how you feel in the morning. I will bring you some vegetables and meat shortly,' Yarran said.

They left to allow Hobbs to rest a while longer. As night came, signalled by the darkness and faint glimmers seeping through the crevices of the wooden walls, Yarran reappeared, carrying a plate with thin strips of meat and small potatoes.

'Goanna,' Yarran said, handing him the plate.

Hobbs played with the strange meat with his hands, which looked similar to dark chicken meat. Without giving too much thought to eating the lizard, hunger took over, and he greedily finished the entire meal.

'Good, isn't it?'

'Yes, surprisingly, it is. Tastes like chicken.'

Yarran took the plate from Hobbs, and just before he left the room, he turned back. 'Thank you for letting me come with you. Are you still okay to leave tomorrow? I still have the horse I found and brought you here with. It has been well-fed and rested.'

'Yes, I think so. One more good night's sleep and I will be okay enough to ride.'

With his stomach full and his body still aching for more rest, Hobbs' eyes became heavy, and he allowed himself to fall into another deep sleep.

His eyes fluttered open, greeted by the embrace of the soft grass beneath him. Above, a thick oak tree cast a cooling shadow, and a slow breeze calmed the heat of the day. At that moment, a profound sense of peace enveloped him. As he sat up, he surveyed the green hills that surrounded him, and suddenly, he felt completely isolated, and a shiver ran down his spine.

'Emma?' he called. 'Emma? Where are you?'

He looked around again, but he was alone in the vast expanse of the field. In a panic, he stood up desperately and searched the area, but there was no sign of Emma or anyone else.

'Henry,' a male voice called from behind the tree.

Hobbs pursued the voice. 'Edmund? Is it you?'

Miller stood proud and tall, wearing his black tunic uniform. His slender face smiled weakly back at him.

'You're okay!' Hobbs said, but as he rushed over to embrace him, his legs suddenly froze. All he could do was remain fixed to the ground, six feet away, unable to get any closer.

Suddenly, a red mark appeared on the centre of Miller's tunic. It grew rapidly, expanding across his entire torso, and Hobbs saw it was blood. Miller was now silent and expressionless as blood flowed heavily out of a growing wound and dribbled down the front of his tunic.

'Edmund, no!' Hobbs cried, reaching out for him, but he was still too far away and still frozen to the ground.

Right in front of Hobbs, as the blood continued to flow, Miller's legs buckled, and he collapsed on the ground. His eyes, vacant, white and cold, looked back at Hobbs.

Hobbs felt a gentle touch upon his back, prompting him to whirl around sharply, his senses still tingling with remnants of panic.

'Emma!'

She appeared by his side and stood with him as Miller's body lay still on the ground. She wore a long white dress and was barefoot, pacing gracefully over the soft grass toward Miller's body before looking back at him.

'There's nothing you could have done, Henry.'

'Stay with me?' he pleaded, reaching for her hand, but she was just out of reach.

Hobbs jolted awake, drenched in sweat and surrounded by the potent scent of tea tree oil still filling the room. His bandages, tightly wound around his body, remained clean and free from fresh blood. He was healing well, physically, yet despite the progress his body made, his mind remained ensnared by exhausting dreams. He eased back onto the pillow, resigned to the fact he would be awake for the rest of the night.

THIRTY-TWO

As the sunrise burst through the cracks of the wooden hut, it roused Hobbs from the depths of a deep sleep. Though his body still ached, there was an improvement in his mobility as he slowly lifted himself from the thin mattress. It was enough for him to travel anyway, and he needed to find Walsh as soon as possible.

When Hobbs emerged from the hut, he discovered Yarran standing by one of the gold carriage horses, preparing for departure. It was a warm morning, and while Hobbs still wore his blood-stained white shirt, Yarran wore a fresh, light flannel shirt and black trousers. His long hair cascaded freely, gently grazing his shoulders.

'Do you want to eat, or shall we leave?' he asked.

'Let's leave. I have much to catch up on already. Are you sure you still want to come?'

'Yes. I am often away for long periods. I am happiest when I am wandering through all parts of the mountains.'

'Okay, let's go then. We can share the horse, but I will not be able to ride very fast.'

'I expected as much. Even while riding at a steady pace, we can still make it to the bottom of the mountains by tomorrow. We will camp overnight.'

'Yarran, first take me to where you found me. I want to see it.'

'Are you sure? I thought we would bypass it. From here we can take a slightly different route this side of the mountains to avoid it.'

'No. I need to see it.'

As they rode together, Hobbs's journey proved far more un-comfortable than he had anticipated. Every so often, he found himself compelled to stop, needing to inspect his bandages and allow himself moments of stillness to ease the discomfort.

Not long into their journey, Yarran declared they were close to the scene of the ambush. Hobbs nodded and soon sensed an unsettling stillness in the air. Yarran was right. They were nearing the very spot he had almost lost his life. The place where the two guards and Edmund Miller were slain.

A little further along, Yarran pulled the horse to a stop and Hobbs slowly climbed down, wincing at the pain in his side. His eyes fixed on the scene before him and he ambled closer as though in a trance. The silence was eerie. Having listened to bird song during the start of their journey, there was now not a sound. The ground by the narrow dirt road was burnt and stained with ash, while the remnants of the gold carriage remained exactly where it had come to an abrupt stop when Russell and Palmer were first assaulted by the flaming bottles. The fire had destroyed the walls, and all that stood was a blackened frame. Walking closer, Hobbs winced at the large volume of dried blood splashed across the ground and burnt grass. What blood was his own, he could not tell. He surmised at some stage, the blood from each of his company had blended together. Grief consumed Hobbs once again as he squatted to the ground, revisiting the ambush in his memory. The sound of gunshot, the screams, the searing heat of the carriage fire. The cold eyes of the assailants behind their hessian masks. It was all too much, and Hobbs broke down.

Yarran, who had stood at a distance, rushed over and helped Hobbs stand.

'At least someone found the scene. I just hope James is aware and has taken responsibility for the bodies,' Hobbs said, wiping the tears from his eyes. 'I cannot process this scene dispassionately, Yarran.'

'I searched the area for clues when I found you. Aside from the bullet lodged inside you, I found nothing of use,' he said.

Hobbs scanned the scene again before lowering his head. 'I'd like to continue on now, Yarran. The memories are too fresh to remain longer.'

Continuing on their descent from the eastern peak of the Blue Mountains towards Springwood, Hobbs remained silent, and Yarran, as though sensing the need for his peace, did not speak. They eventually came upon a suitable spot to halt their travels for the night.

'I'll light a fire,' Yarran said, climbing down from the horse before offering a steady hand for Hobbs to follow. 'You rest.'

In moments and with practised ease, Yarran had gathered twigs and, using a flint, started a fire. 'There is a stream just down the hill there. I will look for fish,' he said as he found a long stick and began sharpening it with a small pocketknife.

'With that?' Hobbs asked.

'Nature gives us all we need,' Yarran said, holding his newly crafted spear with a smile, before shuffling toward the stream while Hobbs rested on a soft patch of grass.

Twenty minutes later, Yarran reappeared, holding two medium-sized fish in his hands. He then fashioned a makeshift spit and positioned the fish over the flames of the fire. Within moments, the fresh aroma of roasting fish wafted through the air.

'That's very impressive,' Hobbs said, warming his hands over the flames. 'Where did you learn how to do that?'

'I have learned everything I know from my ancestors. Knowledge preserved and passed down for generations. There is so much about this land white people either don't understand or perhaps choose not to understand.'

Contemplating this, Hobbs shrugged. 'Yet you still learnt English and speak it so well.'

'I like to learn. And as I said when we met, it helps me find work as a tracker, although our people have little need for money. I do it because I enjoy exploring the bush. Honestly, my people often become frustrated with me. They seem to think I am foolish for learning and practising English and helping the white farmers.'

'So your village? That's your family?'

'Yes. Although many are not related by blood in the typical sense that you would view family.'

Hobbs nodded. 'Different from the concept of family I am used to, but I understand. Your family extends to everyone in your community. What about are your birth parents?'

'Dead. When I was very young. Infected by a white man's sickness.'

'I'm sorry.'

Yarran gave a faint smile and nodded before removing the first fish from the fire and breaking off a fillet. 'Here, have some fish. It's good.'

'I have spent my whole life in England,' Hobbs said, taking a bite. 'I knew very little of what occurred here when my countrymen arrived, and I expect that those in power manipulated the information sent back home to portray the British as less cruel and hostile. It must make you angry.'

'In a way, yes. I just want my culture to continue, but I fear it is being taken from us,' Yarran said, taking part of the fish for himself. 'I want people to be aware of it and understand the importance of the land the way I do. But it is difficult. The white man does not want to learn. They take in excess of what is necessary, and it is killing this land. I fear it will only become worse as more arrive here.'

Hobbs nodded, a tinge of discomfort creeping in as he realised Yarran was referring to his own ancestors. It was part of the problem, after all. He knew all too well of the wastage and excess back home that was no doubt brought here, too.

'How do you say fish in your language?' Hobbs asked, now even more eager to explore Yarran's culture.

Yarran smiled. '*Guya.*'

'*Guya,*' Hobbs repeated, trying to enunciate the intricacies of Yarran's native accent.

'Yes, good. You know, Henry, you aren't like most of the white people I come across. You also seem to appreciate the land, and you showed me kindness.'

'I do not judge people by their colour, but by their values. You are a good young man, Yarran, and I owe you a debt. You saved my life.'

'So why did you come here? To be a policeman?'

'No. I'm not a policeman. Not anymore. I'm a convict.'

'Oh,' Yarran said, eyebrows raised in surprise at the revelation. Hobbs imagined his mind was ticking over the reasons for his imprisonment, likely beginning with the worst level of offending.

'No, it's nothing like you may think, I assure you. You have nothing to worry about. I was a policeman back in England, and I'll save you the complete details, as my story is long. Essentially, some people who wanted to see me gone framed me for a crime I did not commit, and then they sent me here to be out of the way.

James Walsh, my old colleague and friend, found out I was here and took me away from the prison to help him investigate these murders.'

Yarran looked deeply at Hobbs for a moment. The gaze made Hobbs feel a little uncomfortable. It felt as though Yarran was looking past his eyes. Assessing every word he just spoke. He then broke his stare and nodded, content with Hobbs' reasoning. He returned the subject to the investigation at hand. 'Do you think you will find the men who are committing these murders?'

Hobbs ran his fingers through his hair and felt the patches of dried blood still clinging to his scalp. He shook his head. 'I am worried I am no longer skilled enough, Yarran. That I've lost my edge. Or that I've lost the fiery determination I once had in my career. These men have beaten me once, and I am still no closer. My plan to set them up during an ambush failed horribly. But what I know is I will do everything I can. I'll do it for Edmund and every other man who was just doing their job and was brutally killed without mercy.

'And I will help,' Yarran said without a trace of doubt in his voice.

'Yes, and you will help.'

As he ate, Hobbs' mind wandered to Emma, and a wave of sadness washed over him as her memory intertwined with the guilt he still carried from the murder of Edmund Miller. A guilt he knew he would carry for a long time. Miller, a fine young man with a promising future, bore an unsettling resemblance in appearance and attitude to Detective Constable Benjamin Webster. With both deaths occurring under his watch, his remorse was compounded. Choosing not to burden Yarran with these personal reflections, he quietly indulged in another bite of fish.

'This is delicious, Yarran, thank you.'

'Thank the stream. She gave them to us.'

'You talk about the land and water like it is alive. Why is that?'

'The land is a part of who we are. Without it, we are nothing. I respect the land and all creatures as I would respect a person. Now, how are you feeling?'

'A little sore still, but Yemmel did fine work.'

'She is very skilled. You will feel like yourself again soon.'

'Well, I'll try to get some sleep; we have another big day of riding tomorrow. I need to speak with James as soon as possible.'

Hobbs slept reasonably well under the stars and awoke refreshed. The soft grass beneath him had been surprisingly comfortable, and his body continued to repair itself well. As the morning dawned, the calls of magpies filled the air from the branches overhead. Looking around, Hobbs saw the horse contentedly grazing on shrubs nearby, yet Yarran was nowhere to be seen. Unconcerned, Hobbs assumed Yarran hadn't wandered too far, and he looked for the stream Yarran fished in yesterday to wash his face, body and clothes while he waited for his return. Walking down the gentle slope of the grassy terrain, he found the narrow stream, its waters trickling downhill towards the east. The water was cool but refreshing in the warm morning, and Hobbs scooped a handful and washed away the remnants of dried blood from his skin, though his once-white shirt bore stubborn stains, now a deep, earthy brown hue. Removing the shirt, he carefully splashed water on his torso, which now bore deep blue bruising spilling out from the bandages, which fortunately didn't feel anywhere near as bad as they looked.

Upon his return to the campsite, Hobbs spotted Yarran standing by the horse, evidently prepared to depart. Nibbling on a small, round piece of fruit, Yarran glanced up as Hobbs greeted him with a morning wave. Yarran nodded in reply and tossed another piece of fruit towards Hobbs.

'*Miidyum*,' he said. 'Tomato.'

'Thank you,' Hobbs said, taking a bite into the juicy flesh.

'Ready?' Yarran asked.

'Yes. My clothes will dry along the way. I expect it to be quite warm today.'

Hobbs mounted the horse, and he immediately sensed a significant improvement in his physical condition from the previous day. Though bruised and still in pain, he found himself more mobile, moving with greater freedom and flexibility.

They continued riding east through the second crime scene, where patches of dried blood persisted, lingering on some shrubs by the side of the narrow passage. Their route led them through the town of Springwood, its quaint streets passing by in a blur as they maintained their course. Beyond, they traversed the terrain until they reached the site of the initial crime, where shortly after, Hobbs felt the incline begin and recalled being near the very foot of the mountains just before Penrith.

'Where should we go?' Yarran asked from the back of the horse as they reached the Penrith town limits.

'Straight for the police station. I expect if James has returned from Bathurst, he will be there.'

As they rode through the town centre, Hobbs couldn't help but notice the uneasy stares cast their way by the townsfolk. The sight of a dishevelled white man, his shirt stained with blood, riding alongside an Indigenous companion on horseback was clearly an anomaly in these parts. Yet Hobbs refused to allow the glances to disrupt him.

As they approached the front of the small police station, Hobbs spotted Walsh and Palmer conversing by the front door. The sheer relief on both their faces, which quickly turned to confusion, told Hobbs he would have a long story to tell.

THIRTY-THREE

Almost rendered speechless, Walsh rushed over to Hobbs as he dismounted from the horse.

'I can't believe it. Where have you been? We had no idea what happened to you, and after what I found on my way back, well, I thought the worst. It was carnage at that scene, Henry. How did you make it out alive?'

'I was with Yarran here. He found me unconscious, and his people took me in until I was back on my feet,' Hobbs said. His eyes suddenly dropped, and he couldn't maintain eye contact. 'James, it was a mess. The entire plan was a disaster.'

Walsh glanced at Yarran and nodded appreciatively. His gaze shifted to Hobbs. 'I know, and I'm sorry. But you're alive. However, we need to discuss what happened out there. With Edmund and the two guards slaughtered, we are really chasing our tails here. Too many people have been killed, but you have no idea how relieved I am to see you again.'

'I probably should be dead. The entire attack is burned in my mind, and it will stay with me forever. James, I know you need the details for the investigation, but I don't know what to say. I feel sick with guilt.'

Yarran moved a little closer. 'I'm sorry, inspector and sergeant, when I came across Henry, the other men were already dead; there was nothing I could do.'

Palmer's disappointment was noticeable as he shook his head, and Hobbs couldn't help but imagine he had worn this expression from the very moment he realised the planned takedown of the killers had gone awry.

'James, meet Yarran. He is the reason I am still alive,' Hobbs said.

Walsh smiled and shook Yarran's hand.

As they entered the police station, Constables Bryson and Davidson greeted them with stares laden with silent acknowledgement. News of the botched sting operation had obviously reached their ears as well.

'We will have privacy here,' Palmer said, escorting them into a small room with no windows, filled with stable equipment and piles of old paper. 'The constables know what happened, yet I would prefer to continue this conversation in private.'

Walsh was the first to break the tense silence. His words rushed as though he had been holding his breath since the moment he laid eyes on Hobbs, finally exhaling the weight of his thoughts. 'Henry, I thought you were dead. When I reached Lithgow, I heard reports of a gold carriage crime scene. I rode with the Constables there and came across the gruesome sight. My heart sank seeing poor Edmund dead, but when I couldn't find you, I didn't know what to think.'

'If it was not for Yarran, I would be dead,' Hobbs said, waving his hands over his blood-stained shirt. 'I was stabbed and shot. They were too fast for us. They got to the gold guards before Edmund, and I even got out of the carriage.' Hobbs sat down on an old wooden chair in the corner of the office and put his head in his hands.

'I'd do anything to take it all back and still have Edmund here. He didn't deserve to die like that. He was a good man.'

'He was indeed,' Palmer said.

Hobbs recounted his version of events to Walsh and Palmer to the best of his ability. However, the specific details remained somewhat foggy in his memory. A lump formed in his throat as he reached the part where he collapsed in agony beside Miller's bloodied body, but was gracious toward Yarran when recounting his rescue.

Walsh nodded his head when Henry had finished and turned to Yarran. 'Thank you for all you have done, Yarran. I expect you would like to return home now. We have much police work to discuss.'

'He is staying to help,' Hobbs said before Yarran could answer for himself.

'Excuse me?' Walsh asked.

'James, trust me on this. Yarran can help, and I insist on it. He is a brilliant tracker, and we need him. Even after being face to face with these men, I am still no closer.'

'No, I will not have more people hurt under my direction.'

Yarran raised a hand and intervened. 'Sir, I am here of my own free will and fully understand the risks. I just want to help.'

Walsh didn't respond, and his silence spoke volumes as he settled on the edge of the desk. Hobbs interpreted this as an agreement, a familiar response from Walsh whenever he endorsed a course of action. Turning to Yarran, Hobbs nodded, signalling for him to stay.

'I'm sorry this happened to you, Henry, but no one blames you, do you understand?' Walsh said.

'I understand fine, but I do not accept it. Edmund was my responsibility, and I failed him. Have you spoken with his wife yet?'

'Yes. I arranged for all three bodies to be taken to Doctor Andrews so the examinations could remain consistent. And Mrs Miller, yes. I spoke with her yesterday morning. I won't lie to you, Henry. She was distraught.'

Hobbs lowered his head again.

'But she knew the risks his job entailed.'

'That does not bring him back.'

'Henry, I need you to remain sharp and focused with me, okay?'

Hobbs looked back at Walsh with an expression of both sadness and a sudden look of determination. 'I will do everything I can. You know I will.'

'Well, first, how are you feeling?'

'I'm still a little sore, but I have been told my wounds are healing well,' Hobbs said, looking back at Yarran.

Yarran nodded.

'What did you find staying back at Bathurst?' Hobbs asked.

'Nothing unusual. I observed the records being well kept and in order, and I didn't notice anyone trailing you from the mines out of Bathurst. You were well and truly alone. It doesn't seem like an inside job with the gold guard or Mint.'

'So whoever attacked us was waiting for us or had come from another town?'

'All I can say is they did not follow you out of Bathurst.'

The room went suddenly quiet. Hobbs was in deep thought but stumped on where to go next. Looking around the room and seeing silent, blank faces, he knew he wasn't the only one.

'Henry, can I talk to you in private for a moment?' Walsh eventually said, opening the door and leaving for his allocated makeshift office before Hobbs could respond.

Hobbs motioned for Yarran and Palmer to remain behind while he followed Walsh into the office and shut the door behind him. They both sat down on the same side of the desk and looked out the window toward the stables at the back of the station.

'It is such a relief to see you well, Henry,' Walsh said. 'I honestly did not know what could have happened to you. I feared the worst.'

'As did I. And honestly, it appeared we didn't stand a chance. I think in the melee. However, I shot one man in the shoulder, but it wasn't enough. If it wasn't for Yarran, I would be dead. I really feel like he has something to offer to us here.'

'If you say so. Henry, three separate murders, seven dead, including a police officer in the commission of his duties, and then yourself, nearly dead, and we are still no closer to solving this case. They weren't coming from Bathurst. I know that much. We have no witnesses and no other evidence. This is getting out of hand, and I'm truly stumped.'

'I thought my plan would work, James, and I am sorry.'

'I don't blame you. I said that. I allowed the plan to continue; as dangerous as it was, I thought it could have put a stop to this, too.'

'You know, James, in the darkest part of my mind, when I was alone and recovering with Yarran's people, I worried I put my life and Edmund's life at risk because I was reckless. For a moment, I thought I was going to die. I saw Emma as I drifted in and out of consciousness, and to be honest, I wanted to stay with her. I did not want to come back.'

'What are you saying, Henry?' Walsh asked, eyebrows raised.

'I may have created this high-risk plan because part of me knew how dangerous it would be, but also a part of me didn't care. I was an impulsive fool, James, and I think I knew that all along. But now look, my foolishness killed Edmund.'

'I don't believe that for a second, Henry. I don't believe you would ever have purposefully endangered a life, so I will not hear of talk like that. That's not the person I know.'

'You don't know me anymore, James!' Hobbs yelled, slamming his fist into the desk and standing bolt upright. In that instant, rage consumed him. Irrational rage. Where was his old friend when he was alone and in grief? The sight of Emma's murdered body flashed before his eyes again. James had no idea what he had genuinely been through and the loneliness he still suffers from.

Walsh remained seated and unflinching. Hobbs saw a softness in his eyes and quickly calmed himself. He knew it wasn't James' fault, and his heart was in the right place, but there was a truth to his comment. Hobbs knew part of him died when Emma did. He was not the same man he once was.

'I miss Emma, James,' Hobbs continued, his tone gentle now. Exhausted even. 'Every time I close my eyes, I see her, and it hurts. I don't know what I'm supposed to do. How can I go on? Maybe deep down, I don't want to keep going on. It's possible that's why I endangered my life. I thought Emma's memory was keeping me going, but now I just don't know. Not having her is like a perpetual torment. Maybe I just don't care about myself anymore. But it just ended up killing Edmund, and here I still stand. It's not fair.'

His eyes welled up with tears, and Walsh remained silently sympathetic. Hobbs scratched his head and wiped his eyes dry.

'I'm not thinking straight! I'm tired. I'm distracted,' he said.

'Listen,' Walsh said, tugging on Hobbs' sleeve and pulling him back down into his chair. 'I know you're hurting, I do. But the man I know is still there. We will get these people; it's what you do, and it's who you are. Even without Emma, you'll push through, but I need you to stay with me on this.'

'I want nothing more than to find them now, for Edmund's sake. I want to give it everything I have.' Hobbs gazed out the window, observing the horses in the stables as they chewed on fresh hay and a thick bush that extended into the back of the stables. He pondered his last words and whether he actually had enough left to give.

Walsh shook his head. 'Henry, look at me. It may have been years since we worked together, and I know you've been hurt beyond imagination. I can see the way you are tormented, but this is who you are. These people will not stop. You said so yourself. They will kill more innocent people. Good people like Edmund. Tomorrow I have an appointment with Doctor Andrews. Come with me and let's get to work.'

'Before I do anything tomorrow, I need to speak with Edmund's wife. I need to apologise.'

'You don't need to apologise, Henry.'

'Yes, I do,' Hobbs said as he stood up and left the room, slamming the door behind him.

THIRTY-FOUR

A crowd of rowdy gold guards roared aggressively through the small Bathurst tavern. 'We ain't working anymore! This is getting out of hand. We are sitting ducks out there!'

The two dozen guards had convened in the pub, settling in for a night of drinking, with discussions about their precarious position following the murders of so many of their colleagues. As they sat around the long wooden table, empty beer glasses piled up, as did the tension in the room.

'I'm quitting! No job is worth this!' a young guard roared over the crowd.

Another cried, 'We won't have to wait too long until they slaughter us right here at Bathurst while we guard the gold stored here.'

Word of the planned meeting had reached some of the Royal Mint representatives, prompting them to attend to assuage the concerns of the men gathered there. Clarence Pearson was present and trying his best to manage the rowdy crowd.

'Please, everyone, listen up,' he said, nervously rubbing his round head. 'We can work around this. We will double the number of guards on each trip.'

'That's not enough. We have heard of the details of these murders,' one had said. 'I, for one, do not want to be stabbed to death. No gold is worth that.'

'We will double your pay,' Pearson pleaded.

The crowd gave off a loud, resounding groan.

'You can't just pay us off!' another called out.

'We have more gold than ever; it cannot stay here. It needs to be delivered to Sydney,' Pearson pleaded.

'Then deliver it yourself,' multiple guards called out at once.

Pearson sighed and stood up from the table, followed by his assistant, John Grover, and brushed through the crowd and left the pub. He stood on the street and took a deep breath. Grover, an accountant by trade, had been busy spending the day crunching the numbers and identified that if they slowed gold deliveries, it would not take long for the Mint to cease payments to the miners for their fresh finds. He was already a nervous-looking man, and as he decided on what to say, he scrunched his thin face and played with his thin moustache.

'Sir, we can't manage our operations without the completion of deliveries for much longer,' he said as he straightened his round glasses, which were slipping down the end of his nose. 'If we can't deliver the gold, and the Mint tells us we can no longer issue payments, we are going to have a full-blown riot at the mines.'

'What would you have me do, John?' Clarence snapped.

'I don't know, sir. I'm simply reporting my calculations.'

'I know the calculations, but we are running out of options. Word has spread of these murders so fast that no person would dare take the job. We must report the issue to the Mint in Sydney and ask them to advise us. For now, we continue issuing payments and stockpiling the gold here. Then we pray to God that we can keep the miners satisfied because if the Mint tells us to cease trade, they will not stay patient for long, and things will become very violent.

As Pearson wiped the sweat from his forehead and thick neck, a couple of men who had also left the meeting inside the pub approached him.

'Mr Pearson?' Daniel Fleming, a veteran guard, said. Fleming, a middle-aged, heavy-set man with a thick moustache and a round stomach, greeted Pearson with an anxiousness in his body language, shifting his weight back and forth.

'Oh, hello, Mr Fleming, what can I do for you?'

'Sir, Walker Pullman and I would be willing to make a delivery,' he said as Pullman stood beside him, nodding. Like Fleming, he was middle-aged and slightly overweight. He had a completely bald head, but maintained a thick, dark beard that trailed down to his chest.

'You would?' Pearson asked, unable to hide the surprised inflection. 'But with everything occurring, you are fine with this?'

'I understand the concerns of my colleagues in the pub, and frankly, I don't blame them. However, suppose you double our pay, as you said, and also double our firepower. If you manage this, we will do it,' Fleming said while Pullman nodded in support.

'And you are fine with this too, Pullman?' Pearson asked.

He nodded. 'We both really need the money, and Daniel and I have been doing this for a few years now and have met plenty of bandits on our routes before. We can handle ourselves.'

'Okay then. Double pay and we will double your weaponry. You leave tomorrow morning.'

As Fleming and Pullman walked away, Grover cast an anxious look at Pearson.

'Are you sure about this, sir? Throwing more money at struggling men just to deliver the gold. This will be very dangerous.'

'We have no choice; we need to make the delivery, and I just have to trust they will be careful, prepared and safe.'

Hobbs invited Yarran to stay in the living room of their cottage. Apologising for the limited space, however, Yarran expressed his gratitude and assured Hobbs that he would be perfectly comfortable.

After a restless night plagued by guilt and sleeplessness, Hobbs woke Walsh just as dawn broke.

'James, wake up and get dressed. I want to speak with Mrs Miller now.' Hobbs said, standing over his bed, already dressed in a fresh white shirt and dark trousers.

'Henry, you don't have to do this,' Walsh said, yawning and rubbing his eyes.

'I already told you the contrary. Hurry, and let's go. Yarran can stay here for now, and when we get back, we will visit Doctor Andrews together.'

Hobbs and Walsh proceeded in silence, their footsteps echoing softly as they made the short journey until Walsh pointed at the Miller house as it loomed ahead in the distance.

'You are sure about this, Henry?'

'Yes,' Hobbs abruptly replied before shaking his head and rubbing his eyes. 'Listen, James, I'm sorry for lashing out the other day. I'm just feeling the pressure here. I'm not sleeping well, and with everything that happened with Edmund, I'm not thinking straight.'

'Apologies are not necessary, I understand. We are all feeling the pressure. As for everything else, I cannot say I understand how you feel, but contrary to what you may think, you are not alone.'

'Come on, let's just go,' Hobbs said.

The garden in front of the Miller residence remained meticulously tended, and the colourful flowers adorning the front of the pristine white house like jewels glistened in the morning dew. Walsh guided the way through the garden toward the front door while Hobbs followed as his gaze swept across the facade of the house. Despite the tranquillity of the morning, Hobbs noticed the curtains were drawn and an eerie stillness pervaded the air.

As they reached the front door, Walsh glanced back at Hobbs, who responded with a solemn nod. Hobbs then removed his hat, ran a hand through his hair to smooth it back, and straightened his shirt.

After a couple of knocks, the door creaked open, revealing Jane Miller clad in a thick black dress that pooled around her feet and trailed along the wooden floorboards. Red-rimmed tired eyes and a disheveled bun with stray strands framing her haggard face revealed she hadn't slept in days. Despite the signs of weariness and sorrow, Hobbs glimpsed remnants of the attractive, kind-hearted woman he believed she once was. Yet now, grief seemed to consume her entirely.

'Oh, hello, Inspector Walsh,' she muttered in a dreary tone, not making eye contact.

'Good morning, Mrs Miller,' Walsh said in a solemn tone matching hers. 'I am very sorry to trouble you this morning, but there is someone who would like to speak to you.'

Before Walsh could introduce Hobbs, he stepped forward and gave a slight bow.

'Mrs Miller, my name is Henry Hobbs. I am assisting in this investigation, and I know your husband. I was hoping to have a few moments of your time this morning.'

She nodded, stepping aside to make way for the pair to enter without uttering a word.

Hobbs and Walsh stepped into the house, finding themselves in the front living room. They stood in the centre of the room for a moment until Jane ushered them to sit. They settled into the soft armchairs by a small fireplace filled with ash and the remains of two burnt out, blackened logs.

'Tea?' Jane offered, seemingly out of a courteous habit, as there was no inflection in her question.

'No, thank you, Mrs Miller,' Hobbs said. 'May I sit?'

Jane nodded and remained standing, clutching nervously at her arms she had folded across her chest. 'Please, join me Mrs Miller.'

She sat on a long sofa opposite Hobbs and stared out the window while her fingers twitched in her lap. She barely made eye contact, and Hobbs sensed her unease and distress at their visit, coupled with her lingering grief.

'Mrs. Miller, I was present with Edmund when he was murdered, and I need to express my sincere apologies to you. Your husband was a brave man and an excellent police officer.'

Hobbs watched as her eyes became red, and tears pooled in the corners of her eyes. She looked at the floor and continued to play with her hands on her lap while a single tear fell and splashed on her knuckle.

Hobbs continued. 'What I wanted to say to you is that I am truly sorry for what happened. I believe I am to blame for what happened to Edmund.'

Walsh winced and exchanged a nervous glance with Hobbs. Hobbs quickly turned his attention back to Jane, who had now fixed her gaze squarely on Hobbs. Despite her silence, her eyes seemed to beseech him for answers. Hobbs paused for a moment, anticipating a response, but still she remained silent.

'It was my plan to ride in the back of the ambushed carriage. I thought it would finally stop these men who have been murdering the gold guards, but I was deeply mistaken, and my actions cost your husband his life. Even though I knew the risks, I continued with my plan. I hope you can forgive me.'

The silence in the room reached a painful level as Mrs Miller continued to sob quietly, still without speaking.

'Mrs Miller, we were not to know what...' Walsh began.

'No, James, stop,' Hobbs said, waving his hand towards Walsh and leaning further in his chair. He looked Jane directly in the eye. 'There are no excuses, Mrs Miller, and I am overcome with feelings of guilt.'

She wiped the tears now running down her cheek and sniffled quietly. 'You did not kill my husband, Mr Hobbs. Those awful men did. I understood the risks of his job, but how did you avoid injury?'

'I did not, but if my injuries were not so incapacitating, I would have done anything I could have to save your husband.'

Jane Miller sobbed and sunk further into her seat.

'Is there anything you need?' Hobbs asked.

She sniffled again and shook her head. 'No. The funeral is this afternoon, and I suppose I will leave for England soon after. I have no other family here.'

After a moment of reflective silence and with no more words left to say, Walsh stood up. 'We shall leave you to grieve then.'

Hobbs stood up and smoothed his trousers. 'If there is anything I can do, please send for me.'

Jane stood up, too, and looked deeply into Hobbs' sorrowful eyes. 'Mr Hobbs, find these men.'

Hobbs replied unflinchingly. 'Yes, Mrs Miller. I will. I promise.'

As soon as they had left the house, Walsh turned to Hobbs in frustration. 'You shouldn't have promised her that.'

'What could I have done?'

'You do not make promises you may not be able to keep.'

'James, she needs hope. And so do I. We have to find these men. For Edmund. I don't know how, but we will find them, and I will hold them to account for what they have done.'

THIRTY-FIVE

Walsh rapped sharply on the door to Doctor Andrews' surgery, which caused an echo through the quiet street as Hobbs and Yarran stood behind him, waiting patiently. Yarran, having borrowed one of Walsh's pristine white shirts, opted for a more relaxed look compared with Walsh and Hobbs, leaving it untucked as his long, dark curls cascaded past the collar.

Hobbs peered through the window beside the door, noting the darkness and stillness within. It was evident that Doctor Andrews had yet to begin his regular medical practice for the day. Soon, he saw the young medical assistant, Fred, emerge from the back of the office, his usual anxious expression writ large upon his features.

'Good morning,' he said as he opened the door. Hobbs noticed that his focus was drawn to Yarran.

'May we come in, Fred?' Walsh said, walking past before he even answered.

'This is Yarran,' Hobbs said, addressing the question he knew was on Fred's mind. 'He is working this case with us.' Yarran nodded and Fred smiled nervously. 'Where is the doctor?'

'Doctor Andrews is out back. He has been expecting you.'

Fred led the way through the surgery, guiding them to the last room. As Hobbs entered, the familiar and distasteful smell assailed his senses once again.

'Good morning, Doctor Andrews,' Walsh said, walking to the white workbench where three bodies were lying flat covered by white, bloodied sheets. Andrews's white apron, stretched taut over his round stomach, bore the same crimson stains as the sheets.

'Good morning,' Andrews replied gruffly, bustling about the room with a sense of urgency. Hobbs observed as Andrews briefly cast a glance at Yarran, but the stranger seemed to warrant no further consideration in the busy doctor's mind.

'Now, I have conducted autopsies on the two men from the previous murder and also the three more recent attacks, including our Constable Miller. His body will be collected soon for his funeral this afternoon. The first two men are no longer here, I'm afraid. We have returned them to their families to be buried. Here,' Andrews said, passing a small metallic object to Walsh, who held it above his eye level and examined the small object.

'I dug this out of the first two bodies. Appears to be what is left of a bullet. From a rifle, no doubt.'

'Looks like what's left of a .550 conical bullet,' Hobbs said, taking the crushed remains of the bullet from Walsh and holding it up in front of his eye.

'How do you know?' Andrews asked.

'Because I had one in me too,' he said, fetching his own retrieved bullet from deep inside his pocket.

'You didn't tell me you had that,' Walsh said.

'Well regardless, it is a match, I would say. Although a common bullet, looking at these two, they are possibly from the same gun,' Hobbs said.

'Yes. I spoke with Sergeant Palmer last night, and he told me what happened. How are you feeling, Mr Hobbs?' Andrews asked.

'A little sore, but mending well. Yarran's family took care of me.'

Andrews glanced at Yarran and scoffed.

'You don't trust traditional medicine, doctor?' Yarran asked directly, but in a tone Hobbs could only describe as maintaining courtesy.

'No. 'No, I do not,' Andrews said, now taking the time to look Yarran up and down carefully. 'I have studied medicine for years, and there is no evidence of anything outside of modern science that could cure a man of such injuries.'

'Well, look at me,' Hobbs said, lifting his shirt to reveal neat stitch marks and the healing tissue of his puncture wounds. 'I would call this a job well done. In fact, without Yarran's people, I would probably be dead.'

Andrews shrugged, his contempt clear on his face, but Hobbs paid little heed to the old doctor's demeanour, remaining focused on his examination of the bullet. Walsh spoke to break the growing tension. 'What else can you tell us, doctor? Please begin with the murders of the guards before the last attack involving Constable Miller.'

Andrews nodded. 'The cause of death was exsanguination. Now, they were also both shot in their legs, however, this did not kill them. From my examinations, I believe these shots were merely to distract or slow them down, as they would not have been instantly fatal. They did, however, have ruptured tendons from the wounds which would have made their legs fail, rendering them almost incapacitated. From the entry wounds, I can see they fired the shots from a distance, given there was no evidence of muzzle burn or gunpowder residue. These leg wounds bled excessively, whereas many of the stab wounds were made post-mortem given the lack of moving, oxygenated blood. The cuts to the carotid artery were the fatal wounds on both. So summarising, from what I can see, the shots were made peri-mortem and the voluminous stab wounds on their bodies, post-mortem.'

'Same as the first two murders,' Hobbs added.

'Yes. So after the slash to the throat, each man was then stabbed multiple times, and these wounds ruptured almost every organ in their bodies. Ordinarily, they would have rapidly lost several pints of blood, causing them to bleed out, but I believe they bled to death from their necks first. Interestingly, there were defensive wounds on both the larger man's arms and hands which were not seen on the first two bodies.'

'Yes, I noticed this. So he tried to fight off the attackers?' Hobbs said.

'I would say so, yes.'

'So unlike the first murders, where the victims were unknowingly attacked and killed in a surprise blitz attack, the attackers shot these men first and then attacked them face-on.'

Andrews nodded. 'It would seem that way.' In my opinion, the stab wounds are consistent with the same knives as I reported during the first autopsies. About six inches long and extremely sharp. The wounds were incredibly clean and narrow.

'So it's possible the attackers also have wounds on their bodies?'

'It's possible, yes. I found small traces of blood and skin underneath their fingernails. Likely from a scratch during the struggle. I have to be honest with you, I have seen nothing so violent in all my years.'

Judging by the look on the doctor's assistant, who appeared horrified, tucked up and hiding in the corner, looking pale just from the recount, the doctor was speaking truthfully.

'Now as for the other two guards and young Constable Miller...'

'That won't be necessary, Doctor,' Hobbs said, not wanting to hear the details he had already seen with his own eyes. 'I witnessed the attack and I have already relayed what I saw to Inspector Walsh. We provided some element of surprise, and I saw the three attackers, however, all were wearing face coverings. They shot the men dead in front of me and then nearly killed me after. I shot one of them in the arm. After Edmund and I surprised them by firing back, I expect they fled the scene quickly, without checking if I was actually dead.

'Yes, and as you said, Mr Hobbs, the cause of death was gunshot wounds. I found the same ammunition as the one retrieved from the other bodies and your own leg.'

'And they had no time to mutilate the bodies,' Hobbs declared. 'As I said, they were startled and quickly fled.'

'Is there anything else you can tell us, Doctor?' Walsh asked.

'I'm afraid not. These men are extremely efficient, and their stabs are quick, yet deliberate and with no sign of hesitation. Now, unless there is anything else, I need to finish up here in time for Constable Miller's funeral.'

'No, that's all for now, thank you, Doctor,' Walsh said.

When Hobbs left the office, followed by Walsh and Yarran, he was all grateful to inhale fresh air and receive a burst of warm sunlight on his face.

'I don't understand the excessive stabbing, all post-mortem,' Walsh said.

'They enjoy it, James,' Hobbs said. 'I expect they would have done the same to us if it had not been for Edmund and I surprising them. That, along with the growing carriage fire.'

'But why?'

'Because they are deranged, James. The killing is what they are seeking. We always thought they killed for the gold, but I now believe it is the other way around. How else can you explain the overkill? Sure, they take the gold, but it is not what they truly seek. Remember the message on the carriage written in blood? It's as though this is a game for these men.'

Hobbs considered more of his theory and when he had collected his thoughts coherently, he stopped and looked at Walsh and Yarran.

'Hear me out. I saw three men attack us. Now logic tells me one of them has to be in charge. The organiser, or possibly the recruiter, but there has to be a hierarchy. If someone wants the gold, he knows he needs to take out the gold guards, so he finds two people who are willing to kill. Men who are even excited to kill. The leader gets the gold, and the other two are likely rewarded also, but they get to satisfy their desires. That is their true prize. These people enjoy killing.'

'Enjoyment in killing people?' Yarran asked.

'Yes.'

'It's an interesting theory, and I suppose it fits the crime scenes.' Walsh said.

Hobbs continued. 'And James, occasionally we saw this type of repeated killings in London by people who felt compelled to kill without logical reason.' It was just for the sheer thrill and joy. I believe these men have created their own world that simply revolves around their perverse desires with no care for their fellow man. We had a word for them in Scotland Yard: monsters. There is no other way to describe them.'

'Okay,' Walsh said, 'I'm starting to agree, but it still doesn't get us any closer to finding them, though. Homicide investigations back home were very different. The streets of London were busy. We had witnesses and plenty of leads to follow. Is there anything at all you can remember about them?'

'No, not really. It all happened so fast. I recall the man I shot, though. He was a heavyset man, but that's all I can remember. Now their impulses have been hindered, which is a problem because if these men are truly as I think they are, they will not be pleased about not being able to complete their overkill.

'I just pray they don't lash out again soon,' Walsh said.

'If we can't stop them, James, they will.'

THIRTY-SIX

Yarran decided not to attend the funeral, reasoning to Hobbs that his lack of acquaintance with Edmund Miller would make his presence there seem out of place. In addition, he surmised that his attendance might inadvertently divert attention from the solemnity of the occasion, drawing unnecessary questions and distractions.

Leaving Yarran to explore Penrith on his own, Hobbs and Walsh made their way to the local cemetery south of the Nepean River. There, they found a gathering of about fifty people already assembled. Among the attendees were local business owners and townsfolk who had crossed paths with Edmund during his brief tenure as one of the local constables. Clad in sombre attire, the mourners wore a uniform sea of black, with men donning black suits and women adorned in long black dresses and veils. Among the unfamiliar mourners, Hobbs spotted Constables Bryson and Davidson standing solemnly alongside Sergeant Palmer. He noticed a few other uniformed constables whom he had not yet had the opportunity to meet. They all wore smart black tunics fastened with large silver buttons. Standing behind the constables, Chief Inspector Noland cut a striking figure in his black tunic. With hands clasped behind his back, he stood in solemn silence, his gaze fixed upon the ground. As Hobbs observed Chief Inspector Noland's stoic demeanour, he couldn't help but ponder the thoughts swirling within his mind. The string of murders within his jurisdiction, now compounded by the loss of a local constable, undoubtedly weighed heavily on him. Hobbs surmised that beneath Noland's grief, there simmered a potent undercurrent of simmering rage fuelled by the frustrating lack of progress in the investigation. He knew the game all too well. Politics would soon take over and Walsh would eventually have to provide answers why these murders have not yet been solved.

As the midday sun disappeared behind thick clouds, the temperature dropped. As the chill took hold, the pastor wasted no time in commencing the service, sensing the imminent threat of rain. Clad in a long black robe adorned with a white collar and sash, he stood solemnly beside the thick black coffin and the gaping hole in the ground. Wisps of his balding hair fluttered in the breeze as he clutched a leather-bound bible tightly to his chest. With a sombre nod, he began the service with an opening prayer.

Jane Miller stood beside the pastor, her figure cloaked in the same sombre black dress she had worn earlier in the morning. Clutching a single red rose in her trembling hand, she sobbed quietly, her gaze fixed mournfully upon the casket before her. As the opening prayer drew to a close, the pastor nodded solemnly at Jane. With a trembling hand, she placed the red rose atop the coffin, positioning it tenderly where Edmund Miller's head would rest.

Closing his bible softly, the pastor recited rehearsed words honouring the memory of Miller. 'Edmund Miller migrated to the colony of New South Wales with his wife, Jane Miller, in order to pursue a career in law enforcement. He found both a passion and aptitude for serving the community, and his colleagues found him to be a brave man with exceptional investigative skills and wit. He was a loving husband and a friend to us all. Although over time we will forget his face, we shall not forget the memory of the brave Constable Edmund Miller who died in the line of duty, acting with nothing but true valour. Let us now have a moment of silent reflection as we pray for Edmund Miller, who is no doubt watching down from us in heaven by God's side.'

Hobbs and Walsh bowed their heads in unison with the rest of the attendees. Under his breath, Hobbs whispered another apology, his voice barely audible as a single tear traced a path down his cheek.

As the pastor concluded the final prayer and the coffin was lowered into the ground, the crowd dispersed, while some lingered and offered their condolences to Jane Miller. Hobbs observed her growing overwhelmed with emotion, the weight of grief clear in her weary expression. Gazing upon her, he couldn't help but empathise with the profound sense of sorrow and loneliness she must be experiencing at that moment. He knew the feeling all too well.

'Something isn't feeling right, James,' Hobbs said as they ambled through the cemetery, away from the crowd.

'What do you mean?'

'The way the three sets of murders have taken place. Their timings have been meticulous. Sure, we gave them a surprise on the last one, but to me, it seems they knew exactly when these gold deliveries were going to be made. Who else would have access to this scheduling information?'

Just the Royal Mint, the gold guards themselves, and the police also receive copies of the schedules. I receive routine copies of them in the Sydney office, so I know when a valuable carriage is to be expected entering my patrol.'

'Anyone else?'

'No. When I spoke with the Mint staff at the gold mines, they assured me they kept a very close watch on their transport operations.'

'Maybe it's the routine, then? Too regular?' Hobbs asked.

'Perhaps, but maybe these people are patient and they wait. There really is only one route over the Mountains into Sydney. It has always been dangerous. The Mint knows this. That is why the guards carry weapons. Robberies are a constant risk.'

'But not brutal murders,' Hobbs added.

'No. Maybe we can arrange for them to vary their routine?'

'Maybe, but as you said, maybe these men are patient. Even if we tell them to hold off on deliveries for a while, the gold will build up at Bathurst and that will cause a problem on its own, not to mention the security risk and pressure mounting from the Mint.' Hobbs sighed and rubbed his brow, feeling fatigue and a headache growing. 'We really need a breakthrough, James.'

'I know, but where do we go from here?'

'What about the gold trade?' Hobbs asked. 'We try a different approach. Instead of chasing the men, we follow the proceeds of their crimes. How would one dispose of stolen gold? I expect they would want to part from it as soon as possible. It would be too traceable otherwise, and a direct link to the murders. So, it would need to be converted to Pounds as soon as possible. They probably have a connection to a gold trader or smelter.'

'I agree, but I'm afraid that is like finding a needle in a haystack. Since the gold rush, there have been illegally run smelting operators all over the colony for those who do not wish to use the Royal Mint. Some may even offer a better trading price, and often, they do not ask questions if the price is right.'

Hobbs nodded. It was a long shot, but he knew the gold must be traded somewhere.

'But where?' Walsh asked. 'The farms around here would make for an excellent clandestine gold operation. Plenty of space and privacy. So there could be countless people in this area who would buy gold and then resell it onto the Mint, or perhaps even a jewellery maker directly.'

Hobbs nodded. 'Well, let's find every single one of them then.'

THIRTY-SEVEN

As the day wore on, Hobbs found himself alone with his thoughts. Yarran embarked on a quiet walk, tracing the edges of the Nepean River, while Walsh retreated to the dining room, penning a lengthy letter to Helen and his boys. As Hobbs reflected on Walsh missing his family, he couldn't help but feel a pang of emptiness at his own sense of loss. Despite being consumed by his own grief, Hobbs couldn't shake the sense of isolation that seemed to envelop him, causing him to withdraw further into himself.

Deciding that he had little appetite, Hobbs skipped dinner, opting instead for a soothing shave and a long, hot bath. As he undressed in the bathroom, he carefully removed the bandages, revealing that his wounds were healing well and showing no signs of infection.

Continuing to examine his battered body, Hobbs winced as he surveyed the scars that marred his back and shoulders, a painful reminder of the many floggings he had endured. Yet, as agonising as these physical wounds had been, they paled in comparison to the deep-seated mental scars he carried within him. In the solitude of the moment, he pondered the challenges that awaited him after he resolved this case. He had no family. No purpose. The notion of being sent back to Cockatoo Island loomed ominously in his mind, though he clung to the hope that James would intervene to prevent such an outcome. Yet, deep down, he knew that his old friend could only do so much. The continuing thought of isolation gnawed at him, reminding him of the inevitable reality that he would soon be on his own once again. Overwhelmed by a built up wave of frustration and despair, he gripped the edge of the sink tightly before burying his face in his hands, muffling a scream of anguish.

Overwhelmed and utterly exhausted, Hobbs felt the weight of the murders bearing down on him, each one refusing to release its grip on his conscience. Consumed by guilt and haunted by the belief that the blood of Edmund Miller stained his hands, he could no longer contain the flood of emotions that surged within him. He thought of Emma once more, and with tears streaming down his face, he surrendered to the grief that enveloped him, his sobs echoing in the empty confines of the bathroom.

As soon as the bath was ready, Hobbs immersed himself in the warm water, dragging his clothes in after him for a hasty wash. The sensation of the clean water was a welcome respite, and he submerged his face beneath the surface, relishing the brief moment of silence weightlessness. Yet, even in the warm embrace of the water, he couldn't escape the relentless turmoil of his thoughts. It was a fleeting illusion of peace, a temporary reprieve from the storm raging within him. He knew he couldn't remain submerged forever; eventually, he would have to resurface and confront the harsh realities awaiting him above. He took a deep breath, splashed his face one last time and climbed out, hanging his wet clothes over the edge of the tub. Wrapping a towel around his waist, he headed toward his bedroom.

'James!' he called out.

'Yes?' Walsh called back from the dining room.

'I'm going to get some sleep. See you in the morning.'

'You don't want to eat? It's only early,' he called back.

'No, I'm tired and I have a headache. See you in the morning. I'm sure Yarran will be back shortly.'

'Oh alright then, goodnight.'

Within five minutes of his head hitting the soft pillow on the thin bed, Hobbs was asleep.

Once again, Hobbs found himself transported to the familiar embrace of a lush green field nestled within the idyllic English countryside. The tree's broad, leafy branches cast a cool shade, bathing Emma as she stood beneath its expansive canopy. She remained perfectly still, her small smile radiating warmth and affection. Her vibrant green eyes, brimming with vitality and life, met his gaze with a familiar twinkle that stirred his soul. With a surge of longing, Hobbs moved towards her, but a weight that seemed to drag at his legs hindered him. Despite his determination, Hobbs found himself rooted to the spot, his feet fused to the grass, leaving him stranded several feet away from his wife. He suddenly felt a gentle tap on his shoulder and quickly turned around. It was Edmund Miller. He wore his full black police tunic and cap. His eyes were cold and cloudy and seemed to stare straight through him. His face seemed to be drained of all its colour. Miller didn't speak, he just raised his hand up the length of his tunic and collected the blood which was dribbling out fast from several bullet holes in his torso. With his hands soaked in blood, he looked at Hobbs.

'I'm sorry, Edmund. I'm so sorry,' Hobbs pleaded.

He turned around, looking for Emma only to find the grass was dead again and the tree was completely barren of any leaves.

'Emma, I'm sorry.'

Hobbs jolted awake in a state of panic, the suffocating darkness of the room pressing in on him. Overwhelmed by despair, he felt as though the weight of his burdens was becoming unbearable, threatening to crush him beneath its relentless grip. Sweat drenched his chest and neck, yet an icy chill sent shivers coursing through his body. Rubbing his eyes, he fumbled in the darkness, searching for his shirt to ward off the cold. Slipping into a shirt, and with a shaky breath, he made his way down the hallway.

Entering the dining room at the back of the house, he found the small wooden cabinet nestled next to the dining table. With trembling hands, he flung open the doors and searched the cluttered shelves with a sense of urgency, his heart pounding in his chest until he found what he was looking for.

The dining room was still dark, and the unopened bottle of whiskey was more appealing to Hobbs than it ever was. He sat at the table and placed the bottle in front of him, staring at it with both contempt and desire. It had been a long time since a drink and he vowed he would never touch alcohol again, but with everything he had struggled through, he felt he had nothing left to keep him going.

'Everything okay?' Yarran asked, startling Hobbs as he appeared out of the darkness and joined him at the table. He wore the black trousers he had on during the day, but was shirtless.

'Yarran, you frightened me.'

'Sorry, I heard a noise,' he replied nonchalantly. 'What's that?'

'Oh, that's nothing, just a bottle of Scotch.'

'Oh okay. I don't drink alcohol,' Yarran said matter-of-factly.

'Honestly, neither do I, anymore. But I think I need it tonight.'

Yarran's gaze bore into Hobbs, and for a fleeting moment, Hobbs felt as though his innermost secrets lay exposed before him. It was an uncanny sensation, as if Yarran possessed an innate ability to discern the hidden truths that dwelled within others. Despite knowing nothing of Hobbs' tumultuous past in England, there was a profound depth to Yarran's understanding, a keen insight that transcended mere words. In Yarran's presence, Hobbs couldn't help but feel a sense of vulnerability, as if his soul lay bare and exposed to scrutiny. Though they hailed from vastly different worlds, Yarran seemed to possess an intuitive understanding of the pain and turmoil that weighed heavily on him.

After a moment had passed, Yarran leant over the table and whispered to Hobbs. 'Perhaps you shouldn't drink tonight. It is possible you will regret it.'

Hobbs remained silent, his discomfort palpable as he grappled with the unexpected scrutiny, followed by a deep sense of shame.

'There was a time, Yarran, where I drank just so I could forget,' Hobbs said.

'But why would you want to forget? We should hold our memories and cherish them. They are a part of who we are, who we were, and who we will become.'

'Because sometimes the memories hurt.'

'You've lost someone very close to you?'

'Yes. My wife.'

'I am sorry for your loss.'

Hobbs nodded and looked back at the bottle. 'She was murdered. Her death was the one case I could not solve.'

'I am truly sorry, Henry. What is her name?'

'Is?' Hobbs asked with a raised inflection.

'Yes, *is*. She will always be with you.'

Hobbs stared at the whiskey bottle, complementing the amber liquid inside. *Emma.* He repeated her name in his mind several times.

'What made you eventually stop drinking?' Yarran asked.

'It just led to a series of disasters, and it was slowly killing me.'

'And you didn't want that?'

Hobbs twitched involuntarily. Yarran's astute observation had struck a chord within him. He had never consciously analysed his decision to quit drinking, nor had he ever fully understood the underlying motivations behind it. In his darkest moments, when despair threatened to consume him, he had sought solace in alcohol, clinging to its numbing effects. Yet, even amidst the haze of intoxication, a small ember of hope had flickered within him, and perhaps, deep down, he had never truly desired the oblivion that alcohol promised.

'I guess I didn't.'

'You have dreams, don't you?' Yarran asked.

Hobbs felt a startling shiver run down his spine, and he held Yarran's gaze for a moment before answering. 'How did you know that?'

'The first time I saw you, I could see you were carrying a burden. I'm not here to tell you not to do something, but just remember, you have a purpose. As does everything on this land. You need to find that purpose, but with the work you do, and all the people you help, I think you have already found it.'

Hobbs regarded Yarran with a mixture of surprise and gratitude. Although Yarran was still somewhat of a stranger to him, there was an undeniable sincerity in his demeanour and Hobbs couldn't help but feel a sense of comfort in his presence.

'And the fact you never solved this case, can you accept that?' he said.

'That I do not know. My wife deserved justice, and I could never give that to her. Now, from all the way out here, there is not much I can do about it, although my old team vowed to never stop working the case.'

'Well, I still hope you find a way to move on with your life. You deserve that chance. Goodnight, Henry.'

'Goodnight, Yarran.'

As Yarran left, Hobbs pondered the weight of their conversation as a sense of bewilderment lingered. Uncertain of what to make of the unexpected exchange, Hobbs grappled with conflicting emotions. Yet, in the midst of his confusion, a newfound clarity emerged. With a decisive gesture, he set aside the bottle of Scotch and made his way back to bed.

Hobbs remained awake for several more hours, trying to understand his decision to put the bottle down. He felt strangely different. Not better exactly, just different. It felt as though the dormant sense of purpose he had once possessed still lingered within him, patiently awaiting its moment to resurface.

THIRTY-EIGHT

The morning unfolded with a straightforward plan: consult Sergeant Palmer, whose intimate knowledge of the local area surpassed all others, to ascertain potential locations for gold trading outside the purview of banks or the Mint.

Arriving at 9 a.m, with Walsh and Yarran, Hobbs found Palmer on his own, seated behind the thick wooden enquiry counter.

'Morning sergeant,' Walsh said, 'everyone out already?'

'Good morning. Yes, patrols started early. Do you need anything?'

'As a matter of fact, I do. I was hoping you could help us....'

Before Walsh could complete his sentence, Chief Inspector Noland burst through the rear doors of the police station, his face flushed crimson with anger, his neck straining against the confines of his snug collar.

'You two, a word. Immediately.' He then fixed his gaze squarely on Yarran, his features clouded with a perplexed expression, but it was evident that his thoughts were preoccupied with other matters. 'You, get out.'

'It's okay, Yarran. Just wait for us at the house,' Hobbs whispered.

'Something wrong, sir?' Walsh asked.

'My office, now!' Noland stormed toward the back office designated for Walsh's investigation, a space that he knew rightfully belonged to Noland for his own tasks in Penrith.

Walsh and Hobbs trailed behind Noland, entering the office to find him seated behind the desk, his broad back facing the window, engrossed in a stack of paperwork. Hobbs, who still harboured his contempt for the man, with reminders of his former commanding officer, slouched into the chair opposite the desk, meeting Noland's gaze with a steely resolve. Meanwhile, Walsh stood nearby, his posture rigid with apprehension, hands clasped behind his back and his body rigid.

'I don't recall inviting you to sit,' Noland growled at Hobbs.

'My feet ache,' Hobbs quickly retorted, and from the corner of his eye, he saw Walsh wince. Hobbs knew aggravating Noland would not be productive to the investigation, but at that moment, he didn't care.

Foregoing the temptation of a fruitless argument with Hobbs, Noland simply glared back at him before shifting his attention to Walsh.

'Walsh, you're done. You're off the case. Head back to Sydney immediately.'

'Excuse me, sir?'

'You're out. Sergeant Palmer brought you out here to solve these murders, and you've made no progress. There have been more murders under your nose, and you do not even have so much as a suspect. You too, Hobbs. You're out. Go back to wherever it is you came from.'

'Sir, I don't understand. We are working as hard as we can,' Walsh said.

'So you clearly have not heard? Another attack on a gold carriage occurred sometime last night. Locals alerted the Springwood Constabulary to it first thing this morning. That's four separate attacks, and the Mint is in a serious panic, as is the Governor.

'What? More murders?' Walsh said in an alarm. Rubbing his forehead wearily, and a tinge of unease crept into his tone as though he was grappling with the realisation that they were falling alarmingly behind in the investigation.

'That's right. Along the same route. Two middle-aged guards. We believe most other guards refused to work, and this pair likely accepted the job for more pay. And now we are a fraction away from a full-scale riot out there in the mines. I have received word that the Mint is already discussing ceasing their operations temporarily. No Mint means no payment to the miners. Your incompetence has a flow-on effect, in case you failed to realise.'

Hobbs acknowledged the immense pressure that Chief Inspector Noland must have been facing, especially given the intricate web of politics surrounding Mint operations. However, despite understanding the gravity of Noland's predicament, he harboured no sympathy for the arrogant man. With each word he spoke, his fists tightened and his face reddened.

'Were the murders the same as the last? Evidence of overkill?' Walsh asked.

'Not that it is your business anymore, inspector, but yes. It was horrendous.'

'Who will run the investigation now?' Hobbs asked.

'I will. Palmer recruited you without my permission, and that was clearly a mistake. Now I'll sort out the mess you both created. Get out of my sight and don't let me see you anywhere near here or at the crime scene. Walsh, you're lucky you still have a job. Now, where are the autopsy reports from Doctor Andrews?'

Walsh froze, as though he was unable to decide what he could say to absolve himself. 'Ah, it's here,' he said, picking up a pile of papers from a small table near the door. He extended the documents toward Noland, offering them for his review, but the Chief Inspector ignored the gesture, steadfastly remaining seated in his chair.

'Just leave them there on the desk and go.'

'But, sir...' Walsh started.

'That will be all, inspector. Get out.'

Hobbs stood up and patted Walsh on the back. 'Come on, let's go,' he said as he opened the door and pushed Walsh out first. He turned and eyed Noland once more before slamming the door as hard as he could.

'Is everything okay?' Palmer asked as Hobbs and Walsh walked towards the front of the station.

'Thank you for all your help and hospitality, sergeant. I have been told to return to Sydney. We have been removed from the case. I'm afraid there was another murder.'

'Another murder?'

'Yes, near Springwood again. Apparently, someone called the local constables to the site this morning after discovering two bodies. It sounds like the same men we have been hunting. Noland will run the investigation now.'

Palmer looked flustered and, as though he struggled to find the right words, he eventually offered his apologies.

'Well, it was great to see you again,' Walsh said, shaking hands with Palmer.

'Nice to have met you,' Hobbs said, also shaking hands.

As soon as they stepped out of the station, Walsh unleashed a thunderous roar of frustration, the pent-up tension and exasperation finally finding release in his outburst. 'More people are going to die with that fool running the investigation.'

'Don't worry, James, we will solve this.'

'Are you being serious? Were you not in the same room as I was? We are out.'

'You may be out, but as I remember, I don't work for Noland. Neither does Yarran. I'm going to first go look for the crime scene. After that, I'll continue to look into any gold traders in the area.'

'You can't do that and you don't even have the details of where it is. Henry, if Noland finds out you were there, he will find out who you really are and personally drag you back to Cockatoo Island, and there won't be anything I'll be able to do. He will then likely have you charged for hindering his investigation.'

'Well, no one will see me. I'll take Yarran to visit the crime scene. He knows the land in the Mountains better than anyone and with his help, I'll find it. I'll wait until tonight and they will not see us. I didn't want them to kill again, but for each crime scene they create, they are eventually bound to make mistakes, and with Yarran's keen eye, I want to have a good look at it.'

'Henry, I can't let you do this. This is my career at stake here. If you're caught....'

'I know. That's why I'm not asking you to come. You'll never even know we've been there and neither will anyone else. Besides, when we find these men, and we will, not even Noland will be able to stay mad. His job is likely on the line too, so solving this will keep the politicians at bay.'

THIRTY-NINE

Hobbs and Yarran occupied themselves with quiet patience, seated on the plush sofa in the living room of the cottage. Their gazes drifted idly out the window, watching as the sun slowly fell over the horizon. Meanwhile, Walsh busied himself in his room, packing his belongings to prepare for his return to Sydney. However, Hobbs remained resolute in his decision to stay, bound by a promise made to Jane Miller that he was determined to honour.

Hobbs glanced at Yarran beside him, reflecting on his narrow escape from succumbing to the whiskey and disaster that might have unfolded if he had taken a drink, which had been tempting him dangerously. Now safely returned to its place in the cupboard, the unopened bottle served as a reminder of the perilous temptation he had narrowly avoided. Determined not to venture down that path again, Hobbs resolved to maintain his distance and preserve his control. He had work to do, and he needed every ounce of his coherent wit.

'Yarran, put this on over your shirt. It will help us conceal ourselves better,' Hobbs said, standing up and handing him one of two long, black police tunics he had found in the cupboard inside his bedroom. He wondered how long someone had stored them there as they smelled musty, but they would suffice and allow them to blend into the night.

'We'll sneak around the back of the police station. You take James' horse and I'll take mine. No one will know.'

'Are you sure about this?' Yarran asked, fastening the buttons tight around his torso.

'Absolutely. I think it's dark enough now. Let's go.'

As 9 o'clock neared, the antiquated police station had long since shut its doors for the night. Sergeant Palmer and his wife resided in the quaint cottage next to the station, poised to spring into action in the event of an emergency. However, with the silence of the evening settling in, the night promised to unfold with no further police activity. Under the canopy of a clear night sky, adorned with bright stars, Hobbs and Yarran navigated their way to the stables at the rear of the station. Upon arrival, they found Walsh's horse nestled in a comfortable sleep towards the back of the stables. With a gentle touch, Hobbs eased open the stable door and extended a reassuring pat to the horse's nose. Startled from its sleep, the horse jolted awake, emitting a startled twitch and a sharp snort.

'Hey, it's alright, calm down, we are just going to go for a ride. Yarran, take her. She's usually not this startled, but she'll settle. I'll prepare mine.'

Yarran approached the horse with a calm demeanour, his touch gentle as he stroked her head and whispered soothing words in his native tongue. The horse seemed to respond positively to his presence, its mood softening under his gentle touch.

Finding a few old apples nearby, Yarran offered one to the horse, who eagerly accepted the treat, devouring it in two swift bites.

'I don't know where we are going to find this crime scene, Yarran. I expect the bodies and the carriage would have been removed by now, so I am going to be guided by you to find it. We will take the same route the gold carriage would have taken and continue west until we find it. Do you think you'll be able to locate what's left of the scene in the dark?'

'I expect so. If blood was spilt on the land, and there was a disturbance, I will find it.'

'Let's go, I'll follow you,' Hobbs said, mounting the saddle and following Yarran around the side of the police station and quietly trotting past the station. As they ventured into the night, the streets were quiet and shrouded in darkness. Even the local pub, which had bustled with activity earlier, now lay dormant, their doors firmly shut for the evening. Despite the eerie stillness, Hobbs and Yarran maintained a steady pace, and the horses trotting, echoing softly against the deserted streets. It wasn't until they were certain they had left the township far behind them that they quickened their pace, eager to put distance between themselves and the town.

Navigating through the foothills of the Blue Mountains, they ascended the steep incline for nearly two hours. As midnight approached, the atmosphere grew laden with moisture, and the dense canopy of trees obscured what little light remained in the sky, enveloping the bush in an impenetrable darkness. As they pressed on, their horses quickening to a steady canter, Yarran was the first to discern the shift in the surroundings. He eased the pace to a walk, prompting Hobbs to follow suit.

'You see something, Yarran?.'

'We're here,' he replied, climbing off the horse and patting its body, keeping it perfectly still as he examined the surrounding ground.

'Are you sure?'

'Yes. I can see the blood on the ground and branches. And here, I can see the tracks from the carriage. It remained stationary here for a long time. Two men were killed in this spot.'

Hobbs trailed behind Yarran, his senses heightened as he surveyed their surroundings. Despite the darkness, his eyes had adapted, allowing him to discern the subtle details of the terrain. As they advanced, he noted the gradual narrowing of the road, a familiar pattern reminiscent of the scenes of previous murders they had encountered.

'Looks familiar,' Hobbs said.

'No, this is a different spot,' Yarran said, examining the dirt.

'I mean, the area itself. It narrows here at this point. The trees and bushes come right up the road's edge. Like another funnel that the carriage would have had to pass through while allowing plenty of hiding spots for an ambush, just like the last murders.' Hobbs quickly glanced over his shoulder. 'Are you sure there is no one around?'

'We are alone. No one has been here for several hours. These horse tracks are old.'

Hobbs crouched down to inspect the ground where Yarran had pointed, trying to find the faintest details despite the darkness. When he did, his heart sank. Pools of dried blood stained the dirt road, their dark hues stark against the pale moonlight, while crimson splatters covered the leaves of the bushes lining the roadside.

'Look at this blood spray,' Hobbs said, crouching down and running his fingers through the stained leaves. 'It pools all the way back on the road and then reaches the edge where the bushes started. They must have been killed by a rupture to the carotid artery again, bleeding under high pressure.'

Hobbs remained crouched low to the ground, his focus un-wavering, as he meticulously surveyed the area for any further clues.

'Here was the first body and the second over there near those wheel tracks. That must have been from the carriage.'

'What else do you want to look for?' Yarran asked.

'Just anything that doesn't belong.'

Yarran's silent contemplation intrigued Hobbs, but he respected the man's intuition and allowed him the space to interpret the subtle cues of the land. Turning his attention back to the task at hand, Hobbs relied on his tactile senses, feeling the texture of the dirt beneath his fingers and meticulously examining the surroundings for any sign of disturbance. With each careful sweep of his hands, he remained vigilant, attuned to even the faintest indication that might offer a glimpse into what occurred.

As Hobbs continued to comb through the crime scene, uncertainty clouded his mind, leaving him to question the motives behind his actions. Was his decision born out of frustration or defiance against the chief inspector's orders? The previous crime scenes, though gruesome, had yielded nothing tangible. No weapons, no clothing, no witnesses – just eerie emptiness. Frustration bubbled within him, finding release as he struck the bush before him with force, his fingers then running through his hair in a gesture of exasperation.

Standing amidst the dense trees, Hobbs strained to catch a glimpse of the stars above. The bustling streets of London, where challenges revolved around pollution, conflicting witnesses and rain rather than the rugged wilderness of the Australian bush, had shaped his entire career in homicide. Here, though, there was nothing, only a deafening silence. As frustration mounted, Hobbs grappled with the daunting task of finding those responsible with no solid physical evidence compounded because he now operated beyond the confines of official police jurisdiction.

Suddenly, the moonlight reflected something on the ground. *'What is that?'* Hobbs muttered to himself, looking down at the imprint of a horseshoe in the dirt. He brushed away some of the dirt covering the small object and called Yarran over.

'Dhin,' Yarran muttered under his breath as he was crouched on the ground next to Hobbs.

'I'm sorry?' Hobbs said.

'A berry,' Yarran said as he carefully brushed some more dirt away from the shallow print and carefully picked it up. It had suffered slight damage to its form from being partially buried under the dirt.

'But where is the berry bush? This seems like the only one here.'

Yarran examined the small berry closer, holding it toward the moonlight barely creeping through the canopy.

'So? What do you think?' Hobbs asked, looking at the small, partially crushed red berry.

'It's a berry from the Asparagus Fern. They rarely grow this far up the mountains. The climate is wrong, but regardless, the bush it would have come from is not around here.'

'So where are they found?'

'Look I have seen them scattered throughout the entire mountain range, but they don't thrive and produce berries of this size so far up here. I would say this one came from much further east in the very lowest part of the mountains where it's warmer and sunnier, but more likely from around the riverbanks in the Penrith area and beyond.'

'Asparagus Fern you say, here let me have a look?' Hobbs said, reaching out to handle what was once a round berry, less than half an inch in diameter. 'It actually looks familiar, but I can't quite place it. Are you sure? It's pretty damaged, it could be another type?'

'No, I know all the berries around the entire region. Look, you can see the black seed inside it. I promise you, they don't grow like that, and with that size around here.'

'So what are you saying?'

'I think it got stuck in a horseshoe and it was left behind here?'

'But it came from the east?'

'A berry of this size and form? Yes. It would be unlikely it was dragged all the way here from anywhere further west.'

Hobbs rose to his feet, his interest piqued by the inconspicuous berry. Suddenly, a memory stirred within him, triggering a cascade of connections in his mind.

'Oh, God, I know where I've seen these berries before.'

'Where?' Yarran asked.

'They overhang the back of the stables at the Penrith police station.'

FORTY

'Henry, these plants grow all over the Nepean area.' Yarran said, following Hobbs, who was charging back toward his horse.

'That's fine, but I can tell you this. These berries grow by the police stables and I have seen them scattered across the floor of the stables. The office James was using overlooks on the stables, and I knew I'd seen them before.'

Hobbs understood it was a slim chance, but in the current stage of the investigation, he grasped at anything to pursue. These murderers had operated with meticulous precision, possessing an intricate knowledge of the gold transports, including routes and schedules. Yet, this seemingly insignificant berry stood out—a potential oversight. Its presence hinted at a lapse, a deviation from their calculated approach. It suggested the involvement of someone intimately familiar with the area, perhaps even a member of law enforcement. Hobbs couldn't fathom how he'd overlooked this before. The perpetrators were methodical and well-versed in the terrain, which made the berry's appearance all the more intriguing.

The murders were violent, yet intentionally controlled, he thought.

In his mind, there was no doubt.

The men they had been seeking were police officers.

Hobbs recognised the urgency of discussing this revelation with Walsh and strategising their next steps. However, with Noland's strict prohibition against their involvement, he anticipated significant obstacles ahead. The unsettling notion of police complicity in these murders sent a chill down his spine, but he was determined to pursue the truth, even if it meant navigating treacherous waters.

Hobbs urged his horse into a rapid gallop back toward Penrith. As they approached the town limits, they eased into a brisk walk, allowing Yarran to catch up and ride alongside Hobbs.

'We need to be really careful, and really quiet,' Hobbs said.

As the first light of dawn broke over Penrith, the darkness seemed to linger, casting an eerie atmosphere over the town. A heavy silence had accompanied the long ride back, and as Hobbs dismounted his horse, he felt a deep sense of frustration. Despite the new knowledge of who might be involved in these murders, there was still no clear and identifiable suspect. Hobbs knew he would have to tread carefully with his theory. His experience had taught him that crimes involving the most trusted of public officials never ended well.

They abruptly halted their approach about one hundred yards from the police station when Hobbs noticed a flickering candle and movement near the front door.

'Yarran,' he whispered before dismounting. 'Take the horses down the street, away from the station. Someone is in there. I don't want us being seen.'

As Yarran stealthily led the two horses away, utilising the cover of darkness for concealment, Hobbs sought refuge behind a tree encircled by dense shrubbery, affording him a clear view of the station.

Sergeant Palmer stood outside the station, his presence at such an early hour puzzled Hobbs, and he speculated whether Palmer had worked through the night or was starting his day unusually early. Regardless, Hobbs remained hidden, hoping Palmer wasn't involved. Despite seeming honourable and competent, Hobbs couldn't afford to trust anyone until proven otherwise. In his mind, until proven innocent, everyone was a suspect.

He remained crouching low at the base of the tree until Yarran quietly rejoined him.

'What is it?' Yarran whispered.

'I'm not sure yet,' Hobbs replied.

After a moment, Hobbs saw Palmer pull the front doors closed and walk behind the station toward his house. 'Okay, I think he is going home.' Let's go.'

Hobbs moved cautiously towards the station, with Yarran following closely, his movements even quieter. Yarran's experience navigating the bush had honed his stealth skills, allowing him to move silently through the still street.

As they approached the large wooden gate at the side of the station, Hobbs lifted the latch with utmost care, opening it just enough to slip through. Before stepping inside, he scanned their surroundings one last time, ensuring they remained undetected. Satisfied that they were alone, he motioned for Yarran to follow. Together, they crossed the grassy area behind the station, and in the distance, Hobbs spotted a cluster of large, bright green Asparagus Ferns growing wildly. Among them were the unmistakable small red berries he had seen at the crime scene.

The stables were full, and the horses were all sleeping soundly. However, as Hobbs approached, he inadvertently stepped on a twig, causing some of the horses to startle awake with frightened snorts.

'Shhhh,' Hobbs whispered toward the restless horses. 'It's okay, it's okay.'

He headed straight for the pen on the far right of the stables, where the Asparagus Fern was overgrown and encroaching into the pen. Scanning the ground both inside and outside the pen, he noticed hundreds of the tiny berries scattered about, many of them flattened from being stepped on.

He noticed the large Palomino in the pen staring back at him with its large, glassy eyes. Carefully, he unlatched the wooden door and stepped inside, gently patting the horse along its muscular body.

'Check the other pens, Yarran, and tell me if there are berries scattered on the ground like this one.'

Yarran nodded and stared at the pen to the left and worked his way down the line.

'Please don't be true,' Hobbs whispered to himself.

As Hobbs crouched down and examined each of the large hooves, it was even darker inside the stables. The front legs were clear, but it was what he found on the rear left leg of the horse that made his blood run cold.

Yarran returned and shook his head. 'No. This one is the only pen with fallen berries. The fern hasn't spread beyond this one.'

'Yarran, look here.'

As Yarran crouched down alongside Hobbs and looked at the left hoof, he noticed it too. In the dim light of the stables, there was no mistaking the two small droplets of dried blood on a white patch of hair on the back of its hoof.

Yarran's touch was gentle yet firm as he ran his hands over the horse's legs and up to its large body. He circled the horse, examining every inch of its form while keeping it calm and still.

'There's no sign of any injury at all. This blood has come from something else.'

'I feel like my suspicions have come true,' Hobbs said. 'This horse was at the crime scene.'

'It could be from something else.'

'I won't take that chance. With the same berries found here and the crime scene, now the blood. I'm now convinced.'

'Who rides him?' Yarran asked.

Hobbs rummaged through the pouches on the saddle at the side of the stable and found some old papers and a notebook. Reading the name of the owner on the front page, he let out a sigh and ran his fingers through his hair, feeling a mix of frustration and determination.

'Constable Victor Bryson.'

FORTY-ONE

'Henry, are you sure?' Walsh asked in a panic, still jolted awake by the rushed and noisy entry Hobbs and Yarran made into their cottage.

'Yes, positive. It all fits now. I don't know Constable Bryson very well, but from what I have seen, he's arrogant and much too confident. He is of a low rank in the force, so he seeks his urge for control and dominance elsewhere.'

'To suggest police involvement in these murders is very serious. Where do we even take this?'

'I'm not sure yet, but what I know is we can't trust anyone.'

'You need to be sure before we go any further,' Walsh said, as though issuing a stern warning.

Walsh walked over to the kitchen sink and splashed cool water on his face. He looked out through the window. The orange glow of the rising sun cast a weak light through the house. He sat down at the round kitchen table with Hobbs and Yarran and rubbed his head wearily.

'Run me through it again.'

'I found the berry at the crime scene. As Yarran said, it was too far up in the mountains for this species to be growing berries this large.'

Yarran nodded in support.

'We then snuck into the stables of the police station here and sure enough, the berries matched. Then if I wasn't already sure, there were trace amounts of blood on the hoof of Bryson's horse.'

'And you are sure it is his horse?'

'Yes, his notebook was in the saddle next to the horse. Everything else then fits. Shooting me with the conical round. It comes from a Pattern 1853 Enfield, which the police carry.'

'That's true, and I also carry one, Henry, so do many others. It is a widely used rifle.'

'Explain the berry and the blood, then? Plus, who knows the schedules of the gold deliveries? Police. You said so yourself.'

'Maybe he attended the scene himself in response to the murders?'

'All way up the mountains? No chance. Plus Noland said the local police from Springwood responded, he mentioned nothing about Penrith police.'

Walsh sighed. 'Everything you're saying may fit. However, we need more. I don't want to bend evidence to fit a hypothesis. We need to be very careful. The political repercussions could be enormous if we started accusing police officers with insufficient evidence.'

'I understand, but I'm not wrong.'

'I should speak with Palmer,' Walsh said. 'I need to find out where Bryson was at the time of the murders.'

'No. We know there are three involved. Besides, I saw Palmer at the station before we went in. What was he doing there at such an odd hour? We cannot trust anyone.'

'Well, after you left, I spoke with him before I went to bed. He told me about the fresh murders, two gold guards who apparently volunteered to make the trip for extra pay. Daniel Fleming and Walker Pullman, both veteran gold guards. They were slaughtered in the exact same manner as the others, but surely you can't suspect him. I have known him for years.'

'Until I prove otherwise, I will suspect all of them.'

'This is big, Henry. Really big.'

Hobbs and Yarran remained silent, giving Walsh the space he needed to process everything.

'Okay,' he said, slowly nodding. 'Okay. But we do this carefully. If you are wrong, I don't want anyone to know you were investigating police officers. I will not jump to any conclusions, but do what you need to do. Follow him and see what you find. You'll need to be careful. Noland doesn't know you are still looking into this. He is already on edge and this will set him off, especially if we point fingers at his men. You'll have to follow this up on your own. I'll try to stay here for as long as I can, but I won't be able to stay for more than a day or two without raising suspicions.'

'Yarran and I will watch Bryson for a while. We will take care. No one will know we are following him. Trust me.'

'I do, Henry. I do. Just be careful.'

Hobbs nodded. 'I'll need your rifle, James.'

Hobbs swiftly established an optimal surveillance position with Yarran in the dense foliage elevated behind the Penrith police station. Their strategy was simple: remain concealed and observe the stables. Bryson would inevitably retrieve his horse for patrol duty at some point during the day. Despite having a defined jurisdiction, it still covered a sizeable area, and Bryson's patrol did not involve heavy supervision. Nevertheless, Hobbs was ready to extend his surveillance efforts beyond those geographical boundaries, especially if Bryson ventured deeper into the mountains.

Hobbs checked Walsh's rifle for a second time and placed it on the ground by his side. 'Yarran, I am going to rely on you to track Bryson should we need to follow him. We can't get so close that he will see or hear us. Chances are he is probably both irritable and cautious given his involvement, so he may be hyper-vigilant. Do you think you can do that?'

'A heavy horse like his, definitely.'

'Good. If we need to follow him on horseback, we just take the first one we find tied up at a local store. We can worry about returning it later. For now, we wait.'

Hobbs leaned against a sturdy trunk, settling onto a cushion of soft foliage, bracing for an extended stay. Their concealment was effective; they could remain undisturbed for as long as necessary. Perched atop a modest elevation, their vantage point afforded a partial view, sufficient to detect any activity around the stables. Exhaustion gnawed at him, yet determination surged through his veins, keeping weariness at bay. He was acutely aware that his body would soon succumb to fatigue, having endured nearly twenty-four hours without rest, and he knew he would soon have no choice but to sleep.

'We could sleep in shifts,' Yarran offered, as though sensing Hobbs' fatigue. 'You should go first.'

Hobbs nodded appreciatively and settled himself further into the base of the tree.

'How are your wounds healing?' Yarran asked, seeing Hobbs wince and touch his stomach as he reclined.

'Still hurts, but with each day, I'm feeling better.'

'Good. Try to rest. I will wake you if I see anything.'

The midday sun stirred Hobbs from his sleep several hours later, its rays piercing through the overhanging branches that had provided some shelter. It took a moment for his eyes to adjust to the brightness, but the brief respite offered by sleep was a welcome refreshment.

'Okay, Yarran, it's your turn to rest,' Hobbs offered.

'Thank you. I still have not seen anything.'

Hobbs maintained his vigil while Yarran slept, and for several hours, there was no sign of activity. He wondered if he had missed something, but the occasional movement of the Asparagus Fern at the edge of the stables suggested that Bryson's horse was still inside, tugging at the leaves.

As the day neared its end, frustration set in from the tedious watch. Yarran woke up, and Hobbs briefed him on the lack of any significant developments.

'Why do you think he has not left for the day?' Yarran asked.

'I'm not sure. Perhaps he was simply managing the cells today or doing paperwork rather than being assigned a patrol.'

'Does that happen?'

'Yes, an officer needs to remain at the police station during the day, and perhaps it was Bryson's turn to...hang on, what's this?' Hobbs said, suddenly alert.

Yarran poked his head up and looked at the stables.

'Not there, look just to the left, that's Bryson, I'm sure.'

The figure was hard to discern from their vantage point because of the distance, but Hobbs recognised the familiar gait and frame. It was Bryson. He was walking along the side of the station, onto the street to the left, and heading in their direction.

'What is he doing?'

'He must have finished for the day,' Hobbs said.

'He won't see us here,' Yarran said, 'but he may see movement, so we need to stay still.'

Hobbs and Yarran remained crouched in the bushes, hidden from Bryson's view, as he strolled past them. He seemed entirely unaware of their presence.

'Let's follow him,' Hobbs said. 'Give him a head start and then let's see where he goes.'

After what felt like an hour but was probably less than a minute, Hobbs and Yarran emerged from the bushes and trailed behind Bryson as he walked through the bustling town centre. The streets were teeming with activity, mostly men finishing work for the day or heading to the pub. Despite attracting some attention due to their unusual pairing, Bryson continued forward without looking back. They maintained a distance of about one hundred yards as they observed Bryson turning into a narrow street behind the local school.

As they reached the intersection, they nearly lost sight of Bryson until Yarran found him in the distance. He was disappearing into a small, white cottage about halfway down the street. It blended seamlessly with the other houses along the road, all single-storied structures with spacious front gardens enclosed by low wooden fences.

'It must be his house,' Hobbs said.

'Do we wait here?'

'Absolutely. But we can't get too close.'

'Where should we stay?'

'Near the intersection. It doesn't matter if we don't see him leaving the house, so long as we see him enter the town centre.'

'What if he goes the other way?'

'I doubt it. Statistically, covering the town centre is our best option. Bryson doesn't know we are following him, nor would he believe he is a suspect. I expect he will continue his usual business. Can you find us a suitable spot to hide?'

Yarran walked back to the intersection and returned a short time later. 'Perhaps the chapel just down the street? If we stay behind the bushes down the side of the building, we will see the top of Bryson's street. No one should be there at night.'

'Perfect.'

Their spot among the overgrown hedges at the side of the chapel provided ideal cover. It was quiet, and judging by the state of the grounds, no one had ventured down the side of the building in quite some time. They settled in as comfortably as possible and waited.

For another hour, they continued to wait, and just as darkness settled in, they spotted Bryson approaching the top of the street.

He stopped, looked around for a moment, and waited.

Even from a distance, Hobbs could tell Bryson looked irritable. He paced in circles, his movements restless and agitated.

He was waiting for something.

FORTY-TWO

Victor Bryson stood on the street, his demeanour tense and impatient. He had shed his dark police uniform for more casual attire—denim pants secured by suspenders and a loose-fitting grey shirt. An intriguing addition was the brown leather messenger bag he clutched, its weight evident by the way it sagged at the bottom. He shifted the bag from one hand to the other, his movements betraying his growing restlessness.

In the dimly lit street, Bryson's impatience was palpable. He fidgeted nervously, his hand darting into his pocket to retrieve a pocket watch. With a quick glance at its face, he hastily stowed it away again, his eyes scanning the empty road with growing unease.

'What do you think?' Yarran whispered, still keeping an eye locked on Bryson.

'I don't know, let's wait and see what happens.'

In the distance, Hobbs noticed a broad, male figure approaching, moving swiftly but stealthily through the shadows.

Cloaked in all black, the figure's identity remained a mystery to Hobbs, shrouded in the veil of the night. A heated exchange ensued between him and Bryson, their gestures animated and wild, punctuated by furious pointing at the hefty bag clutched in Bryson's hand. As they spoke, Hobbs observed the newcomer's stature, his build echoing that of Bryson, however his hair darker and blended seamlessly with his attire. Though his anticipation grew, Hobbs remained composed, his body taut with tension, his gaze unwavering as he awaited the crucial moment when the man would turn and reveal himself.

'Come on, turn around,' Hobbs whispered.

As Bryson's agitation mounted, he shifted restlessly on the spot, his grip tightening on the bag he held. Gesturing emphatically, his accusatory finger singled out the figure clad in black. Hobbs watched intently, sensing the confrontation reaching a boiling point.

'Things look like they are getting heated,' Yarran said. 'Do you think this meeting has anything to do with the murders?'

'My gut tells me yes. Bryson has to be involved. I just wish we could get closer, but let's just see what happens.'

As the tension seemed to ease between Bryson and the man in black, they drew closer, their voices hushed. Hobbs strained to catch a glimpse of the man's face, but all he could discern was the back of his head. Despite the urge to get a better vantage point, he remained rooted in his hiding spot, well aware of the risk of detection or disturbing the pair.

A moment later Bryson strode away, and the man in black followed, but not before casting a scrutinising glance down the deserted street, granting Hobbs a fleeting glimpse of his face.

'Oh, God,' he said.

'You know who he is?'

'Yes. It's Gerald Davidson. Dammit. Constable Gerald Davidson. Bryson's partner. This is worse than I thought.'

GOOD LUCK

The message written in blood on the gold carriage suddenly became even more chilling.

'You really think both officers would be involved?' Yarran asked.

'It's beginning to look that way. When I first met them, they just seemed a little strange to me. Cocky and overconfident. But also young and naïve. I never would have suspected this, though.'

'Should we go back and tell James?'

'No. We don't have time. Come on, let's give them a head start and then we will follow them to see where they go. Something is happening tonight and I have a feeling that it must be connected to the murders. They were too tense and agitated for this to be a social meeting.'

Hobbs and Yarran maintained their silence, crouched in hiding, observing Bryson and Davidson as they strode down the long, dark street. Once the two men disappeared from view, Yarran cautiously peeked over the rough bush that had concealed them, now leaving them exposed at the side of the chapel.

'I can see them in the distance, about two hundred yards away. They have quickened their pace.'

'Let's go. Stay on the other side of the road and don't get too close.'

They moved swiftly and quietly, maintaining a close watch on Bryson and Davidson. They used the cover of darkness to their advantage, staying close to the shadows of residential fence lines and beneath the canopy of overhanging trees which obscured the moonlight.

Bryson and Davidson pressed on in silence, their steps quick and agitated. As they arrived at the edge of a sprawling intersection, marking the transition from the urban to the rural landscape of Penrith, they paused briefly.

'You left me waiting too long,' Bryson said. 'We needed to get rid of this gold long ago.'

'Well, we are doing it now, aren't we?' Davidson replied.

'I'm thinking even old Arthur is going to catch onto us soon,' Bryson said.

'He probably already knows, but the greedy old geezer wouldn't care. Anyway, if he so much as hints at saying anything about us, I'll slash his throat. Besides, he has plenty to lose should he slip his tongue.

'What's he giving us today?' Bryson asked.

'I already spoke to him in advance. Told him we will have two hundred ounces for today, with more to come later. He'll pay us out at fifteen pounds an ounce. This leaves a huge profit for him so don't worry about his allegiance, we are making him very wealthy too.'

Bryson's ears twitched suddenly. He turned around sharply but found nothing in the darkness. 'What was that?' Did you hear something?'

'No,' Davidson shrugged.

'Behind us.'

They both turned around, but all they could discern were the outlines of trees swaying gently in the breeze.

'I thought I heard something,' Bryson said cautiously.

Davidson shook his head. 'You're just on edge. We both are. Even with Walsh and his convict mate now off the case, things are still heating up.'

'No, you're right. We're fine. No one, especially now, will even get close enough to us to suspect anything. Now come on, we're running late.'

As Bryson and Davidson resumed their walk, Hobbs and Yarran stealthily emerged from a long shadow, maintaining a safe distance as they continued their pursuit. Transitioning from the sheltered confines of the town, they now found themselves exposed in the open expanse of rural Penrith. Where once tightly packed homes offered ample cover, they were now traversing sparse fields with little concealment.

'That was close,' Hobbs said. 'Wherever they are going, though, they must be near. There isn't much out here.'

'Just farms, mostly sheep and wheat in these parts,' Yarran whispered. Yarran's long, black hair glistened with sweat as they moved cautiously, his hand wiping his damp forehead before taking a deep breath. Hobbs pressed forward, focused on their pursuit. He kept Walsh's rifle low by his side, its barrel tracking with each step of his right leg.

'There, look there, they've gone down a long road leading to a farmhouse,' Yarran said.

Hobbs narrowed his focus, tracking Bryson and Davidson as they traversed the long, winding dirt road toward the isolated house. When the coast was clear, he and Yarran stealthily trailed behind, hugging the edges of the road to minimise their visibility.

The farmhouse stood as a small yet well-maintained cottage, painted in a subdued shade of off-yellow. Nestled at the heart of an expansive plot of land, it sat approximately three hundred yards from the main road, linking the town centre to the local farming district. As they approached, the only source of light visible seemed to emanate from the front of the cottage, however as they drew nearer, a barn behind the house came into view, its double doors flung wide open. Within it, a blazing fire pit cast its warm glow, illuminating the interior of the barn.

The immediate vicinity of the house, despite the rugged dirt road they had crept along, bordered by tall grass and thriving wheat, was meticulously groomed by the homeowners. A neatly trimmed patch of grass encircled it, while vibrant rose bushes and assorted colourful plants adorned the front.

Hobbs and Yarran stopped, pausing at a safe distance of about fifty yards from the farmhouse and the open barn adjacent to it, hiding within a patch of tall wheat to the side of the road. Unlike the cottage, the barn, constructed from weathered wood and coloured a deep brown, appeared neglected with the paint peeling from the sides. Inside, old tools and cast iron farming machinery cluttered the hay-strewn floor. Within the barn, Hobbs watched from afar as Bryson and Davidson conversed with a man of approximately sixty years. Short and stocky, he sported a near-perfectly round stomach that strained against a dark leather apron, the length of his greying beard tucked neatly into it.

'Let's see if there's a side window we can peek through. I need to see more of what's going on inside,' Hobbs said.

Silently, they crept diagonally through the dense grass and tall wheat stalks, inching closer to the side of the barn.

FORTY-THREE

Arthur Henderson had been expecting Bryson and Davidson. As they arrived, he preoccupied himself with adding coal to a roaring fire beneath a large, heavy cast-iron bowl.

'You're late,' Henderson said, setting down another iron bowl down beside the fire. The heat inside the barn was intense, and Bryson and Davidson wiped their already sweating brows as they approached him.

'Never mind that,' Bryson spat with a tone of hostility. 'All the gold is here regardless of our timing.'

Arthur Henderson lived a life of relative solitude. His wife kept away from his barn, where he conducted most of his work. While he tended to his wheat fields by day, his profits barely covered his expenses. However, it was during the gold rush that he found his fortune. Isolated on his farm, he clandestinely smelted and refined gold from illegal traders, charging a percentage fee for his services. He then sold the cleaned gold pieces to jewellers and investors across Sydney. Despite the Royal Mint's dominance in the gold market, high taxes and limited accessibility pushed individuals like Henderson to find lucrative loopholes. Henderson understood that gold possessed the remarkable power to evoke primal greed, turning even the most dignified individuals into creatures of avarice. He had no trouble finding eager buyers willing to pay for his services, offering them a substantial discount compared to the Mint while still securing a handsome profit for himself.

Bryson remained puzzled about where Henderson's profits disappeared to. Henderson himself appeared disheveled, often emitting an odour of oil and sweat, while his unkempt beard gave off a putrid smell. The barn, where Henderson conducted his business, was in complete disarray. Bryson and Davidson had never entered the main farmhouse, as Henderson insisted on keeping his business dealings and clients strictly private. Despite the unassuming appearance of the small house from the outside, Bryson couldn't help but wonder if Henderson was hoarding mountains of gold and money hidden or buried somewhere on the property.

Bryson opened the weighty satchel he carried and started withdrawing handfuls of pure, unrefined gold sourced from the latest murder in the Mountains.

'Set it down there and let's have a look,' Henderson said, wiping his greasy hands on his dirty apron.

Bryson deposited the gold onto an aged wooden workbench next to a set of scales and small metal weights.

'Fifteen pounds per ounce,' Bryson said.

'Yes, as we agreed. Set it on the scales and let's see what we have.'

Hobbs and Yarran navigated through the tall grass and wheat, their path guided by the roaring fire emanating from the distant barn. As they approached, they located a lengthy, grimy window roughly midway along the barn's exterior. With caution, they crept toward it. Although the dirt on the window provided some concealment, it also obscured their view. After careful inspection, Hobbs identified a small, clear patch in the bottom left corner of the window, while Yarran found a similar space in the bottom right corner, closest to the barn's entrance.

Despite some obstruction from large machinery and a thick wooden column positioned in the centre of the barn, Hobbs managed to catch a glimpse of the scene inside. His observation confirmed his earlier deductions. Inside the barn, Davidson stood with his arms folded, while Bryson meticulously placed lumps of gold onto a balancing scale. An elderly man adjusted the other end of the scale with weights, jotting down notes on a piece of paper.

Hobbs and Yarran looked at each other and nodded.

Hobbs continued observing silently, planning to tail Bryson and Davidson once they left the farm and report their movements to Walsh upon their return. They would then plan their coordinated arrest of the pair. Dealing with the old farmer could wait; Hobbs suspected there was likely more stolen gold hidden on the property. The Royal Mint and the government would likely want to personally prosecute the man responsible for unloading the stolen gold.

After a moment, it seemed that all the gold had been weighed and recorded. The old man began placing the gold lumps into metal trays and then made his way to another workbench near a roaring fire in a deep pit.

From his window vantage point, Hobbs strained to keep track of them as they moved behind one of the large wooden pillars in the centre of the barn, obstructing his view. He attempted to shift his position along the window, searching for a clearer angle, but the limited visibility hampered his efforts. Then, as he adjusted his footing, a thick twig snapped loudly under his boot.

In that instant, his stomach churned and his heart leaped into his throat as he realised the men inside had turned their attention toward the window.

Hobbs swiftly ducked below the windowsill, pressing a hand firmly over his mouth to stifle any inadvertent noise. Meanwhile, Yarran crouched down on his side of the window, shooting a sharp glance to the left as his eyes widened with a mix of fear and frustration at the unexpected noise. Hobbs berated himself for his carelessness, cursing silently as he hoped fervently that the men inside couldn't spot them amidst the darkness and grime coating the window. Holding his breath, he anxiously waited for a moment, hoping that they hadn't discovered them. Hobbs cautiously raised himself up and peered through his clear patch in the window. Straining to see, he scanned the interior of the barn, but there was no sign of anyone inside. Carefully turning his head to get a better view, he continued to search, yet still found no trace of the men inside.

Suddenly, Hobbs heard a horrifying sound that sent a shiver down his spine. Yarran had let out a startled gasp as Bryson's powerful arm yanked him away from the windowsill just as Hobbs turned around. Despite his attempts to resist, Bryson's strength was overwhelming and all Hobbs could do was watch Yarran's body tense with fear as a six-inch blade was pressed against his throat.

FORTY-FOUR

With his heart pounding in his chest, Hobbs pushed through the surge of fear and urgency. He couldn't afford to falter now. In a swift motion, he raised his rifle, aiming the barrel directly at Bryson's head from a distance of fifteen feet.

'Tough shot from there,' Bryson spat as he tucked most of his face behind Yarran. Davidson and the elderly farmer stood beside Bryson. Their expressions hardened as they focused their gaze on Hobbs, their stance suggesting readiness for any potential threat.

Hobbs recognised the gravity of the situation. With Davidson likely complicit in the murders and the old farmer standing beside him, they were all aligned against him. The odds were not in his favour, and with Yarran being held at knifepoint, it was far from an ideal situation.

'Drop the knife,' Hobbs said as calmly as possible. Hobbs drew upon his experience in handling similar tense situations. He understood that panicking or escalating the tension further would only make matters worse. As Bryson's thick forearm tightened around Yarran, Hobbs saw his face turn red and his breathing became laboured. He winced as the sharp knife was now being pushed harder against his neck, drawing a small amount of blood. Hobbs was then met with a silent yet desperate plea for help from Yarran's gaze.

'I've done it before. I'll do it again,' Bryson said.

Memories of the masked men, their failed arrest attempt, and the brutal violence came flooding back to Hobbs. Recollections of Edmund Miller's fate and his own near-death experience fuelled a potent mixture of rage and fear coursing through him as he tightened his grip on his rifle. Confronted with two of the murderers, he couldn't shake the nagging question: who was the third? Could it be the farmer standing ominously nearby? Despite the torrent of thoughts flooding his mind, he knew he had to push them aside and focus on one thing: ensuring Yarran's safety above all else.

Hobbs swallowed and then forced himself to speak calmly. 'I don't doubt that for a second. I know about the murders of the gold guards, the murder of Constable Miller and the attempted murder of myself, but if you kill Yarran now, you have nothing left to bargain with.'

'Why are you here?' Davidson yelled, pulling out his own knife, identical to the one currently held across Yarran's neck.

'We know all about you. Inspector Walsh knows too. We all know what you've done, and it is not just us who know you are here,' Hobbs lied. 'It's over.'

Davidson's eyes twitched and his face contorting with panic. Yet even in his agitated state, he looked unstably dangerous.

'Don't listen to him,' Bryson said. "If that were true, they would have already arrested us.'

'Drop your knives now,' Hobbs repeated.

Davidson's breathing quickened and Hobbs sensed he was becoming increasingly flustered.

'He's lying,' Bryson said.

Hobbs now detected a weakness in Davidson, but kept his rifle pointed at the exposed part of Bryson's head. He knew he could never make the shot, but Yarran was frightened. For his sake, Hobbs kept him at the centre of his attention, but he knew he needed to change the status quo and remove Davidson from the situation. He would have to deal with Bryson later.

'Although, we don't know about you, Constable Davidson,' Hobbs said. 'This all comes as a surprise to us here. We know you have not killed anyone. It's Bryson we are after. Just drop the knife and leave. You too, farmer. This doesn't concern you either. Both of you, just walk away now.'

For a moment, silence hung heavy in the air. Hobbs hoped the glimmer of freedom would be enough to shift the balance of power from a three-against-one confrontation to a more negotiable one-on-one situation.

Davidson continued to tremble and gave a quick glance toward Bryson.

'Look, Bryson is the one I have my gun pointed at. Not you, Davidson. Walk away son, this doesn't need to concern you.'

'Don't call me that. I'm The Banshee. The Banshee, got it?'

Hobbs shrugged, pondering the meaning behind the odd title, but not wanting to agitate him further, nodded. 'Alright, Banshee, listen to what I'm saying. You can walk away right now.'

'Shut up. Just shut up and let me think,' Davidson yelled, his face still twitching erratically.

Hobbs thought he had him. He knew he was moments away from completely dropping his guard and allowing the power to shift in his favour.

'Banshee!' Bryson yelled. 'He's tricking you!'

Suddenly, Davidson did something unexpected, plunging the already tense situation into further chaos.

He released a guttural, anguished scream and in a desperate move, he seized the old farmer by his apron, using him as a human shield. With a vice-like grip, Davidson held the man in a chokehold from behind, pressing the knife menacingly against his throat. The farmer whimpered in terror as Davidson's firm hold began to cut his air supply.

'*Shit,*' Hobbs thought. The situation had escalated dramatically, leaving Hobbs facing two desperate and deranged men, each holding a hostage at knifepoint. In a matter of seconds, he knew he had lost any control over the situation he thought he once had.

Hobbs felt the weight of the situation bearing down on him. These were ruthless men, driven by violence, and he knew they wouldn't hesitate to kill. The standoff had shifted, leaving him with little leverage. With only one shot in his Enfield rifle, he couldn't afford to miss. The reality of the close-range encounter loomed large in his mind. In this scenario, a knife had the advantage over a firearm. As he pondered his options, each potential course of action seemed to lead to a darker outcome than the last.

Hobbs maintained his focus, his rifle steady as he kept it trained on Bryson. Every breath became shallow, his attention solely on ensuring Yarran's safety, despite the perilous situation.

Davidson's grin sent a shiver down Hobbs' spine as their eyes locked in a chilling exchange. 'Time for you to go, Henry Hobbs. You failed,' he said.

'I'm not going anywhere until you let Yarran go.'

'You have no leverage here,' Bryson said. 'So here's what's going to happen. You drop the gun and maybe we will make this end quickly.'

Hobbs maintained the steady aim of his rifle, but he felt the strain of its weight bearing down on his tired arms, and his muscles ached with the effort. He needed to do something very soon.

'You enjoy killing don't you?' Hobbs asked, thinking of anything to avert their attention.

With the situation in Bryson and Davidson's control, their unnerving smiles widened, revealing a disturbing glimpse into the sinister pleasure they derived from the standoff.

'It's wonderful,' Bryson said. 'Having a man's life in your hands and ending it with a swift and easy slash of a blade. You could never understand.'

'I understand better than you think. I can tell you why you enjoy killing so much. Have you not wondered where the thrill comes from?'

'It doesn't matter!' Davidson snapped, tightening his hold on the farmer. The old whimpered again as the knife pushed further into his neck.

'Are you sure?' Hobbs asked, softening his tone. 'It really is quite fascinating. I thought you would like to at least know that. You see, in London, I have interviewed many people like yourselves, and I have found many interesting facts about men who kill.'

Bryson's grin quickly faded, replaced by an expression of intrigue, his eyes narrowing as he studied Hobbs intently.

'Shall I tell you?' Hobbs asked.

'Go on then, enlighten me,' Bryson's voice cut through the tension, his face inching away from the cover provided by Yarran. As he did so, he eased the pressure on Yarran's throat, a subtle relaxation that Hobbs saw him notice.

In a split second, Yarran sprang into action, lifting his arms and forcefully pushing Bryson's knife-holding hand away from his throat. With swift agility, he dropped his weight to the ground, breaking free from Bryson's grasp.

Hobbs, poised and alert, wasted no time. With precision, he squeezed the trigger, sending a single round straight into Bryson's forehead. Bryson crumpled to the ground, dead in an instant.

Davidson, in a frenzy of panic, slashed the throat of the old farmer and shoved him to the ground, where he lay, bleeding out rapidly. With his only leverage gone, Davidson found himself standing in front of Yarran and Hobbs, his knife still dripping with blood.

'You're out of options, Davidson. Drop it.' Hobbs said. His expression darkened as he glanced briefly at the lifeless farmer at his feet. Though a fleeting sorrow crossed his face, he knew there was no time to dwell on it. Davidson remained armed and dangerous, and Hobbs had spent his only shot.

Hobbs reacted swiftly as Davidson charged towards him, screaming with the knife raised high. With a quick crouch, Hobbs brought the butt of his rifle crashing into Davidson's stomach, causing him to double over in pain, winded.

The fight, however, was not over. Davidson, acting on desperation, seized a moment of strength and lunged at Hobbs, driving his body forward and tackling him to the ground, still clutching the knife tightly.

Hobbs found himself in a dangerous position, with Davidson now on top of him, straddling his body. Hobbs tried to hold his arms down, but Davidson's strength was apparent as he wrestled free and raised the knife above his head, poised to strike. But Hobbs, determined and quick-thinking, reacted swiftly. As the blade descended, he grabbed Davidson's wrist, blocking the strike and applying pressure to immobilise him. With a forceful punch to Davidson's jaw with his free hand, Hobbs aimed to disrupt his balance, but it was ineffective. Davidson remained on top of him, still intent on driving the knife into Hobbs' chest.

Yarran made his move, seizing Bryson's knife from the floor beside his lifeless body. With a sudden burst of speed and determination, he drove the blade forcefully into the middle of Davidson's back. As the knife punctured his body, he howled in agony. With wide eyes of shock and pain, his hold on Hobbs weakened, allowing him to push Davidson away and get to his feet.

Hobbs swiftly kicked Davidson's knife out of reach, then took a deep breath before kneeling down and seizing him by the shirt. Blood trickled down the corners of Davidson's lips as he coughed, a twisted laughter bubbling from his throat.

'You have really got yourself into a mess here, Hobbs,' Davidson muttered in a pained choke.

'What do you mean?' Hobbs asked, shaking his weakened body. 'Who else is involved? The old farmer?'

Davidson's laughter echoed amidst the thick blood oozing from his mouth. His deranged eyes remained wide, but his complexion paled, and his breaths grew increasingly strained. Hobbs recognised the ominous signs: Davidson's time was running out.

'How's your stomach?' he smirked. 'I thought I killed you. Can't say the same for Miller.'

'Who else is involved?' Hobbs yelled, pulling harder on Davidson's shirt.

Grinning, Davidson coughed up more blood.

Hobbs struck Davidson across the face, but the strike only made him laugh and spit more blood down his chin. 'Who else is involved? There's a third. Tell me now!'

'You have no idea how far this goes,' Davidson said weakly. Hobbs watched as the grin faded from Davidson's face, replaced by a vacant stare. Still holding him by the shirt, Hobbs felt the life slip away from him until he took his last breath and went limp as the pool of blood continued to grow around him.

FORTY-FIVE

Hobbs rolled onto his back and drew three deep, slow breaths, trying to calm his racing heart. With a wary glance at the motionless form of Davidson lying beside him, he confirmed once more that the man was indeed dead. The six-inch blade remained firmly lodged between his shoulder blades.

Yarran stood over Hobbs and extended a hand, pulling him up to his feet. Hobbs gave him a grateful pat on the shoulder. 'Thank you, Yarran.'

'You saved my life, too. He was strong. I couldn't so much as wriggle free. Those things you said to them, about why they kill? Do you truly know the reason?'

'No. But I needed some way to distract them. I'm glad you caught on and found the opportune moment to give me the clean shot.'

'What about the farmer?'

Hobbs briefly glanced at the body of the old man, and then something occurred to him. 'Hold on a moment.'

Hobbs crouched down and opened Davidson's shirt. He pulled back the sleeve of his right arm. 'Nothing.'

'What do you mean?' Yarran asked.

'One of these men should have a gunshot wound on their upper right arm. Before I was stabbed, I shot one of them. Check the farmer, will you?'

Hobbs ran over to the body of Bryson and checked the same area. No gunshot wound.

'Anything?'

'No wound on the farmer's arm,' Yarran said. 'Are you sure the farmer wasn't involved? Maybe you missed when you fired.'

'No, I definitely hit him. Besides, at first, I thought the farmer might have been one of the three killers. I knew one was a larger, slower man, but it was something Davidson said that unsettled me.'

'What's that?'

'He said *you have no idea how far this goes.* I think the farmer was just someone they were offloading the stolen gold to. No. Whoever else is involved must be someone more than just a local farmer.'

'Henry, he was probably just taunting you. Probably the same reason Davidson wanted you to call him The Banshee.'

'He definitely was taunting me, but there has to be some truth behind it, and the injured man is not here.'

Hobbs stood back up and tried to clear his thoughts. 'Let's look through the barn.'

Hobbs and Yarran entered the barn through the open sliding doors, their footsteps echoing softly in the cavernous space. They searched the area, moving tools and inspecting various items scattered around. Hobbs's eyes fell upon the satchel bag Bryson had been carrying. It lay flat on a workbench next to a heap of dirty lumps of gold. He picked up the bag and examined it for any clues, but it was empty now, the gold already removed. With a sigh, he dropped the bag back onto the bench and continued his search, scanning the area for anything of significance. Meanwhile, Yarran occupied himself by sorting through an old toolbox nearby. The crackling fire in the large pit cast flickering shadows across the barn, illuminating several locked metal boxes scattered around its base.

'Yarran, pass me a hammer.'

Of the several hammers in the large metal toolbox he was searching through, Yarran handed Hobbs the heaviest one that appeared homemade with a solid cast iron head.

With a forceful swing, Hobbs shattered the hinge of one of the boxes, revealing its contents within. His eyes widened at the sight of piles of cash and small fabric bags neatly arranged inside. Digging through the stash, he uncovered several more bags similar in appearance and promptly emptied their contents onto the ground. The metallic clinks of small, shiny nuggets of gold echoed through the barn as they spilled across the floor. Upon closer inspection, Hobbs noticed the nuggets were meticulously cleaned and polished.

'This gold hasn't been recently mined. It has undergone refinement and cutting. Probably for sale to jewellers. My best guess is Bryson and Davidson used the farmer to swap their stolen gold for Pounds.'

'Which means the third killer is still at large?' Yarran said.

'Until I prove otherwise, yes.'

'So what do we do?'

'First, we need to tell James. Get these bodies taken away from here. Probably come back in the light of day and keep looking around for some more clues.'

'Without warning, a female voice screamed from the entry to the barn. 'Who are you?'

Hobbs and Yarran swiftly turned around, startled by the sudden presence of a woman. She appeared to be in her sixties, with short, greying hair, her chubby figure wrapped tightly in a dressing robe. In her hands, she held a small caliber long rifle.

'Madam, please put the gun down,' Hobbs said, raising his hands in surrender. 'We are with the police.'

'Police? A scruffy-looking Englishman and a ragged Aboriginal boy. You are thieves,' she spat. 'Where is Arthur?'

The realisation hit Hobbs: the woman before him was the farmer's wife. In the intensity of the standoff, he had failed to consider the possibility of other people living on the property.

'Madam, please, I am telling you the truth. My name is Henry Hobbs, and we are investigating several recent murders and the theft of gold. Now please, put the gun down. We don't want anyone hurt.'

'Where's Arthur? Where's my husband?' she demanded, now levelling the rifle directly at Hobbs and Yarran, alternating between the two in a hasty panic.

Hobbs took a step closer and kept his hands raised. 'I'm sorry to inform you, madam, but your husband is dead.' We did not think anyone else was here. I am very sorry.'

'What?' she said, trembling, as tears filled her eyes 'Arthur is dead? You killed him?'

'No, I did not kill him. Please lower the gun. Let's sit down and talk.'

The woman's sobs grew louder, her tears flowing freely as she struggled to comprehend the chaos unfolding before her. 'What did you do? What did you do?'

Hobbs continued to pace cautiously toward the woman with his hands still raised. 'No, please, we did not kill your husband, we...'

A gunshot suddenly rang out, sending a shock through the tense atmosphere of the barn. Reacting swiftly, Hobbs lunged forward, seizing the rifle from the woman's grasp. With a swift motion, he tossed the weapon to Yarran for safekeeping. The woman's emotional outburst continued and her sobs echoed throughout the barn as Hobbs subdued her, preventing any further attempts to resist. Eventually, exhaustion took over, and Hobbs released her as she collapsed to the ground.

'I heard a noise, so I came out.' she sobbed. 'What did you do to my Arthur?'

'We did nothing, I promise you. We are working with the police. There are two men just outside the barn, down the side near the wheat fields. They killed your husband. I am truly very sorry.'

She darted towards the side of the barn, with Hobbs and Yarran in pursuit. When she caught sight of her husband's lifeless form next to the bodies of Bryson and Davidson, she collapsed onto his chest and wailed.

Hobbs rushed over and helped her to her feet. She was covered in his blood and the colour was already drained from his face.

'Please, you don't want to see him like this,' he said. 'I will have a doctor come and take him away. Let's get you inside so you can sit and rest.'

She remained unresponsive, and Hobbs gently supported her weight as he guided her toward the farmhouse. She sobbed heavily, her gaze continually returning to her husband's lifeless form, almost resisting Hobbs's efforts as she strained to rush back to him.

They eventually made their way through to the back door of the house, which opened into a small kitchen with a round wooden table in the centre of the room with fresh-cut flowers in a glass vase. Hobbs guided the woman to a chair, helping her sit as he settled opposite her. Yarran joined them, taking a seat beside Hobbs at the table.

'What is your name?' Hobbs asked.

'Eliza. Eliza Henderson,' she sobbed.

'Mrs Henderson, I am very sorry for your loss, but it is important I ask you some questions, okay? Was your husband involved in trading gold?'

'Gold? Heavens, no, you are mistaken. He is a farmer.'

'Did you recognise the other two men out by the barn?'

She shook her head firmly. 'No.'

Hobbs looked back at Yarran and rubbed his chin.

Mrs Henderson frowned, as though in deep thought, before changing her answer. 'Actually, wait a minute. I know them. Yes. Oh, God.'

'You know them?'

'Yes, they were police constables.'

'Yes, they were. Have they been here before?'

'A few times, I've seen them when I have been washing up in the kitchen, or tending to the front garden. They have visited Arthur in the barn. He never told me why they were here. I just assumed they were looking for lost livestock, or that Arthur had made some kind of theft report. We often have vagrants trespass our land as they head toward the gold mines out west. So why are they dead? What is going on here?'

'Mrs Henderson, those two police officers killed your husband. We believe they were selling him stolen gold.'

'Stolen gold? This is absurd. Arthur knows nothing about gold.'

'We believe he did. He had a secret trade on the side buying and selling gold and he had been dealing with these two police officers.'

'Impossible,' she said stubbornly.

'Mrs Henderson, some more police, and likely the Royal Mint will need to come back here and search the house and the barn.'

'I don't understand all of this. Why was Arthur killed?' As tears streamed down her cheeks, Eliza Henderson trembled with a mix of confusion and disbelief evident on her face.

'The men he was dealing with. The police officers. They felt threatened, and they panicked.'

Hobbs watched as she buried her head in her hands, the weight of her grief causing her entire body to trembling. It became quickly apparent she was unaware of the secret life her husband had led.

'Mrs Henderson, we need to go now and report this back to the police station. Is there anything you need?'

She continued to cry and refused to make eye contact.

'Please stay in the house for now. We will have the doctor stop by soon, then some police to make sure the barn area is cleaned as soon as possible. Again, I am very sorry for your loss.'

FORTY-SIX

H obbs and Yarran hurried down the dirt road, putting distance between themselves and the farmhouse. Despite the darkness, the faint glow of light still emanated from the fireplace by the front window of the small cottage. Hobbs shivered thinking about the bodies of the three men, dead and surrounded by pools of blood. Among them were two disgraced police officers.

'Are you sure you're okay?' Yarran asked as they reached the top of the street and made their way back toward the town centre.

'Fine. You?'

'I'm okay. It must have been very difficult speaking with the wife, though. Especially given police officers were responsible for her husband's murder.'

'It was. None of this was her fault, and although her husband was involved, she clearly was not. I do feel sorry for her and I expect she will never be whole again.'

'And you are certain the farmer was not involved in the murders?'

'Yes, I really think he was just buying and selling their gold. The way Davidson and Bryson disregarded him, and then slaughtered him. He was not part of their team. In saying that, he was not an innocent party. He played an important role and must have had some knowledge of how the gold was sourced. He dug his own grave.'

'But it still doesn't make your job any easier?'

'No, it does not. We should go straight to the house and tell James. We need to wake the doctor and have him attend the farm immediately and collect the bodies. Eliza Henderson should not have to see them there in the morning.'

Hobbs and Yarran quickened their pace, eager to return to the cottage. As they approached, it neared midnight, and the sudden sound of Hobbs bursting through the front doors roused Walsh from his sleep.

'What's going on?' Walsh asked, eyeing a wired Hobbs who was now pacing back and forth in the kitchen. Blood was drying on his hands and once white shirt. Equally jittery and covered in blood was Yarran, also pacing as he ran his fingers through his long hair.

'I was right, James. It was Bryson and Davidson.'

'What? What are you talking about?' Walsh muttered groggily as he rubbed his eyes.

'It was them. The murderers, we saw them trying to sell their stolen gold to an old farmer just outside of town.'

'You did?' Walsh asked frantically, suddenly wide awake and alert. 'And Davidson was also involved? Good God. What happened?'

Hobbs settled at the kitchen table and recounted every detail he and Yarran had witnessed, from Bryson's appearance at the top of their street to his encounter with Davidson, culminating in the tense standoff at the farmer's barn.

'Now all three are dead,' he added. 'We need Doctor Andrews to get there immediately and remove the bodies.'

'Are you both alright?' James asked, his body rigid, clearly still grappling with the events of the past several hours, most of which had unfolded while he had been sleeping peacefully.

'Fine, we are both fine. We did what we had to.'

'I can't believe it. And the farmer, was he involved?'

'Yes, but Yarran and I have discussed his involvement in the actual murders. None of them had a gunshot wound from when I fired on them, the farmer included. I don't believe he was involved in the murders, but I'm sure he at least knew of them.'

'I'll have to report this to Palmer.'

'No, James. We can't rule him out yet. We can't rule anyone out. Another killer is still out there.'

'What would you have me do? He needs to know. He will find out anyway when two of his constables are reported dead.'

Hobbs sighed. Walsh was right. They couldn't keep this quiet for long. 'Fine. But we speak with him together. At least if he's involved, we can gauge his reaction.'

'Fine. First, I will wake the doctor and then we will speak with Palmer.'

'James, tell him to be cautious. The farmer's wife is there, and she is understandably both distraught and very confused.'

'Understood. You both wash up and change your clothes. There's blood everywhere. Yarran, you can find something to wear in my room.'

'I'll meet you at Palmer's house in thirty minutes. Do not go in without me,' Hobbs said.

Walsh nodded. 'I still can't believe all this is happening.'

'Believe it, James. I imagine it will only get worse. I am still replaying the last words of Davidson. *You have no idea how far this goes.* We need to be careful.'

Hobbs made his way to the bathroom with a jug of cool water and filled the small porcelain basin. He peeled off his blood-stained shirt and dropped it onto the floor before splashing handfuls of cool water on his face and neck. The sensation was a relief. As he ran his fingers through his hair, blood trickled into the sink, forming a small pool at the bottom.

Hobbs surveyed his options among the three shirts Walsh had purchased for him upon his arrival in Sydney. One shirt was now stained with blood, another was torn to shreds from when he was stabbed and left for dead at the hands of Bryson, Davidson, and the elusive third person. This left him with the last shirt, which remained soiled with dirt and sweat despite a recent wash. With little choice, he selected the best of the three, the sweaty, dirt-stained shirt, and settled in the kitchen to await Yarran.

Yarran returned moments later, wearing one of Walsh's dark blue shirts, and settled at the table next to Hobbs.

'I think you should stay here, Yarran. try to get some rest. James and I will speak with Palmer alone. If he's involved, things could get messy.'

'I understand. Just come and find me if I can be of any help.'

Hobbs left the cottage and stationed himself outside the Penrith police station, positioned on the corner of the street where he could observe Palmer's house. Despite hoping Palmer wasn't involved, he remained anxious, troubled by Davidson's final re-marks.

You have no idea how far this goes,'

The words echoed in his mind, sending shivers down his spine.

A moment later, Hobbs saw Walsh jogging toward him.

'Doctor Andrews and his assistant are on the way to the farm. They will take the three bodies back to his practice tonight.'

'Good. Are you ready to speak with Palmer?'

'Yes, let's go.'

'James listen, I know he is your friend, but I need you to be prepared for the worst.'

FORTY-SEVEN

Walsh led the way as they walked through the front garden, enclosed by a well-kept, white picket fence bordering the property right next door to the station. Like their own rented cottage, Palmer's home was owned by the police, reserved exclusively for the town's sergeant. Considering the late hour, Palmer was probably asleep inside, and the curtains at the front of the house were pulled closed.

Hobbs prided himself on his ability to read others, but so far, he had determined Palmer to be a good and honourable man. Perhaps he had been out of the game for too long, or Palmer had successfully fooled him. Either way, he was about to find out.

Walsh knocked loudly on the door, but there was no answer.

'Sam, wake up, it's James Walsh.'

Walsh persisted with the knocking, and eventually Hobbs heard footsteps on creaking wooden floors. Palmer answered the door, dressed in a nightshirt and flannel pants. His eyes were bleary and red.

'What is it?' he asked. His tired voice sounded rough and deep.

'We need to talk,' Walsh said matter-of-factly.

'What's this all about?'

'Not here. Can we come inside?'

'My wife is asleep, James. This can't wait?'

'I'm afraid not.'

Palmer, though clearly disoriented, opened the door fully and welcomed Walsh and Hobbs inside. They trailed behind him through the hallway, passing several closed rooms until they reached the kitchen and dining area at the back of the house. Its layout mirrored that of the police cottage where Hobbs and Walsh were staying.

Seated around the small, round wooden table, Hobbs took the lead.

'Bryson and Davidson are dead,' he said.

'What?' Palmer replied, his expression shifting from sleepiness to alertness. Hobbs watched his every move, searching for any hint of a reaction.

He continued. 'They were two of the murderers we have been searching for. I followed them tonight with Yarran and saw them trying to sell off their gold.'

Palmer shook his head. 'I don't understand. Why did you...If Noland found out about...'

'I don't care about the local police politics right now. I had evidence to suggest Bryson was involved, so I followed him, and that's when he met up with Davidson. They turned a knife on Yarran and killed the very person they had been trading gold with. Davidson then tried to kill me.'

'This is outrageous. I can't believe what I am hearing now. They are dead?'

'Yes. But now we have another problem. There were three men involved in these murders. I saw them myself, masked by hessian sacks, yes, but there were three of them. We now have two dead. So who's the third?'

'You're asking me?'

'Yes,' Hobbs said, leaning further over the table and folding his hands together. Walsh remained silent while Palmer was becoming restless, but took a breath, composed himself and looked Hobbs in the eye.

'Mr Hobbs, are you asking me if I'm involved?'

Hobbs remained silent, holding Palmer's gaze steadily, waiting for further explanation or reaction.

Palmer slammed his hands on the table. 'How could you accuse me of something so terrible? There is no way I'm involved! I knew nothing of what Bryson and Davidson were doing. Are you sure you are correct? It just can't be.'

'I *am* correct, sergeant.'

Walsh finally spoke, taking a softer approach. 'Look, Samuel, help us out here. We are still looking for a third murderer. Now that we know two police officers were involved, we need to suspect everyone.'

'This is absurd,' Palmer grunted. He stood up and walked toward a wooden writing table at the back of the dining room. Hobbs stood up quickly and tensed his body, prepared for a physical confrontation.

'Calm down, Mr Hobbs, here look at this.' Palmer flicked through a pile of paperwork on the writing table and handed him a piece of paper.

Hobbs scrutinised the document meticulously. It was a police report penned by Palmer, detailing an incident he had responded to one evening after his shift. The report detailed a conversation Palmer had with a local farmer along the banks of the Nepean River, who had reported the theft of two sheep.

'This man came into the police station to make a report of livestock theft. You can see on my report I have signed and dated it on the same day Constable Miller was murdered. Also, look at the farmer's statement. Signed and dated the same. Ask him if you like. I was not anywhere near the Mountains.'

Hobbs resumed his seat, reading the report again before passing it to Walsh. Palmer returned to his seat and folded his arms. He looked bitter. 'Satisfied?'

'No,' Hobbs said.

Palmer rose quickly, slapping his hands furiously on the table. 'No? What is the matter with you two? How could you still suspect me?'

'Show me your right shoulder.'

'I beg your pardon? You come into my home in the middle of the night, suggesting I am involved in these murders. I show you proof I was not, and now this?'

'Your right shoulder, show me. I shot the third man in the shoulder. Now show me yours.'

'I don't believe this,' Palmer grunted, clearly growing more agitated. He pulled his nightshirt up to his neck, revealing an injury-free shoulder.

'There. No gunshot wound. Can you lower your suspicions now before this becomes beyond offensive and absurd?'

Hobbs paused a moment before answering. He then nodded his head. 'Okay.'

'Okay?'

'Yes, okay, Sergeant Palmer. We are clearly looking for someone else. I see that now. I apologise for any offence, but I needed to be sure.'

'Sorry, Sam,' Walsh said. His face turned red as he handed back the livestock theft report to Palmer.

'I am sure a man such as yourself can understand why we needed to ask these questions.' Hobbs said.

Palmer shook his head and looked directly at Walsh. 'You should have trusted me, James. We have known each other for a long time. I never would have done something like this. I still cannot believe Bryson and Davidson were involved. They were often brash and overconfident, but to commit these murders? I never would have suspected them.'

'You know them better than we do. Is there anyone they associate with often? Someone you do not trust or know very well?' Hobbs asked.

'No. I mean they go out together on their patrols, and given the large area we cover, there is a level of autonomy and trust extended to all my constables, but I have never received a complaint about them or seen them with someone I do not know.'

'Davidson wanted to be called The Banshee,' Hobbs added. 'Have you heard this nickname before?'

Palmer shook his head. 'No. Banshee? Never.' He stood up and fetched a glass of water from the kitchen. He drained the glass and leaned on the kitchen bench. 'This is terrible. Bryson and Davidson?'

Hobbs and Walsh nodded. For the second time that evening, Hobbs recounted everything that happened at the Henderson farm, including the examination of the men's arms and the missing gunshot wound.

Palmer closed his eyes and rubbed his head. 'News is going to travel fast. This is going to be devastating. I always thought they were good, competent officers. They spent a great deal of time together and they would be absent for prolonged periods, but that was normal for all my constables. I never would have thought they could do something like this.'

'The Bryson and Davidson I saw tonight were dangerous and reckless men. Whatever you thought you knew about them was all a lie.'

'I am going to have to send for Noland immediately. The Chief Inspector needs to know about this. I would prefer he heard it as soon as possible from one of his own men before the news made its way to his office.'

'I'd like to speak with him too,' Walsh said.

Palmer winced. 'I don't think he would be happy to see you after your last meeting.'

'Sergeant, two police officers have been murdering people up and down the mountains and they are now dead. He will need all the help he can get, so let me worry about Noland. The fact we are still here and prepared to continue our investigation with tenacity will probably come as a relief now.'

'So, what do we do now?' Palmer asked.

Hobbs stood up. 'Where did Bryson and Davidson live? I need to search their homes.'

'Davidson technically lives with his mother and younger sister not far from here, but I believe he spends much of his time at Bryson's cottage, which he inherited when his parents died a few years ago.'

Hobbs began for the door. 'Take me to Bryson's house.'

FORTY-EIGHT

H obbs' mind raced uncontrollably, a relentless torrent of thoughts that left him feeling increasingly overwhelmed. He couldn't remember the last time he had a proper night's sleep. The brief, restless nap he had taken under a tree at his surveillance vantage point seemed like it had happened days ago. Now, both physical and mental exhaustion were taking their toll, clouding his thoughts and slowing his reflexes. Despite the fatigue, Hobbs knew that searching Bryson's residence might be the crucial step in uncovering the whereabouts of the elusive third member of the group. The problem was, he did not know what he was looking for. Would it be a document, a hidden compartment, or some obscure clue? The uncertainty gnawed at him, but he understood he had no choice but to press on. The stakes were too high, and failure was not an option.

Palmer joined Hobbs and Walsh on the street a few minutes later, now dressed in his uniform and carrying a lantern. He appeared alert, his eyes sharp and focused despite the tension in the air. Hobbs couldn't quite discern Palmer's state of mind – whether he was stressed, panicked, or simply hadn't yet processed the information he had just received. Regardless, Hobbs now trusted Palmer. In an investigation such as this, he knew he needed all the allies and resources he could muster, and Palmer's presence was a reassuring addition to their team.

'Bryson only lives a few minutes from here. Follow me,' Palmer said, raising the lantern.

Palmer walked briskly through the dark, quiet streets, his lantern casting long, flickering shadows on the cobblestones. Hobbs and Walsh followed closely behind, their footsteps echoing in the still night. Palmer finally stopped in front of a poorly kept cottage, a stark contrast to the neighboring structures that were much better maintained.

Damp moss obscured the cottage's brown brick facade, giving it a forlorn, neglected appearance. The grass in the front yard was overgrown and dead in sporadic patches, a testament to a lack of care and upkeep. A wooden balcony wrapped around the cottage, its paint chipped and weathered. It looked so fragile that it appeared it would collapse the minute any of them set foot on it.

Hobbs approached the cottage first, urgency overriding caution. He broke into a jog as he ascended the creaking, rattling stairs, each step protesting under his weight.

'Mr Hobbs,' Palmer began. 'We really shouldn't enter without a valid court authority.'

Hobbs didn't turn back. He fixed his focus on one of the front windows. Straining his eyes, he tried to penetrate the darkness within, but the pitch-black interior revealed nothing. The house seemed to swallow the light.

'Does Bryson have a family?' Hobbs eventually asked.

'I don't believe so,' Palmer replied.

'Well, sergeant, he's dead with no relatives. This is now a deceased estate, so I wouldn't expect a complaint. Plus, time is critical. If our third offender finds out what happened tonight, it could set off a chain reaction of panic and more killings.'

Palmer remained silent, casting a glance at Walsh, who merely shrugged, struggling to conceal a smirk.

Hobbs hustled back down the creaky balcony stairs, his mind set on gaining entry. Spotting a large rock among the overgrown grass, he picked it up and hurled it through the window next to the front door. The sound of shattering glass was deafening, echoing through the silent street, but Hobbs didn't care. He charged toward the broken window, pushing his arm through the jagged opening to unlock the door from the inside.

Palmer and Walsh followed closely behind, the lantern's glow casting a warm light on the hardwood floor and revealing a small combined living and dining room. Hobbs took in the sparse yet tidy interior — a contrast to the neglected exterior. Beyond the main room, he could see a modest kitchen, and further down a narrow corridor, two rooms with their doors closed. The cottage had sparse furnishings, with only a small, round wooden table and two armchairs taking up the space.

'Bedrooms,' Hobbs said, pointing down the hallway.

They made their way down the dimly lit hallway, following the steady beam of Palmer's lantern. When they reached the first room, Hobbs saw a narrow bed pushed against the wall, neatly made with a thin woollen blanket draped smoothly over it. Beside the bed was a wooden closet, its doors standing wide open. Palmer carried the lantern closer to the closet, but halted before reaching it. Even from a distance and with the gentle glow of the lantern, he could see it was empty.

'What are we looking for, Mr Hobbs?' Palmer asked.

'I really don't know,' he said, looking at Walsh who had remained silent, just shadowing Hobbs, allowing him to process his thoughts. 'Just anything that might give us a clue about our third person. I do not even know if this cottage would contain such evidence, but I need to be sure.'

As they reached the next bedroom, Hobbs observed a bed of similar size pushed against the back wall. However, this room seemed more lived-in. The wooden cupboard held police tunics, and Hobbs thumbed through them with a sense of contempt, disturbed by the thought that someone from the police force could commit such heinous crimes.

A disarray of loose papers cluttered the small writing desk next to the wardrobe. Hobbs sifted through them quickly, his gaze catching on a small, leather-bound book nestled among the sheets. This piqued Hobbs's curiosity as he reached for it.

'Sergeant, some light please.'

Palmer hurried over and set the lantern down on the desk, leaning in to peer over Hobbs' shoulder. Hobbs carefully opened the leather-bound book, revealing pages filled with a jumble of scribbled notes. The handwriting was haphazard and densely packed, hinting at frantic or disorganised thoughts.

'That's Bryson's handwriting,' Palmer said.

Hobbs scrutinised the text on the first few pages of the book, which comprised general, work-related notes. They were mundane and offered little in terms of immediate insight. However, his pulse quickened when he reached the fourth and final page.

This page was different: it contained a journal entry scrawled in messy handwriting, interspersed with blobs of spilt ink. Hobbs read through it once in silence, absorbing the text. He paused for a moment, letting the gravity of the contents sink in, as his mind raced to process the implications of what he had just read.

'What is it?' Walsh asked.

Without looking up from the book, Hobbs read aloud, 'When I killed for the first time, I struggled to process the emotions behind it. I felt whole for the first time in my life, and a rush of power I never knew was possible. This was now who I am. The Ghoul. Why? I do not know. Will I stop? I cannot possibly. For much of my life, I have had no purpose, but now, Banshee and I share a blood lust that will not be tamed. I know no other way. I can't stop. We can't stop, but for the first time in my life, I feel bliss for The Shadow guides our way and watches over us.'

They remained silent for a moment, the only sound in the room being the heavy, ragged breathing of the three men.

'Is that it?' Walsh asked.

'That's it,' Hobbs said, flicking through the book and finding empty pages.

'Why would he write that?' Palmer asked.

'I cannot say. I am not sure when it was written. Perhaps after Bryson and Davidson's first murder. When that was, we may never know. I do find it interesting he refers to himself as The Ghoul, and makes reference to whom I assume is Davidson as The Banshee. Perhaps names they gave themselves as part of their murderous personas.'

'That doesn't take us any further,' Walsh said. 'It is frightening indeed but it tells us nothing useful. What do you suspect he means "The Shadow guides our way?" Is that a metaphor?'

Hobbs closed his eyes. His mind raced as he reviewed the text over and over in his mind. Suddenly the pieces fell into place. 'It is not a metaphor. It is a name. The name of the third killer. It is capitalised in the writing. Bryson and Davidson referred to themselves as The Banshee and The Ghoul respectively. The Shadow must refer to the final member of the group.'

'That makes sense,' Walsh said. 'Still, there are no clues as to who his real identity.'

Hobbs nodded and scanned the rest of the room, but found nothing further of significance. They continued their search throughout the cottage, turning over every corner, but there was no additional evidence to identify the third murderer.

In the kitchen, Hobbs's frustration reached a boiling point. He slammed the last cupboard shut with such force that it shattered the glasses on the shelf. The crash reverberated through the small space, making Palmer and Walsh gasp at the sudden noise.

Leaving the cottage, Hobbs paused outside, burying his head in his hands. His mind felt stagnant, paralysed by the weight of their lack of progress. The frustration and exhaustion left him struggling to determine their next move.

'Henry, it was worth a try, but now we all need sleep,' Walsh said.

Hobbs took a deep breath and nodded, acknowledging Walsh's point. He knew that letting his fury take over would only hinder their progress. Despite this, he couldn't shake the frustration and shame of consistently being a step behind in the investigation. Each breakthrough seemed to be followed by a significant setback, and the weight of his repeated failures loomed large, particularly his inability to solve Emma's murder.

As he marched out of the cottage, he sank to the damp grass, crouching with his head buried in his hands. The burden of the investigation, while still battling with himself with Emma in the forefront of his mind, was becoming almost too much to bear.

The light from Palmer's lantern illuminated the front yard as he approached. 'I still need to report what occurred to Chief Noland. As Inspector Walsh said, get some rest.'

Hobbs stood up, took a deep breath, and nodded in silent agreement. He turned to see Walsh exiting the cottage and gave him a brief nod before walking back on his own.

FORTY-NINE

Wired and unable to sleep, Palmer sought Noland himself as soon as Hobbs left. He chose not to send a messenger for fear of any mixed messages. This was delicate news, and he needed to speak with Noland personally. Palmer quickly dressed and headed straight for the police stables. He rode as hard as his horse would allow, making his way up through the bottom of the Blue Mountains toward Springwood.

Hobbs found himself unable to sleep, his mind overrun with a barrage of thoughts that kept him staring at the ceiling for hours. Eventually, he pinpointed the source of his restlessness: fear. Fear that police officers were involved in the gold guard murders and the attempt on his own life. Most of all, though, he was afraid of the elusive third person still lurking somewhere out there. The Shadow. The identity of this third person haunted him. Was he as deranged as Bryson and Davidson? Would he go into hiding, blending into the darkness like his namesake, or would he erupt in fury when the news inevitably reached him? These unanswered questions flooded his mind, and he could not push them aside. Hobbs had hoped Davidson's dying breath might reveal the third member of their group, but now he felt as if he were back at square one, with no leads on who this mysterious figure might be.

The memory of each murder played vividly in Hobbs's mind, the sheer brutality of each one sending shivers down his spine. Then, his thoughts turned to Edmund Miller, and inevitably, to Emma. With these images filling his thoughts, Hobbs found himself caught between the terror of staying awake and the dread of what dreams might await him if he dared to sleep.

As the morning sun cast its gentle light through the gap in his curtains, Hobbs rose from his bed and dressed, feeling the weight of the night's events still heavy upon him. With a deep sigh, he made his way to the kitchen, his steps heavy with exhaustion and his mind still reeling. A strong coffee seemed like the only remedy for the thoughts swirling in his head.

When Hobbs entered the kitchen, he found Walsh and Yarran already there. Walsh appeared crisp in a fresh, white shirt, while Yarran remained clad in the same dark blue garment from the night before, his long hair still damp from a recent wash. Their sombre expressions mirrored Hobbs's unrest, indicating a shared night of little sleep. As Hobbs took a seat, Walsh poured him a cup of coffee, and they sat in silence for a moment, each lost in their thoughts. Outside, the morning air was already warming, evidenced by the wisps of steam rising from the grass. Hobbs took a sip of the coffee, feeling its effects immediately.

'What do you want to do today, Henry?' Walsh asked.

'I have a few things in mind. Perhaps we could see the doctor and have a good look through Bryson and Davidson's clothes. Perhaps there will be a clue. I also want to arrange with Sergeant

Palmer to alert the Royal Mint on the Henderson farm and have another look through the barn and the house in the daylight.'

'Perhaps the police station will have something. I'll start looking through Bryson and Davidson's personal things and paperwork,' Walsh said, draining his cup.

'What about me?' Yarran asked.

'Stick with me,' Hobbs said. 'But stay here for now. James and I will go over to the station and see if Palmer has raised Noland. I'll come back with a couple of horses and get you when we are ready to head out and start these enquiries.'

'And if Noland asks us why you are still here?'

'Yarran, I'm not worried about him. With what we now know, he will have many other things on his mind to worry about us.'

'You want some breakfast before we go?' Walsh asked.

'Not hungry. Let's just go. We have a lot to do.'

As Hobbs and Walsh entered the police station, an eerie silence hung in the air, amplified by the recent deaths of the young constables and the subsequent revelation of their involvement in the string of horrific murders. The usual hustle and bustle seemed absent, with empty cells, and Palmer, typically stationed at the front counter, was nowhere to be seen. They pushed open the door to the office at the rear of the station and found him engaged in conversation with Noland, who had already arrived and was seated behind the desk. Noland's broad smile, framed by his thick, grey mustache, hinted at a sense of relief.

'Gentlemen, come in,' Noland said, gesturing with a thick hand without getting off his chair.

Hobbs and Walsh entered the office and stood beside Palmer in front of the desk.

'I was just saying to Sergeant Palmer here about how grateful we are that you solved the case, Mr Hobbs. He alerted me last night to what had happened, and I insisted on making the trip down here to make sure things in Penrith do not get out of hand. The public will soon hear about Constables Bryson and Davidson, and naturally, they will be understandably distressed and horrified.'

Hobbs frowned at Noland. 'I did not expect such a warm response from you.'

'Well naturally, when Sergeant Palmer told me what happened, that you went behind my back and ignored my directions, I was irate, but I realise you have provided a great service to the community, and for that, I thank you. You too, Inspector Walsh. As disappointing and surprising that police officers were involved, we can now close the case and rebuild the staffing list here at Penrith. Not to mention the pressure will be relieved at the Mint and operations will return to normal. I tell you, they were close to ending their operations, with no one willing to complete the gold transport. We were so close to having a full-blown riot on our hands over murmurs that the miners would not be able to sell their gold.'

'Chief Inspector Noland,' Walsh said cautiously. 'Politics aside, I am not sure what Sergeant Palmer told you, but we still have an unidentified third man still out there. Henry here saw three men attack his convoy and nearly kill him.'

'Yes, and as I understand it, a farmer who was seen buying the stolen gold was also killed. No doubt he was a part of this group. Of course, we will arrange for an inspection of the Henderson farm and recover the stolen gold. Tomorrow perhaps?' Noland looked at Palmer, who nodded in reply.

Hobbs shook his head. 'The farmer was involved in their gold trade, but he was not one of the murderers, that I am sure of. There are still further investigations required.'

Noland shook his head dismissively and smiled. 'No. I won't hear of it. Now you have both performed exceptionally, but that will be all. I will report to the Governor and the Royal Mint personally that these men have finally been stopped. Trade will return to normal and I will make sure, Inspector, that you receive a commendation. You too, Mr Hobbs.'

'Noland, you are blinded by the politics,' Hobbs said.

'Excuse me?' Noland asked, his smile now fading.

'You want so badly to report that these murders have stopped, you will ignore the evidence before you. It would be a reckless and dangerous decision to make while a killer is still out there.'

'Now listen here,' Noland said, sitting on the edge of his seat and pointing his finger at Hobbs. 'The investigation is over. I told you once before to stay out of it and you disobeyed me. Now granted, you did fine work, and you have saved me a considerable amount of pressure from above, but mark my words, you are now relieved of your duties at Penrith, and that is an order.'

Hobbs remained still, staring back at Noland in disbelief at the man's incompetence.

'Once again, I thank you for your assistance,' Noland said coldly.

'Sir, please...' Walsh started.

'That will be all, gentlemen. I wish you safe travels back to Sydney, inspector, and wherever it is you are going, Mr Hobbs.'

Noland pushed himself up from the desk, a slight grimace crossing his face as he did so. Hobbs's stomach twisted with a sudden realisation. His expression remained neutral as Noland smiled at them, apparently unaware of Hobbs's reaction, and gestured for them to leave.

As Walsh exited the office, Hobbs stayed behind, his smile forced as he fought to maintain composure. 'Well sir, if that is your request, we were glad to be of help.'

The smile returned to Noland's face. Hobbs outstretched his arm, offering to shake hands. As they did, Noland winced once more, but his smile remained. Hobbs noted the discomfort but maintained his grip firmly, offering a reassuring nod before turning to leave the office.

Hobbs maintained his grip on Noland's hand, holding his gaze steadily. 'Something wrong with your arm?'

'I'm sorry?'

'I couldn't help but notice you were in a bit of pain when you stretched your arm out in front of you.'

'Oh right. Yes. I fell off my horse a few days ago. Straight onto my arm. It is quite sore, yes.'

'I see,' Hobbs said, releasing his grip. 'Best take care of yourself then.'

'Will do. Thank you, Mr Hobbs.'

Hobbs exited the office and swiftly guided Walsh out of the police station, gripping his arm to quicken their pace.

'What was that all about?' Walsh asked as Hobbs released his grip.

Hobbs gazed at Walsh sternly and kept his voice low. 'Noland is the third member of the group. The Shadow. We are not going anywhere just yet.'

FIFTY

'*You have no idea how far this goes.*'

Davidson's ominous words echoed in Hobbs' thoughts, revealing the sinister depth of the conspiracy. The trail led right to the Chief Inspector's doorstep, to Bernard Noland. Everything aligned: Noland's stature, his physical build, and now the undeniable evidence of his arm injury. Hobbs was convinced; Noland was the third man they had been pursuing all along.

'That is a huge allegation,' Walsh said, as Hobbs continued to hurry him along back toward their cottage.

'Why else would he dismiss the evidence of a third person involved? And his right arm caused him pain when he reached out and shook my hand, exactly where I would have shot him. Listen to me. I know you don't want to believe it, but you are going to have to. He believes the investigation was over, and is now feeling comfortable. He can report that the murderers are dead, and for a time, the killings will stop because he is in control of everything. But eventually, he will start again. He will recruit others, and nothing will change unless we do something right now.'

Walsh ran a hand through his hair and remained silent, clearly processing the revelation just as Hobbs had moments ago.

Hobbs continued. 'We've seen it before James, a criminal group can't work without a clear hierarchal structure. Noland was the leader, that I am sure of, and now he thinks he can close the case and continue undetected while we are long gone. We were dealing with a team of two deranged men in Bryson and Davidson, involved in all this solely to feed their need for violence, and led by the dominating personality of Bernard Noland. A man in a position of authority and power. I should have realised earlier when he tried to send us home and take the case on personally. Why else would he insist on leading the investigation himself? Because he can control Bryson and Davidson and dictate exactly when, where, and whom they kill. He has the power to keep the politicians calm, and also control the concerns of the Mint.'

Walsh shook his head in disbelief. 'Let's say everything you are saying is true. We need to be extremely careful here, Henry. Simply walking in and arresting him isn't an option. We are going to need more than a sore arm.'

'I know. And we can't trust any of the police except for Palmer, who knows if others at Springwood are involved, or will be potential replacements for Bryson and Davidson. We need to find out where he lives and look around.'

'We won't be able to have a search warrant issued without Noland finding out. All the Chief Inspectors are friendly with the local Magistrates.'

'I don't plan on getting a warrant.'

'Henry, I am an inspector of police. Illegally breaking into his house and being accused of obtaining evidence unlawfully is something I can't afford to do.

'You may be an inspector, but last I checked, I'm a convict,' Hobbs said flatly. Besides, I will not break in. I just want to look through the windows. If I find something relevant, I will let you know that way you can get a warrant from a Sydney Magistrate, and keep things perfectly legal and well away from the local courts here. We need to keep any information about Noland away from anyone in this area. Can you do that?'

'Yes, but you would still have trespassed on private property to get whatever evidence you come across. Just because this might seem like a rough and new colony doesn't mean we don't have to follow the Queen's laws.'

Hobbs shrugged. 'Well, maybe I lost my dog and saw it running into Noland's yard. Maybe in my search for it, I glanced in a window. I can't help that.'

Walsh shook his head and couldn't hold back a sly smile. 'You really are one of a kind, you know that, right?'

'Well, at least my intentions are in the right place. We will get Noland no matter what, and before he hurts anyone else or destroys, whatever evidence may remain.'

Hobbs and Walsh hurried back to the cottage, where they found Yarran prepared and eager to continue aiding in the investigation.

'Change of plans, Yarran,' Hobbs said, offering him a seat at the round kitchen table. 'There's been some new information.'

Hobbs recounted the events in Noland's office and reiterated his theory. As he heard it for the second time and saw Walsh nodding reassuringly, he knew Walsh was now fully convinced.

'I never trusted that man,' Yarran said.

'You were right not to,' Hobbs said. 'Now we need some more proof. He's what we are going to do. As soon as Noland leaves the police station, I'll speak to Palmer and get his address. The three of us will find his house and while you two remain nearby, keeping watch, I'll go around the house and look for anything in connection with the murders; stolen gold, blood-stained clothes, hessian masks, anything. If I find it, I will let you know. James will ride to Sydney and get a search warrant, and Yarran and I will keep a close eye on Noland while we wait. We'll watch him all day and night if we have to. I won't let him kill anyone else.'

'And if you see nothing in the house?' Walsh asked.

'Then we keep a close eye on Noland. He thinks we have gone, and he is feeling safe now. I can tell you this: people like him don't stop. He will make a mistake and leave evidence behind eventually, and when he does, I'll be ready. But most importantly, he can't know we are after him. He could become highly dangerous if he feels threatened or closed in on.'

'You really are sure about this?' Yarran asked.

'Positive. This man is responsible for every murdered gold guard, and for the murder of Edmund Miller. He thinks he can get away with it, but we are going to take him down.'

About an hour later, there came a soft knock on the front door, catching Hobbs's attention.

'Expecting anyone?' he asked.

Walsh shrugged and shook his head.

Hobbs moved quickly and opened the door to find Palmer standing on the other side.

'Morning Henry, Noland just left, so I thought I would come around and say my farewells as you pack.'

'Come in,' Hobbs said. 'We need to talk, and we are not leaving just yet.'

'You aren't? Is something wrong?' Palmer asked, following Hobbs into the kitchen.

Once again Hobbs conveyed the evidence suggesting Noland's involvement, initially met with disbelief until he calmly outlined the reasons behind his belief, much like he had done with Walsh and Yarran.

Palmer stood up and rubbed his chin. 'After finding out about Bryson and Davidson, I think I have run out of shock, and I have never liked Noland, but if you are sure about this, you need to be very careful. You are going up against a powerful and intelligent man. If you don't have your evidence sorted, you will fail miserably, and well, inspector,' he said, glancing at Walsh, 'your career will be over. Are you both absolutely sure about this?'

'Yes,' Hobbs said while Walsh nodded affirmatively. 'But as you said, we need to be careful and we will, so what I need right now is Noland's home address. Don't ask questions, just give me the address. Now, where did he say he was going when he left?'

'He told me he was going back to Springwood police station for the rest of the day. He lives in the big red brick house down the street from the station. I'm quite sure it's number sixty, but regardless, it is the largest house on the street. I've never been inside and only seen it once, but I remember the house having tall hedges in front of a wide bay window.'

'I think I know the place,' Yarran said.

Palmer nodded 'Do you need help?'

'Just a loan of some horses for now. I want to have a brief look around the area. Does he live with anyone there?'

'No. He's wife passed many years ago and I know he has children, but I have never seen them. They would likely now be in their thirties, and have likely long since moved away.'

'So when do we leave?' Walsh asked.

'Immediately,' Hobbs said.

FIFTY-ONE

Palmer returned five minutes later, leading three horses, tacked up and ready to depart. Yarran took the horse previously used by Bryson, and Hobbs mounted the horse he had grown fond of, belonging to The Rocks police station. The third horse was Walsh's own trusted and reliable Palomino, which had been enjoying the peace and quiet of the Penrith police stables. Walsh fetched his rifle and tucked it into the side holster of the saddle.

'Just in case,' he said.

They covered the ten-mile distance to Springwood as swiftly as possible, though the journey proved challenging due to the slow and rugged terrain of the lower Blue Mountains, which Hobbs had still not become accustomed to despite so many trips up and down. The route they rode was one where many innocent lives had tragically ended under Noland's orders, and Hobbs simmered with anger but knew he needed to resist the dangerous urge to focus solely on apprehending Noland. He needed solid evidence and to remain vigilant, keeping his mind clear to ensure they put an end to Noland's reign of terror once and for all.

'We are just outside Springwood now,' Yarran called over his shoulder as he led the way.

'Take us to the hotel to tie the horses up,' Hobbs said. 'I don't want to be seen by anyone, especially by the local police. We go on foot from there.'

The town's sole hotel stood as a commanding presence in the town centre – a substantial double-storied brick building, seemingly the nucleus around which the rest of the town had formed. It likely served as a crucial rest stop for gold miners traveling to or from Sydney. Despite the bustling street filled with casual shoppers, the pub itself remained tranquil, anticipating the afternoon surge of patrons. They tethered their horses by a trough outside, affording Hobbs a moment to survey the surroundings and find his bearings within the town.

'Conceal the rifle, James, I don't want to bring unnecessary attention to ourselves.'

'The police station is about half a mile east, and Noland's house is a little beyond that,' Yarran said.

Hobbs nodded. 'Can you take us to the house by avoiding the police station? I don't want anyone from there seeing us.'

Yarran led Hobbs and Walsh northeast, guiding them through the quiet residential streets away from the town centre. After a lengthy walk, Yarran changed direction once more, guiding them toward Noland's residence without having to pass by the police station. As they approached, Palmer's description proved accurate – the imposing two-story house stood wide and tall, casting a shadow over its more modest neighbours. A short white picket fence bordered the front yard, adorned with freshly trimmed, vibrant green grass, the healthiest on the entire street. The sight raised suspicions – how had Noland afforded such grandeur on a police officer's salary? Without exchanging words, Hobbs knew Walsh and Yarran pondered the same question: how deep did Noland's involvement in criminal activities run? It was evident that someone with his salary could not have funded a residence of this stature through legitimate means.

Hobbs noticed the dense hedge providing a veil of privacy in front of the bay window, with "sixty" printed in elegant italics on steel letters beside the wide wooden front door. The street itself was spacious and serene this far from town, flanked by robust eucalyptus trees that cast shadows over every house except number sixty. As the day neared midmorning, the sun was becoming uncomfortably intense, and a gentle breeze was sweeping through, picking up the loose dust and dirt from the road and swirling it in aimless circles.

Hobbs, Walsh, and Yarran scanned the street cautiously, checking for any signs of activity.

'Everything is quiet,' Hobbs said. 'Noland is probably at the station so, James, head west a little and keep watch and, Yarran, take the east. Let me know if anyone is coming.'

Proceeding cautiously, Hobbs kept a close eye on his surroundings as he moved along the side of the house. He noted the layout, mentally mapping out the interior based on the typical arrangement of similar Victorian homes he'd encountered before. His goal was to locate Noland's potential office space, where he could hold private discussions and keep important documents.

Hobbs continued stalking the side of the house, making his way past the dining room with its elegant decor and the well-appointed galley kitchen. As he approached the rear of the house, he kept his senses sharp, listening for any signs of activity or movement. Despite his careful scrutiny, everything appeared normal and undisturbed, adding to the eerie silence that enveloped the property.

Hobbs surveyed the backyard, noting the meticulous care evident in the neat rows of vegetables along the back fence. Yet, despite the well-maintained appearance, there was an underlying sense of sterility that unsettled him. The small shed with its lacquered wood paneling and the iron table and chairs painted in light grey seemed oddly out of place, contributing to the overall impression of an impersonal and unwelcoming atmosphere. Hobbs couldn't shake the feeling that there was more to this house than met the eye, and he resolved to proceed with caution as he continued his investigation.

Approaching the other side of the house, Hobbs found what appeared to be Noland's home office. The room was dimly lit, with deep red wallpaper that matched the rich hue of the thick writing desk positioned in front of a window. Peering carefully through the window, Hobbs focused on a tall bookcase filled mostly with loose sheets of paper and trinkets with only a few books. However, what caught his attention the most was a small paper bin beside the bookcase, which contained blood-stained rags and cotton medical wraps. Instantly, Hobbs formulated a theory. The bullet wound he had inflicted on Noland was still causing him grief. In order to avoid answering difficult questions and visiting a doctor, Noland had likely tended to the wound himself. It was probable that the wound was still bleeding and not healing as expected.

In deep thought, while peering through the window, Hobbs never noticed the large figure looming behind him.

The intense, dull pain of a hard object smashing into the back of his head caught Hobbs completely off guard. Without a chance to grasp onto something or even turn around, he collapsed onto the soft grass underneath the side window of Noland's office, and then everything went black.

FIFTY-TWO

Hobbs groaned as he slowly regained consciousness. His head throbbed with a deep, pulsating pain, and he felt nauseous, his vision grainy with specks of black. As awareness returned, he found himself in a small, dark room, lying on a cold, hard floor. Sharp tips of hay prickled his body uncomfortably. When his eyesight focused, he saw a looming shadow above him – it was Noland. From Hobbs' prone position, Noland appeared formidable, clad in black riding boots, trousers, and his unbuttoned police tunic, revealing his broad chest beneath a white shirt.

Despite his disorientation, Hobbs attempted to speak, but all he managed was an incoherent mumble. Looking around, he saw he was in a small tool shed. He surmised he couldn't have been moved too far and realised that he would likely have been dragged to the shed at the rear of the yard. A private setting for Noland to finish the job. The shed had no windows and the only light which entered was from the cracks in the gaps of the wooden walls and a small candle Noland had lit on a workbench. Next to the candle, Hobbs saw a long black raincoat with small, dried drops of blood on the lapels. Draped over the jacket were a set of knives and a small pile of unrefined gold.

'You have tenacity, Mr Hobbs. I will give you that,' Noland said as he crouched over Hobbs, straddling his body with his thick legs. 'In fact, I am surprised you survived our earlier ambush. I even broke a fence paling over your head and you were only out for a minute or two. You are indeed a fighter.'

Hobbs attempted to take a deep breath, but the weight of Noland's body pressing down on him restricted his chest from expanding fully. Without receiving enough oxygen, his vision slowly faded again.

'I was quite surprised to see you and Constable Miller in the back of that carriage,' Noland continued, a smirk stretching across his face, 'but I wouldn't let your intrusion stop us. In fact, it was nice to see your smug face in pain.'

Hobbs struggled to breathe under the weight of Noland pressing down on his chest.

'And you never give up, do you?' Noland continued. 'I take it you saw the blood-soaked bandages in my office. You really took me by surprise that day when you shot me.'

Hobbs stayed silent, continuing to struggle under Noland's weight.

Noland pushed down harder as Hobbs groaned. 'So when did you figure it out?'

Hobbs said nothing.

Noland chuckled and shook his head. 'Well, it doesn't matter now.'

'You are a disgrace. A murderer,' Hobbs said through clenched teeth.

'I'm afraid you are wrong again, Mr Hobbs. I had Bryson and Davidson for the murders. Killing was their pleasure, and they made the perfect accomplices, eager to do whatever I told them. My pleasure is simple: wealth. But I guess in a few moments, once

I finish you, I will join them in their vice. You should have just left town when you had the opportunity.'

Hobbs attempted to wriggle himself free, but Noland's weight kept him tightly pinned to the ground. The pressure on his recent stab wounds sent hot waves of pain coursing through his body.

He clenched his teeth once again and winced. 'I'm not here alone. James is close by. You won't get away with this.'

Noland laughed. 'The evidence here will simply point to a man who broke into my home, and I did what was necessary to defend myself. By the time anyone comes, my last remaining haul of gold will be gone, and even Inspector James Walsh will not be able to prove anything. I am afraid you both have truly overestimated yourselves. Fortunately for you, I do not derive the same pleasure from killing as Bryson and Davidson did, so I will make it quick, but nonetheless, I feel even I might enjoy this.'

Noland shifted his weight to the right, his fingers fumbling for one of the knives on the workbench nearby. Hobbs felt the release of pressure from his left side and seized the opportunity presented by Noland's momentary imbalance. Ignoring the protests of pain from his body, he acted swiftly. Sliding down under Noland's straddling legs, he positioned his head in line with Noland's chest. Before Noland could react, Hobbs raised both legs and drove his knees into Noland's backside with all his strength. The force propelled the top of Noland's body forward over Hobbs, causing him to reach out with both hands to break his fall.

Capitalising on this moment, Hobbs wrapped his legs around Noland's waist, recalling a technique from underground fighting and wrestling, typically reserved for desperate situations. With Noland off balance and his hands planted on the ground above his head, Hobbs pivoted his hips and executed a throw, leveraging his body weight to topple Noland to his side. In a swift reversal,

Noland found himself on his back while Hobbs now straddled him, gaining a momentary advantage.

Before Hobbs could react, Noland unleashed a powerful left-handed punch that connected squarely with his jaw. The impact sent a shockwave of pain coursing through his head, intensifying the throbbing ache already present, and the specks in his vision returned with a vengeance. Momentarily dazed by the blow, Hobbs found himself vulnerable.

In that fleeting moment of disorientation, Noland seized the opportunity, his hands wrapping tightly around Hobbs' neck in a vice-like grip. The sudden pressure on his windpipe cut off his air supply almost instantly. Hobbs struggled to draw even the shallowest breath as Noland's immense strength constricted his airway. Seconds felt like an eternity as Hobbs fought against the suffocating grasp, his vision darkening around the edges as oxygen deprivation took its toll. With each passing moment, the world faded further into obscurity, and Hobbs knew unless he found a way to break free soon, unconsciousness would claim him, and with it, his chance for survival.

Struggling against Noland's iron grip, Hobbs fought to pry his hands away from his throat, but it was futile. Noland's strength was overwhelming, and despite his efforts, Hobbs couldn't muster the force necessary to break free. His body, already battered and weakened from the relentless assault, screamed in protest with each movement. The throbbing pain in his head only intensified, pulsing with each desperate attempt to breathe. As the precious air dwindled, Hobbs felt his strength waning. Darkness encroached on the edges of his vision, and panic surged within him. Every instinct screamed for oxygen, for release from Noland's suffocating hold, but his body refused to comply. In that harrowing moment, Hobbs realised the grim reality: unless he overcame Noland, he would lose his fight for survival in the void of unconsciousness.

Noland's sinister grin only added to Hobbs' torment, his malicious satisfaction evident in the twisted curve of his lips. As Hobbs's face contorted with agony, flushed with a bright shade of red, Noland's grip remained unyielding, each moment suffocating the life out of him. Hobbs felt a strange sensation wash over him, a surreal lightness that contrasted sharply with the crushing weight of Noland's hands around his throat. It was a terrifying realisation, the dawning awareness that he was slipping away, succumbing to unconsciousness again.

As fear tightened its grip on him, Hobbs locked eyes with Noland. In that desperate moment, fleeting memories flashed before his mind's eye like shards of light piercing through the darkness. He saw Emma, radiant in her light sundress, and Edmund Miller, his expression serene in the memory of their first encounter. These visions, brief as they were, momentarily hid his pain and terror.

Even as Noland's suffocating hold threatened to snuff out his last breath, these images gave Hobbs a surge of resolve. It was a beacon of hope in the darkness, a lifeline to cling to when all seemed lost. Summoning every ounce of remaining energy, he pressed his hands against Noland's shoulders, his fingers seeking out the source of the pain. With a final, desperate effort, he drove his thumb into the gunshot wound on Noland's shoulder, eliciting a primal scream of agony as he collapsed on the shed floor.

In that instant, Hobbs broke free, collapsing to the ground in a fit of coughing. Gasping for air, he sucked in precious lungfuls of oxygen, the taste of freedom mingling with the metallic tang of blood as he fought to reclaim his composure.

'Henry,' a voice called from somewhere close by. It was Walsh, and Noland flinched, hearing it too. With a fresh surge of energy coursing through his veins, Hobbs slowly crawled across Noland's prone body, his fists clenched tight. Despite his muscles screaming in protest with every movement, he pressed on, fuelled by a fierce determination to incapacitate Noland. With a roar, he unleashed a powerful punch, aimed straight at Noland's nose, crushing the cartilage and causing blood to gush. Summoning every ounce of strength he possessed, Hobbs once again targeted Noland's injured shoulder, driving his thumb into the wound again. A sharp cry of agony tore from Noland, echoing through the shed. However, Hobbs was not done yet. With relentless determination, he continued his assault, each strike filled with a burning desire for justice and retribution as his thoughts turned to Miller and each of the guards slain under Noland's hand.

'Henry, where are you?' Walsh called out again. This time, his voice sounded softer. More distant.

Hobbs saw panic in Noland's eyes. 'It's over. Walsh is armed, and he is close by. It's over.'

Noland inhaled deeply and roared as he struck Hobbs with an open palm to his ear, sending him crashing to the floor in a fit of disorientation. Noland stood up quickly, leaving Hobbs on his knees, grappling for coherence. He reached for the workbench and stuffed the gold in his pocket before bursting out the shed doors. Hobbs lunged for Noland's legs to stop him, but he was not quick enough. Noland had escaped. By the time he reached the door of the shed, he caught a fleeting glimpse of Noland rushing along the right side of the house toward the street. Walsh was still nowhere to be seen.

'Henry,' Walsh called out again.

Hobbs tried to stand up, but did so too quickly, causing his head to spin. 'James, back here,' he replied.

A moment later, Hobbs saw Walsh rush into the backyard from the left side of the house. Hobbs sighed, knowing Noland had likely made it to the street undetected.

'Henry, what happened?' he asked, holding Hobbs by the arm, helping maintain his balance.

'Noland got me. We just missed him. He ran out to the street when he heard you coming.'

'He what? What happened?'

'He ambushed me. Dragged me into the shed and, I admit, nearly killed me. Along with the admissions he made as he throttled me, you'll find a blood stained trench coat in there and probably some left over gold, but no matter about that now. We need to find him. At this moment, Noland will be exceptionally dangerous and volatile.'

'Are you sure you are going to be alright?'

'I'll be fine, James,' Hobbs grunted, rubbing the back of his head and his tender throat. 'Go find Yarran. Maybe he saw which direction Noland went.'

A moment later, Walsh returned to the yard, followed by a startled Yarran.

'James told me what happened,' Yarran said, examining the fresh bruises on Hobbs' neck. 'Noland did this?'

'Yes. I'm lucky to be alive, really. But no matter, Yarran. We need to find him'

'I kept a close eye on the top of the street. Unfortunately, I didn't see him.'

'He must have gone through neighbouring properties to stay hidden then.'

'Before he fled, did he offer any hints about where he might go?' Walsh asked.

Hobbs shook his head.

'If you were him, what would you do?' Yarran asked.

'I would probably try to disappear. He left me alive with evidence in the shed, and likely inside his house. He must know he now cannot get away with this.'

'What do you need to disappear, then? Money,' Walsh said. 'You said he left quickly when he heard me. He may be arrogant, but he will not take the chance of us finding all the evidence we need.'

Hobbs quickly looked at Walsh and Yarran as his mind made the connection. 'The Henderson farm,' he said. 'There is still a pile of gold and money there from last night, plus more hidden on the property, I would expect. That's where he's going. One last stop so he can pay his way out of this to disappear a very wealthy man.'

FIFTY-THREE

As they rushed back toward the pub to retrieve their horses, Hobbs took charge, his voice cutting through the urgency of the moment.

'James, you come with me to the farm. Yarran, I need you to stop off at Penrith police station. Fetch Palmer, then meet us there.'

With swift, decisive movements, they sprang into action, each knowing their role. Time was of the essence, and they could not afford to waste a single moment. They sprinted toward the Springwood police station, taking the most direct route back to the town centre. Discretion was no longer a concern, but their urgency was. It was likely that Noland had stopped there first to retrieve his horse and begin his eastward journey, but they couldn't afford to linger and make inquiries with his colleagues. Hobbs trusted none of them, anyway.

They swiftly gathered their horses and galloped back toward Penrith with all the speed they could muster. Noland may have had a head start, but Hobbs was determined to close the gap. The mostly downhill ride, while precarious in some spots, made the trip easier.

By the time they reached Penrith, the horses had become exhausted, but they received an encouraging pat and were urged to press on just a little while longer. Bursting through the town at high speed, Yarran branched off and headed toward the police station, while Hobbs and Walsh continued eastward, entering the rural farming area of the Penrith township.

'It's just a little further, but keep alert,' Hobbs said. 'We have to assume Noland is not too far ahead now.'

'Got it,' Walsh said, reaching for his rifle and keeping a firm grip on the handle, ready to draw quickly if needed. 'Lead the way.'

Hobbs rode a little further until he recognised the Henderson farm from the dusty road. It was eerily quiet, but Hobbs' instincts told him this was where they would find Noland.

In the daylight, Hobbs noticed the expansiveness of the farm and the parched landscape. Yellow wheat and tall, sunburnt grass stretched as far as the eye could see. In the distance, the small farmhouse and barn, nearly five hundred yards away, appeared as mere specks, engulfed by the vast expanse of open fields.

Hobbs dismounted. 'We go on foot from here. Our priority is to stay low and as quiet as possible. We'll use the wheat for cover.'

They soon departed from the exposed road and sought refuge among the tall crops, aiming for the heart of the farm. Walsh kept his rifle close, loaded and ready with a single round. As they waded through the dense wheat fields, their visibility was limited, but Hobbs eventually discerned the track marks from the previous night. The wheat lay crushed and bent where he and Yarran had tread on their way to the barn. Following this familiar path, they proceeded in the expected direction. Despite being only a hundred yards away, the farm remained eerily silent. Hobbs hastened his pace, and Walsh matched his speed, wary of missing Noland should he hastily plunder the barn and depart. In the distance, originating from the barn, Hobbs heard the faint snort of a horse – Noland's horse.

He turned back to Walsh and whispered, 'he's here.'

As they pressed forward in near silence, the farmhouse's roofline emerged into view, followed by the barn situated approximately thirty yards behind. It was then that they heard the piercing, high-pitched squealing. Hobbs halted abruptly at the wheat field's edge, their final veil of concealment.

'What was that?' Walsh asked.

Hobbs winced. 'Sounds like a woman. The farmer's wife, probably. Noland must have got to her.'

Hobbs peered through the wheat, his gaze fixated on the front porch of the Henderson house. A thin trail of blood stained the white door, and there, slumped in front of it, lay Eliza Henderson. Even from a distance, Hobbs could discern the signs of distress - the short, damp strands of her grey hair clinging to her forehead, the laboured pants escaping her lips. It was clear she was in agony. He surmised she had been attacked and tried to seek help, but collapsed as she crossed the threshold. With both hands pressed against her abdomen, she wheezed, each breath a struggle, while blood seeped through her clenched fingers, staining her once-blue dress a deep crimson.

'We have to go to her,' Hobbs said.

'What about Noland? He might be nearby.'

'Just keep your rifle ready.'

Hobbs took a deep breath and sprinted, his heart pounding with urgency as he traversed the open ground, leaving the safety of the wheat fields behind. He dashed the fifty yards toward Eliza Henderson, his mind racing with the possibility of Noland's presence and the danger it posed. Walsh followed suit, his rifle poised at his shoulder, scanning the surroundings for any sign of Noland's looming threat.

Hobbs hurried to the woman, her moans of pain cutting through the air. Her weary eyes struggled to stay open, betraying the exhaustion she felt. Kneeling beside her, Hobbs gently cradled her head, feeling the weight of her suffering in every laboured breath she took. The pallor of her complexion revealed the severity of her condition, and her shallow, pained breathing only heightened his concern.

'Mrs Henderson, it's Henry Hobbs. Do you remember me?'

With a slow nod, Eliza acknowledged Hobbs' assistance, her gaze drifting down to her blood-soaked hands. She was losing blood rapidly from a gunshot wound to her stomach. Hobbs acted swiftly. He removed his shirt, rolling it into a makeshift bandage before sliding it under her hands, pressing it against her stomach to stem the bleeding. Meanwhile, he and Walsh maintained vigilance, scanning the property, Walsh with his rifle at the ready. Peering through the front window of the house, Hobbs found no sign of anyone inside. Save for a faint trail of blood staining the wooden floor in the living room, everything appeared undisturbed.

'Hold this tightly against your wound,' Hobbs said as his once-white shirt turned red, absorbing huge amounts of blood. 'You need to hold firm pressure to stop the bleeding. Now, this is important, Mrs Henderson. I know you are tired and hurting, but I need you to tell me what happened.'

She groaned again as her head rolled back. Hobbs caught it before it hit the ground. 'Mrs Henderson please, it's very important.'

'I heard something in the barn,' she groaned through her teeth as her eyes closed.

'Mrs Henderson, stay awake,' Hobbs said, lightly tapping her cheeks. Her eyelids fluttered, and she slowly opened her eyes.

'I went out to see what it was. I thought maybe the doctor had come back. He was here earlier to take Arthur's body. But it wasn't. It was a big man with a thick moustache. He looked startled and pointed a gun at me. I turned and ran, but he followed me. By the time I got to the backdoor, I turned to see if he followed and then he shot me. I looked into his eyes just after he did. His stare was intense and frightening.'

Hobbs exchanged a knowing glance with Walsh and subtly gestured towards the barn.

'Have you seen him leave, Mrs Henderson?'

'No. Please help me.'

'We will, I promise, but we need to find him first. He's very dangerous and we can't let him get away. Stay as still as you can and we will come back for you.'

Hobbs surveyed the scene, his gaze fixating on the barn nestled behind the house. Its front doors were open, offering a glimpse of the interior where Noland's horse stood, tethered and unattended.

'Here's in there and he's armed, James,' Hobbs said. 'He shot the woman here without reason, therefore he's even more dangerous and desperate. Keep your gun up and be ready for anything.'

FIFTY-FOUR

As a thick cloud obscured the sun, casting a temporary shadow over the scene, Hobbs and Walsh approached the entrance of the barn, careful to avoid making even the slightest sound that might give away their presence. Alongside the barn, the earth bore dried stains, marking where Arthur Henderson, Bryson, and Davidson had met their end. Hobbs positioned himself on the right side of the barn entrance, while Walsh took the left, pressing their bodies against the walls just beside the open doors. Inside, the sound of clanging and rustling indicated someone working hastily within.

Hobbs strained to peer over the threshold, observing Noland frantically stuffing large hessian sacks with gold and cash. Empty metal canisters and toolboxes lay scattered around, their contents looted and discarded. A metal crowbar rested nearby, evidence of Noland's forcible entry into the containers. He was in a hurry to abscond with the loot before making a clean getaway. Hobbs withdrew his head and locked eyes with Walsh, their silent communication conveying their shared understanding. In unison, they nodded, and Walsh raised his gun, ready to confront Noland.

They stormed into the barn in perfect synchrony. Hobbs, lacking a shirt but undeterred, and Walsh, wielding his Pattern Enfield, aimed squarely at Noland's chest.

Surprised, Noland dropped the bag he was holding and swiftly drew his Dougall Transitional revolver from the back of his trousers. Though less accurate than Walsh's Enfield, it boasted a six-round cylinder compared to the rifle's single shot.

'Drop it, Noland! Don't be a fool,' Hobbs said.

Noland twitched. His face was covered in dried blood from his earlier fight with Hobbs, and his disfigured nose was swollen. His eyes darted, and he looked increasingly desperate as he waved the revolver at the two targets before him.

'It's two against one now,' Walsh said. 'It's over. You have been involved in nine murders and the attempted murder of Henry Hobbs, and now you have also targeted the farmer's wife. You have nowhere to go, and I am bringing you in.'

'You'll hang for this, Noland.' Hobbs growled bitterly.

'I'm not going anywhere with you,' Noland said, increasing the speed of his revolver arm, waving it back and forth. Hobbs and Walsh widened the distance between them, making it more difficult for Noland to keep aim as he waved his revolver in a wider arc.

'Stop moving! Both of you! I will not allow myself to be arrested. I'm taking the last of the gold and you'll never find me again.'

Walsh shook his head. 'You are coming with us.'

Noland took a slow step forward to close the distance. 'If you value your lives, you'll walk away right now.'

'Not going to happen,' Hobbs said.

Walsh tightened his grip on the butt of the rifle and applied light pressure on the trigger, ready to fire.

Hobbs held a hand up to Walsh. 'James, I want him alive. Shooting him is the easy way out.'

'I've had enough of your voice, Hobbs. You should have left well enough alone when you had the chance,' Noland said, as he cocked the hammer and focused on Hobbs.

He fired.

The round missed Hobbs' head by a fraction of an inch, shattering through the edge of the barn door behind him. Splinters flew in every direction as he took cover, scrambling as fast as he could outside the barn and away from Noland's line of fire. Walsh was poised to shoot at Noland, but before he could, Noland turned the revolver toward him and fired, again missing. Walsh also sought cover outside the barn doors, on the opposite side from Hobbs. As he ran, Noland fired a third round, shattering the ground and leaving a gaping hole less than a foot from Walsh's feet.

'He's got nothing to lose now, James,' Hobbs said. 'Stay apart. We don't want to make ourselves an easy target.'

Upon hearing Hobbs' voice, Noland fired through the barn wall in his direction as he took fast steps toward the barn door. The bullet smashed through the wall, and wood chips cut his face, but the bullet missed. Rattled but unharmed, Hobbs was thankful the revolver lacked accuracy and that Noland was either a poor shot or too full of panic to steady his hands.

'He's got one round left,' Hobbs called out, counting the rounds Noland had fired upon them, plus the first shot at Mrs Henderson. Walsh nodded. He had crouched down just outside the barn, waiting for Noland to present himself.

Noland's footsteps approached loudly, followed by the sound of rushed and desperate breathing getting closer. Hobbs had nowhere to hide.

Seeing him crouching down by the doors, Noland extended the revolver toward Hobbs, now at less than eight feet away.

Noland cocked the hammer.

Then, Walsh fired.

The single opportunity Walsh had with the rifle was now gone, but it was all he needed. The round struck Noland on his right forearm, forcing him to drop the gun as he screamed in agony. Blood leaked out of his arm quickly and trickled down the sleeve of his tunic, staining it crimson.

Hobbs wasted no time.

He charged at Noland and threw his body into his stomach, driving him to the ground. Noland tried to fight back, but his right arm was now useless. Hobbs grabbed him by the lapels of his tunic and slammed the back of his head into the ground before delivering a powerful punch to his face.

Noland absorbed the blow, spitting blood from his lip. Hobbs delivered another punch to his jaw, followed by a third to his left eye socket, knocking him out cold.

'James, find me some rope before he comes to,' Hobbs said, staring down spitefully at the limp, unconscious body of Bernard Noland.

Walsh ran into the barn, rummaged through the workbenches and returned with a length of white rope.

'Henry, first take that tunic off him. He doesn't deserve to wear the uniform.'

Hobbs nodded and rolled Noland's bulky body over, swiftly stripping him of the black tunic and donning it himself.

Noland's arm wound was now on display, and the large wound on his arm was still bleeding, but the bullet had gone through his forearm, creating an even larger exit wound on the other side.

'He'll live,' Walsh said, but just to make sure he can stand trial and not bleed out, wrap his arm in rope too and stop the bleeding.'

Hobbs took extra precautions in restraining Noland, using an ample amount of rope to ensure there would be no chance of escape. He bound Noland's wrists tightly before wrapping another length of rope around his forearm to staunch the bleeding from the bullet wound. Hobbs collapsed to the ground, allowing himself to catch his breath after the intense struggle, satisfied that Noland was immobilised.

FIFTY-FIVE

As the sound of galloping hooves grew louder, Hobbs's heart raced with both relief and anticipation. Within moments, Palmer and Yarran arrived at the barn, urgently dismounted and rushed towards the scene at the sight of Noland bound and beginning to stir.

'What on earth happened here?' Palmer asked, staring at the bruised and bloodied face of Noland, gently groaning on the ground and barely able to open his eyes.

'It's over, Samuel,' Walsh said. 'It's finally over. Noland here has a gunshot wound to his forearm. We got here just in time. He was packing the last of the gold kept here in the barn by Arthur Henderson and then he was looking to leave town forever with his stolen haul.'

'James! Mrs Henderson,' Hobbs cried, gesturing toward the direction of the farmhouse.

'Go check on her, Henry,' Walsh said before turning to Palmer. 'Noland shot her just before we arrived. She is badly injured.'

Without hesitation, Hobbs sprinted towards the house to assist her, leaving Walsh and Palmer to deal with the unconscious Noland. 'Yarran, come with me and see if you can help.'

By the front door of the farmhouse, Hobbs knelt beside Eliza Henderson, his heart sinking at the sight of her now even paler complexion and the blood that saturated his shirt. He gently touched her shoulder, trying to offer some comfort despite the urgency of the situation.

'Mrs Henderson, it's Henry again. Stay with us.'

She groaned lightly and closed her eyes again.

'Yarran, can you help? She needs a doctor. Take her to Andrews.'

'She won't make it in her current state,' Yarran said, crouching down and peeling back the rolled-up shirt. 'The wound is still bleeding, but I can help. I saw something on my way. Get a sheet from inside, Henry. I'll be right back.'

Yarran swiftly departed from the front porch, darting towards the small garden nestled in the front yard. With determination, he sifted through the various plants and bushes until his fingers closed around the one he sought—a small, yellow flowering plant. Gently, he plucked a few leaves and carefully collected the sticky sap from the stems before hurrying back to the porch.

He met Hobbs, who had returned from inside the house with a thin white sheet.

'Tear me a long piece to used to bandage the wound.'

With utmost care, Yarran removed the blood-soaked shirt once again, eliciting a shallow gasp from Eliza Henderson. From his hand, droplets of thick, golden sap fell onto the wound before he covered it with the leaves, applying them gently yet firmly.

Finally, he tightly wrapped the sheet around her body, ensuring the wound was securely protected.

'What was that?' Hobbs asked.

'Snake Vine. The same plant we used to treat your wounds. It has saved my people for generations. It is for reasons like this that I always pay attention to my surroundings. You never know when nature will be needed.'

Hobbs nodded. 'Will she make it?'

'I think so, yes. This will keep her alive, but there ends my knowledge of natural medicine. We should take her away immediately. Help me onto the horse and I will ride into town right away.'

Carefully, Yarran and Hobbs lifted Eliza Henderson and carried her to the waiting horse. They placed her gently across its back, ensuring she was as comfortable as possible. Once she was secured, Yarran swiftly departed from the farm, riding off back the way he came.

'Sergeant, we need to get Noland back to the cells,' Hobbs said, returning to the front of the barn.

'Of course, I'll leave now and bring back the carriage. Are you alright here? Noland appears to have lost consciousness again.'

Hobbs nodded, glancing back at the motionless figure of Noland, lying on the ground, battered, bloodied, and thoroughly defeated.

After Palmer left, Hobbs instructed Walsh to keep watch over Noland while he inspected the barn. He found two hessian sacks by the door, tied at the top. Hobbs opened them, revealing a mass of cleaned and processed gold. Despite his thorough search, Hobbs found nothing more than opened metal boxes devoid of any more gold while he continued looking through the barn.

Piles of blackened smelting tools, along with iron pots, filled the space, but there was no more gold. Noland had efficiently cleared out the stash.

'Noland must have cleared the barn out completely,' Hobbs said, marching back toward Walsh carrying the two heavy sacks. 'Unless there is gold buried on the property, he bagged up everything in the barn.'

On the ground, Noland groaned behind his restraints and stirred. Walsh ensured he remained subdued by tightening the ropes further until he fell silent once more.

'There must be at least thirty pounds of gold in these,' Hobbs continued. 'Henderson clearly had quite the trade operating out of this barn. There's more than enough here for Noland to have started fresh.'

Hobbs opened the bags and spilled its contents, revealing hundreds of loose gold nuggets. He assumed it was a mix of gold Bryson and Davidson had delivered the night before, and an extra amount Henderson had been stockpiling.

'Must be worth a small fortune,' Walsh said, inspecting the pile on the ground.

'At least several thousand pounds.'

Hobbs began to re-pack the sacks, and while Walsh turned away to check on Noland, he discreetly collected a few of the smaller lumps and put them in his pocket. Not for himself, but for someone else. Nevertheless, he figured it would be best to not mention it to Walsh.

A short while later, Hobbs spotted a wooden carriage being drawn by Palmer's horse, its hooves stirring up clouds of dust as it approached the barn. Palmer rode at the reins, accompanied by a young constable seated beside him. The constable bore a striking resemblance to Edmund Miller, briefly stirring a flutter in Hobbs' stomach. Young, slender, and sporting a friendly smile, the constable introduced himself as Stephen Mercer after dismounting.

'Stephen is one of the fews constables left at Penrith,' Palmer said. 'I expect we will need to recruit as a matter of urgency. Has Noland said anything?'

'He has only just regained consciousness, but he has not uttered a single word since we tied him up,' Walsh said.

'Well, get him up and throw him in the back. He can sit in the cells at Penrith. I'll be writing to the Inspector General of Police as soon as we return.'

Hobbs seized Noland by the scruff of his shirt while Walsh grasped his rope, hoisting him off the ground. In a matter of moments, they threw him unceremoniously into the back of the carriage.

'Here, take the gold and cash too. The Mint would probably be happy to have it back. We'll see you back at the station, Sam,' Hobbs said.

Hobbs and Walsh maintained a close watch on the carriage, ensuring Noland's secure transportation to the station. As they approached the town centre, Hobbs gradually slowed his pace.

'Something wrong?' Walsh called back as he maintained speed.

'No. There's just something I have to do. I'll meet you at the station. You go ahead.'

FIFTY-SIX

H obbs walked through the front garden toward the door of the Miller residence and detected an unusual sense of bleakness hanging over the house. The closed curtains and the faint sounds of rummaging from within added to the somber atmosphere. Hobbs knocked gently on the door.

Jane Miller answered the door after a momentary delay, her weary appearance speaking volumes about the weight of her recent loss. Her eyes, still sunken and bloodshot, betrayed the pain she continued to endure from the passing of her husband. Clad in an all-black dress reminiscent of the one worn at Edmund's funeral, she seemed to be enveloped in mourning.

'Good day, Mrs Miller,' Hobbs said, bowing his head and clasping Noland's tunic to cover his bare chest underneath.

'Mr Hobbs,' she said, standing at the threshold with no offer of an invitation for him to enter. Hobbs knew he looked terrible and probably smelled worse, but she took no notice.

He glanced past her into the dim interior of the house, noting the stark emptiness where furniture once stood.

'I'm heading back to London tomorrow,' she said, waving her hand toward the empty space in the living room behind her. 'With all my belongings donated to the church, I will stay with my parents back home. I've scraped together enough money for a ticket on a ship leaving from Sydney.'

Hobbs truly empathised with Jane's plight. She had sacrificed everything for a new beginning in a distant land, only to have her dreams shattered by tragedy. Now, she found herself alone, isolated in a place that held memories of loss and heartache. It struck a chord with Hobbs, reminding him of his own sense of displacement and loneliness after Emma's death.

'Mrs Miller, I am sorry to intrude like this. I wondered if I could come in and have a word?'

'Sure,' she said, stepping out of the doorway, allowing him to pass her. 'Sorry, there's nowhere to sit.'

'Apologies are unnecessary. I know how hard this is for you.'

'You do?'

Hobbs stood in the centre of the once well-decorated living room. It seemed much larger now, and his footsteps echoed.

'My wife was murdered. Back in London.'

'Oh, I'm very sorry, Mr Hobbs. Very sorry.'

Hobbs nodded and offered a weak smile. 'I know how hard it is to deal with being on your own. For a long time, I didn't want to live, and if I can be honest, I nearly drank myself to death more times than I care to remember. But it gets better. I'm still learning that for myself, but there has to be some truth to it. The pain never goes away, and I still have some dark moments, but you will find a reason for pushing on.'

'Have you?'

Hobbs paused. He was not expecting that question.

'Yes,' he eventually said, hoping his words would offer some solace to Jane, even if he struggled to fully believe them himself. As he saw her half-smile, he felt a glimmer of reassurance. Perhaps there was some truth to his words, after all. He had brought justice to those responsible for the murders, yet despite this success, a lingering sense of emptiness remained with him. For Jane's sake, however, he maintained a facade of hope, knowing that she needed to hear it now more than ever.

Hobbs looked Jane directly in the eye and continued. 'Look, I came here to tell you we have caught all the men involved in the gold carriage murders and the murder of Edmund.'

'Who were they?' she asked cautiously, almost as though she was afraid to know the answer.

'I'm very sorry to say it was three police officers.'

Jane choked a little and began crying. 'Police officers killed my husband?'

'Yes. I'm very sorry to be the one to tell you, but I wanted you to know.'

'Where are they now?'

'Two are dead, and one is in custody. I expect they will hang him.'

'You did as you promised, Mr Hobbs. Thank you for telling me. Thank you for finding them. Although it still does not bring my Edmund back, but I'm glad justice has prevailed,' she said as she continued to sob, clutching a crumpled handkerchief that bore the marks of countless tears shed that morning.

Hobbs remained silent, his head bowed solemnly.

'Why did they do it?' she asked.

'I don't think I can give you an answer, Mrs Miller. Why would someone do such a thing to another human? I simply do not know. Some people are just not rational like you and I. Some people, I have found, are selfish and simply enjoy the misery of others.'

While Jane continued to cry, Hobbs, feeling a mix of discomfort and sympathy, reached into his pockets and retrieved the small lumps of gold.

'I want you to have this,' he said, taking her hand and placing them in her palm.

'What is this?'

'Please don't ask too many questions. It is not proper for me to be doing this, but just take it, please. It is not much, and it will not repair the wounds you have, but if this can make your life in London even a fraction more comfortable, it would have been worth it.'

Jane sniffled and made eye contact with Hobbs. 'Thank you.'

Hobbs nodded and turned to leave. 'Look after yourself, Mrs Miller.'

'And you, Mr Hobbs.'

FIFTY-SEVEN

Yarran stood alone outside the Penrith police station when Hobbs returned. Despite the tumultuous events, he appeared revitalised, neatly tying back his long hair and exuding a sense of ease, casually tucking his hands into his pockets.

'Mrs Henderson is going to be alright,' he said as Hobbs approached. 'The bleeding has stopped, and she should make a recovery.'

'That's great news, Yarran, thank you. You probably saved her life back there at the farm. It was quite impressive.'

Yarran smiled and bowed his head. 'So I take it you will leave soon?'

'I expect so. Although I'm not sure what happens now. James got me off Cockatoo Island, but now the case is closed. I don't know where I'll go. Perhaps they will send me back there.'

As Hobbs pondered his future after the investigation, a sense of uncertainty nagged at him.

'How about you?' he asked.

'I will return to my people. Nothing will change for me. I will continue to hunt, explore, and offer my tracking services where I can.'

Hobbs stretched his hand out. 'It has been my pleasure, Yarran.'

They shook hands and smiled.

'I hope we meet again soon,' Hobbs said.

'I hope we do too,' Yarran said as a wide smile stretched across his face. 'James is inside with Noland. You should go in. Travel safely.'

With that, Yarran left on foot, headed west for the Blue Mountains.

As Hobbs entered the police station, he noticed Palmer and Walsh engaged in casual conversation behind the counter, while Noland sat in silence in the dirty cell behind them. The Chief Inspector, once a figure of authority and pride, now appeared as a disheveled shadow of his former self. Cuts marred his face, and without his uniform, he resembled a sweaty vagrant more than a law enforcement officer. When Noland caught sight of Hobbs, his glare spoke volumes, though he remained silent, his moustache quivering over his bruised lip.

'He hasn't said a word,' Walsh said.

'I guess there's nothing for him to say,' Hobbs said.

'I sent Constable Mercer to report what had occurred to Inspector General McLerie,' Palmer said. 'I expect he will be most interested in ensuring a successful prosecution. He will probably arrange a prisoner transfer to Sydney as soon as possible. What about you two?'

Hobbs looked at Walsh and shrugged. 'I guess we are finished here.'

Walsh seemed to read the uncertainty in his voice. 'Henry, I will not have you sent back to Cockatoo Island if that thought has been on your mind.'

'What do I do then?'

'Come back to Sydney with me. We will work something out. It's nearly Christmas, you'll stay with Helen and me.'

Hobbs nodded. 'My first summer Christmas.'

'Thank you for everything, Samuel. We will stay in touch,' Walsh said, shaking Palmer's hand.

'Please, I must be thanking you. And you too, Mr Hobbs. I cannot express my thanks enough. You are welcome back anytime.'

Returning to Sydney the next day, they were greeted by an overcast sky and high humidity that left them sweating profusely. The bustling streets of the city were a stark contrast to the quieter, more recently familiar surroundings of Penrith and the Blue Mountains.

'Before we head to my place, I just want to stop by the police station first and check up on things,' Walsh said.

As they made their way to the police station, they leisurely strolled along the bustling harbour area. Horse-pulled carriages lined the streets, while workers bustled about construction sites and pedestrians enjoyed leisurely strolls by the water's edge. Upon entering the station, they found it to be just as bustling. Constables were engrossed in paperwork, and all the cells were occupied, mostly by drunks, Hobbs surmised.

'Sir, welcome back,' a young constable said. 'You have a visitor in your office.' He then leant in closer and whispered, 'It's Inspector General McLerie.'

'Perhaps I should wait here,' Hobbs said.

'Nonsense, come with me,' Walsh said, leading him through the station to his office.

The door to Walsh's office stood open, revealing Inspector General John McLerie seated in the visitor's chair. Patiently awaiting Walsh's arrival, McLerie idly perused the titles of the numerous books adorning a tall wooden bookcase that overlooked the harbour. Though Walsh had only met McLerie once before, during a police function, he had formed the impression he was a principled man, dedicated to improving law enforcement in the burgeoning colony. McLerie, a former military man, had assumed the role of Inspector General of Police for New South Wales in 1856. With his tall stature, round face, and a thick white beard to match his hair, he exuded an air of authority tempered by kindness. As Walsh entered the office, McLerie greeted him with a warm smile and rose from his seat in acknowledgment.

'Inspector, how do you do?' he said with a thick Scottish brogue.

'Sir,' Walsh said, shaking his hand. 'Allow me to introduce Henry Hobbs, formerly of Scotland Yard.'

'Mr Hobbs, hello. I have read the prisoner transfer and report from Sergeant Palmer and heard of your involvement in the successful investigation of the gold carriage murders. Most impressive. Come in and have a seat, gentlemen.'

Walsh approached his desk slowly and sat behind it, while Hobbs took a seat next to McLerie.

'The report I received about this matter was most confrontational. That three police, including a Chief Inspector, were responsible for these murders was horrifying to learn, but you two gentlemen have done fine work. Had it not been for your tenacity, things could have spiralled out of control. The Mint would have suffered, and not to mention the gold mines, so for all your hard work, I thank you. I will ensure the safe transportation of Bernard Noland to the Sydney cells, where he will await trial and, undoubtedly, hang for his crimes.

'Thank you, sir, we were just doing our jobs,' Walsh said.

'Yes, and that is what I want to speak with you about. You may not be aware of this inspector, but for some time I have followed your career here in Sydney, and I have been most impressed. You may have heard rumours that I have been drafting the Police Regulation Act, which, when the government passes it, will allow us to unite our police force under a central command, and then divide it into districts. My plan is for a much more cohesive and entirely unified force. The New South Wales Police Force,' he said proudly. 'So what I am saying, inspector, is part of my proposal calls for a specialised unit of highly trained detectives to assist the colony in major criminal offences. Now, from speaking with members of the government, they are in approval of my proposal. It is just yet to be formalised, so in a few short weeks, we should be prepared to amalgamate. Now, what I want is for you to lead this unit. What do you say?'

Walsh's eyes widened, but then he managed a smile. 'It would be my honour, sir, thank you.'

'Well, you've earned it, son.'

'Sir, my colleague here, Mr Hobbs, I am not sure if you are aware of...'

'Inspector, I have been made aware of Mr Hobbs' situation and I assure you, Henry, after all you have done in the recent weeks, in my book you have redeemed yourself. We won't send you back to Cockatoo Island. I am a believer of reformation, and you sir have done just that.'

'I would like to request, with respect, sir, that Henry be part of this investigative team. His skills are incomparable.'

Hobbs felt his heart race, and he looked at Walsh in complete surprise. McLerie simply nodded in agreement.

'I agree. Your skills would be wasted if you weren't, so let it be done. We will have Mr Hobbs here sworn in as an officer and join your new team.'

'Thank you, sir, I'm truly honoured, I won't let you down,' Hobbs said humbly, with a bow of his head.

McLerie smiled and stood up. 'You'll be hearing from me soon, gentlemen. Merry Christmas.'

After McLerie departed, there was a moment of silence between Hobbs and Walsh as they absorbed the significance of the Inspector General's visit.

'Thank you, James,' Hobbs finally said. 'I don't know what to say.'

Walsh nodded and smiled. 'We will have to find you a place to live around here now. So, are you ready to get to work?'

Hobbs smiled. 'Absolutely.'

ABOUT THE AUTHOR

Born and raised in Sydney, Max always had a deep passion for writing. While pursuing a full-time career, he put several ideas for a novel on hold. It wasn't until many years later that he finally brought one of those ideas to life, resulting in his debut novel, *Altered Sense*. With a love for crafting thrilling narratives, Max aims to create fast-paced stories that captivate readers with suspense, intrigue, and excitement. Max still lives in Sydney with his wife and son. When not writing, he spends as much time as possible with his family.

ALTERED SENSE

The loyalties of those closest to him will be tested...

When an unprovoked and vicious assault leaves William Denham at a Sydney hospital with serious head injuries, he soon begins to experience strange visions.
Forced to question his sanity at the realisation that he is experiencing premonitions of violent and horrific crimes yet to occur, those closest to Will are confronted with his newfound abilities, causing fear for his state of mind.
As the visions of these brutal crimes continue to plague Will, he must turn to his friends for help to save the lives of the unsuspecting victims...

"An unnerving and thought-provoking new novel from a talented writer who grips the emotional tension with both hands and doesn't let it go..." Trevor, Indie Book reviewer

DEADLY SENSE

The mind that terrifies him is also his greatest asset...

Following the harrowing events in 'Altered Sense', Will Denham continues to grapple with premonitory visions of horrific crimes yet to occur. However, after a devastating tragedy, he spirals into the depths of despair and refuses to use his gift again. Meanwhile, the city reels under the onslaught of a wave of violent armed robberies, each more brutal than the last. As the violence escalates, Will finds himself at a crossroads - compelled to overcome his inner demons and reignite his abilities to stop them. Continually one step behind the elusive robbery crew, Will makes a chilling discovery as a haunting figure from his past resurfaces. Now forced to confront a life he thought he had left behind, he must navigate a treacherous path to save innocent lives.